ESCAPING ELEVEN

ALSO BY JERRI CHISHOLM

ESCAPING ELEVEN

JERRI CHISHOLM

Entangled Publishing, LLC
10940 S Parker Road
Suite 327
Parker, CO 80134
rights@entangledpublishing.com

Entangled Teen is an imprint of Entangled Publishing, LLC.

Visit our website at www.entangledpublishing.com.

Edited by Stacy Abrams
Cover Design by LJ Anderson, Mayhem Cover Creations
Cover images by
grandfailure/Depositphotos_90723558 and
Hzpriezz/shutterstock
Font Design by Covers by Juan
Interior design by Toni Kerr

TP ISBN 978-1-64937-097-6
HC ISBN 978-1-68281-501-4
Ebook ISBN 978-1-68281-502-1

Manufactured in the United States of America

First Edition November 2021

10 9 8 7 6 5 4 3 2 1

To j.a.p.

At Entangled, we want our readers to be well-informed. If you would like to know if this book contains any elements that might be of concern for you, please check the back of the book for details.

CHAPTER ONE

I hold out open hands, palms down. Inches above hovers half a lemon, and even between pockets of mold, it sparkles with juice. The smell of citrus fills the cell. The anticipation is the worst, or it used to be, when I was small. But now I am grown and so my pulse is steady.

Now I don't flinch as the juice hits my knuckles, as acid seeps into open wounds. I glance sideways, but my face is otherwise indifferent, and I am, too. Only the initial jolt stings, then the pain fades into Compound Eleven's dimly lit corridors.

"Hurt?"

I note how calm his voice is as he squeezes the lemon tight, wrings it so every last drop is pushed free. He enjoys our ritual; at least I think he does.

I stare at him and shake my head.

"Good," he says. My strength pleases him. Then his eyebrows pull together. "Today's fight is getting attention. Are you ready?"

I slap my right cheek; he slaps my left. Just like always.

"I'm not worried," I say, but I pause. My hands clench into fists, and I examine the effect of the lemon juice. Red slashes burn pink. "Why is it getting attention?"

He must sound like a cruel man, my father. But I have been his only child since Jack was sent aboveground. No one can survive aboveground. And so he had only me to shape, and he shaped me into a fighter.

I watch him carefully and see the corner of his mouth twitch. He's excited.

"Your opponent is from upstairs."

"Probably that Upper Mean I beat last—"

He shakes his head before I'm finished. "It's a Preme you'll be fighting."

My back straightens.

A Preeminate, or Preme for short. That is big news. Premes don't fight—they don't even attend the fights, not usually. That would mean descending from the fifth floor to the second, where the Bowl is located, and Premes don't often rub shoulders with Lower Means.

Lower Means like me.

He is staring, waiting for a reaction. Instead I pull up both pants legs and lean back on the narrow bed that used to be my own. It squeaks under my weight. "My knees are skinned. Clean them, too."

"Please," he reminds me.

"Please."

He sighs as he shifts positions, and he looks older than I remember. His movements are stiff, and his hair is graying at the temples, skin pooling under his mouth. He picks up the other half of the rotted lemon from the concrete floor, and I shift my gaze to the ceiling as I wait for a fresh slice of pain. I barely feel it when it comes; I'm too busy thinking about the news.

A Preme.

So it will be an easy fight, short and sweet. Hunter will be pleased; Maggie, too. And Emerald and the other fighters will have a good laugh. I smile in spite of myself.

"Two weeks in your own place now," my father says as he stands. He is tall and so his head nearly skims the ceiling. He throws the rind to the floor as he watches me; I am clean.

"Two weeks tomorrow," I agree.

"Settling in okay?"

My eyes slide over pictures I drew as a child before I answer. They dot the walls of my parents' cell—and pictures of Jack, too. From the early days, before he had to go. And some embroidery work by my mother, hung with pride on one of her better days. The ones that don't come around very often.

"I'm settling in fine. It's nice to have some space to myself." Immediately, I wince. It wasn't a kind thing to say to my father.

But something resembling amusement spreads across his face. "An independent girl, Eve," he says. "You always have been."

I swallow. A feeling I know well makes my stomach squeeze into a hard pit—guilt. I would prefer the feeling of lemon juice lashing my wounds.

"Will you bother with the job tours, or are you settled on fighting?"

"Not sure," I lie. He thinks I'll choose to be a fighter as my job. We must pick in six weeks' time. I am sixteen now; schooling is complete.

But I am not going to be a professional fighter. And I am not going to bother with the job tours. There is no job I will choose. In six weeks' time, I will be gone.

CHAPTER TWO

1000535 right left right left right right right left 11000535. Every ten steps, I mutter it under my breath. Again. Again.

My brain barely registers the thumping of feet close above my head, a sound that grows louder with every passing second. Same for the cathartic thundering of thousands of voices. It isn't my first fight in the Bowl, and it won't be my last. I don't need to pay attention; I don't need to savor it. Not yet.

And certainly I don't need to fear it. Not when my opponent is a *Preme*.

I push into the Blue Circuit training room, where I change, and from there into the tunnel that connects to the Bowl itself. It is a coiled metal half-cylinder where the air is stale, stained with sweat from fighters previous. I can feel it in my nostrils. And it is impossible to ignore the thunder in here; it is visceral. It vibrates my bones.

The ref stands near the door, and though he nods at me, I don't bother with pleasantries. Instead I gaze down the tunnel to the mouth of the Bowl, to where someone warms up at a punching bag.

The Preme. It must be, but I can't know for certain until he takes off his hoodie. If he is my opponent, his arm will be wrapped in red. Mine is wrapped in blue, and it is hidden, too. I am Blue Circuit, classified as an occasional fighter. He is a guest fighter for Red Circuit.

I walk in his direction, my eyes locked onto his back, and with every step I breathe harder. Deeper.

Shit.

I can tell from here. He is going to destroy me.

My footsteps are silent under the noise of the crowd. But he must sense that he is no longer alone, because his head snaps left, his eyes meeting mine. They are piercing yet distant—a seemingly impossible combination.

I look away, go to my punching bag. Deep breath in and out.

In.

Out.

But every time I blink, I see his shoulder blades, wide and vast and imprinted on my brain. He has a fighter's build. Strong. Quick. Tall but not too tall. The lanky ones I can beat; they can't move. The short ones I can beat, too; they lack power.

But the Preme...

He slides beside me as I take my first swing at the bag. The old wounds burst open upon impact. My father will have to clean them again.

"What do you want?" I ask. Another swing. Another tiny burst of blood. I glance at him between punches, enough to see that his eyes are wide set, his face square. Masculine.

But his lips are smooth, and they curve gently. He has a kind mouth, I think. Or he would, if the rest of him didn't glower at me. "Are you awake? I said, what do you want?"

Eyes narrow over a perfect nose—a nose I will soon break. "What do you think you're doing," he asks me, though it sounds like a statement rather than a question. His low voice is clipped.

"What do you *think* I'm doing?" My knuckles crack loudly against the surface of the bag, loud enough to sound over the crowd. I don't understand his confusion, and I don't care about it. In fact, I wish he would leave me alone, because right now I should be thinking only about the match at hand. I should feel nerves fraying the lining of my stomach, clawing at my skin. I shouldn't be distracted, and I can't afford to be, either.

I am about to tell him to get lost when he speaks again: "You're bleeding."

Now I bite my lip, but I can't hold back the smirk that pulls at my mouth. I can't hold back the words bubbling to the surface. "What's wrong, Preme? Never seen blood before?"

He steps closer and grabs the punching bag, holds it still so that my next punch stuns the bones in my wrist. "Listen," he snarls as I shake out my fist, "it's a simple question. Don't think I want to be talking to you, either. You're a waste of my time."

Light hazel eyes cool to brown, and I can see by how he holds his body—so rigid, so plank-like—that I am getting under his skin.

Perfect.

"There's a fight scheduled soon, did you know? Get out of here." He nods up the tunnel, away from the Bowl. Then he turns.

The source of his confusion is now obvious, and I laugh.

"Yeah, I do know," I say loudly. "What do you think I'm doing, warming up to go write in my diary?" I turn my attention back to the bag, still faintly amused, but he grabs my shoulder before I can launch a punch.

"*You're* my opponent?"

I jerk myself free and pull off my sweatshirt, hold out my arm. Blue band.

He is silent as he stares at it. So silent, it makes the roar of the crowd seem louder, like we're being swallowed deep into the earth below Eleven. They are more excited than usual because of him.

"Ass," I mumble, and I expect him to hit me. Mouthing off to a Preme isn't a smart thing to do. But instead, he walks away. Away from the crowd, away from the Bowl. For a moment I watch him, then shake my head. I need to focus on the punching bag and nothing more. I don't know why he distracts me so easily.

One strike. Two. Blood stains the hide. I do it again. Again. My muscles feel warm; they bulge under pale skin. One strike. Two.

When I stop to shake out my arms, I see he is speaking with the ref. I can't hear either one of them, not from this far away, and not over the thunder of feet or the vibration inside my chest. But I can see them through the webbing of punching bags that spreads through the tunnel, and I see the Preme shake his head, see him take a step toward the ref, see the ref step away. Neither looks happy.

It is only when the Preme turns and stares at me that I shift my gaze.

Focus, Eve.

If I want to get in a few good strikes, I need to think. He moves quickly; I can see that. I need to be quicker. Quick like Anil, one of the professional fighters for Blue Circuit. He is small, his wrists no wider than my own. But he wins because of speed, and so I need speed, too.

I need to be good. I can't be anything less or I could be dead.

Behind me, the Preme is back, hitting the bag harder than before. His punches echo easily over the jeering crowd, and the next time I chance a look, I see two things. First, his face is flushed, his eyes fiery. Second, his hoodie is off, red band exposed. I see, too, that his arms are strong, forearms impossibly thick and leading to large fists. I imagine them connecting with my face and swallow.

Now the nerves are there, burning my insides like acid and making my heart slam against my ribs. But this isn't the first time I have been up against someone I know will win. So I bag up my fear and the agonizing anticipation of pain. I put it aside. The only thing I need to focus on is drawing blood. Draw blood from the Preme. It will make Emerald and the other fighters happy: Anil and Bruno and Erick. It will make my father happy.

Just a bit of blood is all I need.

"Ready?" shouts the ref from over my shoulder. He is short with white-gray hair, red-rimmed drinking eyes. My arms drop to my sides, and my stomach lurches. I nod—I am as ready as I will ever be.

He shouts next to the Preme, but the Preme must not hear. He keeps punching the bag—he punches it with enough force to crack my skull. He is angry; there is no doubt about that now. Perhaps it was my attitude or calling him a name.

I watch as the ref moves sideways until he falls into the Preme's peripheral vision. The Preme glances at him, then hits the bag again. Complete and utter insolence, and I smile inwardly—I can't help it. Now the ref says something, something that makes the Preme stop and glare at him.

But finally he turns to face me, blood dripping from large knuckles.

His gaze is cemented low, to the side—not on me at all.

"…Sportsmanlike conduct," the ref says. "Respect…" The same old thing, and I don't bother to listen. In truth, there are no rules. Not in the Fighter Bowl—not even in Compound Eleven.

Violence is a way of life down here, and in the ring, it is even more than that. It is a celebrated form of entertainment. The more gruesome the fight, the happier the crowds. The happier the crowds, the happier the Combat League—the one all us athletes must appease if we want match time. So the rules are simple: There are no rules.

It hasn't always been this way.

There used to be other forms of entertainment, at least before the remnants of civilization moved underground. Football, the books on the fifth floor call it. Or maybe it was baseball. Whatever it was, it required space. An open field, big arenas. There is none of that here. I don't know about the other compounds, but I do know Compound Eleven.

There is only fighting.

The ref orders us to shake hands. I don't have an intimidating face, but at least it looks disinterested, and that can be off-putting. So I stare evenly at the Preme as I extend a bloodied palm. Only he doesn't take it. He doesn't even look at me. Instead he strings his hands behind his head and stares at the metal ceiling. The ref looks as though he will insist upon a handshake—sportsmanlike conduct indeed—but after a second thought, he grabs his loudspeaker and brushes past us into the Bowl. He welcomes the crowd to the match, and they roar. Then he begins the haunting anthem of the compound…

Mother dearest see us staring, stop the ticking clock
Your beauty is unrivaled, from beasts to gilded rock
One more chance for everything, oh the love you shall unlock
Mother dearest hear us whisper, tick tock

Mother dearest see us staring, stop the ticking clock
Your betrayal is still stinging, a path of shame to walk
Women, children cast aside, men you cruelly mock
Mother dearest hear us singing, tick tock

Mother dearest see us staring, stop the ticking clock
Foolish is your thinking, your twisting of the lock
A declaration of war, and us weakened by our shock
Mother dearest hear us shouting, tick tock

Mother dearest see us staring, stop the ticking clock
Telling secrets, sharing lies, your love was just a crock
Set the noose, start the fire, never again to talk
Mother dearest hear us laughing, tick tock

My brow digs together as I wrap my knuckles, as the crowd joins the ref for the last stanza, the one that always inspires anger. The entire compound is founded upon it. I stare at the Preme. He doesn't look my way, and when I throw him the roll of tape, he doesn't move to catch it. Instead it falls to the floor, and he kicks it away.

Now, instead of trying to make him feel uneasy, *I* feel uneasy. Fighters always tape their knuckles. Does he think it will be that quick a match? He faces the Bowl now, his gaze empty and unfixed. He doesn't bounce to keep blood flowing or his muscles loose. He does nothing.

Yes. He must think this will be an easy fight indeed.

I will show him otherwise.

With a deep breath, I turn and face the Bowl myself, and my eyes sweep over the largest room in Compound Eleven, one that spans the second and third floor, even part of the fourth. The only room where the ceiling isn't directly overhead. Black-and-white pendants hang from the rafters, along with large banners advertising upcoming matches—matches between well-known professional fighters.

But this one must be just as well attended as those will be. Row after row, tier after tier, the seats are full. Except nobody sits. They all stand, stomp feet, clap hands. Scream.

I bounce up and down and stare at the raised ring in the center of the Bowl. It is surrounded by blinding white lights that remind me of Preme lights. Lower Mean lights are dim, lone bulbs strung across a low ceiling at too-long intervals, strands of wire hanging between. The bleached Preme floor glitters by comparison. Powerful jobs, elaborate schooling, lavish living quarters. All a far cry from Lower Mean life.

But sport fighting is a Mean game, and most of the fighters are second-floor Lower Means like myself. This is my turf, not his.

I slap myself and relish the feeling of my heart hammering in my throat. I let the screaming crowd fill my ears, the thumping boots fill my veins. I stare at the glowing ring until my pupils tighten, until my muscles twitch.

The ref puts down the loudspeaker and motions us forward.

CHAPTER THREE

Immediately the crowd notices: We've left the confines of the tunnel. We've been released into the wild. If they were loud before, it is nothing compared to now. Their screams meld into one, and it fills my eardrums like liquid lead. It is so loud I can hear nothing at all.

The glaring lights of the ring are still eighty paces away—I know the walk well, too well. A shoestring of space slithers before us, and fingers snatch at me with every step. Some yell, most boo. It is the Preme they are booing, not me. He's the guest fighter, and an elite one at that. It is too bad I will disappoint them in the end.

I will be disappointed, too. I don't like to lose. I wonder, as the faces wash into a blur around me, whether it is a good trait or bad. My mother would say it is bad, that it is petty. Everything is petty, I suppose, when you've been to hell and back. But my father would think it's good, a killer's instinct.

I find Maggie's face in the crowd, and her lips are pressed into a tight line as she watches me. She doesn't smile; she doesn't yell. But she is strong-minded, and she knows I am, too. So she claps and nods encouragingly as I pass. Emerald cheers loudly next to her, and her hand clenches into a fist once our eyes meet. She believes in me.

It is a shame *she* didn't get paired with the Preme. Muscles ripple under her brown skin like she was born for this. She loves it—the fight, the crowds, the pain. She is one of the best, and she might even have a chance against the Preme.

Hunter is next, and his face is paper-white. He doesn't clap; he just gazes uneasily at the Preme. He is fearful for me, and it makes my insides squeeze so hard that I need a distraction.

So I set my face into its most disinterested expression and glance over my shoulder at my opponent. Arms jostle me, but I barely notice, just as he seems not to notice the hands that paw at his chest. I can see it in his eyes. Danger. But something resembling fear, too. They sweep over the crowds too quickly; that is his tell. When his gaze meets mine, I smile. "Scared, Preme?"

He says nothing. His eyes simply tick away, back to the masses. But his lips press together ever so slightly…

The disinterest on my face isn't just for show. It runs deep, and right now it courses from the chambers of my heart through to my extremities. The first punch will hurt, yes, just like the sting of lemon juice. Then I won't notice.

We climb into the ring and face each other under the lights. The ref has yet to follow, but once he does—once he climbs into the ring—the fight will begin. I shake out my arms and jump up and down.

But the Preme just stands there, staring to the side. And once again, he distracts me.

Finally I can take it no longer. "Wake up!" I shout from a foot away. I remember his words from inside the tunnel. "This is a fight, did you know?"

His eyes narrow as they meet mine. "You feel like joking around right now? What's wrong with you?" He shakes his head, and I stop bouncing. My arms drop to my sides.

I take a step closer so he can hear every word. "Are all Premes this pissy? Oh, wait—stupid question."

"Do all Means think it's normal to beat up girls?"

I am silent. Now I know what is bothering him. He must have signed up for today's fight on a whim, having no clue as to the rules—or lack thereof—that surround this most violent entertainment.

"I can't fight you," he adds.

I resume bouncing and smirk. "Who says you're going to beat me up?"

He gives me a look. "Come on."

Something inside me recoils at this unusual boy. At his gentlemanly nature. At his *kindness*. I liked it better when he was calling me a waste of his time. When he refused to listen to the ref. That is the kind of thing I expect from a Preme.

So my arm twitches, and I punch him. I punch him hard, a right hook to the middle of the face. It is a hard smash, completely unprotected. A sucker punch, and the crowd goes wild.

There are no rules, not here. The fight is on.

He stumbles back a pace, his hand moving instinctively to a nose that now bleeds. I wanted to draw blood, and I have. My next goal is to stay on my feet for as long as possible. Do maximum harm until he knocks me out cold.

I do not accept his refusal to fight.

My next punch is knocked away, and it makes my forearm sting. Our eyes meet, and I see he is mad. He meant for that block to hurt. I swallow a smile and attack again, manage to land a hit to his ribs before I'm pushed backward with shocking force. He is strong. The moment he decides to fight,

I am done for.

"Stop it!" he yells. "You're going to get hurt."

I kick the outside of his thigh and see him grimace. "No quitters allowed." I launch another attack, but this time he stirs. His eyes flash, and he punches, lands a firm strike to my cheek before I can land one on him.

It rattles my skull and lights fire to my skin, but then the sensation is gone and there is nothing left but dull, aching bone. I raise an eyebrow. "Looks like you can hit a girl after all."

"It didn't feel that bad, either," he snarls.

He punches me low in the ribs, and I keel over, but only for a second. I force my spine to straighten.

"I might feel bad," he continues, "if you were even the least bit pleasant." He launches forward, and a small bullet of panic streaks through me, but instead of hitting me, he grabs my arms and forces them behind my back. He pushes me against the ropes. It is an unusual thing to do and one I don't resist, not yet.

"You can't move—it's over!" he yells in my ear over the chanting of the crowd. "Tell the ref it's over."

Instead I drive my knee up, making him groan loudly, making his head knock backward with pain.

A heartbeat later, he cracks his skull into my face, and my eyesight is lost in a sea of red. My face is warm and slippery wet. The cheering fans sound a million miles away, and my brain sizzles from the impact. My neck feels like a wet noodle.

He is cruel, I think.

It was a cheap shot, a dangerous one. But I suppose I set the tone, punching before the fight began.

Before I can see again, he releases my arms and hits me square in the stomach. It sends bile to my mouth, and for an instant I'm transported back in time, to when I was just nine years old. It was my first fight, and my opponent was a thirteen-year-old boy, seemingly twice my size and with a fierce temper. The terror is what I remember. The twist of his lip as he toyed with me. I shook with fear, enough that vomit started up my throat, tasting just like now. And then he clobbered me. Strangely enough, I don't remember much about the fight itself. Only the fear before it.

I give myself a shake, force my mind to the present. *Relax, Eve.* The lemon juice has spilled. The first jolt of pain—real pain—has arrived. The rest doesn't matter. Not really.

I block his next punch with my wrist and ignore the stinging of bone on bone, instead landing an elbow under his chin that I know must jar his brain. Then I kick him again, full impact. Guys don't often kick, so they never expect it.

Another punch of his finds me, this one to the jaw. This one hard. It knocks me down, and before I can pull myself up again, he is over me, his chest rising and falling quickly like he has sprinted across the Bowl instead of tossing me around ten square feet of it. Even with blood coating his face, he is handsome.

It makes me like him even less. I try another punch, but he grabs my fist and squeezes it until I wince. Danger streaks loudly across his eyes, much louder than before.

"Stop!" I shriek before I mean to. But my bones will buckle soon.

He freezes. "Stop? Is that what you said?" His head turns to look for the ref. He is desperate to be finished—I can see that. More desperate than me.

I use his momentary distraction to my advantage. My loose fist connects with his eye socket, forcing him back. It makes my knuckles scream, even through the wrapping. But it hurts him more, I am sure of it.

The crowd howls. It is a good fight; I am doing Blue Circuit proud.

"Stop fighting!" he screams at me. Instead I launch myself at him.

He punches me so hard I find myself on the floor before I know what has happened. When I open my eyes, there is only blackness. My palms feel the coolness of the ring floor, and though every cell screams with unbearable pain, I push. Up. Up. Keep fighting. At all costs.

But something hits me on the back of the head. Something hard. It feels solid, cold. Like metal. Are there weapons allowed in here? Maybe it was the Preme's foot. Maybe it was his fist. Maybe it was his head. Maybe I should let sleep take me because that is all I really want to do right now. Get away from his flashing eyes.

If I could just lay my head down.

But it is down, I can feel that now. My cheek is pressed to the floor. Has it always been there?

Perhaps the fight hasn't started yet. Maybe the day hasn't, either. Yes, that's it. I'm in my cell now. Go back to sleep, Eve.

I let my eyes fall shut, or maybe they already were. Next I let myself fall sideways. Down and away. Gone.

CHAPTER FOUR

turn right. Ten paces, left. Seven paces, right. Fifteen paces, left. There is no need to count it out. I know this route like the back of my hand; it will be the thirty-fifth time. This is the corridor where the fluorescent light shudders overhead; it always does. Turn right. This corridor has doors leading off it, important ones, ones I must be mindful of. Everything is important up here on the fifth floor. The Preme floor. Turn right. Another right. I stand before a brushed metal door and enter the code. 11000535. I turn the handle, but there's no give. It's locked; it didn't work. But I already knew that. I have tried that code before.

Now my eyes are awash with light. Sunlight. It is the first time I have seen it, and it squeezes out everything else in my field of vision. It is blinding. I must have found a way into the Oracle after all.

"Why are you smiling?" comes a voice many miles away. It sounds vaguely familiar, though I can't place it. But I have heard it before, I am sure of it.

Slowly my eyes pull open, but I see nothing. No light,

no darkness. Nothing. I close them again. Where am I? I am not trying to break into the Oracle on the fifth floor, I realize that now. And I am certainly not inside the Oracle. I have been sleeping. Dreaming. I open my eyes again and lift my head, but it is too painful. It thumps with blood, and my neck screams.

Moving my hand, my fingers—it's no better. Pounding throbs, sharp aches. All over, in every joint and tendon.

So I am still, except for my eyes that blink and blink, again and again, until slowly vision returns. A lone lightbulb hangs from the ceiling, and a wire dangles from it. So I am on the second floor. That is good. That is my floor. My Lower Mean floor.

But I am not in my cell. The air is different. Thinner. The smell of cleaner lingers.

"How are you feeling?" comes that voice again. I frown. I can't place it no matter how hard I try. I will have to lift my head to see who the speaker is. I take a deep breath and squeeze my stomach muscles, pull my neck. The pain makes me grit my teeth, but right now I don't care who sees.

Until I realize who it is.

The Preme. He sits on a chair beside me, his arm resting easily on his knee. A black T-shirt stretches over his chest.

I draw in a breath and force myself to sit the rest of the way up. Every muscle, ligament, and tendon rallies against my movement, but I am determined. And this time I don't let the pain show on my face. Because I don't know why he is here, with me, and I don't know where *here* is. Two things that put me at a disadvantage.

Straightaway I ask, "Where am I?"

"You should probably lie down."

My eyes slide to his. There is no malice there, not from him. But I can feel it froth in my stomach. Not for putting me in so much pain. He had to. And by the looks of his bruised face, I put him through some pain of his own. A sharp purple line rides under his eye where the skin has split. And a yellow bruise runs alongside his nose and under the chin.

Not bad work, Eve.

In truth, I don't know why I feel so much malice, aside from the fact that he is wearing jeans and looks clean and relaxed, and I am still in the clothes I wore during the fight — blood-splattered and coated in sweat — and in a foreign place with this foreign boy who until now has been watching me sleep.

"Where am I?" I ask, louder this time.

"Nurse's station." He shrugs. "I'm guessing by the way you fight, you've been here before. Am I wrong?"

"And let me guess, you came to gloat. Typical Preme."

His eyes narrow. "You know…" His voice trails off, and he shakes his head.

With some effort, I lie back down on the well-worn mattress. I stare at the ceiling. I don't care what he was going to say; I'm not interested. He is a Preme. I am a Lower Mean. It is ingrained in us not to like each other; it has been ingrained in us since civilization first moved down here all those years ago. Since the wealthiest and most powerful families aboveground established themselves on the fifth floor, and those less fortunate were slotted down here in our own slice of hell. So instead of thinking about him for another second, I think about what I am going to do.

The last place I want to be is the nurse's station. Only losers wind up in the nurse's station after a fight. If word gets around… I need to go. It's bad enough I lost, but to lose to a Preme? I need to go *now*. Except my insides scream in agony every time I move, and it will be a far walk back to my cell unassisted. My head pounds so hard I can barely keep my eyes open, the lighting too much for my warped brain, though it is dim. Lower Mean dim.

Time to ignore the pain.

I shove one foot off the mattress, then the other. I pull myself to sitting, breathing through my teeth as my feet dangle to the floor. Bare toes skim its cool surface, and I focus on this sensation alone.

"Are you kidding?" His back is straight now, and his arms are folded over his chest. "You need to lie down. You need to rest."

"I'm fine," I snap. "And I certainly don't need *you* telling me what to do. Just get out of here, okay?" I let my head fall forward until it rests in my palm and dry scales of blood curl under my fingers. My long blond hair hangs over my shoulder, and it is twisted with burgundy.

He stands abruptly and then sits again. He is strange for a Preme. I can't put my finger on it.

"Here's the thing," he says, and I can hear his low voice tense up like a coil. "When I threw my name in to fight, I didn't know." He stares at the floor, eyes flashing darkly.

"Didn't know what?"

"Nobody mentioned that I'd be paired up against…"

I watch him closely as he runs a hand through his hair. His discomfort is thick between us. It feels good to watch him sweat.

"A girl?" I finally offer.

He looks at me and shrugs. "I had no idea," he says plainly.

I frown. I don't know how to feel. Offended that he thinks I am weak just because of my gender? Touched by his chivalry? I decide on the former. "Don't do me any favors, all right? I fight guys all the time. Usually I beat them. Today I didn't. No big deal."

His voice darkens. "I tried to get you to stop. I kept telling you to stop fighting. But you just wouldn't give up. I had no choice…" His voice fades away, and his gaze licks at my wounds, trickles down the bloodstains.

So this is what it's about. He feels guilty because he beat up a girl. Something they don't do on the fifth floor, evidently. Where they are *civilized*. And now he needs me to tell him it's okay. That I'm fine. No hard feelings.

Only I don't want to appease him. But I also don't want him to think I am weak. "I hope I get the chance to fight you again," is all I can think to say. My voice is calm, earnest, my face once again disinterested. "Now that I know what kind of cheap shots you Premes take."

Quickly his eyes narrow into a scowl. "You punched me before the ref was even in the ring."

I have the sudden urge to burst into laughter. But I hold it in. "Just watch your back, okay? Us Lower Means fight for the fun of it, in the Bowl and out. Preeminates like you are delicate."

He leans forward, and I see anger dart across his eyes. "We're alone right now. Want me to finish you off?"

A hot rush of anger spreads through my chest, but before I can raise a fist, he laughs.

"You think you've got me all figured out, don't you?" he says. "Because I live on the fifth floor and you live down here." His eyes are cold again. They are expressive. Except I haven't seen anything resembling warmth in them. Maybe it is in there, behind a cloud; maybe not. "But here's the thing: Life isn't that simple. You think since I'm a Preme my life is gold, but you have no clue. You think I look down on you, see you as filth, but you're the one doing it to me. You're more preoccupied with being a Lower Mean than anyone else is. Did you ever think about that?"

I shake my head. "I wouldn't know. I don't exactly venture out of Lower Mean territory if I can help it."

"That's a lie." The words escape him quickly, and then he pauses. Like he didn't plan to say them.

"What are you talking about?"

He looks uncomfortable again. The anger in his eyes has faded. "I've seen you before, that's all. In the library." He stares at me. "Or at least I think it's you. It's hard to tell when your face is covered in blood." His lips curl into a smirk.

"Cheap shots tend to do that."

"You didn't give me a choice."

I'm about to tell him there is always a choice, but I hear something from around the corner: the shuffling of feet, low chatter. A moment later, Hunter, Maggie, and Emerald push into the small room.

They freeze when they see who sits in front of me. Or maybe it is my condition that does it.

"What's *he* doing here?" Hunter demands, his gaze shifting slowly from my bloodstained face to the Preme.

Emerald stirs and makes her stance wider. "Get away from her."

The Preme's eyebrows lift. "Why, you think I'm going to hurt her?" His gaze flicks to mine. "Again?"

It stings; he meant for it to. My stupid pride. But he is accepting the fact that he has hurt me—relishing it, even. No longer does he feel riddled with guilt; I can see that. That is good. I don't want his sympathy.

"You just about killed her," Emerald continues. "You know that, don't you? Smashing her face in like that...we have a word for that down here: dirty. Don't think we'll forget."

He raises a hand. "If I wanted to kill her," he says as he stares at me, "don't you think I would have by now?" Strangely enough, there is no anger in his eyes, not now.

Instead they look thoughtful. Maybe he is thinking about killing me. Maybe he is enjoying it.

The room is silent, and all of us are still.

Finally Hunter raises the white paper bag that he holds. "Lemon squares, Eve. Your favorite," he mutters. His eyes linger a little longer on the Preme. Maybe he'd rather not look at me at all. I don't blame him.

"Thanks, Hunter." If there was any fight left in my voice, now it is gone. I just want to sleep. To lie back peacefully and shut my eyes and forget all of this. I want to dream about the Oracle. Dream about being anywhere but here, in Compound Eleven.

The scraping of the Preme's chair wakes me from my daze. He is standing. But before he goes, he bends his face down so it is inches from mine. "Bye, *Eve*. Hope it doesn't hurt too much to chew."

I watch his back as he moves past my friends, glaring at them as he goes. His eyes flash to mine one last time, the slightest grin curling his lips, and then he is gone.

The others rush to my side and fill his place. Whatever spell made things so uncomfortable is broken. It is me and my friends, and everything is okay again. The worst of the pain is over, and from here on out, it will get better.

It can only get better.

"Are you all right?" Maggie asks. She sits next to me and places my hand in hers. There is a bruise on the top of her hand, a strange spot for one, especially for someone who doesn't fight. I don't have the energy to ask her about it.

"I'm fine, or at least I will be. I just need to lie down." I sigh, and weariness wraps itself around my shoulders. "Is he gone?"

Emerald ducks her head around the corner. "All clear," she reports a second later. "What was he doing here, anyway? Dare I ask?"

I shrug, then Maggie and Hunter grab me under the arms and slowly lower me onto the bed. That feels better. A few more minutes here, just to rest my head. And then I'll go back to my cell, where I can heal.

"He probably wanted to rub in the fact that he won," Emerald continues. She shakes her head. "So, how big of an asshole was he?"

I mean to say that he wasn't that bad. Instead I say: "Huge one."

"Figured. Big dude, though, right? You really held your own out there, Eve. Bruno says that even *he*'d have a tough time beating a guy like that. And he's pro."

"Really? He actually said that?" She nods, and I smile. Bruno is seventeen; he picked fighting as his job a year ago. And he's good—one of the best in the League.

"He said that guy can fight. Like, legit, you know? And he's quick." She grins, and dimples pinch in her cheeks. Normally she looks fierce—she *is* fierce. But she's got a sweet smile, something guys are starting to notice. "Not that I need to tell you that," she adds with a wink.

Hunter sits beside me on the bed, pushes my hair from my face, and sets a neatly cut square with powdered sugar dusting the top into my hand. "Eat," he orders. "It'll make you feel better. And since it was no small feat getting it out of the kitchen, savor every bite."

"Damn, that's legit. How'd you even get it?" Emerald asks. "Because Houdini you are not. I've seen you run before, and you're sure as hell not fast enough to make a dash for it."

He shoves her. "I'm faster than you. And my girlfriend works there, that's how." He drums long fingers against his knee, then adjusts his glasses. "I'm pretty sure I've mentioned her. Anita."

Maggie leans forward. "Wait, she's your girlfriend now?

I thought you two were just hanging out!"

A shy smile flickers across Hunter's face. He is all shy smiles. "Well, yeah."

"Is it official? Like Kyle-and-me official?"

He rolls his eyes, and as Maggie makes kissing noises, I focus my attention on the lemon square. The last thing I want to do right now is put food in my mouth; my stomach churns with too much blood. But holding the square in my hand is no better. The bones in my knuckles scream—they must be cracked—yet I know how difficult it is to bend the rules in Compound Eleven, and so I swallow the pain and the nausea and force my hand to my mouth. Hunter is a good friend.

"How'd you know I was here?" I ask once I'm sure I won't vomit.

"Saw the ref outside the Bowl talking to your dad. He told us. Not that it was exactly hard to piece together ourselves. I mean, they had to *carry* you out of the ring."

I place the remainder of the square on my chest and do my best to ignore the heat lashing at my face. "Was he—was he angry?"

Maggie gazes at me. She has an inquisitive look to her. All eyes. Today they look puffy, like she's been crying. "Was *who* angry?" she asks slowly. "Your dad?"

I nod.

"Angry that you lost?" She rolls her eyes. "It was a good fight, Eve. Tell me you know that. Emerald's right: he was a big guy. And older than you, don't forget."

I am silent. He *had* looked older than sixteen. Definitely. It strikes me suddenly that I don't even know his name, let alone anything else about him, other than the fact that he is a Preeminate. And a good fighter.

Maggie is still talking. "If anything, your dad was worried

about you. *Obviously*," she adds when she sees the look on my face.

Right. *So then why hasn't he stopped by?* my brain yells. He knows I'm here, laid up in the nurse's station.

Hunter takes the remainder of the lemon square and passes it to the others. When he turns back to me, he sighs. "At the risk of stating the obvious, that was a shocking match. When you didn't get up at the end, the entire Bowl went quiet. I think everyone sort of thought, you know, that was it. You wouldn't be waking up from that one." He runs a hand through his hair a little unsteadily. He was scared for me. They all were.

"Yeah, everyone went quiet…except for Daniel, Landry, and *Zaar*," adds Emerald as she rolls her eyes. "They weren't exactly what I'd call worried."

"They wouldn't be," I say. Daniel and his friends hate most people, but they have long held a particular hatred for me. The feeling is mutual.

"If it makes you feel any better," Emerald continues, "I think they were the only ones in the entire Bowl actually cheering for the Preme. And that's saying something, right? I mean, the stands were killer full. And man, when you sucker punched him at the start of the match, they…went…*wild*."

I try to smile, but I can feel a wave of disappointment riding in instead. I lost, in a big way. I couldn't even walk out of the Bowl with dignity. They had to carry me. People thought I was *dead*.

Deep breath, in and out. Time to package up my disappointment and set it aside. So I got beat—badly—by a Preme, landed in the nurse's station. He was strong. Dangerous. And I put up a good fight before things slid sideways. I did.

And—this is the most important part—it doesn't matter. Let Daniel laugh. Let my father be disappointed; let him think that maybe, just maybe, if Jack had been born first, he would have beaten the Preme. That he would have made him proud. It doesn't matter, none of it. Because in six weeks—by the end of what civilization used to call summer, by the time adulthood begins in earnest with the selection of a job—I will be gone.

I don't know how, not yet. But I know that my time in Compound Eleven is nearly over.

CHAPTER FIVE

wake to blackness, velvety and thick.

They say that many decades ago, before we were forced underground, the rising sun would gently wake its people — not kill them. I squeeze my eyes shut and try to picture a burning ball of fire, one that lulls me awake with its glow.

It is impossible. I know only blackness.

But I have seen pictures in my textbooks and in the books that fill Compound Eleven's library on the fifth floor. I know it looks like a bright-white light, like the end of a flashlight. I know it is hard if not impossible to stare at. I know it is a four-billion-year-old sphere, one much larger than even Earth...

Still, I can't imagine it. How could one object so many miles away fill the world aboveground with so much light? With so much heat that it is deadly? I must see it to believe it.

Something I intend to do today.

Not that today is different from any other day. It has been months now — months of trying and failing to gain entry to the Oracle, Compound Eleven's only viewing station. The view it offers is of the world aboveground, and it is encased in glass or some other protective material so that it is safe, so that the heat doesn't swallow you whole. That is all I know.

They used to have field trips there for the children; they don't anymore. I remember sitting straighter when the second-grade teacher first mentioned it. I remember thinking maybe *my* class would be permitted to go. I remember feeling inexplicably hopeful.

No such luck. Besides, even if a field trip had been authorized, my parents wouldn't have allowed it.

Because in second grade, I was seven. And when I was seven, my little brother, Jack, was thrown aboveground for being in breach of the compound's *one child per family* policy, a policy designed to curb population growth, a policy that uses forced abortion and even sterilization to ensure compliance. Sometimes, though—sometimes a second pregnancy can be hidden from the Preeminates in charge. From Commander Katz and his comrades. Sometimes life can be hidden, too. But Jack was not so lucky, and so my parents would never have allowed me to view a world that saw his final breaths.

My own breath hitches in my throat at the thought, and I push it down, down. Instead I comfort myself the same way I have for the past nine years. I think about the remote possibility of a miracle. I convince myself that maybe… somehow…*he* found a way to do what all else can't. Survive.

Silly. And senseless. Similar to my preoccupation with the world up there. Silly. Senseless.

Sure.

But for nine years, I have thought of little else. I have read more books about it than anyone I know, even my teachers. And now, as I teeter on adulthood, I have decided to finally see in person what all those dusty old books describe. See in person, through the protective walls of the Oracle, the scorching world my little brother was cruelly turned out into.

Since school is over and I have no interest or need for the job tours, I have had plenty of opportunities to attempt entry to the Oracle. So far I haven't been successful, but maybe today will be the day. 11000536. That is today's code. That is what my hopes pin to for now.

It has been three days since the fight, and my bruises have started to fade—those to my body and to my ego. Skin that was punched apart has mostly mended. My muscles are still sore, and my ribs, but now I can move without groaning; I have rested enough. Too much, in fact, because now I am restless.

Restless people make mistakes; they get sloppy. And if I am caught breaking into the Oracle…

Well, I don't know what would happen, not fully. Punishment is decided by the Head of Justice, a Preme position—of course—and from what I've heard, he has a particular hatred for rule breakers. Losing a finger is a definite possibility, maybe worse. Everything, besides murder, is decided on a case-by-case basis, probably to keep us guessing. To allow the Head of Justice discretion to exact his will, offer him an outlet for a bad day or a crummy mood…

For murder, on the other hand, punishment is clear: Murderers are released aboveground. There, the sun will scald them to death, and if it is cloudy, the heat will suffocate them. And if for some reason it doesn't, the land is barren and dry—incapable of supporting life. They will eventually die.

I think of Jack, his smiling face, his delicate fingers inherited from my mother, and I shudder.

We used to play a game together in the evenings: one of us would hide a small object—usually a paperclip—on our body. Pushed behind an ear, shoved down a sock. The other person had to find it, and I still remember how deftly those little fingers of his moved, tucking into my pockets, combing through my hair. I still remember how hard he laughed, how much joy he took from our simple ritual.

Frowning deeply, I turn on the lamp beside my bed and sit upright, pull on my boots. They are heavy with steel, useful if I need to defend myself. First, I tuck in a switchblade — a gift from my father and one I take care of. Weapons are hard to come by in Compound Eleven. Next, I tuck in a small flashlight, in case of a blackout.

The blackouts are to conserve energy, they say, and are becoming more and more frequent. It is something I pay attention to because, though I am afraid of little, I am afraid of the dark.

A secret I guard with my life.

I check to make sure my hair is still braided from the night prior, then rub sleep from deep-set eyes, crescents carved into skin. I yawn. Slowly, my hand drags over the rest of my face, over features that are straight and even and wide. I've been told that I don't look like a fighter, not really. I don't look fragile, either.

Finally I stand and glance in the small mirror that hangs over the desk, one that is cracked along the top and stained around the edges. My eyes look tired, though not from lack of sleep. At least the swelling in my face has gone; I look like myself again, even with a patchwork of color stretching over the skin.

A moment later, I leave the confines of my small cell and lock the door behind me as my eyes scan the hallway for danger. There is none; it's empty. Only the faint buzzing of the neon green sign that hangs opposite my door, letters spelling out *Mean 2*. As if I couldn't tell. The very same number is tattooed on the backs of my hands.

If for some reason I don't escape Eleven by the time of job selections, I will be subjected to more tattoos, ones that will eventually cover my forearms. All lower-floor adults have them, meaning upper-floor managers don't need to learn our names. So they can simply read the bits of unwanted ink to know our position, our family history, our disciplinary record. An information dump, one continually updated as time marches on, and all for the convenience of the higher-born. What else is new.

The tattoos have a far worse connotation for me than for most people, though, and as I remember the sound of skin being scratched into long, tapering pieces, I cover my ears until the memory passes...

I don't know what time it is, but I know it is early. My father has trained me to wake early, and so I do. Maggie still sleeps soundly behind the door to my left, and Hunter too, on the door to my right. Emerald is a Mean, so she lives on the third floor, between the Lower and the Upper Means, and most days she sleeps until noon.

They know nothing about my secret trips to the fifth floor. Nobody does.

I am not quite to the main corridor when I hear it. Footsteps, heavy with speed.

I move to the side of the dimly lit hallway and wait. The concrete wall is cold, enough to make my palms ache, but I don't have to wait long. A young boy flashes in and out of my vision: short with orange hair, something tucked under his arm. A heartbeat later, there is another flash, this time all black. A guard. He is holding something long and metal.

A baton.

I step into the corridor when they have passed and gaze after them. Just in time to see the guard raise the baton over his head and smash the boy to the ground. The boy crumples and then rolls. The guard smashes him, again and again. The thing under the boy's arm was a loaf of bread, and now it lies still and forgotten.

Soon the boy will, too. I can't see the tattoos on his hands from here, but he's probably a Denominator from the first floor; they are always hungry.

Maggie and Hunter think I should try to be a guard, think that I would be able to secure such a position even though it is an Upper Mean fourth-floor job, even though Lower Means like me are never granted such authority. My fighting background helps my chances, they say, and my volunteer work feeding the Denominators — Noms for short — does, too.

I think I would rather die, I tell them.

In fact, I would rather die than hold any position down here, because every Mean job ultimately does one thing. It serves the Preme leaders, the people responsible for what happened to Jack. I refuse to serve them, not for a day, not for an hour, not even for a minute. I refuse to kneel before them and pledge my service. I refuse to have a painful past branded forever along my skin. So I will have to escape Compound Eleven before that time comes.

Six weeks. Six weeks to find a way out.

Tick tock.

I take a deep breath and turn away from the violence. There was a time when I would have interfered. Called out, told the guard to stop. Stepped in front of the kid. That natural inclination to right wrong has been beaten out of me, though. It is every man, woman, and child for themselves. I understand that now. Perhaps other compounds are less cruel, but ours is not.

Ours is cruel.

As I take my first step, the boy groans, low and guttural, and it reaches my ears over the dull thuds of metal against bone. My stomach curls; my vision twitches. My voice bursts from my chest before I can force it down again. "Get away from him!"

When will I learn, when will I learn.

The guard freezes with his baton suspended in midair. His head swivels in my direction. Black marble beads glare at me, and then his spine straightens. The boy is barely moving at his feet, but there is life in him yet.

I swallow. I am in no condition to defend myself. That is the biggest downside to fighting at the Bowl: how vulnerable I am in the hours and days that follow. Weak from expending every last molecule of energy, then another mile more. No, I cannot fight. My only chance is to run.

Perhaps the guard will let me be. He won't let both of us be, though. He needs to take his rage out on one of us, and I decide quickly it had better be me. "Coward," I say loud enough for him to hear, and then my muscles contract and expand and I am running up the main corridor as fast as my boots will allow.

The lightbulbs are strung at long intervals, and every third or fourth is burned out so that I pass in and out of a cloud of darkness. My boots smack against the cold cement floor, the guard's steps echoing close behind.

I will veer off the main corridor soon and lose him. I know these halls better than he does, and I'm quick around corners But I need to find someone first.

Finally, bodies up ahead—live ones.

"Go down there!" I yell between breaths to a group in front of me. Women and children. "There's a boy there, hurt. Go help him."

The women scowl at me and draw the children near to their chests as though I might attack. As though I am not currently preoccupied. "Stay away from us," one spits at me as I pass. They are Upper Mean. Well dressed and groomed, the number four tattooed on their hands. They can tell by my wrinkled T-shirt and ripped jeans alone that I am Lower

Mean. That this level is my home.

They will not help the boy.

But an old man with white stubble and a twisted arm nods at me as I fly past. He has heard. He will go. My work is done, my meddling complete.

I dart left, down the corridor that leads to the family cells, my own neighborhood until a couple weeks ago. This one has a pink stripe painted along the concrete walls, and it is mostly covered in wadded-up paper crusted with saliva. There will be more bodies down here, crowds of them; kids tend to wake early, or so I remember. Right now, though—right now it is just the guard and me.

I glance over my shoulder as I run. He hasn't gained on me; he hasn't dropped away, either. But most disconcerting of all is his silence. Most guards shout. They tell me to stop, then they give up. This one is determined.

Dark turns to light, and light turns to dark. A strobe effect, dizzying. No sound but my heart thumping in my ears, my boots slapping the floor. And then a strange thing happens. Part of me thinks about giving up. Slowing my pace. I see myself coming to a stop, letting the guard's fury find me, baton cocked. I see myself lying in a pool of red, waiting for death.

He is closer now.

A rush of adrenaline finds me, and I push on, the will to live still burning bright. Sometimes I wonder if it is better to be alive and caged or dead and free. I guess if I'm fighting for my life right now, I believe the former.

It is always better to be alive.

Weary muscles sear with pain, and my lungs burn. Running from guards when I was small was something of a pastime, something fun. Now I just want to be free of him—of all of them. I want to be left alone.

Up ahead is my out.

Children kick a ball around; parents supervise, they mingle. More and more appear from their cell doors as I watch, ready to start the day, and the crowd grows thicker. Kids laugh, and babies scream. This is my chance. I push several feet into the crowd, then duck behind a cluster of women, and from there I jump after another group trailing that. I don't look back or let my eyes scan for my foe, I just keep moving, weaving through bodies with my head low, losing myself in the sea of people.

"…And last month's allotment was stolen right out of my hands," complains a woman loudly in my ear.

"No respect," mutters her companion.

Then a thumb digs painfully into bone until I wince. A heartbeat later I swivel and put all my force behind a blow to the nose. I hear it crack over the noise of the children. A perfect strike. The guard is stunned and distracted, and I yank myself free and disappear through the crowd, running harder than before. Now, just like that, the stakes are raised. Now he will shoot, if he gets a clear line.

I force my way through a group of boys playing with a handmade hacky sack and veer right, down a tight-fitting corridor. That is when I notice another guard up ahead—a female one, something of a rarity. Those belonging to Compound Eleven's guardship are mostly men—men hungry for clout, domination, the right to rule with brutal force. But it is impossible to mistake her for anything else. Black combat boots and fingerless gloves, knee and elbow pads of the same color. A protective vest full of artillery pockets. And lastly, the face mask. A flat piece of metal painted matte black with two holes for the eyes. Except the guards never wear them; they are too uncomfortable, so instead they hang around the neck to be used as needed.

More disconcerting than any of it, though—a gun in one holster and a baton in the other.

But I am smiling because I know there is a supply closet just ahead, down a corridor to my left. If it's locked, I am dead. If it isn't, I have a chance. A good one.

The female guard looks up, and her eyes latch onto mine through strands of stringy brown hair. Then her head arches, and she spots the guard behind me. Automatically, and just as I knew it would, her hand reaches for her weapon. There are no sanctions she or the others would face for killing a Lower Mean like me, not in practice. Head of Security Jeffrey Sitwell may preach protection for all, but everyone knows the guards are here for one reason: to keep safe the ruling floor. I am not a Preeminate, not even close. I am disposable.

Quickly I throw myself left, speed down a short corridor with a single door at its end. The supply closet will be connected to other hallways, and that is why it is worth the risk.

Don't be locked, don't be locked, don't be locked.

They hardly ever are—most of the locks don't even work. Nobody around here wants to steal a broom. My legs drive me to the end of the corridor, and an unsteady hand shoots forward. My stomach seizes up like an elastic band has been wrapped around it.

Don't be locked.

It opens easily, and I jump inside, grab a handful of mops, and jam them under the door as far as they will go. It will slow the guards, and that is the best I can hope for. Next I turn, and as a gunshot rings out, as it cracks the door I have just wedged shut, I jump over a trash bin and pull open the door straight in front of me. I hear the guards shouting—that and their guns firing again into the small room—but I am gone.

I run quickly, my boots carrying me down one hall and into the next. I keep going and going, longer than I have to, rolling up my sleeves as I go, even changing my hair so that it falls loosely past my shoulders. I am more risk averse now that I am older. Finally, with half of Floor Two separating me from that supply closet, I let myself smile. I shake out my muscles, shove my hands in my pockets. I even think about telling Maggie and Hunter about my adventure later, how it will remind all of us of old times.

Hunter refused to run from the guards when we were little—maybe he was too afraid, or maybe he just knew better. Whatever it was, he kept himself out of trouble, played the system to his advantage. Still does. Maggie and I, though, spent many hours of our early childhood on the run, causing a ruckus in a supply closet or smuggling treats out of the cafeteria—nothing serious, just enough to attract the attention of a nearby guard. And once we'd shaken him, we would hunch over with laughter.

The guards were less ruthless back then. Everyone was. But as time beat on, agitation grew—the sort of toxic agitation I attribute to life quarantined inside an underground box. Now people are miserable; they are mad, particularly on the bottom floors, where life is most difficult. The fourth-floor guards have a good life —too good, as far as I'm concerned— so I don't know why they are more sadistic now than they were. Maybe they're sick of putting up with shit from the rest of us. Or maybe they've always been this way and I was simply too young, too naive to see it.

It has been a few generations since civilization moved underground, and they say our generation is the worst. We are too far removed from it. We don't appreciate the gift of life we have been given here, firmly below the earth's crust. We don't realize how tough life was aboveground. How much had to be sacrificed to start over somewhere safe.

Perhaps. But it's not as though we are unfamiliar with the details. They teach it in school—drill it into us from an early age. I know the story of our inception as well as anyone.

It all began when the writing was on the wall. When it became clear that within decades, crops would be in a permanent state of ruin. Cities would be awash with ocean water. Young and old and everyone in between would be killed by smothering heat, by viruses festering in skyrocketing humidity. Panic spread; denial, too. Governments teetered as they rushed to turn back time. Humanity started to come undone.

But first, an idea was born: to transfer society underground and away from it all.

Governments wouldn't hear of it; their focus was aboveground, their revenues earmarked for efforts to cool the earth. Yet still the idea of an underground society persisted — it grew into a movement in its own right, populated by those who correctly predicted that the governments' efforts were in vain. But such a vast project required vast funds.

And so the wealthiest, most powerful members of the movement banded together, our so-called saviors — they agreed to finance every aspect of the new society, on one condition. That it would be theirs to rule.

Early proposals excluded the indigent entirely — space was reserved for only those who could afford it, something our teachers conveniently left out of their lectures. But I know the real story from whisperings in the corridors, from our elders and the elders before that. I know that eventually the wealthy realized they would need muscle to build the compounds, laborers to clean them, workers to fill the underground factories where goods would be made, where genetically modified food would be produced. And so, because of necessity and nothing more, those of little means were invited in — offered a chance at survival, so long as they abided by the rules. So long as they inhabited the lowest floors, so long as they asked for little.

Our saviors indeed.

When the indigent agreed to such harsh terms, they probably didn't realize how deeply they would be oppressed or how dire their circumstances would be. And they couldn't know then that all their descendants would be sentenced to the same cruel fate. So when the time came, when the clock finally ran out on Planet Earth and the last embers of aboveground civilization turned to ash, down they came, rich and poor and those in between, and a new order was established...

They say we can't understand. I suppose we can't, and so misery abounds.

All around me, I see evidence of it: faces touched with strain, eyes tomb-like and empty. Even the sound bites are depressing:

"Oh, Billy? He hung himself at the equinox."

"We ran outta diapers. We've been reusing them dirty till the compound authorizes more."

"His broken arm was never set. Don't you see it sticking out funny?"

With intention, I drop my gaze to the floor, hum the compound's anthem loudly under my breath. Time to circle back to the elevators; time to go to the fifth floor.

To the Oracle.

CHAPTER SIX

I kick an empty can all the way back to the elevators and find them busy. The cafeteria is on the third floor, and people are waking in droves now, heading up for breakfast. I have barely eaten since the fight; my jaw has been too sore, my appetite too sparse. Right now I just need to get upstairs to the fifth floor. I just need to try today's code: 11000536.

Usually I take the stairs—they're always empty—but I am too sore, especially now. So I board the elevator and try to ignore the feeling of shoulders pressing against mine, the breath of many mingling and rising. I blot away the remaining blood from my knuckles and run my fingers over broken scabs. That guard deserved a broken nose. I am happy that I was the one to give it to him. I am angry that I had to.

The doors slide open at the third floor, and the elevator clears out. Perfect. Except Daniel spots me through the crowd, and he jumps aboard before the doors can close. My muscles tighten and my breathing quickens, but the rest of me is still. Impassive.

He is an Upper Mean, tall with curly hair cut short, and

he smells like bitter, astringent soap. Otherwise he is plain and unmemorable, except for an evil streak that cuts through him like acid. To describe him as heartless would be too kind.

"What do you want," I say as the elevator glides upward. My voice is sour.

He shoves a piece of toast into his mouth and smirks. "Haven't seen you around for the past few days, Eve. What happened? Did you get an ouchie on your face?" His fingers reach toward my bruises. I grab his wrist.

"Touch me, and I'll destroy you," I say quietly.

He laughs. "Hard to believe that, sweetheart." He pulls his hand free and makes a point of wiping it on his pleated pants. "Heard you had to get medical attention, you were so bad. And against a *Preme*. Maybe you're losing your edge, *Evie*."

I scoff. "You think calling me a childhood nickname is going to get under my skin? Get real, *Dan-Dan*."

Now his hand curls into a fist, and he studies it. He puts on a show that is meant to intimidate me. I don't allow it to. But I do glance at the buttons of the elevator, feeling my muscles unclench when I see we are almost at the fifth floor. I don't have it in me to fight him, not right now, but if I had to—if I *had* to—I would win. I am confident of that.

I was confident of that back in fourth grade when I threw an elbow into his teeth, sick of the endless taunts he leveled against us Lower Means, particularly against Maggie, who I think he had a thing for. It was the first time one of us stood up to him, and it cemented his hatred for me then and there—it serves as the foundation for our endless feud that lives on today.

The doors are slow to open, and when they do, his hand reaches out and stops me—pushes roughly against my stomach. "What are you doing up here, anyway?"

"None of your business."

"What, think you're going to land a job with the Premes?" He sneers, and his face looks so smug I want to punch it.

"I'd have a better shot than you," I say hotly. I know I shouldn't let him get to me, but I can't help it. "My grades are better than yours. I fight, I volunteer. Maybe I'll try for one of those guard jobs you're always talking about," I lie.

"Go back to where you came from, Lower Mean," he snaps. I've hit a nerve.

A wicked smile curls my lips, and then I push past him and into the Preme atrium, where the floors are spotless and the air is clean. "Trash," he mutters, but before I can retaliate, the elevator doors seal into one and he is gone.

Relax, Eve.

But I am rattled; I can feel it in my bones. Between the orange-haired boy downstairs, the guard, and Daniel, I am shaken. I need to breathe. I need to calm down and concentrate. Because today is the day. Today will be the day. 11000536.

I start forward, but I pause at the bronze sculpture of a globe that hogs the middle of the atrium. I have walked by it hundreds of times, but never have I studied it. I know it represents the world, and I know that the small red X indicates our position on a piece of land known as North America, but the whole thing is meaningless. Maybe people used to study this sort of thing when they lived aboveground, but what's the point now?

Slowly I walk around it. Perhaps it *does* have meaning. Because as I stare at it, I see that the world is a very big place, and that Compound Eleven occupies a very tiny sliver of it. Under five square miles, to be precise. The number of other compounds out there must be staggering. And surely not all of them are as cruel as ours.

Now my eyes twist around the atrium in search of

something else—a sign, any sign, any indication at all of where the tunnels to other compounds could be. I don't have to accept Compound Eleven, I already know that. I don't even have to accept the nearby compounds Ten or Twelve. I can keep searching, on and on, for my rightful home…

The thought is soothing, just what I need. So it's with something approaching contentment that I walk past the library, past its large glass windows that let me glimpse the long tables and rows of books inside.

It is my favorite room in the entire compound, even more than the Bowl. Means aren't allowed up here on the Preme floor, just like Noms aren't permitted on the Mean floors, but the rules are relaxed for the library. Our class frequented it as students, and me far more than that. Besides, if it weren't for people like me, the entire place would be obscured by dust.

I don't understand why. The pictures and stories the old books hold of life aboveground, when it was safe, are mesmerizing. Maybe what happened to Jack first sparked my obsession with the world up there, but it has grown into more than that. Now I often spend hours there, doing nothing more than looking at the cities and the streets, drooling over the open and unending space.

By comparison, there is nothing but dimly lit, dirty hallways down here. I suppose that isn't true on the fifth floor. The lights are bright, the hallways sterile. And the walls aren't concrete like they are downstairs; they aren't covered in filth and graffiti. No, these are smooth and plastic and pristine. They glow white. Everything does.

I breathe, and the sequence begins. Right, left, right, left, right, right, right, left. I take my first right. Ten paces, then left. A quick right. It is therapeutic and cathartic, this ritual of mine.

Finally, I reach it…the door to the Oracle's emergency exit.

Normally an elevator would be used to reach the Oracle, one that runs from the fifth floor, but for some reason it is guarded too closely.

I spent weeks trying to get past those guards, but to no avail. Then one day I overheard two of them talking, and I learned about this. A back staircase, it would seem, and the possibility was undeniably uplifting. It took many more weeks to locate the room, or at least what I think is the right room. It runs behind the elevator shaft, and it is locked under code, signs that my suspicions are correct.

I run my fingers over its cool brushed metal. My heart hammers in my chest; I don't know why. After thirty-five unsuccessful attempts to get through this door, there is nothing to be nervous or excited about.

11000536, today's code. I will repeat it again and again in my head until it is time for the next code: 11000537. The worst part is that, since the clock is ticking on my time here in Eleven, I can't be certain I'll ever crack it.

But I suppose I should be grateful that I have an educated guess to work with. It's more than most people have. Of course, most people don't have years upon years of concerted effort deciphering Compound Eleven's codes.

It all started when I was a little girl, when I would help my mother work the food lines for the Noms. The same job I do now, alone. Each time I would watch the guards' fingers hover over the keypad as they unlocked what they referred to as the "feeding dock" for us, and though most were discreet, as they are trained to be, there are a careless few in every crowd. And so with time I got a sense for the code, and I started experimenting when others weren't watching.

The first two digits were easy to see and easy to understand: 11. As in Compound Eleven. The next three are zeroes—fillers, I have come to believe. The next digit is the floor number.

But the last digit, or digits—they link to the specific door. If a floor has twenty doors under passcode, each door will be assigned a number between one and twenty, and there is no rhyme or reason to this final assignment. Trial and error is the only name of the game.

The second floor has only a handful of locked doors—little is valuable on my floor. So through repeated, varied attempts, I have figured out the code to each. I have made headway on the third floor, too. But the fifth floor is different. Valuable rooms abound. Labs are up here. The entire compound is controlled from this floor. The government rules from up here.

I tap in today's code. There could be a hundred locked doors on the fifth floor, maybe more. And so, at my current pace of trying a single code per day, it could be months before I crack it—months that I don't have. Or I could be on the wrong track completely; the code could be altogether different here in Preme land.

On my thinking goes, and so I barely notice when the door clicks quietly open in front of me.

When I do notice, I freeze. If my heart was hammering when I was fleeing the guard downstairs or speaking with Daniel on the elevator, it is nothing to how it feels now. Blood rushes to my brain, and I must grasp at the wall for balance. I can't remember feeling so lightheaded before.

Deep breath, in and out. I reach an unsteady hand forward and pull open the door.

It is just a room, a dark and unused room. But light from the hallway floods the small space, and with it I see a ladder built into the far wall.

A ladder to the Oracle.

CHAPTER SEVEN

A guard could be by at any second, or even one of the Premes, so I step quickly inside and flip on the light, let the door close behind me. The thumping inside my chest is fast and pronounced… I got in.

I got in.

A glance around the room brings to mind the Mean floors, particularly my own: utilitarian, nothing more. No glowing plastic, no pristine shade of white. Just a stack of orange crates sitting in a concrete corner. *And the ladder.* I stare at it and breathe.

Months and months and months of focused, concentrated effort have led me to this moment. It makes everything else feel inconsequential, even my plan to leave Eleven for another compound before jobs are chosen. For the first time in my life, I am going to see what it looks like aboveground. To that place where Jack was sent. To that place where there is too much space, too much light for me to comprehend. And as far as I know, I will be the only person of my generation to see it.

The truth is, I should have been spending the past few

months working on a plan—something definite—regarding how I will break free from my compound. How I will break into another. Which compound that should be. Instead, I have been consumed with this pet project, a burning, inexplicable desire to see the outside world displacing all reason.

Suddenly, I sway with anticipation. Or maybe it's nerves. Whatever it is, I give myself a shake; I grit my teeth.

Be strong, Eve.

I slap my right cheek, then my left. Better.

One boot starts up the ladder, then the next. Up and up until the emergency exit is within my reach. There is no lock, nothing but a smooth sheet of plywood hinged at one end. I stare at it and frown. What if someone is inside the Oracle right now? Unlikely, I know that. It serves no function that I know of, not since they stopped using it as a novelty for children below.

So a shaky hand shoots up—shoots up and strokes it, finds that it is rougher than it looks. With another breath, I gently push, push. Hinges creak, and I smile. It is opening—it is *actually* opening. I am almost inside the Oracle.

I shove it all the way back, and there is a flash of light, one that makes my eyes squeeze shut, one that makes me fall backward. Down. I land hard on the floor with a thud, and the wind is knocked from my lungs. Excitement is replaced by pain radiating to all extremities, and I struggle to breathe.

What's worse is that when I open my eyes, I see nothing but blazing white. So I blink and I blink, and finally spots of black appear, and finally the spots of black pool into one large spot that opens to reveal the room around me.

Okay. I am not hurt, not seriously, and other than seeing shots of electricity when I blink, my vision is fine. It had been blinding, though, whatever it was that made me fall. Surely it wasn't the sun. If it was, I know why the field trips to the Oracle were canceled. They said it would happen. The earth would grow more and more barren; the sun would burn brighter and brighter. We are not safe from it even under a protective barrier.

Do I dare venture up again?

A silly question, one that makes me smirk. It isn't just the months I've spent trying to get here. It's the years I've spent poring over books that describe the world up there. It's the heart-wrenching knowledge that my little brother took his last breaths there. I am tethered to it, even if I don't want to be. Tethered, intrigued, repelled, and a jumble of a million other emotions.

Stomach muscles draw me upright, and I start toward the ladder once more. But now I am more careful. Each step burns brighter than the last, and so I go slowly; I give my eyes time to adjust. Just as my head nears the emergency door, it happens again. This time I turn away and squeeze my eyes shut. This time I don't let go of the ladder. Instead I climb another step, even as the inside of my eyelids burn red, even as I feel warmth pressed against my cheek.

So it is the sun, a burning ball of fire indeed. I take a few moments to collect myself, then open my eyes a sliver.

It isn't so bad, so long as I turn away. With my heart pounding in my ears, my hands reach up and through the door, onto the gritty floor of the Oracle itself. Muscles spring into action, and I hoist myself up. I crouch above Compound Eleven.

I crouch *above* Compound Eleven. It isn't something I ever thought I would experience.

My eyes are still squeezed into slits, and I am afraid to open them. I don't know why. Perhaps it is fear of shooting white-hot pain through my retinas, but maybe it is more than that. Maybe I am afraid of seeing a red, grotesque plain littered with bones. Or maybe I am afraid that this quest won't make me feel any closer to Jack. Or that there is nothing interesting to see up here in this curious, dirty, warm place. Maybe it is better to stay as I am, full of accomplishment at making it here, and, more importantly, full of hope that something more beautiful than compound life persists in the world.

Lemon juice, Eve. The pain won't be as bad this time. And so what if the Oracle is a disappointment? All of Eleven is a disappointment. What's the difference?

So I open them slowly, keeping them trained on the floor, where the light is dullest. I can tell without looking up that it is brighter here than anywhere in the entire compound, even the fifth floor. I have never in all my sixteen years had so much brightness filtering through my pupils. Perhaps they will burst.

But after what feels like hours, my eyes adjust. I blink, and they open wide, still staring at the planks running below my boots.

I take a deep breath and lift my gaze.

I haven't moved in more than a minute, and I'm not sure my heart is pumping properly, I feel so faint. When I swallow, it feels like acid burning my throat.

In front of me is a slanted wall made of nothing but a thick sheet of glass in the shape of a triangle. And through the glass is the most magnificent thing I have ever seen.

When movement finally finds me, I inch forward, barely daring to breathe. Barely daring to blink. What if I do and all of it is gone? What if it's a dream that I wake from? Never to return again…

But the floor underfoot is true, and one step turns into

several, and finally…finally the glass wall is in front of me, and I raise both hands—I reach out and touch it. My fingers draw back at its warmth, but then they relax into it. Not burning hot, no. Just warm. A special technology, I remember. One that protects us from the murderous heat out there.

Out there. It might be dangerous out there. It might be killer and cruel. But it is poetry. It is artistry. It is grace.

It is life like I have never known.

There is no low-hanging ceiling. No broken lightbulbs. No unending concrete. There is no waste of red and no collection of bones.

I stare through the glass at a cord of brown that clings to the Oracle just left of my fingertips. From it bursts flaps of vivid green. Like no green I have ever seen. It is electric, and it is alive. Beyond it is a solid-looking growth with haggard skin, one that has soldiered through the earth perfectly linear, one that bursts into a million different offshoots as it reaches for the sky. Olive circles coat it at all angles, shuddering constantly, swaying in imperfect, perfect rhythm.

I have seen it before, in my books. It's a tree. I am sure of it.

Something black and violent bursts from behind it, and I jump, I swear, but then I see what it is and I smile, then laugh. I laugh for a long time as my eyes watch it go, as they find another, as they seek out even more. Birds. They must be birds. They can fly, and not many creatures can, according to my sixth-grade teacher. Insects can, but they are tiny, barely visible. Yes, those are birds.

So much freedom, so much latitude, so much space. I close my eyes and picture myself flying with them, my belly skimming the green on the tree, the breeze pushing my hair back and filling my nose. Tickling my skin. But I know the sun would scald me and the heat would suffocate me, and it is a wonder that even the birds can survive.

That scalding sun that shoved me down the stairs and filled my eyes with white-hot pain remains behind me, and I am careful to keep my gaze away from it. I have no need to look that way, not right now. Next time. There is enough to see here on this side of the Oracle. There is more to see than I could have ever imagined.

I take a seat and push my palms into the glass. I watch the birds. I watch the circles of green sway and tick. I watch the colors mix and mingle and change with every movement.

I thought it was better to be caged and alive.

I thought wrong.

CHAPTER EIGHT

When I am sure the hallway is clear, I slip out the door and shut it firmly behind me. 11000536. That is the code. That is the only code I need to remember. My heart beats in my throat, but this time it isn't with fear. It is with pure joy, and it feels foreign, it feels intoxicating.

An hour or more must have passed with me sitting up there, doing nothing but staring at the brilliant world aboveground, warm but otherwise safe under the protective prism of glass known as the Oracle. I could have spent many more hours there, perfectly at peace, but I can't be gone too long or the others will start to wonder. Maggie and Hunter know I wake early.

I want to tell them, I do, but I know that I won't. It is my secret—my beautiful, wondrous secret—and I smile to myself as I stream through the corridors toward the atrium. My secret to be shared with no one.

"Eve?"

I freeze at the sound of my name, then I laugh. I laugh because suddenly it sounds unfamiliar. Alien. Like I have met this Eve person before, but I don't know her well.

I am no longer in the Oracle, I remind myself; I am back in Compound Eleven, on the fifth floor where I don't belong, where I'm not allowed. Eve is me, and the speaker is someone I recognize. *Him* The Preeminate. The one from the fight. One I thought I would never lay eyes on again.

I turn, vaguely hoping my face is disinterested, passive. Except I can barely contain my excitement. All I can think about is my secret, and I can only hope he doesn't notice.

His wide-set eyes stir as we face each other, but otherwise his face is even. He wears a plain black T-shirt and blue jeans, and the bruises on his face have all but disappeared. "You look different," he finally says.

I resist the urge to burst into laughter. If only he knew. I don't simply look different, no. I *am* different. I can feel it in my veins.

Of course, he is probably talking about my face — no longer swollen — or maybe it is my loose hair or my unsoiled clothes. It doesn't matter which it is. Nothing matters, now that I have seen aboveground.

He takes a step closer and squints like he is trying to see deep inside me. "What are you doing up here?"

"Library," I say automatically. "I was in the library. I go there sometimes, remember?" I shrug.

"Library's back that way." He points behind me.

"Yeah, well, I decided to stretch my legs."

He nods like he doesn't quite believe me.

"Writing a book?"

"Your face looks better," he says instead of answering. "I take it you're feeling okay?"

This time I can't help the laughter that bubbles up in my throat. It tips through the air between us. I am more okay than I have ever been. "Fine, thanks," I mumble, fully aware of how crazed I must seem but unable to bring myself to care.

He stares at me, and a crease forms between his brows. His flashing eyes are like X-rays, but even they can't see my secret. I am sure of it.

"Where were you?" He takes another step closer. Now there is only two feet of space between us, and that is strange because the hallways up here aren't narrow. It is strange because it feels like there is something magnetic between our bodies, but I can't tell if it is pulling us together or pushing us apart. All I know is that we are connected. Maybe fighting a person has that effect.

I shake my head. "I told you. The library."

"Your face is flushed."

"So?"

"So you're lying."

I scowl. "Nobody asked you, Preme."

"My name's Wren, by the way."

"Okay. Nobody asked you, Wren."

He shakes his head, but that gentle mouth of his hides a faint smile. Then he holds out a hand. "Nice to officially meet you, Eve."

I stare at it, at the smooth skin unblemished by ink. Premes aren't subjected to such debasing markings. The last time I saw this hand up close was at the Bowl, and it was cocked. It was coming toward my face, and when it landed, my face exploded in pain. Except that it didn't explode, because here I am, speaking with this strange boy, and before I know what I am doing, my hand extends forward.

It feels small in his, my forearm unusually narrow. But instead of making me feel weak, it makes me feel strong. I can't understand why.

Only after I shake it do I notice the gun gripped in the other.

"Shooting range," he explains as his gaze follows mine.

"What do you mean?" I take a step back. "Are you a guard or something?" Preeminates are never guards—such a position is beneath them. But that doesn't mean they can't be. He is a Preme; he can be whatever he likes.

But he shakes his head. "One of the perks of the fifth floor, I guess."

"Guns?"

"Guns."

Underneath our boots, there is a loud roar, followed by a chorus of angry men and women. Protests. They have been happening more and more; unrest in Compound Eleven is rampant and growing by the day. Floor Two is particularly vocal, demanding better conditions, more allotments, respect. As far as I know, Katz and the other leaders don't bat an eye in return.

I ignore the chanting and frown under bright lights. I should be mad. The Premes get to carry guns, and the rest of us don't. It isn't fair; I know that. But my eyes still radiate with sunlight, and I can't summon the will for anger.

Wren is talking. "Is being a guard something you're interested in?" One hand runs through light brown hair. Then he leans against the wall with the gun hanging easily by his side. "I assume you'll be picking a job next month, seeing as how you're not working and not in class right now."

"I finished school a few weeks ago," I agree. My gaze follows every move he makes, from the way his fingers tap gently against the plastic wall behind him to the way his neck arches when he looks at the floor. Suddenly, my experience in the Oracle begins to fade. Suddenly, the fact that I am standing in a hallway with the boy who beat me to a pulp becomes apparent. And we are having a regular conversation, seemingly, except that I am a Lower Mean and he is a Preme. A *Preme*.

I feel like I am betraying everyone I know.

"A few weeks ago?" he says. "Yeah, me, too. So I guess that would make me two years older than you."

It would. Premes go to school until they are eighteen, Means until they are sixteen, Noms until they are twelve. "Wow," I say. "I didn't know pretty boys could do math."

"And I didn't know you thought I was pretty." He grins.

I roll my eyes. "Two years older. Well, no wonder you won in the ring, then."

He tilts his head like he's considering it, and I take the opportunity to stare at his straight nose, the one I smashed blood from while the ref wasn't looking. It has healed without a trace. And the cut under his eye has disappeared, leaving smooth and even skin in its wake. Maybe I am disappointed by this, maybe not.

Now he's watching me examine him. "What?" His low voice is quiet.

I cast my eyes quickly away. "Nothing," I mutter. As blood rushes to my face, I turn toward the atrium. "I should go."

His back straightens so he no longer leans against the wall. "You're not heading downstairs right now. Listen to them." He is referring to the protesters who grow louder by the second. Any moment now, the shouting could be interrupted by a spray of bullets from the guards, a reminder that insubordination is not appreciated by the Premes in charge, that revolt will be met with ruthless and indiscriminate force.

"I'll be fine," I say sharply. I don't need him looking out for me, that much I know.

"There's the Eve I remember. Are you ever not fine?" Before I can turn my head or feel the full twinge of defensiveness rising in my stomach, he laughs. "If you're thinking about applying for a guard—"

"I'm not," I interrupt. "I'd rather die."

He raises an eyebrow. "Okay. Well even so, if you'd like to learn how to shoot…" The hand holding the gun gestures to me.

"Are you serious?" I blurt out before I can stop myself. "You'll show me how?"

"If you're interested."

Of course I am. But why would he do something like that? I am a waste of his time; he said so himself.

So I shake my head and shrug. "Somehow I doubt they let Means into the shooting range."

"You're with me. Come on, it'll be fun." He doesn't smile, and he doesn't wait for an answer. He just turns and heads to a corridor I haven't been down before.

You're with me. What does that mean? He's a Preme; of course he gets special treatment. Or is there more to it than that?

I stare at the back of his head and exhale. I can't go. I need to get back downstairs before people ask questions. I need to relive my time in the Oracle before it fades from my mind. I need to not betray all those who are important to me by hanging out with someone like him.

Instead my feet kick after him. My body has an unfortunate habit of disobeying my brain.

CHAPTER NINE

"Is this a trick?" I say as I hurry after him. The corridors are quieter up here than downstairs, even with the rhythmic shouts of the protestors, and so I hear my boots squeak against the polished floor with every step. Downstairs, they don't squeak; they crunch, from dirt or glass underfoot.

He half turns, and his eyebrows inch up.

"You know. An easy way to finish me off."

I say it mostly as a joke, but he doesn't laugh. Instead he looks serious. "You think I'm a monster." He says it not as a question but as a simple fact. A grave one.

In truth, I don't know if he is a monster or not. I don't think so, or I wouldn't be following him into the depths of the fifth floor. I tell him so. "Besides," I continue, "I've already been shot at today. If you want to join in, go for it. No hard feelings."

He gives me a look. "Very funny." I am silent, and he slows his pace. "You were kidding, right?"

A small smile turns my lip. I don't know why I feel like joking around with this boy who is a Preeminate, who beat me to a pulp in front of thousands of people, but I suspect my time in the Oracle has something to do with it. "Kind of. A guard did shoot at me this morning. But if I'm being honest, I would prefer it if you didn't join in."

I expect him to ask me what I did to deserve it. Because if a guard is shooting at a Lower Mean, it must be her fault. But instead he shakes his head, a faint look of amusement spreading across his face. "I'm beginning to think you're suicidal. That or an adrenaline junkie. Hard to say which."

"Life's different down there," I reply evenly.

He nods. "Fair enough."

Our ears fill with more shouts from below, punctuated only by the sound of our boots. His legs are longer than mine, and even though he has slowed his pace, I must hurry to keep up. Out of my peripheral vision, I glance at him, and it strikes me that he doesn't look like a Preme. He moves like one, and he has the confidence that comes with this floor—the easy saunter, the head held high—but his clothing is casual enough to be Lower Mean. A T-shirt and jeans, just like me. Except his jeans aren't ripped, and his shirt is crisp.

Finally, he slows in front of a door. It looks like the door I just broke through, except it isn't locked. He pushes it open, and I follow him inside.

A long room, coated in black foam panels and darkness. Targets hang at the far end, white with black concentric circles, and light shines on them but nowhere else. After the brightness of the Oracle and the Preme hallways, the lack of light here is unsettling.

"Why's it so dark?" I ask quietly. My breathing is steady, but my pulse is not.

He looks over his shoulder at me as he walks to a far table, past two others who load bullets into their weapons. They don't bother to turn their heads as we pass, but I see they are older men, around my father's age. "What's wrong, Eve? Afraid of the dark?"

"Of course not," I lie. "It was just a question."

The shouting from below has vanished. It is because of the soundproofing in here—no sound can penetrate these walls. Even my cell in the middle of the night isn't so silent. It pulls at my eardrums; it presses against my head.

The sharp burst of a gun a few rows down from us punches through the air, and I jump. My hand lands on the smooth skin of his arm before I can jerk it away. "Sorry," I say quickly. "It's just because of earlier. When I was shot at." I can't tell him the truth. That I *am* afraid of the dark—or worse, why. I take a deep breath and will myself to get a grip.

My eyes adjust to the darkness enough to see him staring at me. He is grinning. "You sucker punch me in front of thousands of people, yet you're sorry for lightly touching my arm?"

I stand up straighter. "Okay, I guess I'm not sorry. I just wanted to make sure you knew that…"

All of a sudden, I am grateful for the dark. It hides how jumbled and uncertain I feel.

"Yes?"

"Well, that I didn't actually mean for—"

"Eve?"

"Yeah?"

"Take the gun." He grabs my hand and pushes my fingers apart, and cool metal sinks into my flesh. I have never held one before—only stared at them in the guards' holsters—and it feels foreign. Foreign yet comfortable.

It is solid but not heavy. Smooth but not slippery. Cold. So cold it is grounding.

Wren shows me how to hold it and then how to stand. "Aim at the target, pull the trigger, and don't move the gun when you fire."

"That's it?"

"That's it."

I do as he says, but the gun jumps as the bullet is released. It misses the mark by a mile, and my ears ring from the silence the blast leaves.

"You can't let the gun kick like that. You have to hold it steady."

"And how am I supposed to do that?"

"Move your hands up higher, for starters. And grip tighter."

I do as he says, but my second shot is no better.

"You have muscle, don't you?"

I glare at the side of his face. "You're lucky I'm preoccupied right now, or I'd punch you."

"As a little reminder of that muscle, I'm guessing?"

"That's right."

My next shot hits the target, barely, and the one after that, too. Wren watches with his arms crossed, but I barely notice. Instead I focus only on what I am doing. It is a powerful feeling, to shoot a gun. It is wonderful. But it is also a grave responsibility, and the thought of the guards today pointing and shooting at me makes my stomach awash with acid. I see now how worthless I am in their eyes. How truly disposable. How lightly they take this power of theirs, gifted into their palms. They have internalized it in the cruelest way.

I hate the guards now more than ever, something I didn't think was even possible.

"You haven't moved for a while," Wren says. "Everything okay?"

"Yeah. I'm just thinking about... I'm just thinking."

After a few moments, he nods. "Okay." He clears his throat. "So, Eve, if the thought of becoming a guard makes you want to die, what exactly *do* you want to be?"

I place the gun down on the table. My eyes have adjusted to the low level of light, and I am no longer fearful.

Then I notice that the others in the shooting range have cleared out; it is just the two of us. Typically, I don't like to be alone with someone I barely know, especially if that person is significantly stronger than I am. And he is that. He has beaten me senseless once before, and he is capable of great violence. Emerald was right; the headbutt to my face could have killed me. But I look him in the eye and see none of the anger I witnessed before.

Even in the darkness, though, they flash. They flash, and something stirs behind them that I can't quite identify. Could it be danger?

Is he, to use his terminology, a monster?

I think he is dangerous, and I think I ought to be careful, but once again my gut tells me that he isn't a monster. Should I trust my gut?

He steps forward so that more of his cheekbone catches the light from the opposite end of the room. It makes him look animalistic. "Are you going to answer my question?" he asks.

"What? Oh, yeah. Um, a job. I don't really know."

"Tell me you're not going to be a pro fighter."

"Is that supposed to be a jab? Because I can beat a lot of people."

He walks past me and picks up the gun. Our shoulders brush. He slides a bullet into the chamber, then gazes at me. "Do you really think I need to be reminded of that? As someone who has been on the receiving end of your punches, I know very well, thanks."

His first shot hits the bull's-eye.

"Okay, so why shouldn't I be a fighter, then?"

"Are you always this defensive, Eve?"

"Maybe."

He laughs, and it is quiet and rumbly. "You shouldn't be a fighter because it's brutal, that's why. Do you like pain? Do you like waking up in the nurse's station covered in blood?"

I scoff. "Easy for someone like you to say."

"Yeah, maybe it is. But surely there are other jobs for Means that are better than that. You should consider them." He picks up another bullet and shoves it into the gun. "Been on any of the job tours?"

"Nope. Don't plan on going on any, either. You?"

His eyebrows pinch together. "What do you mean by that?"

"I guess I mean that I don't really care about picking a job at selection time. Maybe I pick one, maybe I don't. Maybe this bullet hits the target, maybe it doesn't." I take the gun from his hands and wrap my own around it. "You obviously don't need any practice," I add by way of explanation.

This time I hit the target only a few inches from his strike.

"Impressive. So, what do you do with yourself, then, if you aren't bothering with the job tours? Other than fighting for the fun of it. Oh, and pretending to be in the library."

I give him a look over my shoulder. "I do go to the library, actually. A lot of the time."

"To do what?"

"I don't know, read?"

"Read what?"

"You ask too many questions, Preme."

"Come on."

"Okay. About life aboveground, mostly." I think of the Oracle and smile. "You know, before everything moved down here."

He is silent, so I turn and see that he is staring at me. His eyes are thoughtful. They aren't hard; they aren't even cold. Just thoughtful. Still he says nothing, and so I keep talking.

"And I do other stuff, too. Hang out with my friends, train for the Bowl, work the food lines for the Denominators."

"Is that volunteer?"

I nod and turn back to the target, take another shot. Another successful strike. I am getting the hang of it. "For as long as I can remember," I tell him. "I used to do it with my mother. Now it's just me."

"Want company next time you go?"

The suggestion is unexpected, and I put the gun down hurriedly and face him. He stands close enough that even without adequate light, I notice a thin scar that runs along his jaw, the stubble that reminds me he is two years older. "Seriously?" I say. "You want to help give food to the Noms?"

He shrugs. "Sounds interesting enough. And sometimes, Eve," he says as he picks up the gun, "it's fun to try new things."

I peer at him through the dark, expecting to see something cruel shooting through his eyes. That perhaps hanging out with a Lower Mean nobody like myself is something new to try. Something to laugh about with his Preme friends later. There *must* be an explanation along those lines.

But instead, his eyes are earnest. I can't figure this Preme out.

CHAPTER TEN

The darkness claws at the back of my throat. It suffocates me, like there is a sock wedged behind my teeth. Like a tether is twisting around my neck. My hand twitches at my side. It wants to reach over, turn on the bedside lamp, but I resist the urge. I have resisted the urge for a long time, ever since my father decided I was too old to be afraid of the dark. So I am not going to indulge myself now.

Time for sleep, I try to remind myself. But it is hard to slow my thoughts after a day like today. My time in the Oracle is too fresh, like a wound that still drips blood. Whenever I close my eyes, I see the trees swaying, the birds soaring.

I feel more caged in now than ever before.

A tear falls against my pillowcase before I realize I've spilled it. It's the unknown that scares me right now. What awaits in another compound. Whether I can even make it to another compound in the first place. Because though others have managed to go before me, though they have located the tunnels, forced their way through, well...their exits have become the stuff of legend. They are the outliers. Most people who try to break out of our compound and into another receive a back full of bullets before they make it very far.

What if I *do* make it, only to have them send me back to Eleven? What if the compound I stumble into is even *worse*?

Another tear follows in the same path as the first. There is no need to wipe it away, not really. I am alone. When I lived with my parents, I would have to hide the tears; I would have to stifle the sobs. My father wouldn't tolerate it. Only when Jack was sent aboveground did he give allowance, and even then, not for long. Crying is for those who can't manage their emotions, he said. Those who are strong manage them always.

I know that.

So even though there is no need to wipe away the tear, I do. I am strong. I flex my arm and run a hand over bulging muscle, an easy reminder of my strength. Strong body, strong mind. His words.

Am I, though? I am tough and muscular and a good fighter because I have to be. Because I am a Lower Mean and because my father has trained me to be. I have known no other way. But what if I didn't have to be? Do I enjoy punching people?

Part of me does. I am powerful, self-sufficient; I rely on no one. And I like that. But I don't lust for blood the way someone like Daniel does. I don't take joy in seeing someone else suffer under my hand.

A sob rings out from my chest and through the darkness, sudden and sharp. I can't manage my emotions; I am weak. My father bred me to be strong and fierce, but it is a charade. I am not cruel enough. My heart beats, and it craves peace and the kindness of others; it does. And all around me is violence.

The tether circling my neck tightens, but this time it isn't the darkness doing it. It is life.

On one of her good days, my mother would tell me to

cheer up; she would say that the lights will come on in the morning. But it makes me feel no better. In fact, it makes a pang of guilt underline my sorrow. It is selfish to leave. It is cruel to my parents, especially after what they have endured with Jack. Cruel and inhumane and merciless.

But she is wrong about the lights. The lights left her the day Jack was sent aboveground, and they haven't been turned back on since. Not in years. Instead, darkness has swallowed her whole, pulled her into a pit that she can't crawl out of.

I can't stay here and wait to be pulled in, too.

I sigh. Just for tonight, I will give my heart what it wants. And then I will be Eve again tomorrow, disinterested and cruel and self-sufficient. I shift my weight and turn on the lamp. Light floods my ten-by-ten cell, one left mostly undecorated. There is a small patch of embroidery over my bed, but otherwise the walls are intentionally bare. Since I refuse to serve Commander Katz, there's no sense in getting too comfortable here; I will be gone soon.

I slide my socked feet into boots and pull on a sweatshirt. When I open the door, I am cautious. It isn't against the rules to be out of bed at night, but it isn't encouraged, either. Guards view night-wanderers with particular disdain. Besides, the hallways are not well-lit during these hours, and danger never lurks far.

Maggie is with her boyfriend Kyle tonight—she is with him every Friday night—and so I turn toward Hunter's door. I wipe the last of my tears away and knock, three sharp raps followed by three soft ones. A code from when we were young.

The green neon light opposite turns me into a shadow, and I watch my head swivel back and forth as my ears listen for the sound of footsteps. Other than my breathing, though, Compound Eleven is calm. It is quiet, for now.

A few moments later, Hunter pulls open his door. "Sorry

I took so long," he mutters as he zips his hoodie over a bare chest. His hair is crumpled on one side, adding to the boyish good looks that girls adore him for, and his voice is groggy. "What's up? Is everything okay?"

"Sorry to wake you, but…can I stay here tonight?"

"A sleepover?" he asks as he pulls me inside. "It's been years since we did that."

I force a small laugh. "I'm sure it has been. I don't know why we stopped," I add, then I follow him under the covers. They are warm from his body.

"Maybe our parents thought we were too old for it."

"Maybe."

"They probably didn't bank on us winding up in cells right next door to each other."

I lift my head from his pillow and motion around me. "Speaking of which, you've done a nice job with the place."

He gives me a look. "You mean hanging the periodic table on the wall? Thanks."

"Well, yeah, that," I say, smiling. "I don't know—it feels like you, that's all. Maybe it's all the books." Hunter enjoys the library as much as I do, except since his interests extend beyond life the way it used to be, up there, he is far more well-read than I am.

"Or maybe it's the balled-up hoodies on the floor," he suggests.

"Yeah. Could be that."

He rolls onto his side so that we stare at each other, his nose only a few inches from my own. "Is everything okay?"

"It's fine. Everything's fine."

"Eve, you always say that. What's going on?"

I shrug. "Couldn't sleep. Thought maybe I could use some company."

"Okay," he says slowly. "I mean, yeah. Of course. You're

always welcome." He offers me that famous shy smile. "Maggie and I were looking for you today. Where'd you get off to?"

"I spent most of the morning visiting my folks," I lie. "And I took a nap in the afternoon."

"I've hardly seen you since you fought the Preme. Are you healing okay? Any lingering injuries I can help with? Don't forget that kink in your hamstring I fixed." And he draws his hands out from under the sheets and regards them, clearly still impressed with himself.

I laugh, easier this time. My muscles uncoil as I stare into eyes that are intimately familiar. "Hunter, come on. It's me. I said I'm fine. Now, shut your eyes and go to sleep."

"Your wish," he begins solemnly, and I join him for the rest—"is my command."

Grinning, I ask, "Do you remember what book that was from?"

"Nope. Just that we spent an entire year repeating it roughly four hundred times a day—"

"And pretending to grant each other wishes with our imaginary wands," I finish. I poke him. "Don't tell any of my fighter friends that story."

"I'll take it to the grave," he agrees, poking me back.

After another moment, he leans over me and switches off the light, and my eyelids burn black. It's okay, though. Because even after we finish whispering our good nights to each other, I can hear him breathing beside me, in and out, and that is enough.

I roll onto my back and let myself drift away.

CHAPTER ELEVEN

"**D**o you guys ever wonder what else is out there?" I ask as I toss a ball into the air with my right hand and catch it with my left. The motion snaps the scabs apart on my knuckles, and I stare at them.

Hunter closes the book he has been flipping through for the past ten minutes and stares at me. "What else is out there. What do you mean?"

Maggie and Emerald sit on the floor of my small cell, and Hunter and I share the bed. I ignore my bleeding knuckles and chuck the ball up again. The ceiling is so low it bounces back at me. "I don't know. Like, in other compounds."

"I do," Emerald says, lifting her head from the game of War she plays with Maggie. "Sometimes. They say Compound Twelve is next door, right? I mean, I wonder if it's…"

"Better?" I offer. "Because this one sucks, in case you guys haven't noticed."

"I was going to say different."

Hunter nudges my leg. "If you're thinking about what happened to Jack, then yes, I agree with you. Beyond that, I actually think it could be worse. Case in point—it's not like we're starving."

"Speak for yourself," mutters Emerald. "After hitting a punching bag for hours, I'd literally *kill* for seconds."

Hunter grins.

"And besides," adds Maggie, "we have one another."

I give her a little sarcastic smirk.

"Hey, I have a point," she insists as she lays down a card. "I mean, obviously things down here aren't great. Remember that guy I saw last month? The one with his skull caved in?" She shivers. "Literally, I'm still having nightmares. But we have one another, and that's saying something. So maybe which compound you're in or which floor you're on doesn't matter so much. It's the people that make it, you know?"

I catch the ball and hold it tight. She's right, in a way. My friends and family are the only things stopping me from trying to leave Compound Eleven this very second. They're the only reason I've stayed for the past nine years, since Jack was taken and everything changed. But come job selection, now less than six weeks away, it won't be enough—nothing could be. Nothing could be worse than serving those who ordered Jack's removal, or kneeling before them, or being branded with a past I want to forget.

I need to go—it is in my blood. Especially after the Oracle.

The Oracle has made me feel more caged in, yes. But it has also made me deeply hopeful, and for the first time in years.

Maybe other compounds have more viewing stations. Ones that people can go to whenever they want—that aren't guarded or locked like here in Eleven. Maybe the compounds are extended aboveground. Maybe they have evolved to have less hierarchy, less injustice. Perhaps there's less violence, even. And more freedom, more latitude. Because I need it. Every cell in my body screams for it.

I need to spread my wings like the birds. I need to *breathe*.

Hunter is staring at me, and his blue-green eyes are uncharacteristically dark. He straightens his glasses and says: "I knew something was wrong with you."

"Nothing's *wrong*, Hunter. I'm just…curious."

He sighs—he knows me too well. But he doesn't push it. "You haven't been on any of the job tours. Come with us today; we're going to the press room."

"The press room? I thought you wanted to work in the kitchen."

"I do. You'd be surprised at the amount of chemistry that happens behind those doors."

"Sadly," interrupts Emerald, "he's not talking about romance."

"But that doesn't mean I'm not going to explore other options," Hunter continues, his tone serious, even as Emerald and I chuckle. "That's the whole point of these tours. Come on. It'll be fun. We'll make you love Compound Eleven again."

"Again? Did I ever love it in the first place?"

"You should come today, Eve," Maggie says. "It actually sounds pretty neat." She lifts her head and stares at me, and I notice a patch of yellow-brown beside her left eye. "It's a Mean job, but I've heard of people from our floor getting jobs there from time to time. I think you might actually like it."

I am silent, and her lime green eyes narrow. "Are you even listening to me?"

"Where'd you get that bruise from?"

Her fingers jump to her cheek. "What bruise, this?"

"Yeah, that. Obviously."

"Oh. I don't know." She looks nervous. Maggie is pretty and smart and confident. Never is she nervous. "I ran into the door yesterday. Maybe it's from that."

"What door?"

"My door. My cell door."

"You ran into it."

"Yeah. Like, when it was open. The edge, Eve. Like this." She holds an open palm perpendicular to her face. "See what I mean?"

She is a terrible liar.

"Wow, Maggie," Emerald sneers. "You know Eve is the blond one, right?"

"Very funny."

I lean back on the bed and toss the ball into the air again. "How are things with Kyle?" I grimace as I say his name, but only after making sure she isn't watching. The truth is that I don't like Kyle. Never have. He is an Upper Mean, and he makes sure I and the others don't forget his position above us. No matter that we are Maggie's best friends.

Her head jerks like I've slapped her. "Kyle? Things are great with Kyle. Why do you ask?"

"Haven't seen him around lately."

"He's just super busy with work and his friends and things." She shakes her head and lays down another card. "Boys. Am I right?"

"We're not the best ones to ask," says Emerald with a smirk. She looks at me—neither one of us has had a boyfriend before. "It's because we're fighters, right, Eve? Guys are intimidated by our muscles." She flexes her arms, and the room fills with laughter.

Yes, I will miss them when I go.

Maggie and Hunter I've known for as long as I can remember—they lived a few doors down growing up, we had classes together, we played together on the weekends. I've logged more time with them than my own parents. And Emerald—she was my first friend in the Combat League, one I was immensely grateful for in those early days when fighting for sport was new, terrifying. We've been inseparable ever since.

I shut my eyes, but they flick back open as a scream fills my ears, one that is loud enough to pierce the thick cell walls that surround us. I pull myself up, but Hunter's hand lands on my chest. "Stop, Eve. Just lie back and wait it out."

I push him away and jump to my feet.

Emerald stands, too, the card game forgotten, but she only does it to block the door. "Forget about it," she instructs. Her laughter is gone, and her voice is stern. "It isn't our fight. You're going to get yourself killed."

They are only doing this because of my encounter with the guard the other morning. I thought they would get a kick out of it when I told them, but instead they exchanged looks and reprimanded me for meddling. And maybe they're right. Holding the gun and firing at the target upstairs, something I did not share with them—it made me realize how vulnerable I am. How easily I can be killed by the guards. I need to remember that.

"I take it you didn't learn your lesson a couple days ago?"

"What, not to meddle?"

"That's the one."

I shrug. "They're getting out of control, those guards. Someone needs to rein them in."

"Yeah, well, that someone isn't going to be you." She folds her arms across her chest. "You already did your part when you broke Black Eyes's nose." Her face breaks into a grin. "You've got an impressive punch, girl. I'll give you that."

Hunter knocks me across the shoulder. "Speaking of the guards, you need to stop making enemies out of them. First of all, they're not all bad. Statistically speaking, it's impossible. Second, they're going to start to recognize you, and you won't be able to go anywhere. Not even the cafeteria."

I snort. "Only a *coward* would worry about that."

"You're calling me a coward now?"

"Looks that way, doesn't it?"

We glare at each other, but after another minute, the hallway falls silent. Possibly the fight has gone elsewhere, possibly someone bleeds outside my door. I sit down and stare around at my friends. "Everyone happy? It's over—you won."

"Don't be like that," says Maggie. "You almost got killed the other day. We're your friends, and we care—"

"It's fine," I interrupt. "Let's talk about something else." I bite my thumbnail. "Anything. What time is the press tour?"

"In half an hour. Will you come?"

"No thanks."

Slowly, Maggie gathers up the deck of cards from the floor and shuffles them. She sighs. "Eve…"

"The compounds are connected by tunnels, right?"

She stares at me. "Some of them. I mean, the ones that are close to each other. Why do you want to know?"

"There are jobs there, aren't there?"

"Oh. I mean, yeah." Relief lifts her shoulders. "Yeah, there are. Like, construction and maintenance jobs, definitely. Is that something you're interested in?"

I shrug. It isn't something I have thought much about, but it could be one way into another compound. Possibly.

"You and Emerald will probably go pro, though, don't you think?"

"I will," Emerald says quickly. She straightens her long legs and pulls at the muscle. "But I'm still doing the tours, just like Hunter said. It's called options, Eve." She winks at me.

I lean back and toss the ball into the air again. "What do you think tunnel maintenance is, smartass? An option. But yeah, I'll probably go pro if they'll have me. And they might not—losing to a Preme didn't exactly help my ranking."

It is easier if they think I will become a professional fighter. If that is what it takes to keep them off my back about the job tours, so be it. Not that I want to lie. I don't. Not to my best friends. But I can't tell them the truth—they would never understand, not in a million years.

"Blue Circuit would hire you tomorrow," Emerald insists. "Besides, you know what a bleeding heart Bruno is. He already thinks we're practically family, and we're just occasionals."

"Nobody wants a weakling on their team."

"Eve, you're far from a weakling. That Preme was good. We've been over it already."

I just roll my eyes again. "So, Maggie, which super-awesome Lower Mean position will soon be yours? Manufacturing lightbulbs? Watering potato plants?" I am not speaking off the cuff. Because the term *job selections* is a charade. A misnomer, one that suggests we have the power to choose whichever job we like. The reality is that no matter how hard we work in school, no matter how strong our applications are for an upper-floor position, the only jobs we are truly eligible for are Lower Mean ones. Almost always, we end up working the factory floor or the greenhouses. We end up as line cooks or cleaners or fighters for the Combat League.

In other words, we *are* allowed to select a job…so long as the job comes from a Preme-approved list of jobs nobody else wants.

She hits my foot. "Cut it out. Besides, you know how hopeless I am at making decisions. You guys have no idea how lucky you are to have something to fall back on. The kitchen, the Combat League…" She sighs. "I mean, it's the rest of our lives we're talking about."

"Yeah, no pressure or anything," says Emerald, and somehow I manage a short laugh.

Hunter, meanwhile, is still.

"What's with you?" I say to him. My voice is heavy, the laughter gone.

"Take a guess."

"Don't be so touchy, Hunter," I snap.

"Don't be so secretive, Eve. I know something's going on with you."

"I already told you—there's nothing going on. Can you just lay off?"

He stands and stares at me. "Sure, no problem. But next time you want to have a sleepover in the middle of the night, put some ice on your face first so it isn't so obvious you've been bawling your eyes out." Then he walks out the door, slamming it behind him.

It rattles my skull, or maybe it's his words—whatever it is, I roll onto my side with my back to the others. After a few minutes, they mutter goodbyes and follow him out.

I don't know who is right and who is wrong. Maybe I shouldn't have called him a coward; maybe he deserved it. Maybe I should confide in my friends; maybe it's too dangerous. Maybe as I stand on the precipice of adulthood, I am changing. Yes, maybe I am.

I roll onto my stomach and swear loudly into my pillow

CHAPTER TWELVE

Later, I lean against the wall in the main corridor, near the elevator bank. The Lower Mean lobby, it is called, although there is nothing different or special about this slice of hallway. Certainly it's nothing like the Preme atrium. Except it does have a sculpture.

Cast of bronze, I think it is supposed to be a tree. It looks nothing like the trees aboveground, though. It is rendered in jagged lines, has no grace, no movement. And every so often a body hangs from it, a victim of violence whose killers thought to place them on display, perhaps to send a message, or perhaps just for the fun of it…

All I know is that the sculpture is stained with blood and other bodily fluids, and every single time I glance at it, a feeling of nausea starts up in my stomach. How I hate Compound Eleven.

This is where I told him I would wait. Not that I expect him to show. Not really. Feeding the Noms is far from glamorous, far from interesting by any standard. But he wanted to see it, and so I hope he comes. That way we will be even. Square.

He showed me how to shoot; I show him this slice of hell. And then we can go our own ways, never to see each other again. Perfect.

I tap my boot against the concrete floor as bodies swarm past, their voices washing over me like water, barely noticed. Some laugh, others bicker, kids shriek. A symphony of unwanted noise. The neon sign hanging opposite blinks quickly, and I look away. Normally it reads *Mean 2*, just like the one hanging across from my cell. Right now, the *A* is dead.

I check my watch. He has three minutes, and then I go, with or without him.

"Look who it is," says a voice in my ear. "Oh, and will you look at that," it continues as I glance sideways at him. Daniel. He slams a hand on the wall close to my head, and evil glints in his eye. "Landry, take a look, man. Eve is healing up nicely, wouldn't you say?"

Daniel's friend Landry shoves into position in front of me, and over his shoulder I see Zaar. I hate all three of them. Landry stands so close, I can smell meat on his breath, and it mixes with Daniel's acidic soap so that I gag.

"Get away from me."

Landry smiles, and then his eyes trickle slowly down my face in a way that makes my muscles tense up. Tales of sexual misdeeds follow him closely, not that the authorities care. In fact, Landry and Daniel are both keen on becoming guards— probably Zaar, too—something they all will likely accomplish, given their status as well-connected Upper Means. Perfect. How fair and how just life in Compound Eleven is.

"Don't know, Dan," says Landry slowly. He has short blond hair and still gray eyes. "There's some bruising on her cheek, right there. Too bad. I like them fresh. *Pristine*." He leans closer like he might kiss me, so I pull up my hand and smash the back of it against his face. Just a slap. A warning shot.

"Don't stand so close," I whisper, "or you'll have bruising of your own. Understood?"

His face turns red, and I can't tell if it is from my strike or from boiling anger. Probably both. But he contains himself. He rubs his cheek and exchanges a sly smile with his friend. "She's got an awful lot of attitude for a Lower Mean, doesn't she?" He crosses his arms, and I see that those gray eyes are icy. "Perhaps we ought to teach her a lesson. Come on, Eve. A little spanking, that's all I'm thinking."

I open my mouth, but Wren appears beside me, and words of rage freeze on my tongue.

Daniel's spine straightens, and he smiles. "Look, Landry. Maybe we won't have to teach her a lesson after all. This is the hero who put her in the nurse's station, remember?"

Landry pulls a sad face as he stares at me. His eyes don't move from mine. "Shame, though. It would be kind of fun."

"Next time," Daniel says to Wren, "do us all a favor and finish her off, okay? I can't quite express my disappointment when I got word she pulled through." He winks at me and sticks out a hand in Wren's direction. "My name's Daniel, by the way."

Wren stares at him thoughtfully, eyes flashing. Then he turns to me, disregarding Daniel's waiting hand. "Ready?"

I lean my body weight forward, off the wall. Probably Daniel is confused as to why the Preme and I are meeting. Probably he is angry about being rebuffed by Wren. But I don't bother to look—I just elbow him out of the way so I can pass.

He turns around to shove me, but I am already gone.

"Hey, Eve!" he shouts through the crowd. I don't turn, but I pause in my step. "Watch your back, okay? There's this giant red X painted on it, and nobody seems to have given you the memo."

I walk on, leading Wren silently through the crowded main corridor. It is the widest on the second floor but also the busiest. A red stripe lines the concrete walls, an artery, and the Lower Means are the blood cells that infuse it with life.

Only once we turn onto a quieter corridor does Wren speak. "Nice backhand you have. Is there a day that goes by when you're not fighting or being shot at?"

"Guess not," I say darkly.

"Who were those guys?"

"Does it matter?" I kick at a piece of garbage on the floor, my mood sour. Daniel's comment about the giant red X plays again and again in my mind.

"It's called making conversation," he replies levelly. "Something you might want to work on."

I eye him. "Let's just get this over with."

I turn down a corridor where most of the lightbulbs overhead are burned out. I hate this corridor. The ceiling is particularly low, dirtier and dingier than the rest of the second floor—and that is saying something, since it is dirty and dingy to begin with. I look at Wren out of the corner of my eye. His head almost touches the ceiling, but otherwise he looks relaxed. Surprisingly so. Most Premes would be unable to hide their disgust.

I stop in front of the steel door that leads to the feeding dock. "It's right here," I say. "The guard should be by any minute to unlock it." Technically what I have said is true. I do have to wait for a guard to unlock it, since to do otherwise would be suspect. But I know the code.

We both lean against the wall—opposite sides—and I turn away from him, staring up the hall instead, waiting for the guard to appear. It is always a young female guard, not much older than myself. The junior guards get the boring jobs like unlocking doors for volunteers. Melissa is her name, and she has bright pink hair and a nose ring crafted from wire. She's not bad, for a guard.

Never is she late, and so of course today will be the day.

Finally, the sounds of footsteps and whistling draw near, and it crosses my mind that perhaps it will be a different guard today. I stare up the hall and wait. A figure appears and turns in our direction, black clothed and combat ready. His frame looks familiar. And even from down here, I can see he has black beads instead of eyes.

"Shit." I turn on the spot and swipe the elastic from my hair. *Shit.* It's him. Of all the goddamn guards in this godforsaken compound, I get him. *Him.*

The asshole guard who shot at me. If he recognizes me, I'm dead.

Wren moves quickly toward me and wraps both arms around my head. "Shh," he whispers in my ear before I can resist. He teases my loose hair with his hands as his forehead rests on mine. Inside my chest, my heart hammers uncontrollably, and every muscle spasms with anticipation. What if, what if, what if?

I don't know what exactly Wren is doing, but I think he is trying to help me. It isn't in my nature to accept help, but right now I am desperate.

"Here to feed the Denominators?" the guard asks once he nears. His voice sounds bored. He has two purple lines running under his eyes and a swollen nose. So I did break it— badly, by the looks of it. My eyes are trained on him through gaps in my hair, gaps in Wren's arms. Him and his baton. Him and his gun.

"Yeah," Wren replies heavily as he strokes my hair. I get it; we look like lovers. And I am mostly hidden, wrapped in his long arms.

Except I can't relax enough to make it convincing. Every

cell in my body screams to break into a run, to get away from this man who would enjoy killing me. Every instinct is to flee or to fight, but that would be worse. I have to be brave, but the worst part is that the only thing I keep thinking is how good Wren smells. Like soap, but not like the soap I use or that Daniel uses. This is a masculine smell and a safe smell and one that makes my muscles unclench against their will.

The door squeaks open, and my heart leaps. Soon he will be gone.

But as he turns, my eye catches his.

"Do I know you?" he asks. Black beads blink. The lone bulb overhead flickers as if reminding me to think. Think. Don't just act; don't punch and run, then figure out how to pick up the pieces.

"No," I say with as much attitude and angst as I can muster. Then I bury my face into Wren's chest the way I have seen Maggie do with Kyle.

"Stand up for a second so I can have a look at you."

"She said no, all right?"

My ear is pressed to Wren's chest so that when he talks, I feel the vibration inside me.

I tense up at his words. Guards don't like attitude   not that it tends to stop me from giving it to them. Probably all he has to say is that he is a Preme. Flash him the back of his unmarked hands. That ought to stop the guard from bothering us. When Wren opens his mouth again, this is what I expect him to say. Instead he says, "She's having a rough week, okay? She's been sick. Do you mind?"

Part of me cringes. It would be easier if he would just say who he is. What he is. But part of me likes that he isn't, too.

"Whatever. Shut off the lights when you're done," the guard mutters. His footsteps are heavy as they echo into the distance, and with every step, I feel a weight lift from my shoulders. My breathing slows. I wait until I can no longer hear the echoes before I push back from Wren. His arms drop quickly.

I stare sideways, decidedly not at him. When I speak, it is barely audible. "Yeah, so…thanks. That was actually pretty decent of you."

"Don't sound so surprised."

I raise my chin an inch. "Well."

"Well what?"

Now I do look at him, at his square jaw, wide-set eyes, the kind curve of his mouth. "Nothing. Listen, let's get going, okay? They don't like it when I'm late. Noms don't exactly get a lot of food." I start through the open door, but Wren's arm shoots in front of me, blocking my path.

"Eve, come on."

"What?"

"Aren't you going to tell me what that was about? I don't think I've ever seen anyone move that fast. Nice disguise, by the way." His gaze lingers on my hair, and then he shoves his hands into his pockets and shakes his head.

A small shudder of laughter bursts from my mouth. I didn't even feel it well up in my stomach, but now it is all I can do to hold it in. He watches me laugh with his lips curled into a smile, and I feel like a lunatic, but I don't stop.

When I finally do, I am lighter. "That was the guard who shot at me a couple of days ago," I explain. "If he recognized me there… I don't know. I'd probably be dead."

"So I just saved your life?" A grin flashes across his face.

"Hardly," I scoff. "If you hadn't done that, I would have figured something else out."

"No doubt."

I look at him. Is he being sarcastic? Or does he really believe I am capable? It doesn't matter, of course. But I feel something spreading inside my stomach that is warm and uncomfortable. Or rather, it is perfectly comfortable—pleasant, even, and that is what is so unsettling. Perhaps the stress of the situation and the relief I feel now is what is causing it. Or perhaps it is the Preme's smell still lingering in my senses.

He clears his throat. "What?"

I have been staring. I walk quickly past him and through the door, down a flight of stairs. *Get a grip, Eve.*

At the foot of the stairs, a yellow bulb illuminates a small cubby—the feeding dock. A long table the width of the room is pushed against the far wall, and over it is a partition slid shut. The rest of the room is concrete and unremarkable. On top of the table sit silver food trays with a stack of brown paper next to them. Several bags of dinner rolls sit on top.

The kitchen staff bring it in before the feeding; it is my job to wrap up what's inside and pass it out. Usually, the food reserved for the Noms is stale and unpalatable—surplus from the Mean cafeteria, table scraps from whatever is served on the Preme floor. Space in the compound's artificial greenhouse is limited, and so fresh food is bestowed down here only once or twice per year. But still, what I pass through the partition is food. Still, it is sustenance.

I fumble for my elastic and draw my hair into a ponytail. They shake, my fingers. It must be from the guard. Surely it isn't from Wren standing behind my shoulder. He is close enough that his chest is only inches from the back of my arm and I can feel his breaths, in and out. I shouldn't care where he stands. In fact, I don't.

Suddenly, his fingers run up and down my arm, near the bulge of my biceps. I tense up at his touch, my stomach muscles clenching so tightly that they pull me forward. I force myself to stand straight again. "Yes?" I ask. I try to make my voice sound relaxed and nonchalant. Instead it comes out as a squeak.

"Bruising is still pronounced," he says quietly. "Will you fight again?"

"I've got another match in a couple days." I glance down at my arm and see that it is stained purple. "Once those are gone, there will be plenty more to take their place, don't worry."

"Do you like it?"

"Fighting?"

"Yeah."

I shrug. "I'm not complaining."

"That's different from liking something. Why do you do it, then? I know you said fighting is a way of life down here, but you're not forced to fight in the Bowl."

I grab a piece of brown paper and scoop in a half portion of lentils as I think about his question. "I read once that before civilization moved down here, parents used to sign their kids up for music lessons." I look at him and shrug. "Well, it's like that. I've just always done it."

"You've just always done it," he repeats.

I nod. "Grab some paper. A small scoop goes in the middle. Fold it like this."

I demonstrate a couple of times, and he joins me.

"So your parents started you fighting early."

"My father did. As soon as I was old enough. You have to be at least nine, or the League won't allow it."

"How decent of them," he says drily. "Then what? I suppose you took to it?"

I snort. "Hardly."

"What's that supposed to mean?"

"It means that whenever I get punched in the stomach, hard enough to bring up vomit, I go back to that first match. Except back then, I vomited from fear." I pause. "Don't forget

I was only nine years old."

He is silent, his hands moving slowly over brown paper. His low voice is restrained when he finally speaks. "I punched you in the stomach."

For a moment, my hands are still, and I stare at the food packet I hold in my palm. He did punch me in the stomach. Hard enough to bring up bile, hard enough to send my memories backward.

"Did you…?" he starts.

"Do you really want to know?"

"No."

I resume preparing the food packets, and when he speaks again, his voice is harder than before and he has changed the subject. "So you never told me the full story with that guard. Surely they don't shoot at Lower Means for target practice."

I stiffen.

He must notice, because he quickly adds, "I was joking, Eve."

"Yeah, well, easy to joke about when you don't live down here." My pile of food packets greatly outnumbers his; he is slow.

"Are you always like that?"

"Like what?"

"So defensive. So quick to evade a question. Talking with you is a bit like pulling teeth—no offense."

I slam down the packet I am working on and turn to him. My arms cross as anger shoots through my chest. "You want to know why that guard was chasing me? Okay, Preeminate, let me tell you. A little boy—a Denominator who we're about to give food to—stole some bread, and that guard caught him. He started bashing the kid's skull in, so I said something, okay? Happy you asked?"

Wren stares at me, then his eyebrows dig together. "That's

it. You said something."

"I told him to stop. That's it."

"And he chased you. He *shot* at you."

"Welcome to life as a Lower Mean. Be grateful you were born on the top floor." With that, I lean forward and slide open the partition. Heat has filled my face and my chest. He is a Preme. He is from an elite society that has never known hardship. He is from a society that handed Jack a death sentence. I want to hate him, I really do.

But when I see the hungry faces pooled in front of me with hands extended, my anger breaks. It isn't fair that I complain about my station as a Lower Mean. It isn't, because the people pushing for position in front of me, the ones whose ancestors had no money or assets to leverage into a spot on a Mean floor, have it much, much worse. For with the construction of the compound long complete, these people now serve little purpose to the Premes.

Unlike the Means, whose lifework is spent ensuring that the compound and its hierarchy endure, the Denominators are seen as expendable. They are *treated* as expendable—the elevator doesn't even go to their floor. Like the fact that they are living, breathing human beings is completely meaningless. I've even heard whisperings from upstairs about how they could all be blown away and nobody would miss them. About how it would actually be a net benefit, with fewer mouths to feed... The total indifference, the inexcusable callousness—it makes me sick.

In front of me, frail arms reach upward, snatching air, waiting for me to place a small packet of lentils and a roll into their palms. There is no sense in giving them larger helpings—the kitchen only prepares so much. Bigger portions for some means mouths go hungry. I have tried it before, and it did not end well. Anger, riots, gunshots.

I shudder.

The Noms at the front of the crowd are never pleasant. These are the aggressive and greedy ones—the ones every floor has, I think. I don't know any of them by name, and I like it that way. Sometimes they yell if I am late. Sometimes they yell just for the sake of it. But today they are quiet—maybe because Wren is beside me and he is big and so obviously strong. They take their food without thanks and shove off through lighting dimmer than even what I am used to. More Noms move forward to take their place. Wren works quickly now, filling packets at the same pace as I hand them out.

The last ones to collect their lunch are the nicest. These ones I have gotten to know. These ones I feel sorrier for.

"Hi, Monica," I say when I see her pale, pointed face. "Where's Mr. Avery today?"

Avery is her young son, and he calls me Miss Eve. He is small and sweet, just like Monica.

"Nothing to worry over," she says in her lilting way. "Just that he isn't feeling well, not lately." Creases scatter around her eyes, and there is a deep line between her eyebrows. Her voice is tight.

It's no wonder. Too many people who get sick down here on the first floor don't recover; treatment and aid are almost nonexistent.

"It's you we ought to be talking about," she continues. "I heard you took quite a beating in the Bowl—Jules told me. I wish you'd stop with that, a nice girl like you. Feeling better, I hope?"

Beside me, Wren tenses up. I can see his back straighten, and the muscles covering his forearms go rigid. His fingers clench into fists.

"It was no big deal," I say quickly. "Here. Tuck this under your sleeve for Avery. You can eat it if he doesn't want it." I check to make sure nobody is watching and shove an extra packet and roll to her. We aren't supposed to give out portions to anyone not in line, but I think of Avery's tiny voice and his dimples and I am happy to break the rules.

She nods. "Thanks, Eve," she says softly. "You've got a good heart to you, you know."

She turns, and I watch her until she is gone, just in case anyone saw me give her extra. It would make her a target, and she couldn't defend herself; she is too frail. Wren watches her go, too, his face tight, and I wonder what he is thinking.

"Hey, kiddo. Who's the hottie? Finally get a boyfriend or something?" I blink and stare at Jules's round face. She's a Nom I befriended years ago, a daring one who doesn't mind breaking the rules. Often, we spar together or hit the bags in the Bowl. I pass along clothes to her when I am through with them; I sneak her into the Mean cafeteria from time to time. She makes me laugh always. And never does she complain about her station.

"Who has time for boyfriends?" I say as I pass her a packet.

She rips it open and tilts half into her mouth. "You should try it sometime," she says as she chews. "They're a great distraction—especially the ones who are easy on the eyes." She winks at Wren. "So, you're not going to introduce me?"

"She has a habit of avoiding questions, I've noticed," Wren says bluntly. He sticks a hand forward. "My name's Wren."

"Jules. Nice to meet you."

She shifts her gaze back to me and pointedly lifts an eyebrow. I change the subject before she can say anything more, my cheeks burning pink as it is. "Want to sneak upstairs later? Bring your boxing gloves; I need the practice."

"Can't. I've got a hot date of my own. See you, Eve. Bye, Wren." With another wink, she is gone.

Thirty more parcels are passed through the partition

before I slide it shut. "That's it. Was it as fun and exciting as you anticipated?"

I am being sarcastic, but he turns to me with a level expression. "It was even better."

"Even better," I repeat. My fingers drum on the table. All at once, it dawns on me, and the revelation leaves me cold all over. "You plan to work in government."

"What makes you think that?"

I shrug. "The fact that you're here. I suppose having knowledge of the lower levels would be an asset on your job application."

He laughs, low and rumbly. "That's not why I'm here, Eve. And you're wrong, for the record; I don't want to work in government."

I tidy up, my mouth pressed into a line. If he doesn't want to work for the government, why is he here?

"You know, a normal person would ask what it is I do want to do."

"So what do you want to do, then, Wren?"

"I don't know, actually." He scratches his neck. "Something in computers, maybe?"

Computers. Those mighty machines brought underground to ensure goods could still be produced, genetically modified food, too. The ones that keep the compound humming, the ones completely unknowable to those of us on the lower floors. "Sounds like you've put a lot of thought into it," I mumble. "I'm glad I asked."

"Very funny. Dare I bring up your own job aspirations again?"

"You don't dare, no. Listen, the kitchen staff will come get the trays. We can go now." I lead him up the stairs and make sure to leave the lights on—just to piss off the guard. I won't be back until he is reassigned; that much I know.

Then we walk along the corridor where Wren hid me from view. It feels like days ago, even though it was less than an hour prior. I remember his clean, masculine smell and clear my throat. Soon we will part ways, and it is very likely I will never again see this strange Preme.

"Why were you on my floor the other day?" he asks into the silence. "Before we went to the shooting range."

The question catches me off guard, and I freeze. "I told you," I say slowly. "I was at the library."

He turns so he faces me, then says, "You were well past the library."

"I was lost."

He crosses his arms and squints at me. "Hmm. Given your track record for finding and causing trouble at every opportunity, you are surprisingly bad at lying."

I go to protest, but he holds up a hand. "Come on. I've never seen anyone look like you did that day. Your eyes…" His gaze finally breaks from mine, and something resembling discomfort passes over his face.

"What about my eyes?"

He shrugs. "They were…on fire. Like you had just done something, I don't know, big. I *know* you weren't in the library."

A smile catches my lips before I can set them straight. If only he knew. But I just shake my head. "I'm sorry, Wren. I don't know what you're talking about."

I make to walk again, but he grips my arm. "I know what's back there," he says quietly. His eyes burn into mine. "Not many people know, but I do."

My head shakes back and forth. Instinct. How does he know, how does he know? Maybe he is wrong. Maybe this is a test. I keep shaking my head. No.

He leans forward, and his grip on my arm tightens until it hurts. "It was the Oracle, wasn't it? That's where you were."

Still my head shakes, and though I can feel my mouth hanging open, I don't have control enough to close it. Finally, I snap to my senses and swallow. It burns my throat.

Think.

I could run. I could punch him. Fear streaks through me so loudly that it clouds my thoughts—he knows, he *knows*. He could turn me in. He could blackmail me. He could do anything.

How could he know my secret? It is *my* secret, nobody else's.

There is no sense in running from him; he's too fast. There is no sense in attacking him; he will win. I need to remain calm, that is what I need to do. So, as calmly as I can, I wrench my arm free from his grasp, my eyes spewing hatred as I do. "Don't come near me again," I hiss, and then I shove past him. Down the hall. Gone.

"Eve. Wait."

For some reason, I do. I think it's his voice. Always it is low and smooth. Usually it is cold. Hard. Right now, it is soft.

"I know about the Oracle's emergency exit because of my mother. Her department oversees the solar panels aboveground. Nobody else knows."

I turn to him and fold my arms. "Okay. Great, Wren. Great. You know my secret—you figured it out. Congrats, okay? You can turn me in now."

He laughs, and it sounds cold and hard, like the Wren I know. "If I wanted to hurt you, I'd go about it in a much more direct fashion. You can relax, Eve. Your secret's safe with me."

"Right."

He scowls. "And what exactly do I have to gain by turning you in?"

"I don't know. A funny story for you and your Preme friends to laugh about?"

He shakes his head. "You think I'm a monster; I get it. But rest assured, I have better things to do with my time."

I shrug. I am desperate, and the feeling is unnerving. So I force my spine to straighten, then square my shoulders to his. "Tell anyone, and I'll kill you, understand? And trust me, it isn't an empty threat."

His eyes flash, but he is calm. "Fine. So. How did you get inside?"

"With the code, genius."

It is a sarcastic response. But instead of reacting to it, he simply nods. "I suppose it wouldn't be impossible to figure out. No doubt you've seen enough guards open the feeding dock to pick up on patterns. Probably some of the digits are constant between doors. Compound Eleven. That would be part of it. The floor number would be in there too, am I right?"

I stare at him. His wide-set eyes make him look fiercely intelligent, but it isn't just show. He *is* intelligent. Still, I am not about to give anything away, so I say nothing. My jaw is set.

"When are you planning on going again?" he asks.

"To the Oracle?"

He nods, his eyes not moving from mine. Gold shines from his pupils, outward streaks that glow. They look like the sun. His eyes are the sun.

Don't stare too long, Eve, or they'll blind you.

"I don't know."

"But you will go back, won't you." It isn't a question. There is no need to answer.

Of course I will.

CHAPTER THIRTEEN

Zaar stands in front of me with his knuckles taped. He is a guest fighter—only his second time in the ring. He has black hair and pale skin, and his eyes look at me without emotion. He may be friends with Daniel and Landry, but he lacks their evil streak. Not that he is much better. He goes along with whatever they say, whatever they do. In fact, I don't think he is capable of experiencing an independent thought whatsoever. I stare into his eyes and see neither wickedness nor a sense of decency. They are empty slits.

I spent the morning with Erick, the two of us training under Anil. Erick is my age, and he is a hobby fighter like me. An occasional. Anil is a year older. He told me that Zaar has a bum left knee, to exploit this weakness as soon as the match begins. I don't know how he knows this, but I believe him. I would trust Anil with my life.

Erick and I train together often, and so he knows what a hard time Daniel, Landry, and Zaar give me. How they torment me. He knows how much I need to win, and he wants me to win, too. That is why he has been studying on my behalf.

First thing this morning, he opened his books, showed me how my roundhouse kick would be better presented as a sharp side kick. How I will generate more power if only I can master the technique. So we practiced it again and again, too much in fact, because now my quadriceps tingle with fatigue.

I hop up and down. Now is definitely not the time for fatigue.

The crowd is much smaller and quieter than when I was here last. Zaar is an Upper Mean, but a lot of guest fighters are Upper Means. They are never Premes. Wren was the exception.

Close to the ring sit Daniel and Landry, laughing, shouting words of encouragement to my opponent. I hate them, truly I do.

"Don't die, Eve!" Daniel shouts as the ref moves into position. I snap my knuckles and shuffle my feet back and forth. "At least not quickly. Draw it out so we can enjoy it, okay?"

Something hot prickles my skin. I will show them. I will show them there is no X marking my back. I will crush Zaar. Just to show them.

Zaar's arms twitch with anticipation. I haven't fought him before, but I know I can win. He is lean—lean enough to be quick. But he doesn't have much muscle. And he doesn't have much technique. And he has a bad left knee.

Yes, this is a different fight than against Wren, when I knew I would lose. My lips curl into a smile that makes his empty eyes narrow.

"When I blow the whistle, you may begin," says the ref, and he looks at me pointedly. It's the same ref as last time, and a small growl of laughter ripples from my stomach. I jump up and down, and my heart pounds with adrenaline that courses through my veins. The crowd hollers.

Maybe I was wrong when I was talking with Wren. Maybe

I *do* like fighting.

Zaar pounces as soon as the whistle is blown and clips me in the jaw. Now I laugh loudly. "Was that supposed to hurt?" No sooner do the words leave my mouth than I aim a side kick to his bad knee. Just like Erick and I practiced. Just like Anil said to do.

A perfect shot, and I can hear the snapping bone over the crowd. Blood drains silently from his face, and I take the opportunity to place an uppercut under his chin. And a fist to the eye.

I stare at Daniel and Landry and smile as blood rushes in my ears, as Zaar screams at my toes.

Maybe I am cruel.

The ref calls the match; I am the winner. It took a matter of seconds, and it is hard not to feel a surge of excitement even though I think I should feel guilty. But perhaps I shouldn't. Zaar has taunted me alongside Daniel and Landry for years now. When the others have threatened me, when they shoved me around and hit me for the fun of it when we were kids, he would laugh. He never stopped them.

Suddenly, I want to hit him again. I look down, but he has already disappeared. He is being carried out of the Bowl, and I know where he is going. The same place I was a week ago. I glance at Daniel and Landry and see them speaking to each other, tight-lipped, their bodies wooden.

"Let's go!" Erick shouts from behind me. He leans over the ropes and offers me a hand. Once I climb over, he squeezes my shoulder. "Well executed," he says as he leads me through the crush. His voice is distant.

Bodies sway around us, and they call my name. Their faces blur into one flesh-colored mask, and then Daniel shoves into my path and lowers his head so his dark blue eyes line up with mine. "That wasn't a very smart thing to do, Eve," he hisses at me. But he steps out of my way without another word and disappears into the crowd.

I watch him go—watch his tall frame and curly brown hair be swallowed up by the Bowl. My eyebrows pull together. It was a strange exchange; I would prefer it if Daniel had shoved me, thrown a punch, even. I suppose he wouldn't do anything too stupid, especially not with Erick's club-like arm draped over my shoulder. Or perhaps he knows now what I am capable of. Perhaps he will leave me alone.

"Quick work of our guest," Anil says once I'm in Blue Circuit's training room. He doesn't smile—he never does. "Bruno isn't happy, I should warn you."

"What, with me?"

Anil nods. "You know how he is about clean play."

Bruno is a good fighter, but he only wins by a slim margin each time, even when he can destroy his opponent. He is a gentle giant. I am not.

"Whatever," I say as I tear off my blue armband and have a seat on the couch in the corner. I toss it at the nearest punching bag and notice that the others aren't looking at me. "What?" I finally demand. "You're the one who said to go after his knee, Anil. And I did the exact kick we practiced all morning, in case you didn't notice," I add as my gaze shifts to Erick.

"We didn't say anything," Erick says limply. His eyes still don't meet mine.

I stare at them, and it isn't guilt bubbling in my stomach; it is anger.

The door flies open before I can say anything more.

"What the hell was that?" Bruno demands. He is bulky with muscle that pushes against his brown skin with every movement. His neck is so thick it strains the opening of the T-shirt he wears. Right now, it bulges with veins.

I scramble to my feet. "What the hell was *what*? I'm just doing my job, Bruno—we got the win. Besides, what's it to you? The guy's scum."

"You broke his knee. He's going to be laid up for months. I don't care how big a jerk he is—nobody deserves that." He crosses his arms, and I feel like a child being scolded. The feeling makes me hot in the face. "And don't get me started on the last few sucker punches," he adds.

It is unfair. It is unfair, it is unfair, it is unfair.

Isn't it?

"Nobody put you in charge," I say. "If the League wants to stop stuff like that from happening, they can change the rules. But you and I both know when we step into that ring, anything can happen—broken bones included."

He stares at me like I am barely human. Like he can't quite recognize what I am. "You shouldn't need rules to tell you not to do that, Eve. I thought you would have the decency—"

I push past him and out the door before he can finish. He is wrong. He doesn't know the full story. He doesn't know that I had to send a message to Daniel and Landry. He doesn't know, and that is why he doesn't understand. Nothing more.

Without thinking about it, I head in the one direction I know my fight will be well received.

"Certainly makes up for your loss against the Preme, doesn't it?"

I nod as I hold out my fists, knuckles up.

"Unclench your hands, Eve."

I do as he says. The lemon juice is barely noticeable—my knuckles have mostly healed from my fight with Wren, and today wasn't enough to do any new damage. Still, he cleans them. It is just something we do.

My mother didn't see the fight—she never goes. It's a good thing; she wouldn't be impressed, I am sure of it. Not that I feel guilty. I don't. I was justified in breaking Zaar's knee, and for the uppercut and the punch at the end. I was.

I watch her as she does embroidery in the corner, mumbling something about a clock under her breath. Her shoulders are hunched forward, and her neck is bent down at an awkward angle as she studies her stitches. It is something she started doing after Jack was sent aboveground, and now I can't imagine her doing anything else.

Back then, she was different. Back then, she laughed, loud and often. She chatted noisily with friends at mealtimes. She sang me songs, she told me stories while I sat on her lap, imaginary ones with happily-ever-after endings that helped me sleep at night.

All that changed once Jack was taken. The laughter died. Friendships were discarded. No more songs or stories, no offers of comfort. Nothing.

I stare at her and see my own future in Compound Eleven flash in front of me. I gaze upon her misery and see it turn like a wagon wheel into my own. A cycle of despair—that's all that awaits. Good thing, then, I have already decided to go.

"You should go down in the record books for that one," my father says.

I stare at him hollowly.

"Fastest time to finish a match," he adds.

I nod. I knew he would be excited. But it makes me feel only marginally better. I spread myself out on the bed that used to be mine. I feel much too big for it, even though I slept in it up until a few weeks ago. They always reassign kids to their own cells when schooling is complete. It's to ready us for adult lives, with adult jobs. "Can we talk about something else?"

He is silent for a few seconds, and I hold my breath. "How are your friends?"

I relax. "Which ones?"

"Maggie and Hunter."

They are my oldest friends, so it makes sense he would ask about them. But I don't want to talk about those two, either. Not really. Things with Hunter are all uncomfortable silences, cool glances.

And Maggie has another bruise that I noticed yesterday. On her arm. A cluster of them, faint but there all the same. Like someone held her tightly. Too tightly. The thought makes me sick.

"They're fine," I say, my voice placid.

"And your friends in Blue Circuit? They must be excited for you to join them full-time, especially after today's impressive display."

Another lie I must tell. My friends in Blue Circuit were not impressed by today's fight. And my friends in Blue Circuit will not be excited for me to join them full-time because join them I will not. "They're good, too."

"Are they excited?"

I sigh. "Yes, Dad. I'm sure they're excited. I usually win, so why wouldn't they be?"

Wren is wrong. I am not a bad liar.

And what a strange thing *that* is. Wren. The shooting range with him, the feeding of the Noms. Why should he spend time with me when he doesn't have to? Are we becoming friends?

A small laugh slips between my teeth. What an outlandish thing to think. Of course we aren't. Perhaps it was all to ease his guilt for beating me to a pulp. Perhaps he was bored. In reality, though, I don't expect to see him again.

Especially since we didn't part ways on the warmest of terms, my back still up about having to share my secret with him. I don't think he will turn me in, though. I have thought about it through and through. He is a Preme of all things, and capable of great violence, but he isn't petty. He was right when he said that if he wanted to hurt me, it would be much more direct. I believe him. But the Oracle was my secret before, and now it isn't. Now this *Preme* knows, too.

"Which Preeminate do you kneel before once you're hired on?"

My head snaps up. "What?"

"For the Combat League. Who do you make your pledge to?"

"Oh. I'm not sure. Whoever's in charge of Recreation, I guess."

"You should find out who, do it proper. It's the best way to get your name on the banners."

Earlier someone stared at me like they couldn't tell whether I was really human. Now I am the one wondering that—about my father. Because the thought of getting on my knees before one of the Premes in charge makes me sick, and it should make him sick, too.

"As for this," he continues, and he retracts his sleeve so that the ink on his forearm is exposed. "There will be mention…"

His voice trails off, and he looks agitated. My mother murmurs louder from her corner. I gaze at my father with my mouth open. For he is talking about Jack, and that is something we don't *ever* do.

Already I know what he is going to say. That there will be mention of Jack tattooed along my own arm. Mention of the fact that he was exiled from the compound for breaching the rules, that he is presumed *dead*. I think of staring at those words every day; I think of my mother's reaction to them when she pulled off her bandages just a week after he was taken…

"Eve."

I startle. "Huh?"

"The tattoo—"

"Yes. I realize."

"Don't let it get to you. Don't let it make you go soft. Think how good it felt to set a match-time record today, taking down your opponent without breaking a sweat. Say it." He nods at me encouragingly. "Say how good it felt."

"It felt good," I hear myself whisper. Then I repeat it again and again, until I can't really remember feeling any other way.

CHAPTER FOURTEEN

I check my watch again. I am impatient; it's in my nature. To my left is a large group of people my age, and to my right is an empty hallway. I stare down this hallway, willing him to show. Of course he will. This is the job he wants.

It is the last thing I want to be doing today. But I need to make things right again with my best friend, and besides, the others are getting suspicious about why I have so little interest in the job tours. I want to tell them the truth—I do. They might even understand my refusal to serve Katz after what my family has endured. But just because they could understand my decision to escape Eleven doesn't mean they'd support it, especially when so many who have attempted it before me have wound up dead.

"Food prep goes now!" shouts a voice from the front of the crowd. My eyes sort through the gathered faces one more time. I recognize most of them—they are all Means of one stripe or another, and all the Means school together. It is only the Denominators and the Premes who are schooled separately. Hunter's face is not among them.

He is never late.

The group pushes through the door to the kitchen, and then I see him.

He walks quickly up the hallway in our direction, stretching a rubber band into complex formations with his fingertips, something I've seen him do a million times before. The sight makes me smile.

"Just in time," I say as he nears, and his eyes lift to mine. Usually they sparkle, but today they are dull. Immediately it strikes me that he is upset about more than just me.

"What are you doing here? You aren't interested in the kitchen." He pauses, taking a minute to put the rubber band away and smooth his blue hoodie, one that has a green stripe through the middle. He adjusts his glasses. "Are you?"

I shrug, and together we join the back of the line that files into the kitchen. The lights are brighter here—Preme bright—and every surface is coated with a matte silver. Our eyes meet and tick away again like we are anything but friends.

"Did you hear about my fight with Zaar? It took about ten seconds to finish him off. Literally." I am not bragging. I don't even want to talk about it, frankly. But I need to fill the silence between us. I need to make things normal again.

He is one of my closest friends, and I need him. I do. My fighter friends at Blue Circuit might be disappointed in me or angry at me or whatever it is they are feeling; I can deal with that, even from Bruno, who has become something of a mentor to me. For now, anyway. I can't deal with Hunter and me not being good.

Because he isn't like the others. He isn't simply a friend. He is so much more.

None of my other friends bring me something special on the last day of May. Always it is something he has traded for, something he has made, something he has been allotted that he knows I would enjoy. One year it was wool socks, thick and warm, my own full of holes that left my toes aching from the cold concrete floors. No matter that his own socks had holes in them.

Another year it was a stack of books he had checked out from the library for me—those he knew I would enjoy and a few of his favorites, too. The year after that it was a small tin of ointment, a remedy for sore muscles, one he secured by trading away a kickball his father had gifted him.

The last day of May is when Jack was taken.

"Zaar? Yeah, I heard." Silence. "Too bad it wasn't Daniel on the receiving end," he adds. His voice is distant.

"Tell me about it."

"Maggie said he's taking it pretty personally, though, if that brings you any joy."

"Who, Daniel?"

"That's what she said."

It does bring me joy, hearing that. If I have upset someone like Daniel, I have done something right. But I already knew he was taking it personally—I could see it in his eyes after the match. He was mad, mad like I have never seen him before.

"How does she know that?"

"Kyle," he mutters, and in my peripheral vision I see his eyes darken. He doesn't like Kyle either, then.

The woman at the front of the group clears her throat. "Everyone starting out begins on chopping duty. Day in, day out, this is where you'll be stationed." She motions to a series of wooden boards, each the size of my bed.

I lean in to Hunter. "Any good with a knife?" I'm trying to be friendly, but he just shakes his head. I squeeze my eyes shut as the woman continues the tour, and I don't bother to listen—I don't care to. When there is a lull I turn once more to him. "Did Maggie say anything else about Daniel?"

"I don't think so. Why?"

"Just wondering. So am I to assume, then, that he and Kyle are friends?"

"Something like that." He pauses, then fixes me with a stare. "You realize he won't hang out with us, right?"

"Obviously. He's so stuck up, I'm surprised he's even dating Maggie."

"No kidding. It kind of makes you wonder."

I look at him sharply. "Wonder?"

"You know, about what his motives are."

"Uh, it's pretty clear what they are. We're talking about Maggie here."

He smiles a true Hunter smile, one that has comforted me for sixteen long years, and my shoulders relax. "I guess. Guys like pretty girls; I get it." His eyes meet mine and dart away again. For some reason I feel my face grow warm, even though the kitchen is cold.

The woman at the front introduces two of the kitchen staff. Probably Hunter would like to hear what they have to say, but instead I nudge him in the ribs. "Have you noticed her bruises?"

He looks at me solemnly this time and nods.

"Think they're from him?" I ask.

He stares at the man speaking, but I can tell he isn't listening. His lips are pressed together too tightly. "We can't exactly ask her," he finally whispers. "Can we?"

I shrug. "I'll kill him if they are."

"Back off, Eve. I agree that we need to do something, but blowing up isn't going to help anyone."

I force my jaw to unclench and nod. "Okay. You're right. I...I've been a little wound up lately."

He looks at me. "Yeah, you have."

I know he wants me to apologize, but I don't want to. I

only apologize when I feel it is warranted, and right now I don't know if it is. So instead I say, "Cut me some slack, okay? Losing to the Preme didn't exactly tickle." I am making an excuse, but I know it is one he will believe.

His gaze shifts, and I watch carefully as he takes a deep breath. I watch his chest rise and fall. Then he nods.

"So we're good?"

"We're good."

I wrap an arm around him as the group shuffles forward, past the burners and a series of refrigerators each larger than my cell, feeling much lighter than before. Just then, a girl with long braids catches sight of Hunter and flashes him a grin. I glare at her, then poke Hunter on the arm. "Hey, is your *girlfriend* here? She works in the kitchen, doesn't she?"

His gaze falls ever so slightly.

"What happened?" I say immediately.

"Nothing serious. She ended things, that's all. I imagine it will be fun working alongside her." He laughs a little, disingenuous.

"Sorry, Hunter. I really am."

"It's not the end of the world."

"Did she give you a reason, at least?"

He mumbles, "She said I was too young or something. I don't know."

"But she's a year older than us, right?"

He nods.

"Okay. Well, a year is a big difference. I wouldn't take it personally if I were you."

"She's already hanging out with someone else." He looks at me, and I understand.

"I'm sorry," I say. "That sucks." Then I pick at my nail because I don't know what else to offer. I don't exactly have any dating experience to draw on, and saying she wasn't good enough for him sounds like a cliché. Something you say to be nice but don't actually mean. Except I do mean it—nobody would be good enough for Hunter.

"Through these doors is the storeroom," the woman up front yells. "Anyone been inside before?"

Silence, and I turn to Hunter: "Did she say the *storeroom*?" He nods.

The storeroom, the room where all the supplies and goods that run Compound Eleven are housed—those brought from above when society was first established, and those produced underground with 3D printers taller than we are. These are the supplies that the compound carefully allots its residents— batteries, toilet paper, T-shirts, even alcohol—though I suspect it's offered mainly as a numbing agent, and only so we don't become too much of a nuisance. The lower the floor, the fewer allotments offered. Volunteer work means a few extra allotments per year, and holding a job means even more.

I already know the code to the kitchen; I know the code to all the doors on the second floor. Or so I thought. But I have never been to the storeroom, and until now I didn't even know its location.

Immediately I grab Hunter's hand and push forward. Talk of his breakup will have to wait.

"What are you doing?" he whispers as I shove through bodies.

I walk faster now. Faces swivel to mine, but my eyes are trained on one spot. The keypad. I need to see the last digits. The storeroom is one of the most important rooms in the compound—one I have only heard about.

"All items that don't fit in the kitchen are stored in—you guessed it—this bad boy. Spare knives, extra flour—the works. You'll be in and out of this room more times than you can count. Only senior members of the kitchen staff can open the door, so you'll have to ask me or Sal—the tall one with the black hat—if you want in. Got it?"

Heads nod. Her eyes sweep over Hunter and me as we position ourselves at the front, but she doesn't look suspicious. She does, however, use her free hand to block her fingers from view.

Still, as her arm lifts, I know the first two digits. 11—the same as every other code. Next her hand drops and pushes against the keypad in three motions. The fillers, 000. The next number is 2—I don't even need the confirmation I receive when her hand inches up.

And then it drops. It strikes twice, and low. As the door opens, I am frozen, thinking. It looked like two zeroes. 11000200. But that doesn't make sense. It isn't in keeping with the rest of the compound.

I understand why a moment later.

The storeroom isn't in keeping with the rest of the compound. It is cavernous, twice the height of the Bowl, stretching all the way up to ground level, surely.

The group buzzes with excitement; it is so different from the low ceilings that usually skulk overhead. And every few feet is a peculiarity. Thick nets slung from corner to corner, goods placed on each one, from floor up to ceiling.

The woman giving the tour grins. "Good news. Kitchen stuff is on the first three nets. These ones right here. Be grateful we aren't at the top, 'cause I'm willing to bet none of you would do so hot with heights."

"How do we get stuff from the middle of the net?" a girl with long red hair asks.

"Two feet and a heartbeat. Climb on in; the nets'll hold your weight."

"How do people get to the top?" I ask next. My neck aches from staring upward. But it is impossible to look away.

"Those things right there." She points to a ladder built into the wall near the closest corner. "There's one on each side. Couple guys work the place if you think the kitchen needs something from higher up. They can scale up pretty quick. Not that you'll ever need anything more. Been working here for thirty years now, and I've never needed nothing the first three nets don't offer."

I stare at her. Thirty years? The thought of working the same job for thirty years depresses the hell out of me. But Hunter is nodding in a way I recognize as interest, and so I swallow my horror, I squeeze his hand, and I nod, too.

That afternoon, I and the others head upstairs to the fourth floor. The job tours are scheduled by the Upper Mean administrators, and so we go to collect forms, timetables. One tour I might actually sign up for is the one that will take me to the tunnels connecting Compound Eleven with other nearby compounds. Twelve is nearby—we share energy with Compound Twelve. Compound Ten is farther away, I have heard—hours by foot. The rest, I have no idea.

The only tunnel job I would be eligible for as a Lower Mean is maintenance. Far from glamorous, but I am okay with that. Really, I just need to see where they run from and how they are guarded. Maybe one night at the end of "summer," on the eve of the so-called *job selections*, I will venture through one of them myself.

Or I could take the maintenance job, and then on my first day leave Compound Eleven forever under the cover of authority, greatly increasing my chances of survival. But I won't be permitted in the tunnels until I've kneeled before the higher-ups and pledged to them my soul, until I've been branded with my family history of deviance. And maybe I could swallow my pride enough to bend a knee, but the thought of going the rest of my life with a reminder of what happened to Jack etched into my skin is too much to bear.

I sigh. Right now, this tunnel scheme is the closest thing I have to a plan for escaping my life down here. Small fragments of hollow ideas.

But I can't let myself go down that hole. I need to believe that my hollow ideas will harden into concrete action. That not only will I bid Eleven goodbye—I will also find someplace better. And if I can't have belief in that, if my hope is extinguished, I will shatter into a million pieces.

My entire existence rests on eggshells.

I nudge Hunter as we empty out of the elevator and onto the fourth floor with Maggie and Emerald close behind, an attempt at playfulness. I don't want to think about the future, not right now, and I want him to feel better, too. I want him to forget about Anita. He gives me a shy smile, and the muscles lining my stomach relax, just as they always have when he smiles at me.

It was smart of me to go today. Not just because I made things better with Hunter, and not just because I saw the compound's massive storeroom. But also because the others have eased up on me. They think I am finally interested in finding a job. We can be ourselves again, at least on the surface. The secrets that divide us are pushed down deep.

"Better hope you don't run into Daniel up here, Eve," Maggie says. "Kyle told me he's super pissed about your fight with Zaar."

"Yeah, Hunter passed on the message. And I think what you mean," I add as I punch her lightly on the arm, "is that you hope he doesn't run into *me*."

She laughs. "Fair enough."

I am joking around, but I am also serious. It is bad enough I have to watch my back for the guard whose nose I broke; I don't need to add another name to the list.

"Speaking of Kyle, where is he?" I ask. "Still too cool to hang out with us?"

"Hey, that isn't fair. He's just super busy, you know? He works all the time. We'll see what that's like soon enough."

"What does he do, exactly?" Hunter asks.

"Construction management. He really likes it, but it's a lot of responsibility. He says it's one of the most important Upper Mean jobs available and that a lot of people depend on him performing day in and day out. So yeah, all that stress can get to him, you know?"

I resist the urge to roll my eyes.

Hunter clears his throat. "Sounds like interesting work. So, things going well between you two?"

We had discussed it at length at the end of today's tour and had agreed to tread lightly. The last thing we want is to lose her as a friend. Still, it is hard for me to be tactful. It is hard for me to keep my mouth closed when I think of what he is doing to her.

"We're getting pretty serious," she says, then turns to him. "Hey, sorry to hear about you and Anita. Emerald told me this morning."

"Oh." His voice sounds suddenly lackluster. "It's not a—"

"It's freezing in here," I interrupt. It's a transparent attempt to change the subject, but I don't stop. "Don't you think? It's the middle of summer aboveground, and it feels like we're living in an ice cube."

Maggie pokes me. "That's our Eve. Always keeping tabs on things up there."

"What's that supposed to mean?"

"Nothing," she says. "Just that you talk about it a lot."

"And look at a lot of weird old books," Emerald adds. The lights are nicer up here—the bulbs are encased in covers that diffuse the light, and there are more of them than on the second floor. It falls gently on her brown skin and makes her eyes twinkle.

"Can't be working on my punches all the time like you," I say as I nudge her.

She flexes her arm, and it is big and strong like the rest of her. "I heard your kick's more deadly, anyway."

I laugh.

Hunter turns so that he walks backward, so that he faces me. "Too bad there aren't any jobs studying the history of civilization. That'd be up your alley."

"Yeah, that or studying the burned-out sauna aboveground," Maggie adds.

"Hey, that stuff's interesting," I protest. I don't bother to add that the "burned-out sauna" is actually the most beautiful thing I've ever laid eyes on.

"Yeah, interesting to you."

"So? Are there job possibilities?"

I shake my head. "I don't think so. At least not that a Lower Mean can do. Some of the Premes study that sort of thing, but that's it. Scientists, I think they're called."

"What about maintenance teams for the solar panels?"

"I think that's all engineers. Upper Means and Premes." What else is new.

I kick at the floor. My friends are right—a job studying aboveground would be ideal for me. A job that involved being in the Oracle. A job that *didn't* involve serving the people who took away my brother. One with no demeaning oaths or haunting tattoos. That sort of job might make me stay in Compound Eleven.

Too bad I was born on the second floor, two floors beneath where we now walk.

"Here, Eve." Hunter holds out the color-blocked hoodie he had been wearing.

"What's this?"

"You said you were cold."

I go to refuse, never one to readily accept help, but think better of it. "Thanks, Hunter. You're the best." I pull it on over my T-shirt, and though it is too big, it feels good. Like I am wrapped in his love. I smile and then reach over to him so we hold each other as we walk.

It feels good to spend time with my friends, our conversation light, mood high. It tastes like a snippet of freedom. It makes me forget about Katz, makes me think for a fraction of a second that I could spend my life here.

A group of young men walks past us. I wouldn't notice them at all, except one stares at me, and it breaks my attention from my friends. Hunter's arms pull me forward, but not before my eyes latch on to Wren's. He walks with two others and his strong hands clench into fists as he stares at me. Gold eyes burn into mine with such intensity I stumble, my lips part, and I can feel his gaze in my ears like a buzzing.

He looks like he did at the Bowl; he looks angry. He *is* angry. I can feel it from across the hall; I can see his eyes flashing as they drill into mine. And then the moment is broken as I am propelled forward and he passes me by, and my heart beats in my chest and in my throat and in a way I can't quite understand.

CHAPTER FIFTEEN

I place my hand on the scanner, and it blinks red. Two flashes. Access denied. The plaque on the wall explains that only Commander Katz, the Leader of Compound Eleven, can open the Oracle's door. Only his handprint will release me.

Not his Deputy, not the Executive Director, not the Deputy Directors or even the Department Heads. All levels of government are useless to me, except for the very top. Not that it makes any difference; to a Lower Mean, the entire government is nothing but meaningless titles and faceless names. Those with power don't often step foot off the Preme floor—why would they? So even if they could help me, none of them would.

I think about the Katz we are gifted with now, Zachary. Ever since Compound Eleven's inception, one Katz or another has been the ruler—power has transferred blindly from father to son, father to son. Probably theirs was the wealthiest family all those years ago, or the most domineering. The most ruthless. Frankly, I don't care about Zachary Katz's pedigree or what his backstory is. I care only that of the thousands upon thousands of people below my boots, only *he* has the authority to release me.

Not that it is much of a release—not really. I wouldn't survive long outside, and so it would be a release to a certain death, just like what Jack must have endured.

Still, as I stare out the glass walls of the Oracle at the swaying trees and the vast spaces, it is hard not to pine for it. Just to see what it feels like. Latitude, to run and scream and breathe in air that hasn't been recycled through thousands upon thousands of other mouths. To feel something called a breeze against my cheek. To look up at nothing but a sky forever away instead of a gray ceiling a couple feet above.

Funny how something that looks so beautiful can be so deadly. In every sense of the word, it seems like paradise. Like an oasis, one that is all mine. Oasis…paradise…

I drum my fingers on my leg as the song comes slowly back to me, the one my mother used to sing to Jack and me before everything changed. It's set to the same tune as the compound's anthem, but instead of accusations, instead of a bellowing of anger against the planet that was once home, this is sung sweetly, intended to lull us peacefully to sleep…

Children dearest hear me whisper, release the ticking clock
Start forth in the darkness, behind the north night hawk
Follow very closely, cross the ragged shards of rock
Children dearest run your fastest, tick tock

Children dearest hear me singing, release the ticking clock
Til you reach the oasis, free you're not to gawk
Once you're there forget your cares, slow your pace to walk
Children dearest ignore the ever, tick tock

Children dearest hear me shouting, release the ticking clock

There the sun can't reach you, green canopies do block
Burbling streams to drink from, a field of hollyhock
Children dearest find the eternal, tick tock

Children dearest hear me roaring, release the ticking clock
Relieve your pain, don't be scared, smash apart the lock
Drift to gentle paradise, it's there that we shall talk
Children dearest side by side, tick tock

An oasis, somewhere out there, safe and free. How deeply I wish it were true…

The sun isn't shining as brightly today, though it is the middle of the afternoon, and so I can take in the scenery from all angles. Through the glass wall in front of me, I see a field with long grass that blows with the wind before giving way to a wide hill. At the base of a hill is a small outbuilding, about the same size as my cell, and on top of the hill sits row after row of solar panels, the ones that run the compound. Someplace beyond, far off in the distance, are dark and crusted mounds that reach toward the sky, their lines pointed and uneven, mesmerizing and menacing all at once.

Next I shift my gaze to the peculiar room around me. In the middle is the elevator shaft, and behind it, the trapdoor. On the back of the elevator shaft hang binoculars, covered in a thick layer of dust. Underneath them and propped against the wall looks to be a first aid kit, but the lettering is so faded, the layer of grime so thick, that I can't be sure. A compass lies next to it, smashed to pieces.

Small details, interesting ones, yet all at once my attention returns to the Oracle's door. So I stand in front of it, trying my hand again and again in the scanner, even though I know it is futile. Endless flashes of red. Denied, always. I am not the leader of Compound Eleven, and this is not a code that

I can crack.

My hands move along the seams of the door, and my fingers dig in, suddenly desperate to be nearer to the outside world. Just as futile.

But maybe, maybe

I tick my fingernails against the glass, drag my palm noisily across it. Yes. A bullet might work. Just to test, to see what it feels like, out there.

Too bad I have no gun of my own to give it a try.

Exhaling, I move to a corner of the prism, where I crouch, then sit with my legs crossed. I have brought a field guide with me today, one I borrowed from the library. From my new vantage point, I am surrounded by nature, and with the guide splayed open in my lap, I can identify all that encompasses me. Those green discs that tick against the glass like music are leaves, and with some effort I am able to identify them as honeysuckle leaves. I smile to myself— tongue the word around my mouth.

Then I flip to a different page. Roots. That is what I see bulging from the ground. From the *dirt*. When I spot a bird in the sky, one of the few creatures to have adapted to the heat, I turn to a section in the book devoted to various species, but the bird outside glides too high for me to identify.

So I consider the sketches beneath my fingers—the songbirds, the eagles, the hawks—and I think again about that song, the one my mother used to sing. I think about the so-called oasis. *Start forth in the darkness, behind the north night hawk.* I touch the illustration of the hawk, then look beyond the hill where the solar panels sit, to the uneven lines mounding in the distance. Ragged lines. *Follow very closely, cross the ragged shards of rock.* I breathe deeply as I contemplate them, then flip through the guidebook until I know for certain. Yes, those ragged mounds way out there, they are rock—they must be. Hard, unyielding, even in the breeze. Next I flip to the back of the book, to the index.

When I finally find what I'm looking for, I gasp. *Burbling streams to drink from, a field of hollyhock.* Hollyhock. Not a falsity at all. Instead it's an enchanting flower, like a shallow bowl constructed purely of saturated pigment. In my head, I picture a whole field of them, and I see it. I see paradise.

I turn back to the outside world, smiling now, slowly identifying more of what surrounds me. Time ticks on, but I don't stop, not until my eyes grow impossibly heavy and I lie back on the floor, wrapped in warmth, and let sleep wash over me.

I dream of the oasis, I wake to the sun's soft glow, and everything becomes clear.

I don't simply want to go outside. I *need* to go outside. I need to escape these walls, even if I am escaping to a probable death. The other compounds I am not interested in. Deep down, I think I always suspected that. Now I can be certain of it. There is only one thing in life I desire.

Freedom.

CHAPTER SIXTEEN

We sit at our usual spot in the cafeteria on the third floor. Hunter sits on the other side of the table, Emerald beside him, Maggie beside me. The others talk, but I can barely concentrate; all I can think about is my time in the Oracle yesterday afternoon. And about my decision. That I am going outside, aboveground, even though it will kill me.

Once you're there forget your cares, slow your pace to walk.

Or maybe it won't kill me. Because after the Oracle, I didn't return to my cell, at least not right away. Instead I studied the sculpture of the Earth in the Preme atrium, then went to the library and located a threadbare topography atlas. And I discovered something. That those shards of rock way off in the distance sit directly north of here…just like the song suggests.

That song, the one my mother used to sing to Jack and me, is crafted on the compound's anthem. That means it came into existence *after* life moved down here. So there must have been whisperings at one time, rumors, for such specifics to work their way into the lyrics. Whisperings that evidently have some grounding in reality…

So maybe I *can* survive. Maybe the oasis *does* exist.

And if it does, what if Jack made it there? If I can find a way up and out, I could make it there, too…we could live out our lives together, on our own terms—

The thought makes me feel more hopeful, more alive, more content than anything the compound has ever offered me.

I look around at the others, at their smiling faces. I can't tell them about this latest development. No way. Maggie might be supportive, but she might not. And besides, she has enough to deal with right now. I glance once again at the new bruise on her forearm. With Hunter, on the other hand, there's no question. He wouldn't support my decision in a million years. And Emerald flat out wouldn't let me go.

I guess I should be flattered. I matter to them. I *matter*. Do I matter to myself?

My fingertips graze the rips in my knuckles from the previous evening. Hours at the punching bag is the culprit, and I can barely lift my arms now to feed myself. Do I matter to myself? Would I be choosing probable death if I did?

The scabs that are starting to form bulge under my index finger. There are no nerve endings in scabs.

Do I matter to myself?

Yes.

I protect myself, and I nourish myself when I'd rather not, so yes. And I am not choosing death. I am choosing freedom. That is the crux of it.

It is what I want more than anything else, and I owe it to myself to get it. Even though it may be short-lived. My decision is final; it is how to achieve it that needs sorting. A bullet will shatter the Oracle glass; it will allow me to step across the threshold, wave goodbye to Compound Eleven confinement, feel fresh air against my face. It will allow me to run north as fast as my legs will allow…hopefully into my brother's arms in paradise. I drum my fingers on the table, grinning at the thought. All I need is a gun.

A gun. There is no shortage of guns marching around down here under the stench of authority, gifting power to those they shouldn't. How difficult would it be to take one?

Difficult. No question. It will require some consideration, some thought. But the slight uptick in my pulse alerts me to the fact that I am onto something. It is the start of a plan, a real one, to turn my dream into reality.

I pick up my fork and glance around. Eighteen long tables jammed into a plain rectangular box with a ceiling too low and a crowd too rowdy. I won't miss it when I go.

"Is everything okay, Eve?" Hunter asks as I pick at a gray, glutinous mound of mashed potatoes.

"Huh? Oh, yeah. Yeah, of course." I force my back straighter and clear my throat. "Emerald, how was your fight this morning?"

She has a puffy eye, but otherwise her spirits are fine, and she looks none the worse for wear. "Easy as pie," she says with a grin.

"A guest fighter?"

"Nope, it was a Red Circuit pro. The one with the spiky red hair, you know her? She's solid but slow as hell. Not to brag, but she never stood a chance."

I force myself to laugh. "You've been racking up a lot of wins lately. Bruno must be happy."

"He is. He mentioned me going pro today after the fight." Her eyes light up with excitement.

"Really? That's great! You deserve it."

"Yeah yeah," says Maggie with a wave of her hand, "that's awesome and everything, but don't think you're cutting the rest of the job tours, because I don't want to be the only one—"

She freezes, her eyes glued to someone or something over my shoulder. I'm willing to bet I know who it is.

"Get away from me, Daniel, or I swear to God I'll break your knee, too," I say without turning around. The look on Maggie's face makes me glance over my shoulder, and when I do, I freeze in my own right.

It isn't Daniel standing there, and it isn't Landry, either. It is Wren.

"Too?" he asks as he looks down at me. His gaze flicks off mine quickly, like he is just a little nervous or self-conscious, neither of which could be true. "Whose knee did you break?"

"What are you doing here?" I ask instead.

He shrugs. "Eating lunch. Is that allowed?" He sets his tray down next to mine and takes a seat. Hunter stares at him like he is from a different planet. Emerald scowls.

There is no sense in telling him that Premes don't exactly eat down here in the Mean cafeteria. He already knows that. A few others sitting nearby glance at him, but I don't think they can tell from looking at him what he is, especially with his hands resting under the table. They can't understand how peculiar his presence is.

"I'm Wren," he says as he glances around at my friends. He adds darkly, "I've come to realize Eve isn't one for introductions."

The others silently switch their gaze from Wren to me. I know exactly what they are thinking. As far as they know, I haven't seen the Preme since our fight, but here we are, having lunch together like old pals. Me and a *Preme*. Yet another secret I have been keeping from them. Is it normal to keep so much from your friends?

After several uncomfortable seconds, Maggie leans

forward. "Nice to meet you. I'm Maggie. This is Hunter, and this is Emerald."

I watch as he picks up his fork and turns it around in his hand. Probably it is flimsy compared to what he is used to. I don't say anything, though. I just watch a muscle in his forearm tick up and down with the movement.

"Are you two friends or something?" Emerald asks slowly, her dark brown eyes shifting back and forth between us.

I shake my head. "Of course not."

"She's right," he adds. "Of course we're not friends. You know, because I'm a Preme and everything." He gives me a look, then returns his attention to Emerald. "Nice black eye. I take it you're a fighter like Eve?"

"Yeah, something like that," she mumbles.

I give myself a shake, try to focus on the rationed portions of unpalatable food sitting in front of me. But Hunter is watching us closely, and a pang of guilt stabs at my stomach. How could I not tell my friends that Wren and I had seen each other since the fight? Why did I feel the need to keep *that* of all things secret?

Emerald shrugs. It looks as though she is the first of our group to accept Wren's inexplicable presence. "So anyway, before the fight, I was hanging in the training room, and Erick mentioned that you and Bruno had a spat. If you want to fight pro, you realize you're going to have to apologize to him, right?"

"I'm not going pro."

"You're *not*? Then how come you're barely doing any of the job tours?"

Too many lies—it is hard to keep them straight. "Okay, well, maybe I *am* going pro. I just—I guess I don't know yet, okay?"

"Okay," she says slowly. "Well, like I said, if you think you *might* want to pick that as your job, you need to apologize. Pronto."

"I didn't do anything wrong."

"Who's Bruno?" Wren asks.

"He's one of the pro fighters for Blue Circuit. He practically runs the team."

"Why's he pissed?"

"Long story," I mumble.

"I've got time."

I turn to him. "What are you doing here, again?"

He thrusts his fork in my direction. "Eating."

"Come on, Wren," I start. But I can feel the eyes of the others, and I stop. I sigh. "My last fight, a couple of days ago. I beat this guy Zaar, one of Daniel's friends—"

"Daniel...the one who introduced himself."

"Yep. Anyway, Bruno wasn't happy with my...ethics."

"Any chance you broke his knee?"

I nod. "That's the one."

"Highly unethical, Eve," he says with a shake of his head. "Quite disappointing, frankly."

"Yeah, almost as unethical as headbutting someone in the face," I retort, and I nudge him in the ribs. Both of us are smiling, but mine evaporates when I see the look on Hunter's face.

"I think I'll be going," he says as he pushes back from the table.

"Don't, Hunter." But I don't know what else to say. He has a right to be mad. I told him on the kitchen tour to go easy on me because of my brutal fight with the Preme. It was a lie, an excuse, and he can see that now.

The look he gives me makes my stomach dive. "I've lost my appetite," is all he says before disappearing into the crowd.

Wren's eyebrows draw together. "Something I said?"

"Don't worry about it," I mutter as I push my plate away. Emerald, who is always ravenous, scoops up the rest of Hunter's lunch and my own. And then, before I can say anything more, I am shoved hard into the table. It catches me under the ribs, and for a second I am breathless

A moment later, I am on my feet and face-to-face with Daniel. Landry stands behind him with his lips curled up at the corners. "If you think you're going to take the last slot from Zaar, you're crazy," Daniel spits at me. "Even with a busted knee, they'd rather have him than a Lower Mean nobody like yourself."

"What are you talking about?" I shout at him.

"He must think you're going after a guard job," says Maggie from beside me. "That you did that to Zaar on purpose, to push him out of the running!"

I laugh a cruel laugh. "You're being ridiculous, Daniel. You think I want to work in the same organization that would hire scum like you and Landry?"

"Watch your mouth, Eve," says Daniel, and his hand grabs the shirt from my chest.

There is no time to react. Wren has him off me before I can raise a hand to defend myself. "Touch her again," he says coldly into Daniel's ear. "Just try."

"Got a bodyguard, Eve?" he shouts as he pulls himself free of Wren's grasp. "Good, because you're gonna need it!" And then he is gone; Landry, too.

"What *was* that?" I yell at Wren above the noise of the cafeteria that reenters my brain like a switch has been flipped. It seems to buzz louder than before.

He smiles, but it isn't a friendly one. It's a sneer, and I am reminded that he is dangerous and cruel like me. "Let me guess, Eve. You didn't need my help—is that it? You don't need anyone's help, right?"

"Something like that," I say, my voice suddenly level.

"What about with the guard. Did you need my help then?"

I don't want to be reminded of my moments of weakness; not by anybody, and especially not by him. So I turn, push through the crowd in the direction of the exit.

But he follows me, and once we're in the hallway, his hand lands on my shoulder.

"Look, it was instinct, okay?" he says into my ear. "You see someone get grabbed like that, and you react. It has nothing to do with you needing help. Or you being a girl. Or me thinking you're weak or something. It was instinct." He stares at me and raises both palms. "Okay?"

I shake my head, but it is only to clear the burning sensation that suddenly stabs behind my eyes. Why I feel like crying right now I do not know. All I know is that I don't need defending. I don't need it, and I don't want it.

"Why are you even here, Wren? You know as well as I do that Premes don't eat down here. And they don't give a shit about feeding the Noms, either."

His eyes narrow. "Are you serious? Come on, you're not that naive."

"What's that supposed to mean?" I snap.

"Come *on*. Why do you think I'm here? Yeah, obviously Premes don't eat down here. They don't help serve food to the Noms. *Obviously*, Eve."

I stare at him. I am at a loss, but this seems to anger him more than anything.

He shakes his head as he pushes by me. "I'm getting a little sick of waiting for you to clue in."

CHAPTER SEVENTEEN

The next day, my muscles ache worse than ever. It is because I headed straight for the Blue Circuit training room after my eventful lunch with Daniel and Wren yesterday, and I passed the afternoon there, sparring with Erick and hitting the punching bags until I couldn't lift my arms any longer. The tears that wanted to fall when I was speaking with Wren—fighting with him, to be accurate—dried up, and I managed to make things better with Bruno, too. It took only a simple apology; my skills as a liar are improving constantly.

Hunter wasn't at dinner last night. And I can't really bear to see him—not now. It was bad enough to have him mad at me when I felt I didn't deserve it, but now…it is worse when I do. Shame leaves a bitter taste in my mouth.

The low ceiling of the second floor skims my fingertips as I reach to touch it. My sore muscles scream in protest, but I ignore them. I am headed for the Oracle. I know I shouldn't go; I can't make a habit of it. Every time I venture there, I venture getting caught. But I can't stay away, especially now that I have a plan to take my exit. I may not yet have the gun in my palm, but it is just a matter of time before I do.

Besides, I need to keep clear of Hunter until he cools down.

The stairs are empty, and I take them two at a time even though the movement makes me wince. It's a good pain, though. The kind of pain I like. Worn muscles are stronger muscles. Strong body, strong mind.

My father's words.

The fifth floor is still, just like the rest of the compound. Protests down below are scheduled for today, but right now it is quiet. I walk past the library, my fingers grazing the glass walls. It is one room I will miss when I go.

I turn through the hallways just as I always have, muscle memory carrying me forward. How I used to long for the right passcode to get into the Oracle. It is strange to think those days are over. That Eve is dead. Now I know the code, now I've seen aboveground, now I've decided to escape—I even know how to do it. I am a different person. Perhaps that's all life is. A series of deaths and rebirths, over and over until we can be born again no more.

"Going somewhere?" rings out a voice.

Something drops in my stomach. Not fear, no. Just dread. I want to be left alone. I want to walk and move freely without being questioned.

"You don't look like you belong up here," the voice continues, and when I turn, he adds, "what happened to your face?" His voice is full of genuine curiosity, and I am reminded that I still sport residual bruising from my match with Wren.

I blink at him, at hair that is yellow, skin pink.

"Wait a second—I've seen you before. You were in that fight, weren't you? With a guy from up here? I was working the Bowl that day. Remember your hair."

Automatically, my fingers start to reach toward my messy

waves. Just in time, I remember the tattoos on my hands and fold them away.

"Yeah, I know you had it pulled back and everything, but still. A guy remembers a pretty girl. Long blond hair, nice face—yeah, I remember."

I frown. Not often do I hear such things, especially from an Upper Mean, like he undoubtedly is. His voice sounds relaxed, but there is something greedy stirring behind his eyes. Something I don't like. Maybe he is a bigger threat than I thought. I try to smooth my eyebrows and lift my voice to an octave considered friendly. "Oh?"

"Looks like it should be fine, though. Eventually. When I watched the fight, I thought that pretty little nose of yours would be coming out your ear."

He laughs loudly, and I blink.

"I'm Ben, by the way. What's your name?"

"Eve." Deep breath, in and out. I still don't know the fifth floor well enough to lose him in a footrace. And I don't trust my fists now that I've seen the power of guns. The feeling of vulnerability makes me lightheaded.

"You're from Floor Two, is that what your hands say?"

I nod.

"Mind if I ask where you're headed?" He takes a step closer.

Another breath. In, out.

"She's looking for me," comes a new voice, and I see Wren turn the corner. His black T-shirt is faded today, and it pulls tightly over his chest. It is an odd thing for me to notice. His eyes don't look into mine, but he walks in my direction, stands beside me before glancing coldly at Ben the guard. "Anything else?"

Ben twirls his baton, then grabs it. His eyes slide pointedly down my body. "Head on downstairs where you belong, save me some paperwork, huh?"

"Sure."

"And take care of that face, okay?"

I swallow a grimace that pulls my lips from my teeth.

"Really nice meeting you, Eve," he adds under his breath. He squeezes my wrist as he passes, and then he is gone.

I glance at Wren. "Are you following me or something?"

He makes a noise of disbelief. "Get over yourself. Oh, let me guess. You didn't want my help there, either, right?"

My arms cross, and I glare at him out of the corner of my eye.

"Right, Eve? Because the way he looked at you there was no big deal, right? There wasn't something on his mind?"

He moves closer, and his head lowers so we are almost eye to eye.

"I can take care of myself." Defiant and stubborn I definitely am.

"Next time I'll wait until he's finished with you, then."

I bristle at his words. Then I shrug. "How'd you know I was here?"

"I saw you walk past the library."

My eyes narrow. "Little early for the library, isn't it?"

"Little early for this, isn't it?" He nods in the direction of the Oracle.

"That's an evasive answer."

"What's it to you?"

I shrug. "Just curious. Not many people spend much time there."

"You do."

"You know what? Just forget I asked, okay? Thanks for helping me out with the guard. Happy? I'll be seeing you."

I walk quickly past him, but he follows. "You're not the only one interested in things, you know. I was reading about a concept called democracy."

"Democracy? Why are you interested in that?"

He shrugs. "I've been thinking about life down here. Down there. The Noms, the Means. I was curious what other models of governance they had before the compounds were established." One corner of his mouth tugs up as he glances at me. "I was also reading about combat, but I didn't think you'd find that as impressive."

I don't know what he means by that. I don't know what to make of this Preme, period. Why would he care about impressing me?

A door opens at the end of the hall, and a girl who looks a couple of years older than me emerges. I wait for her to walk by before I respond. But she pauses when she sees Wren, and her eyes widen. "What are you doing here?" she asks.

He shrugs. "Walking around. You?"

"Getting this from Father's office. I forgot it yesterday when he was giving me a tour." She holds up a purse, one that is completely superfluous, one that would never be allotted to someone beneath the fifth floor. "Please, Wren, please, please, *please* tell me you'll be touring your mother's operation? Father's office and hers collaborate all the time, you know." She wraps her fingers around his forearm. "Think about it. I would be in charge of security; you would be in charge of energy—what an unstoppable team that would make us."

I string my hands behind my back as I consider her. Those delicate features, that red hair—hair that is so long it could be used as a noose—

I shake my head to clear the inexplicable image flashing through my mind, but it draws her attention. "Who's this?" she asks. Disdain rests heavily across her brow as she eyes me.

"This is Eve," Wren says. His voice is level, as it always is.

"She doesn't even look like an Upper Mean."

"She's not. Not a third-floor Mean, either. And for the record, I won't be touring my mother's operation. Not interested," he adds before pulling his arm free and walking past her. Not even the courtesy of a goodbye.

As I follow, I do my best to pass her without expression. But I am weak and cruel, and I smile a wicked smile as I go. She scowls.

When we reach the door to the Oracle's emergency exit, I turn to him. "Why don't you run along to your girlfriend there and I can be on my way. *Please, please, please.*"

He presses his lips into a straight line and looks at the ceiling like he is considering it. Finally, he shakes his head. "I think I'll stay here, thanks. I'm kind of interested to see what the big deal is."

"Sorry, but it's for my eyes only."

He laughs. "You realize I've been before, right? On a few occasions, though I can't say I've ever snuck in through the emergency exit."

The revelation catches me by surprise, and it must show clearly across my face.

"My mother's office, remember?" he adds.

I nod, then turn to the keypad. But my fingers hover; they pause. If I enter the code, he will see it, and he will be able to access the Oracle whenever he wants, too. Do I want to share it?

He is a Preme, seemingly a well-connected one. He could probably access the Oracle at his bidding if he really wanted to. So what if he has the code?

My fingers punch in the digits; I feel him watching and committing them to memory. Then the door opens, and we slip inside. Immediately it strikes me how strange it is that I am here, with him. At the thought, my heart beats harder. Faster. It has nothing to do with him, of course. Just the fact that I am sharing this with someone. Or maybe because it isn't often I am alone in a room with a boy I barely know.

"Everything okay, Eve?" he asks quietly. He is grinning.

"What?"

"You haven't moved in a few minutes."

I force myself forward and will my shoulders to loosen. A lost cause. "Oh. Yeah, I'm fine."

"Okay." His eyes rise to the trapdoor. "After you."

Deep breath, in and out. My boot lands on the first rung of the ladder, and my fingers grip the rungs above my head. There is a fluttering in my stomach that I can't identify, and as I draw myself upward, I can feel his eyes on me, and every move I make feels forced and unnatural.

But once I swing the trapdoor open, that feeling evaporates. The Oracle is darker than I have seen it and full of a sound I cannot identify. I scramble in with Wren at my heels, my eyes searching for the source of the noise. It comes from the glass itself—something is smacking against it, millions of fine pieces whipping it like melting beads of plastic. My fingers stretch out and touch the glass.

"Raindrops," says Wren from behind me. He stands close, and that feeling in my stomach returns.

Raindrops. The fine pieces are raindrops. I stare at them as they cling to the outside of the Oracle. They don't look hard—not as hard as they sound. And they are so shapeless, nothing like the neat teardrops depicted in the books below. Next my eyes travel upward to the sky, one previously so blue. Today it is a dark gray like the walls and ceilings of Compound Eleven, except that it moves and it sways and it is anything but the stifling compound below my feet.

"What do you think?" he asks me.

I stare at the trees as they whip from side to side, as leaves are ripped from them and thrown through the darkened air. The northern shards of rock sitting in the distance are unmoved, but set in this context they seem more ominous than before, cold and leering. "I think…I think it's frightening and beautiful at the same time." My voice is a whisper, barely audible over the rain.

Suddenly, there is a flash of light followed by a deafening crack that sounds worse than the breaking of bone. I step back from the window, and my hand falls to my side, spine straight. This is a side to the world aboveground I haven't yet witnessed. It is cruel and fascinating, frightening and beautiful.

"Lightning. And thunder. It's a thunderstorm, Eve," he says quietly. "It happens from time to time. It will clear."

I swallow, and my throat burns. "How do you know all of this?"

He shrugs, and I notice that the back of my shoulder touches his chest. "I told you. My mother's in charge of the solar panels. I've heard her talk about it, since it interrupts the collection of energy."

"Is it still hot during a thunderstorm?"

"Is it still hot? I don't know. I think so. Planning on stepping outside?"

"Something like that," I murmur. Another burst of light pierces through the sky, and I place both palms on the glass in time for the thunder. I can feel it rattle, and its power and fury make me smile. "I'm not staying in Compound Eleven much longer," I blurt out before I can stop myself. Maybe it's the storm. Maybe it's stopping me from thinking clearly, but suddenly I don't care if he knows. "I'm going outside. Out there. I know I'll probably die. I'm okay with that."

He is silent for a long time, but when he speaks, his voice is surprisingly soft. "Somehow I'm not shocked to hear that."

I look at him over my shoulder without moving my hands. "A normal person, Wren, would ask why."

"Very funny. It's no secret you're unhappy here. When do you plan to go?"

"Before we have to choose jobs."

"Why then?"

"Let's just say that an order was issued from the Preme floor once, and it resulted in me losing someone very important. The thought of serving those people—Katz and the others, producing their clothes, growing their food...it makes me sick."

He nods heavily, like he actually understands. "What about producing clothes for other Means? Growing food for them?"

I shake my head. "Every job down there reinforces a system that I don't support. That I *can't* support. Even fighting pro... It's just a way to keep Means entertained so they don't rise up. It's for Katz, all of it."

He stares intently at me. After a while, he asks, "How're you going to get out?"

I shrug. "I'm working on it. Listen, not that you'll see them again or anything, but don't tell my friends, okay?"

"What do you mean? They don't know?"

I shake my head.

"Wait, let me get this straight. This is something you told me...in confidence?"

I can feel my cheeks burn pink. "I...wasn't thinking."

He laughs lightly. "I guess not. You know, seeing as how we're not friends and all." He pauses, and when he speaks again, his voice is serious. "You're not the only unhappy one here, you know. Leaving—dying—isn't the only option."

"I'm not the only unhappy one... Surely you're not talking about yourself."

"Remember when I said you're hard to talk to?"

"Fine, Preme. You're unhappy, too. Care to tell me why?"

"Hmm. Seems like something I'd talk to a friend about."

I sit down on the floor and stretch out my legs so that my boots touch the glass. I tuck my hair behind my ears. "Maybe we're sort-of friends."

He sits next to me. "Sort-of friends." He nods. "I can live with that. Okay, sort-of friend Eve, what do you want to know about me?"

"Why you're so unhappy."

"Right," he says in his low voice. "Well, I'm not sure I could put that one into words. Could you?"

My eyes are unfocused as they stare through the glass wall of the Oracle. "I'm unhappy because I miss that person I mentioned. I'm unhappy because I feel caged. Trapped. Like I can't breathe, all the time. Like something is wrapping around my neck or sitting on my chest, and no matter how hard I fight it off, no matter how strong I am, it doesn't go away. Not ever."

He stares at the side of my face for a while but then looks away and nods. "Fair enough."

"Your turn."

"Maybe I don't know why I'm unhappy," he says quietly. "Maybe it isn't life in the compound. Maybe it's just…me. Maybe I just…don't like myself."

"That makes no sense," I say quickly, glancing at him. "Why wouldn't you like yourself?"

He shrugs. "So, tell me about this person that you lost."

"Way to change the subject, Wren."

Our eyes find each other, and he smiles. It is the kind of smile that makes me feel like we are the only two people in the entire world. I look quickly away.

Then he leans back so he is lying down, and his large hands tuck under his head. His T-shirt rides up so that an inch of skin is exposed, and it is smooth and golden. It is distracting, that inch of skin, and I feel something inside of me stir.

"You said it was someone important to you," he continues.

I have no obligation to respond. I shouldn't. I shouldn't share something so intimate—not with this virtual stranger. I turn back to the window, but before I know it, I hear a voice, and it's my own. "I had a little brother. Jack. Nobody knew, not at first—my mother hid the pregnancy. But then *they* found out." I pause. "The Premes in charge." Ied Bergess, to be exact. Head of Health and Population Control. And, of course, Commander Katz.

"Don't say what I think you're going to say." His voice is low and husky, and it feels so familiar and warm that I lean back so I am lying beside him. I stare through the top of the Oracle to the gray sky outside. I don't want to remember it, that moment when Jack was taken. But it is impossible to forget...

It had been a good day. School, then a short playtime with Hunter and Maggie. Dinner was near, and I sat on my bed with a well-worn and well-loved doll snuggled in my lap. She had red yarn for hair, and I called her Marlow, my sole toy allotment from the compound. My mother lay next to me, long hair sprawled around her head like a halo, Jack in her arms. "Make me go high," he pleaded. "Evie, are you watching? Mommy—do it quick, make me go high! Please, Mommy!"

She kissed him on the lips, then lifted him into the air so that he giggled; she did it again and again until he laughed so deeply it was almost a wonder he could force air into his lungs. My father was away, working his fingers raw at the plastics factory, manufacturing wall panels for the Preme floor, and so it was just the three of us.

"Evie, did you see? Again, again!" Jack shouted. "Mommy, again! Please!"

My mother looked at me out of the corner of her sky-blue eyes, and both of us grinned. These were my favorite moments. These were happy and secure moments, ones that didn't come often in Compound Eleven.

And so it was then, as if on cue, that our cell door burst open and heavy footsteps drowned out the sound of joy. Men, cloaked in black. Three of them. Vaguely I recognized them as guards, but my confusion didn't snap to panic until a scream erupted from the back of my mother's throat. From the bottom of her stomach.

Instantly I stood. Marlow fell to the floor, forgotten. What caused my mother's anguish I did not know—not then. But it was pure terror, thick and unsettling, and it was upsetting Jack. She would never upset Jack, and so I knew in my bones it must be bad. Very bad.

Still I pled with her—I begged her to settle, all I could think to do. But it was futile. She was already too far gone.

Terrified, I turned to the guards. I saw the nearest one look over his shoulder at the one behind, one who was bald and square-faced, and they exchanged a nod. Curt and clinical. All business.

My mother must have seen it; she must have understood what I did not, because immediately she slid to the back of the bed, as far away as she could make herself in that small concrete box that was our home. One hand held the back of Jack's head, pushed it so hard against her chest I almost cried out. She was going to hurt him, she clutched him so tight. He may have been three years old, but he was fine-boned like her. With her other arm, she held his body, one that now wailed, laughter displaced by fear of his own.

The first guard surged forward. He knelt on the bed, and it squealed under his considerable weight. Then as I watched with a sinking feeling in my stomach, his hands wrapped around my little brother, and they pulled with shocking force. With determination.

But my mother was strong, and she didn't let go; she didn't give an inch, and he slapped her across the face, and the sight made my own wet with tears. Now the chorus of screams was bolstered by my own.

Now I understood.

The guards were going to take away Jack. He wasn't supposed to be here, after all—that was why I was forbidden from mentioning him. That was why I had to pretend he didn't exist. To steal food for him from the cafeteria.

I tried to help. I did. But I was small and weak—something I instantly resented with all the might a seven-year-old could muster, and the bald guard sent me across the room with one hand. Then he helped the other, he restrained my mother, and Jack was finally wrenched from her warmth.

We screamed louder now, our three, a frenzy of white-hot hysteria, but it was no use. The guard holding Jack headed for the door. But still the fight had not left my mother, and she pulled herself free of the guard who restrained her; she leaped from the bed and made to chase after her boy—

For a brief second, a balloon of hope swelled inside my stomach. For a brief second, I actually believed that all would be okay, that those secure moments would be ours once again.

But the third guard turned. He pulled out his gun. Probably it wouldn't have stopped her, except he was smart, and so it was me he directed it toward. Instantly my screams were silenced; immediately my mother was still.

She was still, except that her shoulders rounded in defeat; they curled forward and shook as her tears flooded our small cell.

Off in the distance, Jack screamed our names. "Mommy! EVIE! MOMMM-EEE!" The sound pulsated in my ears like a million hammering needles. But the silence that followed was much, much worse. Vomit ran up my esophagus; it slipped quietly to the floor and over Marlow like a blanket.

When I finally wiped my mouth, I noticed that the guards had left; it was just the two of us. In body, at least. Already I could sense that where it really mattered, I was all alone.

"Eve?"

I startle as I return to the present, as I refocus on the gray sky outside. On Wren next to me. "They took him," I say. "For being in contravention of the one-child policy. Put him out there, to die. A little boy."

The sound of the ticking rain fills my ears, and for a second I think it is going to swallow me whole. I see Wren shake his head, I see his chest rise and fall beside me, but he says nothing. There is nothing to say, nothing that *can* be said to ease the pain.

"I guess that's another reason I need out. It isn't fair, life down there. And besides, there isn't anything to stay for. Not for a Lower Mean. Shitty jobs, violence…that's it. Trust me, I'm not the first one from my floor to try to escape, and I won't be the last. I'm probably the first one set on going out there, though," I add, motioning toward the sky. Once again I think about that song—about the possibility, however remote, that Jack found a way to survive, and that I will, too. The swell of grief I felt from reliving that terrible moment nine years ago is replaced with a surge of hope.

"What about your friends and family?" Wren asks.

I shake my head. "It isn't enough. Nothing will ever be enough. I want freedom more than anything in the world. I want to breathe fresh air and feel it on my skin. Even if it's short-lived, it'll be worth it." *Even if the possibility of finding Jack is so far-flung it defies all logic, it'd be worth it.*

"But your parents…" His voice trails off until it is swallowed by the sound of rain.

"What about them? That it would be cruel to make them

go through it all over again?"

"Well…yeah."

"I need to live my life," is all I say, and my voice is firmer than it needs to be. I don't bother to tell him that my mother is already gone. She already left. I don't tell him that my dad would rather have Jack than me.

"Live your life by effectively ending it?"

"Who knows what will happen out there. I've heard things… Just forget it, okay?" I snap, suddenly annoyed. "You're probably right. But I'm not asking you to understand."

"Okay," he says slowly, and his voice is calm. So calm that my muscles unclench. "Well regardless, I'm sorry you had to go through that—your parents, too. I know what it's like to lose someone."

"You do?"

"I lost my father when I was ten years old."

So his life hasn't been a cakewalk, either. He has known despair; he has experienced loss. Even being a Preme.

All I can think to say is, "I'm sorry."

"Thanks."

"Were you two close?"

"Closer than my mother and I have ever been. Or will ever be," he adds bitterly. "Certainly she wouldn't shed a tear if I were to venture out there." He laughs a short, hard laugh.

I listen to the raindrops for a moment, then raise my head, gaze through the glass to the solar panels that sit on the hilltop. I want to ask him more about his relationship with his mother, but I can sense that he doesn't want to discuss it. So instead I say, "She's in charge of those?"

"Her office is, yes."

"Has she ever been outside before?"

"Not sure. I try to avoid speaking with her at every opportunity."

His voice is hard, revealing his distaste for his mother even more than his words do. That's a good thing, I think. Because without a doubt the woman holds allegiance to her colleague and superior, Commander Katz, and so if Wren were to hold allegiance to her, well…

"What's the building for, out there?"

Wren lifts his head and follows my gaze to the small outbuilding sitting at the base of the hill.

"Control boards for the solar panels," he says quickly before dropping to the floor again. "The engineers do most of their work from there. Making adjustments to the angles, troubleshooting problems. I think they store tools in there, too, for when the panels need fixing."

"So they can walk there safely. And up the hill, even."

"Seems that way."

I nod, then lower my head, relieved to learn that, at the very least, the sun doesn't kill instantaneously. Thunder rumbles, and a gust of wind makes the raindrops beat harder; it makes the glass walls creak around us. The mounds of rock to the north remain impervious.

Since he says nothing more, I use the lull to think over our conversation. I can't imagine why he doesn't like himself, and I can't imagine why his mother doesn't, either. His only remaining parent. I feel something hard against my chest whenever I think about this particular point. Maybe I never realized a Preme could experience misery. But he can, and a Preme he is.

"Wren." My voice is firm. "How come we're hanging out right now. How come you were in the cafeteria yesterday. How come you fed the Denominators. The shooting range. The nurse's station."

"Why do you think?"

I turn my head so that I am looking at him. He doesn't

look at me, though, and so my eyes wander freely over the muscles bulging under his skin, at the broad chest that rises and falls under his T-shirt. "I don't know," I finally say. "Guilt?"

His eyebrows crinkle. "Guilt? For what? Beating you up?"

I nod.

"The nurse's station, maybe. But since then, no. Not guilt. I don't feel guilty for that, not now. It was just another fight for you—I get it."

"So then why?"

Now he does turn his head, and his eyes latch onto mine. "I like hanging out with you." He says it so simply, like when he identified the raindrops outside.

But it is anything but simple. He likes hanging out with me. Does he mean as friends? Surely he doesn't mean as something more. No, surely not. *Obviously* not.

My gaze has cast away, but he is still watching me. I look at him and open my mouth. "Your eyes look like the sun."

He laughs, lighter than before. Genuine. "That's a strange thing to say. Everything about you is strange. My eyes look like the sun," he repeats as he stares at the sky. "You know, if anyone bears a resemblance to the sun, it's you."

"Me?"

"A dangerous, intense, burning ball of fire? Yeah, that sounds like you."

It's my turn to laugh, and I do.

"Or maybe you're more like a thunderstorm. Frightening and beautiful at the same time."

The laugh dies in my throat. He just called me beautiful, and now my heart beats so fast it feels like it has legs and they are pumping as hard as they can, an all-out sprint to the finish. But there is no finish line, and I don't know why it is running in the first place.

"Eve, do you know what a normal person would say when

somcone says they like hanging out with you?"

I shake my head. I don't trust my voice right now.

"They'd say they like hanging out with that person, too."
He props himself up on his elbow and looks at me. He seems
closer now than he did before, and it does nothing to slow
my heart.

Get a grip, Eve.

But then my eyes meet his, and I see the sun and feel like
I am breathing in fresh air. I can feel his warmth against my
skin, and I am reminded that getting a grip is not really an
option right now.

He wants me to say something, but I can't. So I nod, and
I know it is meaningless and childish, but all I can do is stare
into his eyes and keep nodding.

His free hand reaches over, and his fingers glide over my
hair. "I take it that's a yes, you do like hanging out?"

Somehow I find my voice. "Yes." Because it's true. Never
once have I wanted it to be true, but all along it has been.

Still he doesn't move his hand away. I hope he can't hear
my heart thudding. His thumb grazes my temple, and my skin
feels electrified where he touches it, and as his hand moves I
can smell his smell. It is the same as that day we fed the Noms,
when he hid me from the guard. Clean and masculine and safe.

"Come closer," my mouth says. I hear the words like they
are spoken from someone else, like they come from a great
distance. Surely it wasn't me who said them.

His hand freezes. "I can do that," he says slowly, and then
he slides himself over so that his long body is pressed against
the side of mine.

It isn't just where his fingers touch me that feels electrified.
It's all over. Somewhere, my brain screams that he is a Preme,
an impossibly strong one—one who is capable of hurting me.
But he won't hurt me; I know that.

He looks like he is studying me.

"What?" I ask.

"I want to kiss you," he says. "But…"

"But?"

One corner of his mouth pulls up. "But you're unpredictable. And I know how hard you can punch."

I grin, and my hands reach up; they coil around his head, and his hair feels smooth in my fingers. I pull him to me so that the pillow of air separating us disappears, and suddenly his lips are on mine, and they are impossibly soft, impossibly warm. How can they be so soft and warm when he is anything but?

His hand grips my head as he kisses me, his smell is inside of me, and I kiss him back. I have never kissed anyone before and so I don't know how fast or slow to go, but he seems to linger on my lips with every motion and so I match his tempo even though my heart beats against my chest so fast I think I might die.

And suddenly I realize, it's worth the risk.

When he pulls away, my eyes flutter open, and I realize for the first time they were closed. "Wow," I mutter before I can stop myself. "You're a really good kisser."

My head starts shaking as soon as the words are out of my mouth. I cover my face. "I don't know why I just said that. Remember I don't have anything to compare it to, so maybe you aren't that good after all."

"If it makes you feel any better," he says in his low voice, "you're a really good kisser, too." When I uncover my face, I see that he is grinning, and my shoulders relax. He lies down beside me and twists his fingers between mine. The raindrops are lighter now, and they sound like music. Sun bursts from behind the last of the thunderclouds that roll by, and he squeezes my hand, and I squeeze his, too.

CHAPTER EIGHTEEN

"**A**re we going to talk about it, or are you just going to look at your books like a super big weirdo?"

I glance up from a glossy photo of a city street bunched tight with bodies. "Check this out," I say, and I turn the book so Maggie can see. "Protests, outside, from before the world moved down here. I wonder if people were killed in them like now."

"You realize you're completely obsessed, right?" Emerald interrupts as she pushes back from the table. "Like, seriously. I love you like a sister, Eve, but I've got to call it. This place is just as boring now as when Mr. Frasier dragged us here in sixth grade."

I kick her leg under the table. "It isn't *boring*; you could learn a thing or two up here. Besides, you guys said we could do whatever I wanted this afternoon, remember? No job tours scheduled, no fights scheduled, nothing. And I picked this. Welcome to the library." I stick my tongue out at her.

"Excuse me," Maggie says sternly, "but I asked you a question." She crosses her arms, but there is a smile hidden beneath her frown. "And for the record, it was a trick question. Of course we're going to talk about it. What the *hell* is going on with you and the Preme?"

"Yeah, Eve, come on. I thought that dude was the devil after your fight. You said yourself he was horrible. But you guys looked like old pals in the cafeteria. Not to mention him getting up in Daniel's face on your behalf. What was *that* all about?"

I have managed to evade any and all questions from my friends on the subject, until now. They do not know about Wren and me kissing in the Oracle, and it's not something I plan to share with them. I don't want to keep any more secrets from them—I really don't. But as often as I go over what happened with him in my mind, I can't make sense of it.

And I can't tell them anything until I figure it out myself.

"We aren't old pals. We just… I don't know. We've hung out a bit. Hardly at all. But a bit. I guess we're sort of becoming friends."

They both stare at me like I have grown a second head.

"Okay, wait. Wait, wait, wait. A thousand different questions are shooting through my brain right now, and I don't know which one to start with. Define 'a bit.'"

"Yeah, and go piecemeal," Emerald adds. "Don't gloss over everything like you always do."

"Okay," I say slowly. "Well, first he taught me how to fire a gun at the Preme shooting range."

"What? You can shoot a gun?" Emerald cries.

"Wow," says Maggie, and she leans onto her elbows. "Was it romantic? Did he wrap his arms around you when he showed you how to fire?"

I stare at her, then laugh loudly. "Of *course* it wasn't romantic," I whisper after the librarian gives me a warning look. "And yeah," I add to Emerald, "I can shoot a gun."

Maggie's eyes narrow. "Then what happened?"

"He helped me work the Noms' food line. And that's it. That's the extent of us hanging out." I shrug again. "As I said—a bit."

She tucks a foot under herself. "He went to the feeding dock with you?"

"Yeah."

"But, why?"

I shake my head. "I have no idea. He wanted to see it."

"This is all very strange, girl."

"Not really," Maggie says quickly. Her large green eyes shift to mine, and she grins.

"What," I say.

"Isn't it obvious? He's into you. Why else would he do all that? Why else would he come to the Mean cafeteria and then force Daniel off you before you could even blink?"

I don't want to lie, but I also don't know the truth. "I'm really not sure, but I don't think it's because he's into me," I say finally. My voice is firm, even though on the inside I am less certain. Because surely that kiss meant something… "I think at first he felt guilty for beating me so badly in the Bowl. And now we're kind of friends, just like I said. It's no big deal. Look, Hunter and I are friends, and you don't think there's anything strange about that."

"That's a little different—you guys have been friends forever. And he hails from Floor Two."

"Speaking of," interrupts Emerald, "why's he so cranky right now? Erick and I had a math question for him about punching angles, and he completely blew us off. Normally he'd give out his allotments to have an audience for a physics lesson."

I sigh, then turn the page of the book sitting in front of me. A large hill looks like its top blew off, gushing red into a black sky. *Volcano erupting*, says the caption. I have never seen the word before, and I roll it around my tongue before answering. "I don't know. Because he was mad at me for shooting my mouth off, so I told him to go easy on me, since I was still getting over the fight with Wren."

"Meanwhile you were becoming friends with him."

I nod. "It was a small lie, but you can see his point."

Maggie frowns. "Well, I don't think he's super thrilled about how things ended with Anita, so that isn't helping. Give him a couple of days. He'll get over it."

"Nice volcano picture," says a voice over my head.

I snap the book shut, and my spine straightens. My heart hammers in my chest like it is several times too big and will soon break free of its rib-made cage.

"Did I scare you?" Wren asks.

"Of course not."

"Silly question, huh, Eve? Mind if we join you?"

I notice for the first time that two guys who look to be Wren's age stand behind him. "Yes, I mean, no. I don't mind." Maggie and Emerald are watching me closely, and I feel like the word *liar* is tattooed across my forehead. I feel like our kiss in the Oracle is playing out for all to see a foot above me. I clear my throat and try to act nonchalant. "I didn't hear you come in."

"Yeah," he says, and he glances at me as he sits. "I know."

"I mean…what I mean is…"

He presses his mouth together and squints with his fist posed under his chin. I laugh before I can stop myself.

"I saw you from the hall, so I thought I'd say hello. These are my friends, Connor and Long. This is Eve. And these are her friends, Maggie and Emerald." I nod at Connor, who looks nothing like Wren. He isn't very tall, and not half as muscular. He adjusts his glasses the way Hunter sometimes does before saying hello. His eyes dart to Maggie, then to his feet.

Long, meanwhile, is striking-looking, with jet-black hair that hangs over forest green eyes. They shine. "I don't know about you, Eve. I mean, I saw the fight, and I kind of thought you'd fare a bit better than you did against this loser." He pinches Wren under the arm, and Wren punches him.

"Shut up, Long."

"You and I could fight," I suggest, "because considering the size of your arms, I could take you in under a minute. Ever heard of push-ups?"

"Damn!" He laughs, earning himself a disapproving glance from the librarian. "You didn't tell me she had so much attitude," he says to Wren as he sits next to him. "You know, when you've been going on and on and on and on about her."

He winks at me, and then Wren elbows him and says something under his breath that makes Long laugh harder. I can't help but smile, too; apparently Wren has been talking about me. Except that Maggie is staring at me with a look on her face that looks remarkably like triumph.

I force mine to straighten.

"How's the job search going?" Connor asks Maggie as he sits next to her on the other side of the table. He is careful to leave a body space between them, but I don't think he does it out of disgust for her station. In fact, it seems like it has more to do with respect than anything else.

"Terrible," she laments. "I've been on a thousand job tours, and I can't make up my mind. Don't tell me you're one of those people who knows exactly what they want to do."

He smiles. "Sorry. I'm a computer guy, always have been."

She groans.

As our friends chat, seemingly impervious to the differences that separate us, Wren leans toward me. He lowers his voice so the others can't hear. "Any plans tonight?"

I shove my palm over my mouth to stop it from smiling. "What are you thinking?"

"Have you been to the Oracle at night?"

"At *night*?"

"Yeah."

I shake my head. The compound isn't well lit at night. The Oracle wouldn't be, either.

"Neither have I. But apparently the sky is full of these things called stars. Ever heard of them?"

"I've seen them in pictures," I whisper.

"So. Are you interested?"

I am still. The thought of seeing what the world aboveground looks like at night fills me with excitement. Seeing it with Wren, even more so. "It'll be dark, though, right?" The words slip between my teeth before I can stop them.

His hazel eyes narrow. Eyes that match his hair. "Yes," he says slowly. "Is that a problem?"

I shake my head again.

"Come on. Don't tell me…"

"What?"

A grin breaks across his face. Then he laughs. He makes sure the others aren't paying us any attention before he speaks the dreaded words: "You're afraid of the dark."

"No, I'm not," I say quickly. Too quickly. My spine is blade straight, and I try to relax it, but it's welded in place.

Now there's no choice but to go—my ridiculous pride. "So, tonight, then. Yeah, I'm in. What time?"

"Ten. Meet in front of here."

I blink slowly, deliberately.

"We don't have to," he says eventually. He is staring at me, and I know I am being rude. I should be excited. He is asking me on a date, and it sounds perfect. The Oracle at night. With him. Of *course* I want to go.

My eyes dart to Maggie and Emerald; they are deep in conversation with Connor and Long. I look at Wren and see his face is stern. I sigh. "Okay, listen. You might not be completely wrong."

He leans forward a couple of inches. "The dark?"

I shrug. It is so weak, so weak, so weak. When I look at him again, I see he is laughing. "Sorry, Eve. Really, I don't mean to laugh. But of all things…and you…come on, it's funny."

"It isn't funny, it's…" I lower my voice. "It's humiliating."

"I kind of like it." He shrugs. "Now I know you're at least partly human."

"Hey, that's not fair."

He grabs my hand under the table, and the warmth of his skin on mine spreads inside of me. It is weird, this feeling he gives me. It isn't something I can quite understand.

But I do understand that I don't want the others to see, and so I glance quickly around the table as I blush.

"Hiding something, Eve?" His face is stern again.

"Actually," I say evenly, "yes, I am." I look pointedly at him, and his eyes narrow. Then he squeezes my hand and lets it go. Except I hold on tightly and our hands stay entwined, hidden from the others' view but together nonetheless.

The corners of his mouth twitch. "So tonight. I can meet you down on your floor, if you'd like."

"I don't need an escort, thanks."

"How did I know that'd be your response?"

Long catches Wren across the shoulder. "We're going to be late, man."

Wren looks at me, then slips his hand free. "I've got to run. I'll be seeing you."

Before I can respond, he has moved away from the table,

and the seat feels exceptionally empty beside me, and my hand feels exceptionally cold. I swallow. I didn't want to like Wren, not even as a friend. But now we've kissed and we've held hands…and we're meeting again tonight. Just the two of us. A date.

A *date*.

I don't know how I feel about the whole thing, but I can't deny the excitement coursing through me. I just can't.

"It was really nice meeting you," Maggie is saying from across the table.

Connor adjusts his glasses again. "Really nice meeting you, too. Good luck with the job search."

"Thanks! Good luck with the computer gig."

Their eyes linger on each other for a moment longer than they should, and then he is gone and Maggie is a light shade of peach.

I fix her with a stare. "What was that all about?"

"What was what about?"

"Come on, Maggie. You guys were flirting!"

"We were not," she says quickly, and her cheeks turn from peach to a bright shade of fuchsia. "I have a boyfriend, hello!"

"Yeah, well, Connor seemed a lot nicer than Kyle, and that's saying something, seeing as how Connor's a Preme."

Shit.

What is wrong with me? The words hang between us like sour air.

Finally she speaks. "What's that supposed to mean? Do you have a problem with Kyle or something?"

I am already in hot water with Hunter. I can't be in hot water with Maggie, too. "Look, I didn't mean to say that; I'm sorry. I don't even know Kyle. Okay?"

Her jaw relaxes. And then her face breaks into a smile. "Why are you even mentioning the fact that Connor's a

Preme? The fact that Wren is one doesn't exactly seem to be an issue for you."

"An issue for what? I told you—we're friends. We weren't flirting like you guys were."

She exchanges a look with Emerald. "Don't think we didn't see you guys whispering away like schoolkids. That's flirting where I come from. And did you notice that Long said how much Wren talks about you? Yeah. We noticed, too. Don't think you're fooling anyone, okay?"

I am spared from answering by the sight of Hunter pushing through the library door. He returns a stack of books a foot high to the librarian, then, spotting us, takes a seat next to Maggie. He pulls one of the books from the middle of the table under his nose. They are books I've selected—all of them full of pictures of life aboveground, all those decades ago. Before it became uninhabitable.

I hold my breath as I stare at him.

"Thought I might find you guys here," he says quietly. "What's going on?"

"Eve thinks Maggie's crushing on one of Wren's friends, and Maggie thinks Wren and Eve are crushing on each other. They're fighting about it now, if you care to listen in."

"Emerald!" I cry. "We aren't fighting about—about *that*. Right, Maggie?" I don't wait for a response; I set my gaze on Hunter instead. "Listen, Wren and I ran into each other a couple of times since the fight. I guess maybe we're friends. Sorry I didn't tell you."

"It's no big deal," he says, his gaze still anywhere but on mine. "That being said, it is kind of strange you'd even talk to him, following that match. He almost killed you. And beyond that, well. We all know your history with Premes…"

He is referencing Jack, and something inside of me grows hot. I push it down again. "It was just a fight, Hunter," I say quietly. "And yeah, you're right—there is a history there…but Wren had nothing to do with that. He was just a kid when it happened."

"True. But between that and Reneeta, didn't it teach you something?"

Reneeta. It has been a while since I have thought about her. Flowing hair, long skirts, an everlasting smile. She volunteered on the Mean floors, one of the very few Preeminates to make the journey. But she loved children, and so she would lend a hand with childcare from time to time when parents were ill or otherwise detained. Sometimes she would bring us snacks, or even a small toy like a rubber ball. She cared about us.

Until she glimpsed Jack through the door one afternoon when I forgot to pull it tight. And even though I can't prove it, I'm sure it was her who tipped off the Premes in charge about his existence. She hasn't been down to the Mean floors since, which is smart. I'm not sure she'd survive an encounter with my father. Or with me.

"Teach me something," I say carefully. "What?"

Hunter adjusts his glasses and stares at me. "That you can never…*never* trust a Preme."

CHAPTER NINETEEN

I walk through the lower hallways of Compound Eleven with a switchblade clasped in one hand and a flashlight in the other.

Dull beads of orange run along the spot where the floor meets the wall, and so it is possible to move through these corridors without the aid of a flashlight, but that isn't an option for me. In fact, the thought of my flashlight running out of power makes my blood go cold. I really should carry spare batteries, except Lower Means aren't allotted spares of anything. Essentials only.

All around me, shadows run up the walls and leer at me as I sprint past, Hunter's words echoing in my brain with every step. *He almost killed you... You can never...*never *trust a Preme...*

I force them to the side and concentrate on my footing as I climb to the top floor.

It is no better lit than the rest of the compound, and this surprises me. Usually it is flooded with bright light, and so by contrast it looks darker here than anywhere else.

"Trying to flag Ben down?" comes a voice from behind me. I turn quickly with my knife ready, though I know it is Wren. "Wow, you're not messing around," he adds calmly as his eyes sweep over the open blade. "Might want to put that flashlight away."

I swallow. Of course he is right. Being out of bed at this time of night isn't prohibited, only frowned upon. But sneaking onto the Preme floor and into the Oracle *is* prohibited, and attracting the guards' attention needlessly isn't exactly intelligent.

So I turn it off, and we are cloaked in blackness. I can't see Wren's face—the beads along the floor are too dim, and my eyes are used to the unfriendly glare of the flashlight. I feel blinded in a world where everyone else can see. I feel vulnerable, exposed.

"The knife, too," he says quietly.

I am still. All of a sudden, Hunter's warning flashes in my mind's eye. *He almost killed you.* I take a step back and bump into something that sends my pulse racing. It's only the wall, but now the darkness claws its way into my mouth and down my throat until I can no longer breathe. I can feel hands snatching at me just like when I walk through the Bowl before a fight, and they pull me down, drag me lower—

"Eve!" His hands are on my face, and for a moment I think maybe he is covering my mouth and that is why I can't breathe. That he *is* dangerous and mad and murderous. But then I realize they cover only my cheeks and he is speaking and his voice is smooth like butter. "Eve. Hey, come on. It's me. It's me."

I breathe deeply to force oxygen to my brain. My eyes adjust to the darkness so that I can see the outline of his face, and I know he stands close with his eyebrows pulled together.

"Deep breath, Eve. I'm not going to let anything happen

to you. Calm down."

I realize I am still clutching the open knife, and clumsily I snap it shut. "Why can't I have the knife out again?" I ask tersely.

"In case we run into a guard. In case you trip and stab yourself in the eye."

I push the knife into my pocket.

"Take my hand," he says, and I do. He clutches it tight and leads me forward through the blackened halls. My heart thumps uncomfortably in my chest as we go. But I feel better now that he is by my side.

Does it make me weak, to be soothed by his strength? One thing I have always prided myself on—one thing my father drilled into me from a young age—is being self-reliant. I take care of myself and I defend myself and I protect myself, too. And now my hand is tucked into his much larger hand, and he is guiding me forward, and he has promised not to let anything happen to me. To *me*.

It feels wrong, all of it. But it feels good, too. It does. It feels good to let someone else be strong for once.

Fast and heavy footsteps echo behind us, and every cell in my body squeezes into itself. Wren pushes me against the wall, and his hand lies flat against my stomach, forcing me to be still. The footsteps fade into the distance, and I feel the pressure of his hand, its warmth reaching through my thin T-shirt. I can see his eyes through the darkness, just, and they flash onto mine and then away again as he draws me forward once more.

Danger never lurks far in Compound Eleven, even on the Preme floor.

When we reach the door, he is the one to punch in the code. He saw my fingers last time, then, and he put it to memory as I knew he did. He pushes me through, and immediately

I turn my flashlight on and swing the delicious light it casts around the small room. Empty.

"We survived," he says heavily. In the glow of the flashlight, his cheeks look hollow and his eyes flash like warning signs.

"Barely," I mutter.

"Let's get upstairs before anyone sees the light under the door."

I nod and put the flashlight between my teeth as I climb the ladder, swing open the trapdoor. I am not self-conscious today; I am too pent up with adrenaline and fear.

The Oracle is brighter than I expected, considering it has no lightbulbs—no beads, even. I look up and see that it is something coming from above that is offering brightness, and I turn my flashlight off to better see it. White dots that almost shine. Millions of them. And a large circle, also white but smudged with a fingerprint of gray: the moon. This is the night sky. Vast and brilliant and majestic.

Wren closes the trapdoor and stands beside me. He is staring at the side of my face, but I can't look at him. If a mirror stood in front of me, I couldn't look at it, either. "How do you manage during the blackouts?" he asks, and his voice is sharp.

"My knife and flashlight. Any other questions?" My voice is every bit as sharp as his, and I move forward so that I stand directly in front of the glass. So that he is behind me.

"I'm not judging you, but—"

"That's exactly what you're doing," I snap.

He laughs darkly. "If you would let me finish, I was going to say that there's something going on with the solar panels. They aren't collecting energy like they used to. It means the blackouts are going to continue; they may even get worse."

"So I should just get over it, right? My fear of the dark?"

"I'm not saying that," he says in a low voice right next to

my ear. It makes a chill race up and down my spine.

"Look," I say, "as long as I have my flashlight and my knife, I'm fine."

"What about right now? Are they enough light for you?"

I can feel his chin bump against the top of my head, and I know he is looking up at the stars.

In truth, the fear that lurks in the back of my mind rears its head whenever I cast my gaze away from the brilliantly lit night sky. The Oracle itself and the grounds outside are smothered in velvety darkness that makes the hairs on the back of my neck stand upright. But I am not going to tell him any of that.

"Of course," I lie.

"I'll walk you back to your place later," he says, and his voice has lost the edge that was there earlier.

"Not a chance."

"Unfortunately for you, I insist." He moves forward so that he is standing beside me, our arms touching. After a moment, he asks, "How come you haven't told your friends about…this. Us."

"I don't know. I guess I don't really know what this…is." My heart begins to race, but now I don't know if the cause is the darkness or something else entirely. I take a deep breath. "And I don't need an escort back to my cell, thanks. I already told you that."

"Eve, your entire body was shaking."

I turn and start to walk away from him, but his hand lands on my shoulder. "You're human. It's a good thing, trust me, so long as you can handle the blackouts." He sighs. "So, about the other…"

"Hunter thinks I shouldn't even be friends with you. You know, after what happened to my brother."

His body goes rigid, and his eyes flash. "Since I happen

to be a Preme? Do Maggie and Emerald feel the same way?"

I shrug. "They don't care so much. But, you know. You're a Preme; I'm a Lower Mean. The two don't exactly go together."

"Says who?"

There is a gurgle in the back of my throat that sounds close to a laugh. "You know as well as I do that it's true."

"It doesn't bother me." His hand finds the small of my back. "For someone who craves freedom above all else, you seem remarkably willing to fall in line and follow the conventions of this stupid compound."

"I do not," I say quickly, and my eyes race to his. But there is no malice there as he watches me. He seems to study my face under the light of the stars, and I feel my cheeks turn pink. Thankfully they are hidden by blackness. I force myself to stand straighter and raise my chin. "I don't...I don't care. About that. About us being from different floors. It's the rest of the compound that would."

My parents, for one. After what they endured with Jack at the hands of a Preme, they would probably disown me. And the rest of the Lower Means would brand me a traitor—particularly the older generations. The ones who have lived through decades of injustice, who vibrate at the very sight of a Preme, who lead the protests and demand better for our kind from the elite. Yes, if they were to find out, there could be trouble. And then there are the Premes themselves. Their snide comments and sour looks are something I could endure, sure. I might even revel in them. But it would give me no joy to see them leveled at Wren.

Marriage laws, too, are unforgiving. The only way a Preme can marry a Mean is if the Preme forfeits his or her status and relocates to the lower floor. It's the same thing between a Denominator and a Mean. For obvious reasons, then, such unions simply don't happen.

Then there is Hunter. Given his reaction to our friendship, he cannot know about this—whatever this is. Not now and not ever...

See? It's the others in the compound I'm concerned about. *I* don't care that Wren is a Preme. Of course I don't. But maybe I am not speaking the entire truth. Maybe after years and years of knocking the Preme floor and all those who inhabit it, of distrusting them and labeling them as evil, I am worried those closest to me will brand me a hypocrite.

Maybe more than anything, I'm worried that I am a hypocrite.

Then his fingers touch my face and I don't care if I am a hypocrite or not—I am too distracted by the fluttering in my stomach, like a million butterflies are beating their way out. It is a strange saying, that. Civilization hasn't seen a butterfly for decades, but still the expression persists.

"What are you saying, Eve? You don't want...us? This?"

I press my face into his fingers. "No. I'm not saying that. I'm not saying that at all." My voice is low.

"So, you do want it."

I take a deep breath. *Be brave, Eve.* "Of course *I* do," I say hotly.

His fingers wrap around the back of my head, and he moves closer. His lips tickle my forehead as he talks. "But?"

"But...well, I told you. Maybe the rest of the compound doesn't." Now my voice is impossibly quiet yet steady.

"What if we keep it between us, then. Just for now." His is steady, too. "Until people get used to the fact that we're friends."

My fingers shake, but it isn't from the dark. "I'd like that." I'd like that very much.

He nods. "Okay." He pulls his head back a few inches and smiles. "So it's official."

But instead of smiling, I remember that in less than five weeks I will be gone from Compound Eleven, and gone from Wren, too.

"Everything okay?" he asks.

Instead of responding, I fill the little remaining space between us and press my lips to his. I don't want to think of the end—not right now. It is just the beginning; surely it is too soon to be thinking of the end.

I kiss him harder than before. I kiss him until every last negative thought dissolves into darkness. My fingers are steady now, and they push down his chest and under his shirt. The skin of his back is smooth as silk, and as I draw my hands up I feel muscles rippling below. He almost killed me, it's true, but he didn't…and he won't. And feeling his raw strength doesn't make me feel weak, not in the slightest. I am strong. And Wren's strength makes me even stronger.

Every cell in my body begins to scream, but this time it isn't from terror. Instead they are white hot and screaming for more. But he pulls away, and his lips are on my forehead again, and his chest beats up and down with his breaths. "God, Eve," he groans, "What are you trying to do to me?"

"I don't know. I was just enjoying myself, I guess." My fingers dance across his back like they never want to touch another surface again.

"Mmm." Suddenly, he is still. "You realize the moon is currently behind some clouds and it's significantly darker in here…"

"So? Maybe the dark isn't so bad when it's just the two of us."

"Is that a fact?" he asks, and I can hear in his voice that he is smiling. He sits down on the Oracle floor and pulls me with him. I sit on his lap with my arms still strung around his waist. It is impossible to keep my lips away from his, and we kiss again, slower this time.

"Uh, Eve?"

"Yeah?"

"This is a very dangerous position. I'm not sure how much longer I'm going to be able to contain myself, and I take it from the fact that you haven't so much as kissed another guy before, you'd like to take things slow."

"But I'm having so much fun right here," I say, and my voice sounds light. Except that a small pit has formed in my stomach because I know what he is talking about and I know that he is right. And it isn't that I *want* to take things slow; it's that I don't have a choice.

As he has figured out, experienced I am not. In my mind's eye, I see his arms coiled around girls past, and the pit in my stomach grows. No doubt he is experienced, and no doubt my fumbling hands will clue him in eventually as to how uneven our matching really is.

I pull myself off him so that we sit side by side, and together we stare at the night sky, at the stars twinkling overhead as they watch us, at the moon slipping out from behind the clouds.

Don't be foolish, Eve, I tell myself as he strings his fingers through mine. *Whatever you do, don't be foolish.*

CHAPTER TWENTY

Days pass. I train with Blue Circuit, I hang out with friends, but mostly I sneak to the Oracle to stare outside, to visualize the glass shattering into a million minuscule pieces that turn to sand under the heel of my boot. To picture the oasis I will run to, to dream about reuniting with Jack.

Another thing I do is watch the guards who patrol the Lower Mean corridors. I observe their habits, their mannerisms, their movements, my gaze locked always on the guns lodged in their holsters.

If I am going to escape the compound, if I am going to capture freedom, I need to take what is theirs. I need to make it my own.

It won't be easy; nothing ever is in Compound Eleven. Guards tend to be male, and they tend to be large. Not the end of the world—I have fought plenty with the same traits in the Bowl over the years. I know their weak spots as well as I know my own. Still, these ones wear protective gear. They have a baton made of heavy steel at their disposal. They have the very gun I need just inches from their fingertips. No. It won't be easy.

And then, on an otherwise quiet morning, one walks by and my pupils constrict. Melissa. The guard with the bright pink hair. The one who unlocks the feeding dock at lunch, or at least used to. Right now she unlocks for breakfast service, down that underused corridor where the lighting is particularly dim. It makes sweat slip down my back. She is an easy target, almost too easy. More petite than me and without a fighting pedigree.

A perfect mark. So why do I feel so uneasy?

I know the reason, but I don't care for it. Guards don't deserve kindness, none of them. I should be wiser, and I should be crueler. I shouldn't worry about hurting her.

I shouldn't.

Seconds pass, then minutes. I kick the wall and swear. I don't want to hurt Melissa—I just don't. And since inflicting the least amount of damage is not my strong suit, I have some research to do. Wren knows where to find a book on combat; all I have to do is find Wren.

At the top of the stairs I slip into the atrium, the epicenter of the fifth floor, but only after making sure no guards are close by. I tuck my hands that mark me an intruder into my pockets, where they can't be spotted. Most of the Premes don't notice me at all, but a few do. I can feel it in the way they glance at me—they can tell by my manner of dress and maybe by the way I hold myself that I don't belong. Probably they won't bother tracking down a guard, though; it would be too much effort when all I'm doing is standing here.

It is my ego that suffers the most. But then I think of kissing one of their own in the Oracle and have to stifle my smile.

I pass the time in front of the library, I work on a plan for disarming Melissa, I watch faces come and go. And then my spine straightens. Eyes widen.

Wren, with a small child even younger than Avery draped over one shoulder.

He gives me a curious look and kicks my boot. "What are you doing here, Eve?"

"Shouldn't I be the one asking questions?" I gaze at the child, who is fast asleep. Faintly, I notice her smooth cheeks, long eyelashes, and, as I do far too often, I think of Jack.

Wren smirks. "My neighbors were in a jam. And Nell here, believe it or not, happens to like me."

"She happens to like you? That *is* difficult to believe."

His mouth twists into a smile as he watches me. "Mmm…."

"I mean, I just didn't take you for being…you know."

"Good with kids?"

"Bingo."

Deadpan, he says, "I'm full of surprises."

I cross my arms and lean against the wall, amused by this new side to him. "Very interesting, Wren. Maybe a career in computers isn't for you. Have you considered a job in childcare?"

"Funny."

"Maybe I should make a point of waiting around here more often. You know, to see what else I can learn about you."

"By all means—which brings us back to you. Do you have an agenda for today's visit, or did you just miss me?" He grins.

I bite away my smile. "Agenda. I'm after a book."

He is distracted by Nell stirring. She lifts her head and settles it onto his other shoulder. Once her little body relaxes back into sleep, he speaks again, quieter this time. "A book. Let me guess: You want my help finding the library?"

Laughter gurgles in my throat. "I'm after something specific, something on combat. You had a book like that recently. Do you remember what it's called?"

He shakes his head. "I can find it for you, though. Getting ready for a difficult fight?"

"Something like that."

"If memory serves me, you don't need any training on how to throw a punch."

"Not looking for any."

"So what exactly are you looking for?"

I pull myself off the wall and bump his free shoulder with my own. "Just looking."

"What you lack in conversational skills you make up for with intrigue." He bumps me back, and for a moment we just stare at each other, all smiles. Then he uses his free hand to push open the library door, and I follow behind him. Immediately, the sounds of the atrium vanish. It is one of my favorite things about coming here. Like I am entering a whole new world.

Wren leads me past a dozen rows of shelving to the very back wall, where books with broken spines are jammed into every available nook. He scans them silently, and I use the opportunity to watch him.

It is strange, seeing this small child asleep in his strong arms, limbs tipping around him in perfect contentedness. It is completely incongruous with everything I know about him. And yet I am not shocked. Warmth may not exude from him, not at all, but I have glimpsed it in his smile. I have sensed it in his humor. The fact that children like him, that he is helpful to his neighbors…no. That doesn't shock me in the slightest.

A minute later, he hands a frayed and yellowing book to me. *The Art of Non-Weaponized Combat Fighting*, it reads. An illustration of two men throwing punches covers the front. Perfect. I am immediately refocused on the task at hand—disarming Melissa without hurting her. I flip to the table of contents and find the section on stunning an opponent. Nose, neck, throat, solar plexus, kidneys—those are my options. I tap my lip, faintly aware that Wren still stands there. Okay. The kidneys and solar plexus are protected by a heavy artillery vest, leaving me with just the nose, neck, or throat to target. I flip to those pages and begin to read.

Wren begins to laugh, quietly. It is a sound I feel in my stomach. It gives me butterflies, completely distracting me. "I take it my services here are complete, Eve? I really should get Nell back to her parents."

I blush for no reason. "Yeah, of course. I mean, sorry, or—you know. Thanks for the help."

He laughs harder. "My pleasure," he says, supporting Nell with both hands now. We stare at each other a moment more, and then he is gone, and it takes a very long time before I remember why I am here at all.

CHAPTER TWENTY-ONE

My skin prickles with dissatisfaction. This time it isn't over a stolen loaf of bread, or even from hungry eyes. This time even I, with my unwavering knowledge of the atrociousness of the guards, have difficulty discerning who is right and who is wrong.

One of them has decided to join us in the Mean cafeteria. To lean casually against the wall near the door, to enjoy the dampening his presence has on our people as he slings one steel-toed boot over the other. No, he shouldn't be here. He was wrong to have come. But that isn't what causes the prickling sensation running along my arms.

It is because Sully, one of the more outspoken Lower Means, has taken it to heart. I don't know him, not personally, but everyone down here knows his name. Famous for his dissonance, he walks a fine line between life and death, and he takes a singular pride in the fact. His arms, which are covered in sprawling ink from wrist to shoulder, are proof of it. Right now the cafeteria, which usually hammers with chatter and clattering dishes, is quiet. Right now, and just as he likes it, he has an audience.

"You can't let it be, eh?" he shouts at the guard from a few feet away. "Can't let a man eat his goddamn dinner in peace!"

The guard takes his time shifting his gaze. Once it lands on Sully, with his shaved head and missing finger, it meanders on. He whistles, well-skilled at insolence in his own right.

Sully's face sours.

I knock my tongue back and forth against my teeth. Thousands of innocent people sit inside this room. There are children here. Unease prickles louder over my body; it percolates across the entire cafeteria. Hunter places an arm protectively around Maggie. Emerald frowns.

"Come on, Sully, just finish your supper," comes a new voice.

Erick.

He should know better. He should know not to get in the middle of this.

Emerald nudges me. "What's he playing at?" she hisses.

"I'll finish my measly-assed supper when this piece of shit takes his business elsewhere, boy," Sully shouts at our friend.

"There's kids here, man." Erick is on his feet. He has a temper, and right now, it flares. "Don't start something if you don't need to. Go back to your seat and finish your damn supper."

Sully cackles. "You young punks think you've got all the answers. How about you shut the hell up so I can finish my big-boy conversation with our watchman here."

All through the cafeteria, there comes a swell of noise lifting from the floor. Boots, thousands of them, stomping back and forth, back and forth. Usually it is a show of solidarity, this sound. Right now it is a reminder of it.

The guard is unfamiliar with this Mean tradition. His backside immediately lifts from the wall, and his hand hovers over his gun. When banded together, we make him nervous.

Sully can sense his unease, and he uses it to his advantage. Once Erick sits down again, Sully turns to the cafeteria. "Isn't it enough that the ritzy-ass Premes send their watchmen down to our corridors every goddamn day? Watchmen who take what they want, who kill without consequence? Watchmen who make sure we never better ourselves, never have a voice, never get a shot at a little thing called equality?" He pauses to stare around at us, arms spread wide. Slowly, people begin to clap. Someone whistles. He is using his skills leading protests to mobilize the crowd.

"And now this. *This*. Into the last frontier, the one place we can put our feet up and not worry about taking a baton to the teeth." He nods as people cheer, then drops his voice, forcing us to listen carefully to his every word: "The watchman who graces us tonight can't even let us have that. Can't even let us eat our goddamn morsels in peace. Know what I think?" He lifts a hand theatrically to his ear. "Know what time it is?" He is yelling now. "Say it with me, everyone! Time to MAKE. HIM. LEAVE. MAKE. HIM. LEAVE." The chant grows so loud it swallows up Sully's voice. It rings around my head.

People are on their feet. Arms are in the air. Anger is swelling.

"We need to go!" Hunter yells to our four. Others leave the cafeteria in droves—the smart ones. The ones with kids. The Upper Means who have no need for an uprising in the first place. I murmur my agreement but don't move a muscle.

"Aren't you coming?" Maggie asks me as Hunter pulls her up.

"In a minute."

"Eve," Hunter warns.

"I'll stay, too," Emerald says. "I want to make sure Erick gets out of here. You guys get going."

"See you back at our cells in a few minutes," Hunter says. He looks pointedly at me, and I nod.

Left alone, Emerald and I exchange uneasy looks. The guard's hand still hovers over his weapon. His face is rigid. Whatever he was expecting when he decided to take up residence along the wall of our cafeteria, it wasn't this.

Just leave, I scream silently at him. But of course he won't. That would be a sign of weakness, a show of defeat.

Emboldened by the masses now firmly under his control, Sully jumps onto a table and makes a fast movement with his arm. Like he is pulling a knife across his throat. A second later, a wave of Mean resentment launches at the guard. Sully leaps from the table directly at him.

The blast echoes through the cafeteria like a punch, and I scream. But whether Sully is shot I can't tell; the Mean wave hits the guard like a punch of its own, swallowing up Sully or whatever is left of him. It can mean only one thing. More shots are sure to ring out. Mass casualties. A tide of blood. Any second now.

One, two, three…

Nothing.

I see why a second later. It's the way the wave tilts and turns, searching for something—and there is only one thing that could hold such sway with this court.

The gun.

Immediately, I jump over the tables and dart around the group closest to the guard, who uses his baton to beat back his attackers—the rare few not distracted by the missing weapon.

The rest, I see, are not searching productively. They are too busy watching one another. Too worried their neighbor will find it first, too caught up in the moment to remember they are all on the same team. And so from the outside it takes only seconds to lay my gaze upon it.

It hides behind a large brown boot with disintegrating laces. Any moment now, that boot will land on it. It will alert its owner to its presence, and my chance will be gone.

I move quickly, but I am not quick enough. Down comes the boot, and I see the owner freeze.

Before he can examine what rides under his heel, I scream in his ear. I curse him for stepping on my toe; I even shove him. He returns immediately to the mad scramble, no apology proffered.

Deftly, I drop, scoop up the weapon, and push it deep into the waistband of my pants.

A cool sweat slips over my body, leaving me feeling distinctly unwell. What I have just managed was reckless and risky. And it makes me a target—a big one. Now I waste no time at all heading for the exit.

But at the door I bite my lip. It isn't Emerald or Erick I worry over; they can take care of themselves. It is the guard.

He is without a weapon to defend himself. The baton won't be enough, not once the search for the gun is declared futile. He shouldn't have been here. He was tempting fate, the fool. He was taunting us with his power because that is what guards do.

But without his gun, he will die.

Shit.

If I return his missing weapon, he will shoot those surrounding him. I cannot do that. And yet I can't allow him to be killed, either.

Swearing loudly, I run back into the cafeteria and leap onto the table, just like Sully a minute prior. "The guards are coming!" I holler at the top of my lungs.

Some hear—I can see the news move across the cafeteria in small bursts. More importantly, though, Emerald hears; she understands what I am up to. With her much louder voice, she continues the call: "Guards!" Erick echoes it from his end.

The wave falters. For if a pack of guards find them tearing apart one of their own, hundreds of bullets will spray. My job is complete.

I tumble into the Mean corridor and see the elevator doors slide open. A dozen guards file out, masks on and guns ready. They heard the unrest, then—maybe even the gunshot. That or they were tipped off, probably by an Upper Mean. My warning call has proven legitimate.

I should keep walking, but I am rooted in place. It is the way they stare at me. The way their masks swivel in my direction. It makes the metal of the gun tucked against my skin burn like a white-hot iron. It burns so hot I almost cry out...

They let me be. My youthful features don't look like trouble; they hide what I truly am.

My breathing is haggard and hoarse, but I am quick down the stairs and through the main corridor. It is peppered with people, those who left before things went sideways. Soon I will reunite with Hunter and Maggie, and we will wait for Emerald. We will learn what happened to Sully and the guard.

But near to my corridor, I slow. I stop completely. *Fuck the Premes* is painted along the concrete wall, a new addition since the last time I passed. It is nothing out of the ordinary, this message, but still it has me thinking. Under a bulb burned nearly out, I stare at this person's small act of dissidence and think of my own. A guard's gun is in my possession. A *guard's* gun.

They won't let this transpire easily, the Premes. A gun in the hand of a Mean, particularly a Lower Mean, is dangerous indeed. So when the guards can't find it within the cafeteria walls, they will be ordered to search for it—they will frisk our persons, they will sweep our cells. There are no rights to privacy down here; it is a foreign concept. And so storing the gun will be a problem.

A big problem.

I touch the paint—still wet. Paint is hard to come by. There must have been some left over from an official project, stashed in a supply closet. I press my blackened fingertip against my thumb and study the transfer of pigment. Stashed in a supply closet. A supply closet.

No. The supply closets are hardly ever locked; the gun would not be secure. They are small, with few hiding places. They are frequented by the cleaners and by those up to no good.

I tap my finger and thumb together again, faster and faster now…

Suddenly, I am still.

The storeroom.

Essentially sealed under two passcodes, it is the most secure place in the entire compound. A massive room with an infinite number of hiding spots. And only a few visitors.

Now I am running, and I don't stop until I reach the kitchen. I punch in the passcode and slip inside, expecting to meet resistance. Already I have a story—that I dropped something in the storeroom while on a job tour—but it proves unnecessary. With dinner nearly over, the kitchen is quiet, lights are off, and I pull out my flashlight to see. Then come the stomping of thousands of boots overhead, rattling pots and pans and making blankets of dust fall from the ceiling.

The cafeteria runs above. The Means are making a show of solidarity. That is good. They won't turn on one another— they won't finger Sully, if he's even still alive.

Inside the storeroom, I aim the flashlight at the nets. The first three are frequented by the kitchen staff, which means I must go higher. But just as I locate the ladder, I hear something from the other side of the storeroom door.

Voices.

I jump onto the bottom net and crawl to its middle, where I lie facedown on what looks like giant bags of salt.

Staff, most likely, returned to the kitchen.

There's no time to climb higher, and so I begin shifting one bag of salt after another—no easy task, given the close proximity of the net above. Finally, with sweat curling my hair, I wedge the gun nose down between the bottom two bags and restack around it.

There.

Completely out of sight, completely unfindable…at least for now.

The guards can frisk me; they can sweep my cell, turn each of the drawers inside out—they won't find a scrap of evidence of my misdoing. And, more importantly, in four weeks, when it's time for me to bid it all goodbye, when I cannot go another second longer as a citizen of Compound Eleven, all I must do is return here and fetch my key to the stifling, beautiful, deadly world waiting aboveground.

Not deadly, Eve. Not necessarily.

When I slip through the storeroom door, I see two men in aprons standing on the far side of the kitchen, sorting through papers.

"Yeah, and?" the shorter one is saying, staring with interest at the man beside him.

"He's in the nurse's station as we speak. That's the modified chickpea recipe, right there."

"Takes a lot of cumin. Gotta cut that in half or we'll run dry."

"That'll work." The tall man scribbles something on the paper. "I've upped the salt."

"Yep. So, Sully has a new war story, I suppose. He won't mind that. Never shuts up about losin' that finger."

"Took it in the leg, from what I could see. Can't imagine they'll let him off without punishment, though. Not with his background. I'd bet my next liquor allotment he loses his other index."

"At this point he'd be lucky if that's all it was. Take it the guard got hurt, then?"

"What do you think? Gun evaporated and surrounded by a riot of angry Lower Means. Do the math."

My footsteps slow.

"Dead?"

I have to strain to hear his response over the thudding in my ears.

"Just a good lesson, and a well-deserved one at that. When was the last time we had surveillance in the cafeteria? He was looking for trouble, that boy."

A weight lifts off my shoulders, and I exhale.

The short one jumps. "What are you doin' here?" he shouts at me, perturbed.

"Sal let me in. I forgot my flashlight during the kitchen tour." I hold it up to them as I pass. My face is so disinterested, it coaxes the same from them, and a second later I push into the Lower Mean hallway with lightness in my belly.

For a while I walk without a destination. Dazed. But then I grow still. I push my palms to my mouth to hide my smile, fingers bending around tears, barely minding the bodies jockeying for space around me.

I did it. I secured my ticket to freedom, and I didn't even have to lay a finger on Melissa in the process.

Drift to gentle paradise, it's there that we shall talk / Children dearest side by side, tick tock.

I let my hands fall and walk the corridors as I cry openly, happiness unhinged.

Compound Eleven will confine me no longer.

CHAPTER TWENTY-TWO

O nce again, as I sit in the Mean cafeteria, my skin begins to prickle. Once again something unusual happens. Guards. One after the other, masks on, combat ready. They file through the door, they line up shoulder to shoulder, guns in hand and pointed at us.

Immediately, a hush falls. The glutinous mound of mashed potato in my mouth almost makes me gag, but instinctively I know not to draw attention to myself. My body must know it, too, because the potato slides silently down the back of my throat.

And then the last guard files through the door, and instead of carrying a gun, he carries a man.

Sully.

Right now, the leader of Lower Mean dissent is pale, sallow. His leg is bandaged, but the bandage is stained red; bits of debris cling to it as if he was dragged along one of the corridors. Some people call to him; others ask questions of the guards—ones that go unanswered—and then the cafeteria door swings open once more.

This time, the hush that falls feels heavy and oppressive. This time, the fresh round of guards streaming through the door doesn't drag in a gravely injured Lower Mean. This time, it is someone important who walks into our lowly space.

I don't need to glimpse his unblemished hands to see plainly that he hails from the fifth floor, and the others don't, either.

And then from around me, mainly from the oldest members of our Mean society, come knowing whispers. *Katz…!*

I sit straighter, my fingers tighten around the fork that I hold, and I stare at the man rumored to be our ruler. Tall, with a shock of straight black hair. His creased skin is milky white, and his cheekbones protrude; they stretch far wider than the rest of his face. His clothes are well-pressed—no surprise—yet the style is foreign. The fabric is thick and dark, well-tailored. Gold buttons reach from belt to neck—two lines of them, side by side. I don't know what these clothes are meant to signify, but I'd bet a month's allotment they're intended to intimidate.

He shakes hands with the Means sitting closest to him, ones who have no choice but to oblige under the watchful gaze of fifty guards. When he is finished with that, he lifts his arm to the rest of us, something between a wave and a salute. He smiles wide enough to display dazzlingly white teeth, and he acts…he acts like he is well-received. Like he doesn't realize that the reason his head hasn't been ripped from his shoulders is because of those fifty guns.

Much more likely, he doesn't care. He doesn't take our distaste to heart. Whoever he is, he's as apathetic toward our level of adoration as he is toward our plight. Still, that false smile is unnerving. It makes my prickling skin crawl. It makes the fork that I hold start twisting between my fingers.

"Citizens of Eleven," the man begins in a low-pitched voice. "For those of you who've never met me, greetings. My name...is Zachary Katz." Some people gasp at the revelation, some murmur or hiss, some even sound excited. Likely Upper Means. Just as quickly, the sounds are drowned out by the thumping of boots. I sit motionless. Except for my fingers, which twist my fork round and round like they're mechanized.

"I hope I find you well this evening. I hope I find *each* of you in satisfactory spirit," he continues, and there is more edge to his voice than before. "I hope I find each of you enjoying the plate of food placed before you."

There is a slight murmur of assent, and he nods like he is encouraged. "Now, I want you to do something for me. I want each of you to place your fingers alongside your neck"—he demonstrates the motion himself—"and find the ticking of life that doesn't belong. Because your ancestors and mine, they cheated death all those years ago, didn't they? When Mother Earth decided she'd had enough of us, we found a new way to survive. Now, Mother Earth may be easily fooled...but death, not so. Death will come calling whenever I command."

He pulls something small and white from his pocket. He pushes the top of it, and my muscles brace, my fingers clenching the fork tightly. But all that happens is a solitary clicking noise, short and small and easy to miss.

And then, completely on cue, the guard holding Sully drives a fist into his leg, where the bandages are most stained with blood. The scream that erupts from him makes my stomach turn.

When only the sound of Sully's labored breathing can be heard, Katz speaks once again. He smiles broadly. "There is nothing in this world more valuable than peace. Let us cherish it and nurture it." He pulls from his pocket a piece of crumpled paper. As he adjusts it slightly, I see that it is a paper crane, and he places it in the outstretched hand of a little girl. Still smiling, he twitches his thumb, another click sounds across the cafeteria, and Sully is struck with the heel of a baton. When the guards drag him to his feet, his nose or mouth is bleeding—hard to say which—and he looks disoriented. The fork starts twisting all over again.

"I was saddened by what transpired down here yesterday. Saddened, sickened. But I know now, I see it in your faces, that peace will prevail." Katz's arms sweep open. "A show of hands, everyone," he instructs. "Who will let peace prevail so that Eleven can thrive?"

Slowly, hands rise, here and there, just a few. Katz turns side to side, watching and waiting for more. Under his false smile, he looks dissatisfied. His thumb twitches once again.

Click.

Two guards lift Sully's arm straight into the air. For a second, I think that's it, that's all, but then another guard draws a serrated knife, and he uses it to slowly, methodically cut off Sully's remaining index finger. The room inhales and gasps; it almost drowns out the wretched sobbing and small shrieks. Almost.

Now arms rise by the dozens.

Commander Katz has accomplished what he came here for. Fear. Obedience. Submission. Except my hand doesn't lift. It twists the fork in an endless cycle; it twitches with the desire to do what is impossible yet just. *Kill Katz*. Then warmth spreads through the joints, and I see that it is Hunter, that he grips my hand. With his guidance, I drop the fork. Then he squeezes my bones hard enough to make them ache, to remind me where I'm at and what I'm playing. I allow him to lead my hand into the air.

Only then, with each of us conforming to his will, do Katz and his fifty guards sweep from the room. But even in their absence, life doesn't return to its usual rhythm. Katz didn't just break Sully's body—he broke our spirit.

Every damn one of us.

CHAPTER TWENTY-THREE

I saw my father this morning. My mother was there, too—technically, at least. I asked her about that song, wondering where she herself had learned it, but she didn't reply. She just murmured about the time, not lifting her gaze from her embroidery, not even once. It was an image of a simple table lamp casting a yellow glow, and it was more important than her daughter.

Dad cleaned my knuckles and slapped my face, told me he was looking forward to watching me fight. But he was more anxious, he said, to see me fight under a professional title. I lied to him once again and said that I was, too.

In less than a month, my peers must decide on jobs. In less than a month—less than four weeks—I will be free. That was always the plan, and now that I have the gun, I have my plan cemented in stone. No more will I wake from a deep sleep in a cold sweat, thinking that the compound is closing in on me and the beautiful world aboveground is forever beyond my reach. That beautiful world with its field of hollyhock and northern oasis is now firmly within my grasp.

Of course I can't know for certain whether the so-called oasis actually exists. Nobody in the entire compound could know such a thing. But I know from my research in the Preme library that temperatures are more tolerable at night and the farther north you go. I know that, given the specifics rhymed off in the song's lyrics, it has some bearing on reality. I know that, above all else, it gives me hope that I am desperately in need of.

And even though I know how unlikely it is, the possibility that Jack stumbled north when he was pushed out of the Oracle door makes that speck of hope balloon large enough that it could fill all of Eleven.

Sometimes it feels like a shame that I can't just get past what happened to Jack, or that I can't will myself to look forward to a lifetime in Compound Eleven. Look forward to adulthood here, starting a family, holding a job of servitude, whether it be in the kitchen or the Bowl or a factory. Maggie and Emerald and Hunter, they don't dread their futures here like I always have. How they don't, I do not know.

Maybe because their childhood wasn't tainted by tragedy like mine was. Or maybe they are hardwired to be more positive than my brain will allow. Maybe they expect less from life or have taught themselves to extract more joy from its lighter moments.

Maybe they are the ones who are practiced at the art of survival.

But there are others who are unhappy. The protests that rise up every few weeks is one indication, although Katz's visit to the Mean cafeteria may have put an end to that, at least for now. And even Wren isn't content, and his life is far more comfortable than mine. But I remember his words in the Oracle: It is himself he doesn't like. *He* is the source of his unhappiness. Perhaps, then, perhaps if he could see himself in a different light, he could be happy with Compound Eleven life.

It is this last thought that makes me loneliest. It is this thought that beats loudest through my head as I warm up on Blue Circuit's lone treadmill before my scheduled fight. The joy I felt two days ago when I secured a gun still flickers in my stomach, but it is subdued, swallowed up by a crush of emotion I can't begin to understand.

Bruno works at a desk in the corner—he is responsible for our team's administrative needs, and his presence offers the small comfort of companionship, even though he concentrates on a pad of paper in his hands and not on me.

The next time my eyes land on the desk, it is empty, and his voice calls my name from over my shoulder. "Eve!" he shouts again, and I turn my head to look at him. "Your friend's here. She wants to talk to you."

I climb off and wipe the ring of sweat forming around my hairline as I go. "Is it Emerald?" I ask as I near the door.

He shakes his head as he walks past, his eyes not bothering to meet mine. He is still cool toward me, even after my apology, and I resist the urge to scream.

Maggie stands outside the door with Kyle by her side, and my surprise at seeing her is displaced by my dislike for him. Him with his red hair and arrogant eyes. Him with his blue button-up that marks him an Upper Mean just as much as the four printed on his hands. "That's why you shouldn't wear your hair like that, Maggie," he says as soon as I step into the hallway. "You look like you're getting ready for a fight."

"What's wrong with wearing a ponytail?" I snap, and my voice is immediately hot.

"I just said what's wrong with it. It's fine for the gym"—he nods behind me—"but not for day-to-day wear." He turns to Maggie. "If you want to go dumpster diving with a Floor

Two boy, be my guest. I'm sure a ponytail would suit *him* just fine. But if you want to date a higher-born like me, keep it sophisticated."

"I like it up," I say through gritted teeth.

"Okay, guys," Maggie says, and she raises her palms into the air. "You can stop arguing about *my* hair now, thank you." But she lifts her arm and pulls her ponytail free. "It's just the two of us at the fight today, Eve. Emerald and Hunter—"

"You're siding with *him*?" My voice is growing louder, though I mean for it to stay steady.

She looks affronted. "I'm not siding with anyone. It was starting to pinch, okay? And besides, what concern is it to you how I wear my hair?"

"I told you about her," Kyle says quickly.

"Told her *what*?" I snarl.

Maggie shakes her head. "Here, Eve." She shoves my blue armband into my hands. "You forgot this at your parents' place. I saw your dad on our way here, and he gave it to me to give to you."

I take it from her and wrap it around my arm as I stare at Kyle. He thinks he can control her; I know he does. I have heard the sly insults and seen the dark glances. And most importantly, I have seen the bruises. He thinks he is strong, treating her like that.

I am going to teach him a lesson in strength.

"Can I help you with something, Eve?"

"Just wondering if you've ever been in a fight before," I say evenly.

He laughs. "We don't tend to do that where I come from. No offense." But he means offense, and it makes my blood boil.

"Tell that to your friend Zaar. Oh, wait—judging by how quickly I beat him, I guess you're right."

"They aren't friends," Maggie says quickly. "Right, Kyle?

Daniel and Landry and Zaar, they're poison, right?"

He looks sideways at her. "I've told you before, they aren't that bad. You ought to give them a chance."

She is quiet. Her gaze moves to the floor.

"Don't tell her what to do."

"That's hardly what I'm doing. And if by asking me whether I've been in a fight before, you're somehow trying to physically intimidate me, do remember that I am much bigger than *Zaar*." He pauses and fixes me with a stare. "And you."

"And Maggie, too, right?"

"What's that supposed to mean?"

"Yeah, Eve. Where exactly are you going with this?"

I look at her and see something startling in her eyes. Some mix of fear and hurt, and it makes me lose my nerve.

"I'm not going anywhere with this," I say. "Thanks for the armband, and hey, enjoy the match." My eyes are locked on Kyle's as I swing the door shut in his face. Perhaps Maggie will be mad at me for being rude to him. Or perhaps I bit my tongue more than I should have.

"Everything okay?" Bruno calls to me from the desk. My face must betray my anger.

I nod. "Just my best friend and her dick boyfriend."

He crosses his arms from his chair. "That sounds like a good way to lose a best friend."

"Bruno, he treats her like garbage. So lay off, okay?" I swing at a punching bag, and my knuckles smack loudly against the hide.

"All I'm saying is that it isn't up to you to make her decisions. You think he's an asshole; she sees it another way—trust me, I've been there before. Hearing it from you will only drive a wedge between you guys."

When I speak, it isn't with my normal voice. This one is twisted with emotion. "Who put you in charge of me?" I sputter. "Because I can't seem to do anything right in your eyes. I fight Zaar exactly like Anil and Erick suggested, and suddenly you think I don't know the difference between right and wrong. Well I'll tell you what's right and what's wrong, Bruno. What's wrong is when Zaar and his asshole friends make my life miserable every goddamn day because I was born two floors below them. Because they *can*. What's wrong is the fact that that dick boyfriend out there can knock my best friend around without any consequences. That's wrong in my books, and I don't need you or anyone else questioning my sense of decency." I breathe deeply in order to keep myself steady. I will not cry right now. I *won't*.

Bruno leans back in his chair. He runs a hand over his curly hair, and it lands on a chest that is pure muscle. Probably I have said too much. Made a spectacle. Maybe he will berate me and I will have to apologize. Again.

But when he speaks, his voice is restrained. "He's knocking her around?"

I stare at him. It isn't what I was expecting him to say. "Yes."

"We could use someone like you around Blue Circuit, you know," he says quickly, then stands. He walks toward me. "In a professional capacity."

I frown, confused. "The last time we talked—"

"We're a family here, Eve. We don't always get along. We don't always agree with one another—words, actions, whatever. But I have a good feeling about you. I'd like you to think seriously about going pro."

I shake my head. I don't know what to say—there are too many feelings humming through my chest, but I know flattery is one of them. I know that desolate vision of my future in Eleven retracts from sight for just a moment. "Uh, yeah. Okay, I'll think about it," I say, and maybe for a fraction of a second I even mean it.

"And while we're on the subject, I hope one day you find an excuse to beat the shit out of your friend's dick boyfriend."

He smiles, and I smile, too.

I walk into the cylindrical tunnel where I first saw Wren. How strange it is that he is now my boyfriend, and the thought makes my stomach do cartwheels. But I need to focus, because today I will be paired against a Red Circuit occasional fighter named Star. She is Lower Mean, stocky but fast, and I have heard she is dirty. She beat Emerald once and so I know it will be a difficult match.

Wren won't be in the crowd; he and Connor are on a job tour of one of the many Preme computer labs. And as much as I hate to admit it, I am happy he won't be here. I would be nervous with him here. Nervous and distracted—not a good mix for a difficult fight.

One thing I have to look forward to is tonight: a date, and at his place. My heart beats harder at the thought. We will meet in front of the library at eight. Late enough for dinner with my friends to be finished with, early enough that the compound's lights will still be on.

I think of his lips, soft and warm and pressed against mine. I smile.

Star's fists crack against the punching bag, and she grunts loudly with the effort. The crowd at the end of the tunnel is rowdy—I can hear them shouting, but it won't be a well-attended match. We are both occasional fighters, both Lower Means. I unzip my hoodie and toss it aside. I slap both cheeks and think of my father. I tighten my armband and think of Maggie, Kyle.

The old wounds open quickly, and every punch is harder than the last. I don't like to lose, so I won't. Star isn't the only one who can fight dirty, and I see Zaar crumbling under me in my mind's eye. I hear his screams of pain, and I relish in them.

But when the ref gathers us, something inside of me gives way. Maybe it's the love of the fight, if it was even there in the first place. Maybe I am being overly and unnecessarily dramatic. But as I walk into the Bowl and toward the bright lights of the ring, my feet feel as though they are filled with lead, and the desire to be nestled into Wren's arms fills my chest like a syringe has been squeezed into my heart.

No.

No, I cannot go there. Not right now, not ever. I am me. I am cruel. I am a fighter.

I look around at the beating hands that cheer us on, and I let their energy seep under my skin. It propels me forward, faster with every step. Hunter once told me he would die if so many people yelled his name. I know why, right now.

Maggie screams loudly—she must not be mad—and I nod in her direction before my eyes slide over to Kyle. He doesn't clap; he just stares down at me with those pale eyes.

Star stands before me, and I see her stocky legs have tights pulled over them that are acid green; I see she has shaved both eyebrows. Her taped knuckles are stained pink, and she grins like a lunatic. I shift my weight slowly, then faster. I bounce up and down and shake my hands at the wrists. Now isn't the time to be soft, and it isn't the time to be complacent.

I am focused and determined and ready.

Except that I don't see her first punch until it is too late. It hits me hard in the ear, and it feels like a rod has been jammed clean through the other side. She brings an elbow up, and I only just manage to lurch back in time to save my teeth. A kick lands in my stomach, but it hits engaged muscle and so

I barely feel it, and I use her wasted effort as an opportunity to attack her with a punch of my own. I have good aim, and it hits her in the center of the face. I feel her nose give.

It bleeds, and droplets land on the floor that my feet pad over. A guttural noise emerges from her bloodstained lips, and she launches forward, her thick frame barreling into me and knocking me to the ground. It is a dangerous place, the ground. But no sooner do I draw my shoulders up does she grab my ponytail, and I yelp as she pulls me with it: a dirty fighter indeed.

In my state of powerlessness, I think of Maggie and my desire to teach Kyle a lesson. Now, I am calm through the pain. I wait. And then Star moves beside me, and her fist is cocked. I jerk upward and clip her under the chin and hope that she's lost her tongue in the process. Next I grab her shirt and pull her down to me, and we're both on our knees and my ponytail is free. I take a page from Wren's book and smash my forehead into her already busted nose, then jump to my feet before she can see straight again. I kick her—just like Erick taught me, straight in the face—and her head snaps back like her neck has come undone.

She is out. Cold. Another one bites the dust.

My chest heaves as the crowd roars, and I look over my shoulder, my eyes scanning the crowd until they land on Kyle's. I spit and smile, then head back to Blue Circuit's training room to wash myself of sweat and Star's blood.

But once I'm there, I notice something. I am shaking, and it isn't victory or even adrenaline that is doing it. It is fright. Not because I almost lost, but because I almost lost unnecessarily. I almost let myself get soft.

• • •

That evening, I check my reflection one last time in the small mirror hanging in my cell. My blond hair is loose and still damp from my ice-cold shower, all four minutes of it allotted to Lower Means. It doesn't look great, but I am not good at styling it the way Maggie is. I give it a half-hearted tousle and shrug. It will have to do. Next my eyes travel to my nose, straight and wide, and then to my eyes. They are dark blue and set apart. Unremarkable, other than their crescent shape.

My face is unscathed after today's fight. I know I shouldn't care, but part of me is happy about that. One ear still rings with pain, and my scalp burns, but otherwise I am uninjured. Only tired from the exertion it took to beat my opponent.

I check the clock and see that it's time to go. My heart thuds at the thought of meeting Wren, at the thought of seeing his apartment. That's what he called it. An *apartment*, not a cell. But that isn't the appeal, not really. It is seeing another sliver of him that excites me.

I lock the door with unsteady fingers. Perhaps from fatigue, perhaps from nerves, probably a bit of both.

"Are you wearing makeup?" I whirl around to see Emerald standing there with her arms crossed. Shit.

"No. Of course not."

"Yeah, you are. Your eyes look different. And your cheeks are all streaky."

Red creeps up my neck. My hands rub at my face. "They are not."

"Where are you going?"

"Jules. Remember? I told you at dinner. I've got plans with Jules."

"No," she says slowly. "I don't remember that, but okay. So. Jules. What are you two doing?"

I can't tell her we're going to hit up the punching bags. Not after she has caught me with makeup on. "You know," I say instead. "Just hang."

She squints her eyes. "You don't have plans with a guy, by any chance, do you? Say, a good-looking one from the fifth floor?" She leans her head forward knowingly and gives me a look.

"No!" I shout, but I am smiling and I can't get rid of it. "No. Of course not. Besides, we're just friends."

"Yeah right you are. Listen, I won't tell the others, okay?" She winks.

I rock back and forth and then punch her on the arm. "Thanks," I say awkwardly, and then I am gone, past her and down the hall. I wipe the last of the blush off as I go. It isn't so bad if Emerald knows. But Maggie would make a big deal of it, and Hunter...well. I don't want Hunter to know.

I hate sneaking around. I hate lying. But it is hard to feel too bad about any of that right now. It is hard to keep the skip out of my step. I take the stairs two at a time, and I feel like taking them three at a time even though my muscles are heavy.

Still, I am smiling like a fool.

And then the lights go out and all around me is blackness, thick and impenetrable, and I realize I have left my knife and my flashlight in my cell, and that this is bad. So very bad.

CHAPTER TWENTY-FOUR

I don't know which floor I'm closest to. How long was I climbing before the power went out? Probably I'm somewhere between the third and the fourth. Between Mean land and Upper Mean. Possibilities flash in front of me, displacing the darkness, but my brain isn't processing correctly and I can't make sense of any one of them. Instead I stay still, my feet rooted to the concrete steps like one of those trees aboveground, tethered to the earth.

I swallow, and I can feel the pressure in my ears. They are my only useful sense right now. *Okay, Eve. You need to do something.* I swipe a hand in front of me through the black air. It lands limply at my side.

I can't. I can't do anything.

I push a toe forward, and it edges an inch to the side.

It is like I am paralyzed.

Perhaps I am overanalyzing; perhaps I don't need to do anything. Perhaps I can wait here until the lights come back on. And then I will continue on my way to see Wren. Yes, that is what I will do.

The thumping in my chest makes me lose my balance, and my hands fumble for the handrail that digs into my back. Both hands grip it tightly. My feeling of powerlessness in the ring today was nothing compared to now; this is real life. This is true vulnerability. This is terror.

A door pushes open below me, and I hear "fucking compound" hissed under someone's breath. It sounds vaguely familiar, but I need to hear it again to recognize it because my brain is moving impossibly slow. Like molasses that the cafeteria sometimes serves with toast. But whoever it is has a flashlight, and its glow lights up the stairwell. My pupils dilate with excitement as they latch on to it.

When my eyes find the speaker, the giver of light, my pounding heart does not slow. Laughter does not bubble to the surface with relief. Because it is Daniel and Landry, and both slow when they see me, both their spines straighten. As the old saying goes, I feel like the cat just spotted the mouse.

"No bodyguard tonight?" Daniel asks me, and his voice is cold. "That's a shame."

"Don't need one."

"You know what your problem is, Eve?" he asks, and he shines the flashlight up and down along my body. "You're cocky. Do you ever see the other girls acting so tough?"

"Sure I do."

"Nah. Not the butch fighters you run around with. I'm talking proper girls. Like you, Eve. You're a proper girl. Aren't you?"

My brain is moving quicker now, and my eyes dart up the stairs and away.

Daniel is still talking. "And that attitude of yours. Another one of your many faults." He stares at me, but I can't see his eyes. The sockets are a cloud of black. "What do you think, Landry? Cause I'm thinking we ought to teach Eve here that lesson we've been *so* meaning to teach her."

"Back off, Daniel," I manage. I hope they can't hear the agitation bubbling in my stomach. It must be pure acid, because it lashes and burns. All I can think about is the fact that I fought today and how unfair that is. I fought today. Physically I am drained and tired and vulnerable. And it is a horrible thing, to be vulnerable. "Back off or you'll end up like your friend."

"Another thing you ought to pay for," says Daniel, and a sneer curls his lip. As he shifts the glow of the flashlight, I see that evil glints in his eyes.

No more time to waste. I lurch away from them and up the stairs with the help of every fiber of muscle and every last cell pushing maximum energy into motion, but I am not fast enough. Grabbed around the ankle, I fall. My face lands on the lip of a stair, and my cheekbone screams with pain.

Please let that be the lemon juice. Please let the rest of the blows that are sure to come fall over me unnoticed.

"Will you look at that, Landry. Eve is panicking," he taunts. "Thought I'd never see the day. God, it feels good to watch her sweat, although I have to admit it's a bit sad. Pathetic, even." He grabs my other foot and rips me down the flight of stairs until my bare stomach is flush against cold concrete. I am on a landing—probably the Mean landing—and my only hope now is to scream. So I do, at the top of my lungs, but even then, I know it's futile. Nobody will come. Nobody ever comes in this godforsaken compound. It is every man, woman, and child for themselves, and the reality is I don't have enough in the tank to see me to another day.

The back of my head is grabbed; it is smashed into the floor, and my scream is stopped. Cut off much too quickly by pain and shock. Blood seeps into my eyes and between my teeth, and my fingers crawl to my face, my palms offering a bath of much needed warmth. Daniel is on top of me, and his hands grip my arms, and his legs lock over mine.

"Turn her over," comes Landry's voice, and I know that I have no chance. He was my only hope, but his voice gives away his delight. He is on Daniel's side. "I've always thought she had a pretty face."

"Too bad I just smashed the shit out of it, then," says Daniel roughly. "And for the record, Eve, I loved every second of it." And with that, he pulls at one side of my body, and I flip over, my hands still covering my face, holding it together. Still he is on top of me, still I can't move. The smell of his acrid soap chokes the back of my throat.

"Ah, will you look at that," says Landry. "She's playing shy." Fingers touch my bare stomach, lightly stroking back and forth, and a knot twists my insides, one apart from pain and terror. This is a dull and knowing sense of dread.

I thrash around with as much effort as I can muster, the desire to be free drowning everything else that fires through my brain. But it isn't enough. It isn't enough because it isn't a fair fight, not tonight. Not with two of them.

"What do you think of her body?" Daniel asks. I can hear the effort in his voice as he holds me in place, but he is trying to keep it level. Trying to keep it cool. "No complaints there."

"Meh, too hard for my taste. And she's tall, too, right? And flat as fuck, like a dude."

Daniel laughs, cold and sharp, and my hands ball into fists over my eyes as though this will protect me from their evil intentions. Still I thrash, still I try to knock Daniel off me.

"Hey, Eve," he says now. "Hey, Eve—calm down a bit, 'kay? This'll hurt a lot less if you stay still. Trust me, okay?"

"You can't do this!" I scream, and the words erupt from my mouth. They taste like vomit. "You can't do this to me!"

"That's where you're wrong, Eve," he hisses through

clenched teeth. But I see strain in his eyes as he holds me down. He is tiring quickly. "We can do whatever we want because we're Upper Means, and you're a dirty little girl nobody gives a shit about. And let me tell you this," he adds as a small smile curls his lip, "when we're guards, don't think for a second you'll have a moment of peace again. Not when you sleep, not when you eat. Not. One. Second."

But I can't respond because I am screaming again. Landry's fingers curl around the waist of my jeans, and in that moment my legs roar to life, and there is a dull *thud* that is my heel on his chest.

Daniel turns to see what is going on, and with the momentum of my kicking legs, I am sideways underneath him. Almost free.

"Grab her!" Daniel is shouting, but every cell in my body is alight with adrenaline and the tireless pursuit of life.

I am on all fours. I shove an elbow in Daniel's face, I fight, I fight. But then my hair is snatched from behind, and long fingers curl around my neck and squeeze with such intensity that blood vessels burst in my eyes, and the fight is leaving, it is dying.

But I am not ready to give up just yet, and I grab at a finger, just one—and it must be a ring finger, because it is weak—and I bend it back as the world goes dark, and I hear a pop, and the grip around my neck loosens. Oxygen soars to my brain.

I am alive, I am alive, I am alive.

"Fucking *cunt*!" Daniel screams. "She broke my fucking finger!" He is hunched over in the corner, and I run; I sprint up the stairs with Landry at my back, and he pushes me, and he slams my head into the concrete wall, and it is blacker than it was, and it strikes me that I will die here. Never will I say a proper farewell to my parents or my friends or to Wren. Never will I breathe fresh air or feel a breeze against my cheek. Never will I have a shot at finding Jack or tasting freedom.

There is a flurry of footsteps—that much seeps into my battered brain—and maybe yelling, but I am too far gone to make sense of it. No, I must be wrong, because it is quiet now, unless that is my name I hear. It is so faint, it sounds like it is being whispered from the dead other end of the compound, so I can't possibly respond. Maybe it is the trees outside the Oracle whispering my name. I want to whisper back; I do.

But now I am swaying, back and forth, like a clock, or like a tree—one of those talking trees. Yes, that is it. I am whispering my own name, nothing more, and I am alone, always alone. And now my mind is still, and I no longer know if I am moving or awakening, hearing or speaking, sleeping or dying.

CHAPTER TWENTY-FIVE

I blink into a dimly lit room. My head throbs so deeply behind my eyes that for once the darkness is a blessing; light would surely crack my skull in two. Nausea wells up in my stomach from the pain, and I close my eyes again.

Probably I am at Daniel or Landry's place. Probably my hands are chained up—my feet, too. I really should open my eyes. It's a wonder that I am alive at all.

"Eve," comes a low voice, and it is one I open my eyes for, no matter the pain. It is one that sends relief flowing through my veins like sugar. Wren.

He is staring down at me with something dark and animalistic etched across his face.

I try to say something, but it only comes out as a gurgle. The taste of blood coats my tongue.

"Eve," he repeats. "Who was it?"

His voice is so even, his cadence so slow, his eyes flashing with so much violence. I swallow, and it feels like sandpaper, and then I push out three simple words that surprise even me: "I don't know."

"You don't know?"

I shake my head.

He speaks slowly. "What do you mean, you don't know? You don't know their names?"

I shouldn't protect my attackers. Of course I shouldn't. I don't want to, and it isn't my intention. But I have to lie right now because otherwise Wren will do something terrible. I can sense that cruel monster in him right now, see it stirring behind his fiery eyes.

"No. I mean I didn't see them. At all."

He stands quickly and turns from me. Both hands run along his face, and then he strings them behind his head as he gazes at the ceiling. His arms are bulky with taut muscle.

"How could you not see?" His voice sounds desperate.

"I just didn't."

He paces now, and my eyes follow him. I like watching him move, even when he moves in torment, even when I feel like slashing my throat for causing it. But every action of his shines with such gentle, restrained strength that it is impossible to look away. And watching him is a distraction from the pain inside my brain.

"Eve—"

"Where am I?"

He stares at me, and I can tell he doesn't want to change the subject. But he sighs. "At my place. You'll be safe here."

I blink, and his back is to me, and it is getting smaller. "Don't go," I say, and even though I am being weak for wanting him close, for wanting his comfort, I don't care. Maybe it isn't weakness that makes me crave companionship or safety— maybe it is human nature. Those like Daniel and Landry who breathe nothing but destructive, malevolent air, whose blood is clotted with viciousness—maybe they are the mutants.

Maybe I have been trying to be a mutant, when all I am

is human.

Wren looks over his shoulder. "I'm getting you something for the pain. I'll be back."

When I see him next, I think I have fallen asleep for some time, because he is wearing a sweatshirt now with the hood pulled up and he is sitting beside me with his head in his hands. He must sense I am watching him, because he turns to me almost at once.

Next he puts something between my lips and holds a glass to them. "Take this. It'll bring down the swelling."

I do as he says, and the water feels foreign as it drains to my stomach; it tastes like metal. My head burns with less thunder than before, and I feel like I do after a hard fight. Except after a fight I feel strong, and right now I feel anything but. Images of Daniel on top of me race through my mind; the feeling of Landry's fingertips across my stomach stings like acid.

My fingers tremble, and then I realize the shaking comes from the ball in my stomach and I need a distraction. So I push up on my elbows; I lift my raging head and look around. I am lying on top of a bed, and a thin blanket covers me. Blood covers my shirt.

I want to cry, but I shouldn't, because the tears will never stop. Maybe I don't want Wren to see me cry like a child. Maybe I am being a child for caring.

"How many were there?" he asks.

"Two."

He nods. "That's what I thought."

"How…?" I can barely bring myself to talk about it. Saying it aloud makes it more real, too real, and surely it was all a bad dream.

His eyes fix onto mine through the darkness. "How?" he repeats.

"Did I get here."

"I waited a few minutes after the power went out. And then I decided to go meet you." He shakes his head. "I should have gone right away."

I remember footsteps before the world shut off. They must have been his. "They ran as soon as they heard you," I say slowly.

He nods. "By the time I found you, they were gone." His voice is tight and clipped like a belt pulled against itself. He fixes me with a stare. "You're sure you don't know who it was?"

"I'm sure."

"What happened to your knife?"

"Forgot it. Flashlight, too."

"Did they say anything?"

"They had a lot to say." ...*Eve is panicking thought I'd never see the day god it feels good to watch her sweat I've always thought she had a pretty face too bad I just smashed the shit out of it flat as fuck like a dude...* On and on their words rip through my head until I realize that Wren is talking, and I force my eyes to focus on his mouth.

"And, what—you didn't recognize their voices?" he asks. His is heavy with disbelief, or maybe I am imagining it.

I frown. Then I speak as clearly as my blood-coated mouth will allow. "No. I didn't recognize their voices. I didn't see their faces. Sorry."

"One of them had a flashlight, though. I could see it from the top of the stairs."

I shrug. "I didn't notice."

"You didn't notice," he repeats, and his eyes narrow. "You, of all people. You, who is deathly terrified of the dark. You didn't notice that suddenly you could see?"

Burning prickles behind my eyes, harder than before. "I was kind of busy, Wren, fighting for my life, okay? They wanted—" I can't bring myself to say it.

He leans forward. "Wanted?"

I make a face. "What do you think?"

He is perfectly still, like he is carved of concrete. "Did they?"

I shake my head, and when I do, the tears are dislodged, and they fall loose. There is no controlling it, not now. "I got away," I sob. "I was so weak from the Bowl, I couldn't fight them off. But then I did—somehow I *did* get them off me. And then one of them was choking me, and I—"

I catch myself, but only just. I can't tell him I broke Daniel's finger. It would be a telltale sign the next time Wren sees him.

"And?"

"And I got away. Again. I was running up the stairs when one of them caught me, smashed my head into the wall. That must be when you found me." I cover my face with my hands and lie down again, the sobs too loud now to talk over or around. The bed lifts beside me, and I know Wren has gone and I am alone.

I cry until I can't cry anymore.

"Here's a facecloth," comes his voice sometime later. I can't see through the darkness, and I realize my eyes are sealed shut. I take the cloth blindly; it is hot and feels good against my bruised and broken skin. "Have the pills helped yet?"

I nod. "Thanks." When I open my eyes and look up at him, I see his face is still clouded over in rage. "What?"

His eyes are stern, and they beat into mine. "I'm going to find whoever did this to you, you know," he says quietly.

He leans down so that his lips graze my forehead and I can smell his clean scent. "I'm going to find them, and I'm going to kill them."

I say nothing.

He kisses my head and leans back so that our eyes can find each other. "It's late. You should try to get some sleep. You'll feel better in the morning."

Before I can respond, my eyes slip closed, and soon my breathing becomes steady; my pulse slows.

I wake to silence, and for a moment panic seizes me. But then I remember where I am, and the coil in my stomach loosens. My head aches with only a dull thud that worsens when I move, but still it is bearable, and so I sit upright and toss the blanket aside.

Yesterday my muscles served me well, and I rub them slowly as my mind retraces the horrors that now reside inside my skull. That is the problem with trauma: It never ends. It endures in memory.

The mirror over the sink where I wash up shows a face I barely recognize as my own. Black and blue like I haven't seen before; concrete is harder than fists. But whatever Wren gave me for the swelling has worked: The skin is puffy with broken blood cells, but nowhere does the distortion run deep. There is a slash along one cheek, but I wash it and it doesn't begin to bleed again—a good sign.

My neck is the worst of it. Striped blue and yellow, the imprint of fingers holding me in their vise grip. These are the marks that the others will notice.

The thought of seeing Daniel or Landry again makes a

tremor rob my hand of steadiness. I look in the mirror and force my back straighter. I must be strong, and that isn't a problem—not for me. But the shaking doesn't subside, and I think of their warning about not giving me a moment of peace once they are rulers of this compound, with their guns and authority. It is a blessing that I have already decided to go, and before jobs begin. Their threat is empty, meaningless; they just don't know it yet. My mind drifts up and up until I am standing in the Oracle and the trees are swaying under a gentle breeze. I feel the sun in my eyes; I see the glass shattering under my hand. I feel myself sprinting north until I reach a field of hollyhock. Now my breathing is steady again, the shaking gone.

When I leave the washroom, I find Wren sitting on the bed. He is wearing track pants and nothing else, and my eyes linger on his smooth skin. It isn't pale like mine. It is a warm olive, and it mounds over muscle in a way that is almost poetic. Landry is right about my body, though I have never given it much thought until now: It is hard. Straight. It doesn't ebb and flow, it isn't graceful in its beauty, it isn't frightening in its strength.

Wren's is all that and more.

He stands, and I can tell by the way he moves with so little on that he's comfortable in his body, in his skin. "The swelling's down."

I nod.

He walks to me, and his eyes are on my neck, and his fingers go there, too. Gently, they graze the stripes that mark me. His eyebrows pull together so that a line appears between them, a small indentation of concern.

"Is this typical?" he asks. His voice is clipped and unnatural.

"What do you mean?"

"The attack. Is it typical? You know, for Means."

I shrug and even try to force a smile, though I fail. "I told you. It's a way of life."

He wraps his arms around me, and for a moment I forget how to breathe as his bare skin ensnares me. Partly, I don't want to be touched—not right now. But this is Wren, I remind myself, and so I push my arms around him, and my fingers drink in his warmth and the feeling of blood and muscle stirring with every breath. It feels good, better than I thought it would. It is a distraction. A distraction I am desperate for, I realize, and so I focus only on him, on his flesh, on his sturdiness. For a moment in time, I forget the events that unfolded last night. I forget the pain that coats my head and sits inside my chest.

"I can't believe how bad it is. How unfair it is," Wren is saying into my hair. "We're taught it's a different culture down there. That's how they put it. Mean culture is just… different." He sighs.

There is nothing I can say. Violence *is* a way of life. Maggie and Emerald and Hunter, they will feel sorry for me, yes. But they won't be shocked, at least not for long. I was attacked and almost killed, but I am just one of many. I am one of the lucky ones; I survived. So instead I stand taller and pull Wren closer so that our bodies are flush. So that I can smell his skin.

I take a deep breath and push heavy words from my stomach. "Ever kissed a girl with a black-and-blue face?"

He stares down at me, and his face is knotted, perplexed, and then it breaks. He smiles. "I've never kissed a girl like you before, period. No matter the state of your face."

He dips his head lower, and his lips land gingerly on mine, if only for a moment. When we pull apart, I whisper to him, "Do me a favor, okay?"

He nods, his eyes watching.

"Don't feel bad for me. Don't look at me any differently.

Okay? I'll be fine."

"You'll be fine," he repeats. He shakes his head. "I kind of expected you to say that, just not this soon. God, Eve, you're allowed to grieve, you know."

"I already have."

"You just woke up."

I force myself to shrug, a masquerade of nonchalance. "I'm made of steel."

He laughs gently. "Yeah. Trust me, I get that."

I run my fingers along his bare back, focusing on this sensation alone instead of the pain, prying my voice up an octave, forcing it to sound lighter than it is. "And don't even think about feeling guilty for being a Preme. Not now. I mean, I've been putting the guilt trip on you for a while now, and I'd hate to think it was my attackers who finally did it."

He scowls, but his eyes are soft. "What makes you think I feel guilty?"

"You're not a monster," I reply, and my voice is matter-of-fact. Under my fingers, his muscles tense up. But I am too busy pulling him close to pay it any attention.

He kisses me hard this time, too hard for my beaten tissue, and I push at his chest. When he pulls back, I see he is breathing deeply, and there is something exposed in his eyes. It passes quickly.

"Sorry," he says. Then he forces himself to grin. "So, when exactly do you think you'll be feeling better?" His eyes inch down my body in a way that is intended to be playful. He is trying as hard as I am to make things easy and airy and the opposite of what my reality has become.

It makes me smile, his efforts, almost genuinely this time. "Give me a few days, okay?"

He is watching me closely. He nods, then picks up a stack of clothes folded neatly on the bed. "Here," he says. "They'll be big, but at least they're clean."

Once he disappears, I sigh. Then I give myself a shake, carefully remove my bloodstained clothes, and throw them in the trash. The black sweatshirt from Wren is several sizes too big, but it smells like him, and I never want to take it off.

After I roll up the pants, I leave the bedroom and see for the first time the rest of his apartment. I am still as my eyes sweep over a large room painted black, different in every way from my second-floor cell. No, that isn't quite true. Like mine, it is sparsely decorated, the walls empty but for words hanging next to me: *Here in the dark I know myself.* In the far corner, there is a punching bag coated in blood, knuckle tape lying on the floor beneath it.

The room is wider than the main corridor downstairs.

I don't know what to do with so much space; it feels so unnecessary, so superfluous.

"Wow, Preme," I say as I cross my arms. Once more I try to make my voice light, but this time I can't. Sometimes when I'm with Wren, it feels like our differences don't separate us. Like we are the same person, who happen to come from different places. But other times, like now, our differences feel vast. So vast it is a wonder we can see each other from either side.

He has a hoodie on now, and he sits on a sofa the color of concrete. In front of it is a coffee table with a binder sitting on one corner and a gun on the other. "It's no big deal." He shrugs.

"Yeah, it's no big deal. Except that it's *huge.*"

He shrugs again. "Wasted space. I don't spend much time here."

My eyes reach his. "My entire cell is smaller than your bedroom, you know."

He nods. "Come here."

I sit beside him, and he slips his hand into mine. "I wanted to show you something." His other hand reaches for the binder and pulls it close.

"What is it?"

"Remember when I told you my mother's in charge of the solar panels?"

I nod.

"The past couple of years, they've been keeping track of weather patterns. With the aid of these." He swings the binder open, and my jaw drops. It is full of photographs of the sky, and my hands stream over their glossy surfaces, flipping through them with hunger. I see the sun roaring with fire, I see it swollen and orange and barely cresting the earth's crust, I see the moon a thousand times closer than when Wren and I lay side by side in the Oracle.

"This is… This is amazing."

"I thought you'd like it."

"Why are they doing this?" My eyes don't move from the pictures as I speak.

"It has something to do with how poorly the panels have been working lately. They're trying to optimize their effectiveness by studying weather patterns." He shrugs.

"Look at the colors," I murmur as my thumb grazes a photo of the sun sitting low in the sky, pink clouds in front of it. All around it are cascading stripes of purple and red.

"It's called a sunset. Ever heard of it?"

I shake my head.

"It happens at the end of the day. We should watch it sometime." He closes the binder and sits back on the couch with my hand nestled in his. I follow him back, and he kisses me softly.

"Hey," I say, my voice squeaky, "you know how you said you've never kissed a girl like me before?"

"Yeah."

"Have you, you know…" I take a deep breath. "Kissed a lot of girls?"

He presses his lips together as his gaze shifts to the ceiling. Like he is deep in thought. His hand strokes his chin. "Let. Me. Think."

I punch him. "Very funny."

He smiles. "You want to have *the talk*, Eve? That feels like very official boyfriend-girlfriend business."

"Well, you are my boyfriend, aren't you?"

"Known only to the two of us, I might add."

"Well. It still counts." I draw my knees up to my chest. Every time I blink, my face hurts, but I am distracted right now by Wren, and that is a good thing. I don't want to think about what happened. I don't.

"It still counts," he repeats slowly, and then his head nods forward.

"And you already know *my* sad history."

"What, never having kissed anyone before? Come on, it's only a little sad." He nudges my arm. "Okay, fine. Keep in mind that I'm two years older than you."

I shift in my seat. "Okay," I say.

"I've had two girlfriends. One doesn't really count because we were both young. Kids, practically. The other…the other you've actually met." Now he is the one to shift in his seat. His gaze blinks onto mine, but it doesn't stay there for long.

A lightbulb goes off in my head. "*Please, please, please* tell me it isn't her." I hated her when I saw her in the Preme hallway. I hated her long red hair and the way she touched his arm. Now I really hate her.

He runs a hand down his face, then draws his hood up. If anything, it draws more attention to his defined cheek and jaw bone, to his straight nose, his level eyes. "Addison is her name. We dated for a couple of years, on and off. I ended things for good a few months ago."

"She still likes you."

His face is serious as his eyes meet mine. "So? She's nothing to me. Hasn't been for a while." He seems to spit out the words. "Can we talk about something else?" he adds.

I am silent. The only thing I can think about is her. And the fact that he's had a serious girlfriend before. But what should I expect? I look at him and reiterate his words: "You're two years older than me."

"Yeah, Eve. What about it?"

I shrug. "I don't know. Do you think it's an issue?"

"If I'm being honest, it isn't something I've even noticed. Have you?"

"No," I admit. "But Hunter dated someone a year older recently, and it didn't end well."

His eyes are unsmiling as they stare into mine. Finally, he looks away and forces his head up and down. I am about to ask him what is on his mind when there is a knock on the door, loud and completely unexpected. It startles me, and I jump.

It startles me because we had been enveloped in complete silence, because we were talking about uncomfortable truths, because I feel more vulnerable after last night's attack than I ever have before. I startle and reach for his hand before I can stop myself.

He eyes me as he stands. "I thought you were made of steel."

The words sting, and I don't turn my head as he opens the door, as someone enters his apartment. Sometimes Wren is kind, and sometimes he is anything but. I suppose I am no different.

"Where is that binder I didn't authorize you to take?" comes a woman's voice, and it is cold and vaguely familiar. "Tell me I didn't raise a thief, though it wouldn't surprise me in the slightest."

"Nice to see you too, Mother," says Wren, and I know why her voice sounds familiar. Not because I've heard it before, but because they share the same disinterested way of speaking. But where Wren's voice is low and smooth, hers is crisp as ice.

"Drop the pleasantries," she snaps. "I don't have time for it."

"What else is new."

"Don't try me, Wren. The binder. Quick."

"The binder's over there," he says lazily, and I shut my eyes as I feel her gaze land on the back of my head. "Help yourself to it."

Silence.

I don't want to meet Wren's mother. Especially not right now, with my face looking like this. But I grit my teeth, then look over my shoulder, and my eyes meet hers. She is average height and razor thin—not like Wren at all. But her nose is the same; her wide-set, intelligent eyes are his, too. But hers are slivers, and his are the giver of light.

"Mother, this is Eve. Eve," he says with a shrug, "meet my mom." My eyes slide briefly to him, and I see that he is relaxed. There is no warmth his body shows for her, no reverence in his eyes. There is no fear there, either.

"Good God," she says slowly as her gaze meanders down my face. If I blush, it would be well-hidden by bruises. But I don't blush. I stare at her without batting an eye. She turns back to Wren. "Make sure you hide the damage next time."

"Hide the damage next time?" I sputter, drawing myself gingerly to my feet. "You think *he* did this to me?"

She looks amused. "You might be dressed up in my son's clothes, but I can spot a Mean any day of the week. Next time, do remember to hold your tongue until a Preme invites you to speak."

Yes. She is a Preme—an important one, at that. I think about Commander Katz's visit to the Mean cafeteria, I think about a life of misery, I think about Jack…and just like that, my injuries from last night are completely forgotten.

"I'm not sure which is worse," I say bitingly, taking a step forward and completely disregarding her orders. "Being so dismissive of someone so beat up or thinking your own son is capable of it."

"I don't think you know my son very well, then," she says, and as she does, I glance at Wren. I expect him to react to these words, but instead he looks passive. His arms are folded, and he stares at his mother with hardened eyes, yes. But there is no anger in them, no emotion whatsoever.

All at once, Hunter's words come rushing back to me. *You can never…*never *trust a Preme.*

"Are you trying to punish me?" she asks her son. "Bringing this—this creature into your home, dressing her in your clothes? You may as well traipse her around the common areas while you're at it for all the rest to see."

"I look forward to it."

"Be my guest. You'll realize your own foolishness in good time. Do me one favor, though, and keep in mind the company a person like this must keep." She glances once again at me and frowns. "To know such violence…"

"Perhaps you ought to watch your back, then," I say, and my voice is clear and level. "Those who know great violence are capable of great violence."

She smiles. "Perhaps you and Wren share something in common after all." Then she turns to the door. "Bring me the binder within the hour," she snaps at him. Her heels tick against the floor as she leaves.

I stare at him, but his eyes don't meet mine, and he seems lost, like he is somewhere else. "I'm leaving," I say simply as

I follow her out.

He must wake from his daze, because he is behind me in an instant and has my shoulder in his hand. "I'm walking you back to your place."

"You're forgetting," I say as I wrench myself free, "I'm made of steel."

CHAPTER TWENTY-SIX

The next day, I feel better. Lighter in my chest, and my head no longer aches. My face is sore to the touch; it is still black and blue, but already some of the bruising has faded to yellow. It is mesmerizing to look at and reminds me vaguely of the sunset that Wren showed me, where colors bleed into one another, where light and darkness collide.

Yesterday I took the elevator down from the fifth floor and managed to make it to my cell without seeing anyone. My heart thumped with every step, my eyes scanned the faces around me, but there was no Daniel, no Landry. What I will do when I see them, I don't know, yet see them I will. It's impossible not to.

One thing I refuse to do is cower. It is bad enough they will see me covered in injuries they inflicted. I will not let them think they got under my skin.

They didn't, they didn't, they didn't.

Part of me itches to even the score. The fighter inside me—the cruel, violent monster in me. But part of me doesn't want to even the score with Daniel or Landry. It doesn't want to go there, to know such violence ever again. Part of me doesn't want to fight in the Bowl anymore. Part of me just wants peace.

I don't know how to reconcile these two parts of me. And I don't know which side will win.

This morning, though, I am going to breakfast, just like every other morning. Yesterday, I didn't leave my cell, and I ignored my friends as they pounded on the door again and again, on and off. I turned my back on the guards who searched my cell for the missing gun, squeezing my eyes shut as they ran their hands along my legs and under my pillow, taking no satisfaction in my trickery even though it was well-deserved. I slept often, and when I wasn't sleeping I was thinking about the Oracle, the outdoors, the oasis. Whenever darkness threatened to overcome me, I pictured myself there, safe and in perfect freedom, Jack's delicate fingers searching through my clothes for a small object that I hid, just like before, and I was whole again.

I pull on my boots, tuck the switchblade inside; the flashlight, too. The neon light across from my cell shines in my eyes as I leave and turns my white sweatshirt a sickly shade of green. I pull it straight. I smooth my hair that hangs over my shoulder in a braid and breathe in. Out. It is another day, nothing more. *This is Compound Eleven, Eve. Where did you think you were?*

"Finally," comes Hunter's voice from beside me. "Maggie and I were looking for you yesterday, did you know? Emerald kind of—"

He sees my face, and he is frozen, one hand suspended in midair.

"Hunter…"

"What the *hell* happened?"

"Hunter—"

"*Eve*. Tell me." Then, before I can respond, his arms wrap around me and pull me into a tight embrace.

"It's okay," I hear myself saying over and over again, but his head is shaking.

"It's not okay," he insists as he pulls back to better study me. "It's not. Who did it? It wasn't the fight in the Bowl. Maggie said you won easily." His brow digs together. "Your neck. Holy shit, look at your neck. Someone tried to *kill* you."

It feels like there is a stone in my stomach, and the more he says, the heavier it becomes. The quicker it sinks.

"Was it the Preme? It was, wasn't it? I knew he was bad news—"

"What, Wren? No, Hunter, *no*. Of course not."

But he isn't listening. He is banging on Maggie's door over my objections, and when she answers, her eyes are confused and heavy with sleep. Then they land on my face, and suddenly she is awake and just as alarmed as Hunter.

"Oh my God, is this why you were MIA yesterday? Why didn't you tell us? Who was it?"

Too many questions, too much attention. I just want to be. When I speak, it isn't my normal voice; it is one twisted with frustration. "*Stop* it. I'm fine, so just leave it alone." I glare at them, but they only stare back with wide eyes. "Honestly"— and my voice is softer. "Honestly. It's worse this way—you're making it worse. I was attacked. It happens all the time down here, and I guess it was my lucky day. Can we just not talk about it? Please?"

They exchange a look. "If that's really want you want," Maggie says eventually. "Okay. Okay, let me see. Um. I'm going to go get changed. Then breakfast?"

"Perfect," I say. Relief floods my veins. But once her door is closed, I can see that Hunter's face is crisscrossed with concern. He has always been too protective of me.

"You have to at least tell me who it was," he says under his breath.

Of course I can't. There is a chance it would get back to Wren. "I didn't see. It was during the power outage. Can we drop it now?"

He stares at me, waiting.

"Please?"

After a while, he sighs. "Consider it dropped."

I squeeze him around the middle. Maggie emerges from her cell a minute later, and together we move through the Lower Mean hallways. The two of them talk of the job tours taking place after breakfast, but I barely listen. Instead I think of the stairwell; I think how the steps must be stained with blood. *My* blood. "Mind if we take the elevator?" I interrupt once we near the lobby, and they look at me. "My leg's sore," I lie.

They nod. They are good friends, obliging, and I silently chastise myself for yelling at them. Especially when their only offense was caring. I smile appreciatively at both of them.

When we reach the cafeteria, I see neither Daniel nor Landry. The balloon of dread in my stomach deflates somewhat. I don't think I could bear looking at them—not right now. Not yet. But time heals everything, and in another day or two, it will be fine. It will be old wounds; it won't matter to me.

We sit in our usual spot, and I clear my throat. "Any word on Sully?"

Hunter shrugs. "He's recovering. Apparently, he's already coming up with ways to leverage what happened to him into action. More frequent protests, a movement in its own right—you get the drift."

"Mmm. What about everyone else?" I glance around and notice that the atmosphere is more subdued than is typical.

"Things are slowly getting back to normal," says Maggie

between bites. "Talk about an eventful week."

"Yeah, no kidding. So, how's Kyle?"

She gives me a look as she butters her toast allotment—a single piece. "Seriously? Give me a break, Eve." She points the knife in my direction. "I know how much you hate Kyle, I've always known it, but…now I really do."

"Why, what'd she do?" Hunter leans forward with interest. Neither seem to be treating me any differently because of my injuries, at least not now, and I feel lighter, more like myself.

"Yeah, what'd I do?" I ask, smiling. "Oh what, because of the other day? Before the fight?"

"Um, obviously. And after the fight, too. I saw you look up at him after you just about decapitated that loon you were fighting."

"Did Kyle notice?"

She rolls her eyes. "What do you think?" Then she lowers her voice, and it sounds tense. "Look, when you do stuff like that, you're just making life harder for *me*. Okay? It just puts him in a bad mood, and…"

"And?"

"He's just hard to deal with then. Okay?"

I shake my head. "Maggie, trust me. You can do way better."

"Easy for you to say," she says slyly.

"What's that supposed to mean?"

But she is looking over my head, and I turn around to see Wren as he slides into the seat beside me.

"How're you feeling?" he asks heavily, and his eyes comb down my face and linger on my neck.

"Can't complain."

"You know about this?" Hunter asks, shifting forward so he can see around me and to Wren. His eyes dart in my direction.

"Yes."

"When exactly did it happen, Eve?" Hunter asks now.

"I told you: during the power outage. Not last night, but the night before."

"When you were hanging out with Jules."

My eyes lift, and I see Maggie is watching me. Wren is silent by my side. "Yeah. Then."

I could tell them the truth—that I was heading upstairs to see Wren. They already know we are friends, and friends spend time together. But it is too late, and admitting I lied requires more courage than I can muster right now.

"Did she get away?"

"Who?"

"Jules."

"Oh. Yeah, it actually happened as I was heading out to see her. So she didn't have anything to do with it, thankfully."

"And yesterday you just laid low."

"Yep. Rest is best, right?"

"So how does he know?"

"Are you conducting an investigation or something?" Wren demands, sounding annoyed.

My voice is loud: "Can everyone just settle down? I told you, Hunter, I don't want to talk about it."

"Clearly you talked to *him* about it."

I stare at him, exasperated, but then his hand slips into mine, and I feel its warmth, its familiarity, and the guilt for keeping so much from him lately is almost overwhelming. Then Emerald is there, and her eyes are wild, her gaze raking over my wounds but not taking anything in. She sits beside Maggie and drops her head into her hands. The rest of us exchange looks.

"Emerald?" I try. "Is everything okay?"

She shakes her head back and forth, then sits up straight.

Her hands fall away from her face, and she stares at me. "Bruno's dead."

Maggie gasps, but I am still. I don't move; I don't even breathe. "How?"

"Fight in the Bowl," and on the last word her voice breaks and she chokes back a sob. She isn't a crier, Emerald. She wouldn't want to cry in front of us; I know that. So I give her a minute to pull herself together and use the time to do the same for myself.

Bruno. *Dead*.

"He was fighting a Green Circuit pro," Emerald says once her voice is steady. "They were fighting—it was an awesome fight, and then Bruno was falling, and—and—the guy, the Green Circuit guy, he kicked him in the head. Mid-fall. Broke his neck." She is breathing deeply, and one hand snatches at her mouth. "He landed on the floor and didn't get back up."

My head is shaking. The surge of emotion that wants to escape is mounting. It can't be. Bruno *can't* be dead.

When I finally speak, my voice is hoarse. "When did it happen?"

"The fight was yesterday. He passed away this morning." Her eyes are red-rimmed like she hasn't slept. "I've been in the nurse's station ever since. Me and Erick and Anil. I tried to track you down, but I couldn't find you."

"Oh." More guilt, always guilt. "I was...occupied."

"Yeah, by the looks of things, you haven't fared much better than Bruno."

My voice is barely even a whisper. "At least I'm alive."

But she isn't listening; she is rubbing her hands up and down her face. "It could have been you or me, Eve. It could have been one of us in the ring—it was just a regular fight."

I swallow; I push the emotions down deep. "It's dangerous, what we do. We always knew that."

"You weren't there. You didn't see it. It was so quick. One second he's strong and putting up a killer match, you know? And the next, bam. Gone. Forever." Her eyes reach mine, and they look broken. "I don't think I can do it."

"Do what?"

"Go pro."

"Emerald, you love fighting. And trust me," I add, gesturing toward my face, "your life can be over just as quickly outside the ring as in."

She frowns at me, then nods. "Maybe you're right."

Maggie slings an arm around her back. "Hunter and I are heading on a factory tour after breakfast. You should come. You know, get your mind off things."

"Which factory," Emerald asks, but her voice is flat. Distant.

"Clothes, isn't it, Hunter?"

He nods. "Garments, I think they called it."

"Right. We're going on the garments tour. It could be interesting."

Emerald doesn't reply; her gaze is fixated on her lap and many miles away.

Maggie looks at me. "Eve, are you in?"

I shake my head. An automatic no.

Her eyes narrow. "You've been on *one* tour."

"You're counting?" I make a face.

"Someone has to."

"Look, I don't exactly feel up for a tour today, okay? I'll go on more of them soon. There are still a few weeks until we have to decide—that's plenty of time."

She nods. "I guess you plan on going pro anyways, right? Or does this"—she glances at Emerald—"change things for you, too?"

Wren is perfectly still next to me. I just shrug. "Time will tell."

• • •

After breakfast, it is just Wren and me, and I do my best not to think about the last time we saw each other. We'd had a fight—a small one, sure. But I was also reminded of who he is. *What* he is. A Preme, the son of one of Eleven's leaders, a woman I instinctively know can't be trusted. Does it make me trust Wren less, by extension?

It's hard not to let it. Plus, there were her words—odd ones—and the presumption that *he* was responsible for all my bruises...

Maybe I should have gone on the job tour after all. The others are headed there now, Emerald included. There is no use in mourning the dead for long in Compound Eleven. There are no funerals like tradition dictated before civilization moved underground. Already his body will be disposed of. I know she won't be able to think of anything else, though. It is all I can do not to think of him, too. Of our last conversation.

He invited me onto the team, and for a moment I actually considered it. For a moment, I actually considered staying in Compound Eleven.

"What are you doing now?" Wren asks as we head for the elevators.

"I don't know. Polishing my steel."

He smirks. "Funny. Want company?"

I look at him out of the corner of my eye. "What, at my place?"

His gaze meets mine but only for a second. "Sounds like maybe you could use the distraction."

"Don't do me any favors."

"Eve?"

"What."

"You're still incredibly hard to talk to."

We board the elevator only after my eyes sweep the small space for Daniel or Landry. I turn to him. "Whatever. You coming down or not?"

His thumb jams the button for the second floor.

"Did you know Bruno well?" he asks once we disembark. I lead him through the Lower Mean crowd in the direction of my cell. My eyes are peeled for Daniel and Landry, but only because I can't stop them from searching. It is a weak thing to do, a scared one. But still I look.

"Bruno? Yeah. Same team and everything."

"Fighting for sport is rough. Dangerous."

"Yeah. We covered that at the breakfast table."

"Still want to do it?"

"It was a freak accident, Wren."

"That's not why I'm asking, *Eve*."

I look over my shoulder at him as we shove through the main corridor. His mouth is pressed into a thin line.

"Come on," he says eventually. "You've been to hell and back. Maybe put your feet up for a bit."

"And get soft? The only reason I survived what happened the other night is precisely because I fight for sport. Because I'm good at it, because I'm strong."

"True, but since you are hell-bent on leaving the compound soon, why not enjoy your time? Unless, of course, you like to fight."

"Can we talk about something else, please? I really don't want to think about Bruno right now, or the Bowl, or fighting in general."

"How about this. Any chance you'd recognize your attackers if they walked in front of you right now?"

My eyes widen; they search the faces around me, panic playing at my stomach. But they are nowhere to be seen.

Besides, Wren has no idea who it was. How could he? *Get a grip, Eve; it was just a question.*

"I don't know," I say. "Maybe. But what are the chances?" I look at him and drag the corner of my mouth into a half smile. "Right?"

"You're sure you didn't see who it was? Because—"

"I told you," I snap. "I didn't see them. It was dark. I was panicking. Okay? Can you just leave it?"

His face hardens, but he says nothing more until we turn off the main corridor to where the crowds are thinner. He exhales. "Back to your plan to leave the compound. How do you expect to do that, again?"

I glance at him. "Why?"

He looks at me slyly, more playful than before. "Let's just say I have visions of you attempting to kidnap Katz, and it's keeping me up at night."

"Who are you more worried about—him or me?"

"Well, he travels with his own entourage of armed guards, so you do the math."

I shove him. "You can relax. My plan is far less glamorous."

"So what is it?"

"I lifted a gun from a guard, that's all. It's hidden in the storeroom as we speak." I say it plainly, yet the words are touched with pride.

"You think you're going to shoot your way out of the Oracle?" He shakes his head. "It's bulletproof glass, Eve, three inches thick. Compound security was a priority when it was being built, for obvious reasons. Do you really think our forefathers constructed it with ordinary materials?" He must see the horrified look on my face, because he adds: "Impressive work, though. I can't imagine guards give up their weapons very easily. And stashing it someplace outside your cell—also notable. Every bit as calculated as I would have expected from you, to be honest."

I am barely listening. Too much rushing in my ears. Too many specks blurring my vision.

The glass is too thick. Bulletproof. *Bulletproof.*

My plan won't work. My ticket to freedom, gone. Just like that. The field of hollyhock, the oasis, Jack—all of it seems to flicker and fade, just beyond my fingertips…

Relax, Eve. I say it again and again until the tears that prickle behind my eyes dry up. There are other ways out. I will find another way out; of course I will. That paradise will be mine. I will reunite with Jack there. I will.

I will, I will, I will.

"I wish I could say that I feel badly for prolonging your stay down here, but…" He clips me along the arm.

I force a smile in return. "No prolonging," I say weakly. "I'll figure out something."

We walk the next two hallways in silence. It hurts, this revelation. Definitely, it hurts. I feel it in my stomach and my chest and my head. Yet it doesn't gut me as deeply as it should. In another week or two, if I don't find another way out, maybe it will. But right now my senses are too dulled—all of them. Crushed already, I can be pulverized no more.

Near to my corridor, Wren notices the black paint spelling out *Fuck the Premes.* He stares at it and runs his tongue along his teeth. "No wonder you wanted to keep things between us quiet," he says heavily. "It puts you in danger. Why didn't you tell me?"

I snort. "If you think I'm scared about that, Preme, you don't know me."

"Be serious, Eve."

"I am serious. Besides, you don't exactly look like a Preme, so long as you keep your hands in your pockets. What's the difference?"

"But if certain people knew…"

"Yeah," I am forced to agree. "If certain people knew."

In my corridor, the lightbulbs are almost all burned out—two have died since I left for breakfast—and so it is dark, but it doesn't bother me quite like before. Maybe it is because I am distracted by devastating news and brutal disappointment, or because Wren is here, but I don't think so. I think the lemon juice has spilled on my fear of the dark.

"Does someone fix these?" he asks as his eyes comb the ceiling. His arm reaches up and touches a lightless gray bulb outside my cell.

"Eventually."

"I can see why you love it down here."

"Yeah, well, wait until you see in there." I look at him pointedly under the glare of the neon light, then swing my door open. "After you."

Probably it is the first time he has ever seen a Lower Mean cell. His eyes sweep over the small space and quickly latch on to the piece of embroidery hanging on the wall above the bed, my only decoration. My cheeks burn as he stares at the image, as he sees my mother's signature. Silently he moves to the other side of the room, only a couple of steps away, and his fingers graze the objects on my desk: a ball, a book lent to me by Hunter.

He picks up a piece of paper and reads it aloud: *"Death must be so beautiful. To lie in the soft brown earth, with the grasses waving above one's head, and listen to silence. To have no yesterday, and no tomorrow. To forget time, to forgive life, to be at peace."*

He raises an eyebrow.

"It's a quote. From an author. A long time ago." I shrug. "I copied it from a book upstairs."

"Do you believe it? That death is beautiful?"

"I read once that there's no such thing. Death. That it's a change of worlds, nothing more."

"You didn't answer my question."

"I think I did," I say.

He nods and then sits on the bed with his hands running down his face. It looks as though he has accepted my cell for all it is, and with no snide comments or pitying glances. Something else seems to be on his mind.

"So. I guess we should talk about yesterday morning with my wonderful mother. I know you have a lot on your plate right now and—"

He's right; I do. Too much. Too much sorrow that could overwhelm me at any second if I am not careful. I don't want to think about any of it. I don't want to think about our fight or his Preme mother. Maybe I *do* need a distraction… My eyes drink in his thick, olive-coated forearms and the muscles rippling under his black shirt. I see his mouth, wide and kind, just as I saw it all that time ago. My sheets and bedspread are white; it makes him stand out all the more, and suddenly I can't look at anything else.

"Take your shirt off," I interrupt.

He looks up at me. "What?"

"I want to kiss you, and I'd rather do it when you don't have your shirt on."

"Uh. Okay? I actually thought you'd want some sort of explanation for what my mother—"

"Wren. Your shirt."

"You're serious?"

"I am."

He grips the bottom of his black T-shirt and pulls it over his head in one motion. Immediately, I sit down on top of him. "Much better," I mumble. Then I kiss him, and the cloud of darkness over my head retreats just a little. One hand runs down his taut chest, and my pulse quickens because I have never touched a boy like this. The cloud retreats a little more.

But his head pulls back, and he sighs. "I know she was rude to you, but I didn't think you would care about that. It's the other stuff. All the stuff about me being violent that you must—"

My fingers fist in his soft hair, and I kiss him again, stopping the words in his mouth. But once again, he pulls away. "Eve, this is important."

"Not to me."

"Is anything important to you?"

I shrug. "Kissing you. Kissing you is very important to me."

His eyes are hard, and it looks like he might get angry, but then he smiles. He laughs. "You are incredibly strange." His hands wrap around my waist, and his fingers snake under my shirt. "So, are we still taking things slow?"

I want to say no. But then I remember Addison, and a ball of lead forms in my stomach. I feel Daniel and Landry on top of me, and the ball grows heavier. I nod.

"Hmm. It just seems so unfair, though, that if we're going to make out, I have to be undressed and you don't."

I crinkle my eyes.

"Come on," he says, and he lies down on the bed and pulls me with him. Just as I was surprised by his strength in the Bowl all that time ago, I am surprised again by how easily he can move me.

"It's not unfair. Because, you know. You look like that," I say from beside him, and my fingers swirl over his stomach, over the alternating muscle and depression, muscle and depression. My pulse is dangerously quick.

"Like what?" he asks, and his eyebrows are pulled together.

"You know." I kiss him lightly on the chest. "Perfect."

Now he grins. "*Perfect?* Wow, I think that's the first nice thing you've ever said to me." He pulls me close, and his lips are on mine, and his hand rides up my back, under my shirt. It makes a shiver run the length of my spine.

"I don't think you have any idea how *perfect* you are, Eve."

"Come on. Don't do that to me."

"Do what?"

"Bullshit me."

He is kissing me and laughing at the same time. "See? I told you that you had no idea. It's fine. I kind of like it that way."

I am smiling, too, and somehow, even with my plan to escape now blown apart, even with a black-and-blue face and a darkened heart, I feel happy, maybe even desirable. I kiss him harder now and grip his shoulders tightly. He pulls himself around so that he is lying on top of me.

I swallow. It shouldn't remind me of them. It shouldn't. I am strong, and what happened the other night with Daniel and Landry wasn't that bad. It wasn't. I can do this.

Wren's hand runs down my body, and my heart beats harder, but now I can't tell if it's with desire or dread. As his fingers near the waistband of my pants, I know the answer. My eyes snap open, and my hands push hard against his chest.

"What? What's wrong?"

"I don't know." I blink back tears before they emerge. "It's nothing."

He is watching me, and his eyes are dark and thoughtful, an impossible combination.

"It's nothing," I repeat. But still my hands don't move from their spot against his chest.

Finally, he nods. He moves sideways so he is beside me. His lips graze my forehead. "It's okay, Eve."

"It's not okay."

"Does it have to do with—"

"Yes."

He runs a hand over his face. "Look, I get it. It would be weird if it *didn't* have any impact on you, okay? I know you're made of steel and everything…" His eyes narrow, and his lips curl up at the corners. "But I think somewhere deep down in there you're actually, I don't know…human?"

I grasp his hand in mine, and it feels safe and secure. "Yeah. Too human."

"I don't think so." His face is serious. "You're the toughest person I've ever met, but you're good, too. You're hard and soft. I didn't really think a person could be both things at once."

"But you're that way. You're as tough as I am."

His eyes sweep over my face. "But who said I'm good?" Before I can respond, he raises his head and kisses me on the lips. "So," he says into my ear. "Hunter."

"Hunter?"

"Yeah."

"What about him?" I ask. My bedside lamp glows a warm yellow, and it melts into his skin. It lightens his hazel eyes and his hazel hair. It makes his lips look more angular, his chin more square.

"You guys are close?" he asks.

"We've been friends for as long as I can remember. So yeah, I'd say that's pretty close."

"Mm."

I raise my head and frown. "What?"

"It's nothing. It just seems kind of strange for you two to be friends."

"Why? Because he's a guy and I'm a girl, Grandpa?"

"No." He smirks. "Because you're so different."

"Oh." I stare at the far wall, plain and undecorated. Then I shrug. "I guess I never noticed."

"Mm."

"Wren?"

"Yeah?"

"Please tell me you're not jealous." I am laughing; I can't hold it in.

His fingers that crawl along my bare arm are still now. "Of course not."

"Good. Because Hunter and I are practically family—you can ask him—so it would be kind of ridiculous if you were intimidated."

"That's not really the point."

"Well, what do you want me to say? I love him. He's my oldest friend."

"You love him."

"Not like that." I roll my eyes. Because the thought of Hunter being anything more than my best friend is laughable. Almost as laughable as thinking he would feel anything more for me.

He nods. "I know. I know not like that." He runs a hand through his hair, and I watch the muscles in his arm engage with the motion. The fact that I can touch that arm, touch it and squeeze it and kiss it, makes something warm seep through my veins. It makes me never want to leave this spot, nestled beside him.

When he speaks again, his voice is quiet. "I'm not sure where I'm going with this."

"You're intimidated," I say lightly.

"Very funny. I could kill Hunter with my eyes closed."

I look up at him, and he looks at me. He brushes the stray hairs from my eyes.

It is a strange thing to say.

"You could kill him too, Eve," he murmurs into my ear.

A strange thing indeed.

CHAPTER TWENTY-SEVEN

"Are there swings?"

Maggie smiles. "Of course there are swings... although if memory serves me, only half are operational. Don't tell me you're a fan."

"Something like that," laughs Connor. "Wait, is that weird to admit?"

"Not at all." She pauses to straighten her ponytail. "I guess you guys had your own Preme playground growing up?"

He nods. "Are there any on the second or third floors?"

I scoff at the suggestion. Of course not.

"Well, I'm looking forward to seeing the Upper Mean one."

"It won't be nearly as nice as yours," Maggie warns.

"That's okay. The last time we were at ours, oh God. We were probably five years old, right?"

Wren shrugs. "I always went with your family, so you'd know better than I would."

"Yeah, except you were always getting in fights, so we could never stay long."

I glance at Wren and see him shrug. Hunter sits on the

other side of the table beside Maggie, Emerald beside me. Lunchtime in the Mean cafeteria.

"So how do you guys get in?" Connor asks.

"It's left unlocked once a month," I explain as I push peas around my plate. But I am barely paying attention; instead, my eyes dart around the crowded cafeteria for signs of Daniel or Landry. It has been three days since the attack, and I haven't laid eyes on them since. It is just a matter of time.

Making the whole thing worse is the knowledge that I have no way out. No ticket to freedom awaits in my back pocket. I am stuck down here, confined and imprisoned, battered and bruised, and with a giant red X painted on my back.

Worse yet, that X will become much more pronounced once Daniel and Landry are made guards. Before, I had to escape Eleven by the end of what civilization used to call summer because I couldn't bear the thought of serving Commander Katz, or kneeling before a Preme, or being branded with my worst memories. Still can't. But now it is doubly important that I go by then.

"For the cleaners," Hunter adds, and I force myself to nod.

"Right. For the cleaners."

Maggie twists the end of her ponytail. "Yeah, we sneak in after the cleaners are gone, usually ten o'clock. It's usually us and, well, whoever else wants to come. Sometimes it's a big group, sometimes it's small. And always there's booze," she adds with a wink.

Connor laughs. "It's this weekend?"

"Saturday night. Fourth floor, past where the admin offices are for the job tours."

"We're looking forward to it. Right, Wren?"

Wren nods.

"Don't mind him. Like I said, he spent most of his time at

the playground in a fistfight. It's probably bringing back some pretty painful memories. So, any luck with the job search?"

I turn to Wren and drop my voice as our friends continue to talk. "Is there something going on there, or is it my imagination?"

"She's seeing someone, isn't she?"

I nod. "Treats her like shit, though."

"Ah."

I notice that his plate is largely untouched. "Everything okay?"

"Everything's fine."

"You don't have to go, you know."

He looks at me. "To the party?"

"Yeah. It's kind of—"

"If you're going, I'm there." He fixes me with a stare. "Besides, I've never seen you wasted before."

I elbow him in the ribs. "Very funny." But my smile evaporates as two figures push through the cafeteria doors. Daniel. Landry. The noise of the crowd seems to drown away into nothingness, a faint murmur at best, and all I can hear is blood rushing in my ears.

They look perfectly relaxed, perfectly at ease with life. My eyes watch them until they sit at the far end of the table. They can't see me, and I can't see them. But I can feel their presence, feel their viciousness suffocating me, pushing down my esophagus, closing in around my neck like Daniel's fingers did. And now I can't leave Eleven. I have no way out. No way to escape—

I feel like I could vomit. But I'm not doing a good job of hiding it, I know that, and if I'm not careful, then Wren and the others will begin to suspect something. I think Wren already does.

"Did you guys hear the protests this morning?" I hear my

voice say. It sounds higher than usual.

Maggie nods. "I had to take a different route from Mom and Dad's. They were dragging some guy who got killed a few days back. Half the Lower Mean hallways are streaked with blood. Really disgusting."

"A few days?" asks Hunter. "Usually they're pretty quick to get rid of bodies."

"I'm guessing the authorities didn't even realize there'd been a death—"

Emerald's fist slams down on the table, and we are silent. "Can we *please* talk about something else?" Her eyes are bloodshot, and I know without asking that she hasn't been sleeping.

"Sorry, Emerald," Maggie says. "I didn't even think…"

"It's fine. Just change the subject. Please." Her plate, too, is untouched.

The cafeteria door swings open once again, and this time it's Kyle. A moment later, his hands land on Maggie's shoulders.

"Let's go," he says, and I see her body tense up. Beside her, Connor stares at his plate. After a moment's hesitation, she stands, and Kyle gives her a look. "What did I tell you about wearing your hair up? It looks terrible like that. Do you want to date an Upper Mean or not?"

She mumbles something—probably an apology—and I glare at him.

But as he notices my discolored face, his mouth breaks into a sneer. "Looks like you met someone who was a bit bigger than you, huh? Hopefully they taught you some manners."

"Be very careful," Wren says to him before I can speak. His voice is level and restrained—everything mine wouldn't be, if I could pass air through my teeth.

Kyle's eyes flick back to Maggie. "Hurry up," he spits at her.

I want to tell her to stay here, with us. Stay here where she is treated with respect, where she is safe. But I can't, because that would only make things worse for her.

Besides, I am too agitated right now to say much of anything. They are here, *they are here*. My attackers. My foot twitches, and I can't stop chewing my thumb.

When Daniel stands, when he leaves the cafeteria a short time later, I notice two things. The first is that Wren's back straightens. He is watching Daniel as closely as I am. The second is that there is a splint on his finger, one that makes me smile, just a little. Hopefully it is slow to heal.

With Daniel gone, I allow myself a deep breath. Landry, though, remains behind, and I will have to pass him on my way out. I feel his fingers on my stomach, and I want to rip him to shreds. So I focus on breathing in and out until the feeling passes. It wouldn't be smart to pick a fight right now; I am not fully healed. It wouldn't be smart to pick a fight, period. More than anything, I think, I want Daniel and Landry and Zaar to leave me alone. I want peace.

Wren is close behind me when we go, and his presence is steadying.

But when my eyes latch on to Landry's blond hair, he must feel me staring, because his head swivels as I near and his gray eyes come alive with recognition. Recognition of the pain he and Daniel put me through. In an instant, he is grinning and standing, and his arm wraps around my shoulder, and my legs go numb. I am cold all over. Can't move.

"Wow, Eve. Looks like you took it hard, and right in the face. What a shame." Then he moves his mouth to my ear. "Next time I'll see to it that you take it hard somewhere else, too."

The words make me nauseous, but before I can even think of puking or responding or whatever it is my warped brain wants to do, I am thrown forward and onto my hands and knees. I see why a second later.

Wren has Landry by the collar of his shirt, and he is shoving him forward, to the edge of the cafeteria where the tables don't reach. Landry's eyes are wide with surprise, his grin gone, and already his palms are open. A gesture of peace.

Wren's hands unclench and release him; they rise and mimic Landry's. Peace. And then the muscles in Wren's back twitch like they are connected to electricity, and his fist connects with Landry's eye socket.

Landry is thrown backward, but he manages to stay on his feet.

I blink, and once again, Wren's hands are raised, and I can see that he is saying something to Landry. Probably I should do something. Probably I should go over there. But I don't move. I am rooted to the ground.

The second punch breaks Landry's jaw. I can hear it from here; I can see the shock cut through his eyes. And then Wren's free hand wraps around Landry's skull, and he is punching him quickly now, again and again until Landry's knees are buckling and Wren lets him go. He drops to the ground. Calmly, Wren examines his bloodied knuckles; he examines his opponent, who begs for mercy on the floor.

Now my legs are moving, they are propelling me forward, and I can see that Wren is smiling. His chest may heave from exertion, but as he bends over Landry, I know he is not finished with him; he won't be finished with him until the light leaves Landry's eyes for good.

This is why I lied in the first place. This is something I need to stop, even if part of me doesn't want to.

Wren is on top of him, and his eyes flash with danger, and I am screaming his name. But it is no good; the attack continues, and blood splatters over his olive arms, and Landry's eyes are closing. And so I do something I probably shouldn't. I grasp at Wren's fist; I wedge myself in front of him, into his field of vision. His eyes barely register my presence, they are so wild.

"WREN!" I scream. "STOP! STOP!" I slap him across the face, and his eyes latch on to mine, and for a fraction of a second, I am scared for my own life…but then it is Wren who is looking at me, and I know he can hear me. "Stop," I repeat, and I say it as firmly as I can. "Please. Stop or he's going to die. Stop or you're going to be sent aboveground."

And then, before I can process whether or not a Preme would actually be sent out for killing an Upper Mean, I freeze, and I have forgotten about Landry, even about Wren. I have forgotten everything around me and before me. For now I have a solution. Now I have a way out, a proper one. It was there in front of me all along, and now I can finally see it, and I see it firmly within my grasp.

All I must do is kill a person.

And then I am free.

CHAPTER TWENTY-EIGHT

My fist strikes the bag, and the dull thud it makes reminds me of my heel on Landry's chest. And thinking of Landry makes me think of Wren, of Wren nearly killing him yesterday. Maybe he has killed him; I don't know. Landry wasn't moving when I finally forced Wren away. Someone took him to the nurse's station. I haven't gotten word since.

I punch the bag again and feel the wetness of blood.

Maggie is watching me, sitting along the wall in the cylindrical tunnel that connects the training rooms to the Bowl. There are no fights scheduled today; we have the place to ourselves.

"Are you feeding the Noms anymore, or are you done with that?" she asks. Her voice is heavy, not like her normal self.

I finish a set of fifty punches before I answer. "Going today, as a matter of fact."

"So that guard's been reassigned?"

"That's what I heard."

"From?"

"Jules. Apparently he was filling in for Melissa for a couple weeks while she did breakfast duty." I look at her and shrug. "Now Melissa's back to lunches, so I'm good to go."

She picks at her thumb. "You know, you really should apply for a guard job, even if it is a long shot. Especially after what Daniel said about never giving you a moment's peace. Remember?"

"Yeah, of course I do. But I'm not interested," I say between strikes. "Besides, it's an Upper Mean job. They wouldn't hire a Lower Mean in a million years."

"That's ridiculous. If you're a guard, they'll leave you alone, plus you'll be *armed*. And don't tell me the guardship won't at least consider your application. With your fighting record and all the volunteer—"

"Maggie, I'd rather—"

"Die than be a guard? Yeah, I know. So you've said. But maybe you need to start thinking more seriously about what's at stake. Daniel tried to *kill* you, Eve. This isn't the same old shit as when we were kids."

I attack the bag with fury at her words, picturing Daniel's face instead of thick hide, and I feel beads of sweat form along my brow. She's right; it isn't the same old shit at all.

Everything has changed.

"So yesterday sounded pretty wild," she says after a while. I turn and watch her as I catch my breath. Her arms wrap around her knees, and her brown hair falls loosely around her shoulders. She has a black eye, one that is partially swollen shut. "I just can't believe it was Daniel and Landry who did that to you. I knew they were scum, but still. And I can't believe *Wren*."

Her eyes meet mine.

"Wild," I agree. My voice is disinterested by design.

"He's...frightening."

I shrug.

"You trust Wren?"

I give her an exasperated look and then turn back to the punching bag. I attack it with a fresh burst of energy.

What I really need to do is focus. Not on form, not on building muscle, but on the task at hand. I have to kill someone, and in order to do that, I need to decide who I am going to kill. Daniel or Landry are the obvious choices, although possibly Wren has taken care of one of them already.

The thought makes me shiver. His eyes flashing with danger, his calm resolve, that smile—all of it makes me shiver. But mostly because I am not sure I have it in me. Maybe that cruel monster inside me is smaller than I realized. Maybe I am not a killer.

Focus, Eve.

Daniel. Or Landry. But there are other options, too. Other people who deserve to die. That guard with the black bead eyes, for one…

"Can we drop the lies yet, Eve?" Maggie says loudly from the wall. "Or does our lifetime of friendship mean nothing?"

I turn to her, the bag instantly forgotten. My thoughts forgotten, too. "Excuse me?"

"You and Wren are together," she says simply.

"What?"

"Come on. Don't play that. It only makes it worse. I'm your best friend, and you kept it a secret. It's pretty huge, you know—you haven't exactly had a boyfriend before. Why you felt you couldn't confide in *me* of all people, I'll never know."

I stare at her coldly. "Save the lecture on secrets, okay?"

Her arms cross over her chest, and she leans forward. "What's that supposed to mean?"

"Look at your face," I spit at her, and my voice sounds loud and hot. "You think I haven't noticed the bruises? You think the others haven't?"

She blinks at me, frozen, and then she stirs. "I ended things with him." Her voice rings through the tunnel; it vibrates with emotion. "Last night. It's over."

In an instant, I am crouching in front of her. She looks thinner than I remember. Her eyes don't look into mine, and she trembles. Nothing on my tongue feels right or good enough, and so silently I wrap my arms around her and hold her tight.

She doesn't move, not initially, but then her body relaxes into mine, and I can hear her crying, and I don't want to ever let her go.

When her tears slow, I draw back and consider her. She doesn't look like Maggie; she looks like a shell of a person, and if I speak too loudly she'll crack—she'll break forever. "You did the right thing," I say quietly. "You know that, right?"

She nods, but her eyes still refuse to meet mine.

"You didn't deserve that shit. Nobody does," I continue. "Things are going to be better for you now, okay? I promise. This is good, Maggie. This is really, really good."

She blinks away tears and frowns. "Is it, though? I don't want to end up alone. I know how pathetic that sounds, but I don't. And now that we're done with school... We're not kids anymore, you know?"

I force a laugh. "Do you know what a catch you are? And just because school's finished doesn't mean you have to figure your *entire* life out right now. Where's your head at?"

She frowns. "I don't know. But he was just so charming, you know? With his Upper Mean job and allotments and that blue dress shirt..." She sighs.

"Maggie, you're the most amazing person. You can do a million times better than that jerk. You *deserve* a million times better."

She rolls her eyes.

"I'm serious. I'm not just saying that."

"Well. Thanks."

"When did he do this to you?" My fingers graze the swollen ring of purple that doesn't belong on her face.

She shakes her head before answering. "It was after lunch. He was angry—"

"Because of me. And Wren."

She looks away, and her shoulder nudges into a small shrug. "He started apologizing over and over, just like always, promising he wouldn't do it again. But this time was different. This time he went too far." Her eyes meet mine. "He punched me in the face, Eve. He *punched* me."

And then she is crying again, and both her hands cover her eyes, but they can't keep the drops from falling. Nothing can. I feel helpless and useless, and all I want to do is hurt Kyle. Beat the shit out of him, just like Bruno said, but remembering Bruno's words only makes me feel worse—so much worse— and my own eyes burn with tears.

When did life get so complicated? So intense? So *real*?

She sobs. "What if he doesn't leave me alone?"

"It's okay, Maggie," I hear myself mutter. "It's okay. I'll make sure he doesn't come within a mile of you. I'll make sure he leaves you alone. I promise."

She shudders and then looks up at me with lime green orbs that glisten. "I don't know what I'd do without you, Eve. I really don't."

And there's that old feeling again: guilt. Because once I go, I won't be there for her any longer. I won't be able to protect her from Kyle.

Unless I kill him. I could kill *Kyle*.

A parting gift before I go.

She wipes her eyes and shakes her head. "Let's not talk about things with Kyle. I don't want to even think about him—not right now. Let's talk about you instead," she says and forces a smile across her pretty face, a face that should always have a smile on it. "I mean, God, Eve. I can't believe you have a *boyfriend*."

"Yeah. Me neither."

"Have you guys kissed?"

"Maggie—"

"What? It's just a question! Come on, indulge me. I could use some girl talk right now, trust me."

"Okay, yeah. I mean, yeah, of course we've kissed."

She sits up a bit straighter. "Is he a good kisser? He is, isn't he?"

I duck my head, but I can't keep the smile from my mouth. "Yep."

"Like on a scale from one to ten—"

"A hundred."

She squeezes my arm and laughs. "Have you…?"

"No," I say loudly. "No, definitely not." She stares at me with her eyebrows raised, and I shrug. "It's just that, well…I don't know, really."

"If you're not ready, that's totally—"

"It's not that," I say. "I just… I have no idea what I'm doing, and he clearly does, so…"

"Oh God, that is *so* not something you need to worry about. Believe me on this one—there is zero chance that boy will be disappointed by any, um, encounter between the two of you. I've seen the way he looks at you."

"His last girlfriend was different from me, though. Her body. It's, you know."

"No?"

"It's… There's not as much muscle. It's more…feminine."

She laughs, and I stare at her. "I'm sorry. I know I shouldn't laugh. I just can't believe we're having this conversation.

Come on, Eve. It's *you*. Since when do you care about being feminine enough?"

"I don't know. I guess I've never had to think about it before. You know, since I've never had a boyfriend or anything." I stare at my hands. "And something Landry said. During…about how my body looks like a guy…"

"Stop." Her eyes are earnest, and she holds my gaze. "Just stop. I'm not even going to indulge you right now by telling you how beautiful you are, or this or that. I'm not letting you sink that low. Who gives a shit about what *Landry* thinks? You're Eve, and you're strong, and you make no apologies for it. Got it?"

My gaze wanders over the many punching bags hanging throughout the tunnel, most of them stained and threadbare. I nod. "Got it."

"He really cares about you, you know."

I glance at her. "Why do you say that? Because of yesterday?"

"Well yeah, hello. I can assure you, if some guy attacked me, Kyle wouldn't have lifted a finger, let alone beat him to within an inch of his life." She is still. "He also wouldn't hang out with my friends, something Wren seems more than happy to do."

My chest swells at her words, and I shake out my arms to distract myself. "Just don't tell Hunter, okay? He hates him."

"Don't you think Hunter will figure it out? I mean, you have to *really* want to believe there's nothing going on between you two to believe *that*."

"Even so." I pause. "It isn't just Hunter I'm worried about. Don't tell anybody."

"Why?"

I give her a look. "Why do you think we kept it secret in the first place?"

"I honestly have no idea."

"Because he's a *Preme*."

"So?"

"So? So, it matters. You know it does."

"To who? You or him?"

"To me," I say softly. "All my life I've hated them. All of them. And now…"

"And now you've found that you don't hate one. A few, actually, since his friends don't seem so bad."

I feel myself nodding along with her. Maybe it never really made sense to hate an entire society; maybe it never made sense that *all* of them up there were evil in the first place. The actions of the few should never speak for the many—this is something I already know. Besides, what's in a birthplace?

But then a new thought strikes me. "Think about what my parents would say. And other Lower Means, for that matter—like…like Sully."

"Yeah, okay, some might not be that hyped about it, sure. Maybe you don't spring it on your parents anytime soon, but come on. Sully?" She laughs. "I didn't realize the two of you ran in the same circles."

"You know how it is, though," I press. "Premes and Lower Means don't mix. Ever. Nobody will be okay with it."

"So maybe you don't broadcast it. Maybe you don't think too far into the future, either. Just enjoy what's happening. And don't shut out your friends, or his, because all we're going to be thinking is how lucky Wren is to be dating someone as kickass as you."

I roll my eyes and jump to my feet. "I always knew you were full of crap. Now, I need to work on my punches."

"Don't think you're getting off the hook that easily," she calls. "I'll just wait here until you're done, and then we can have a nice, long chat about Eve and Wren."

I shake my head, but it does nothing to dislodge my smile.

When I show up to work the Noms' food line, I find someone is already there. The guard has been by to unlock the door, the lights have been turned on, and the food has mostly been portioned.

"Mom."

She looks over her shoulder and raises an eyebrow. Her features are delicate, not like mine. "Hi, Eve," she says, and her voice sounds like I remember from when I was small. "They told me you quit."

I stare at the back of her head as a million thoughts fly through my own. "I didn't quit. I just…took a break. I've had a lot going on." It is mostly true, this lie. There is no need to tell her about the guard.

"I see."

"What are you doing here?" My voice sounds impossibly weak. "Did you know I was coming today?"

She shakes her head, and something inside me deflates like a punctured balloon.

"I was hoping I would see you, though. You don't come by very often to see your father and me."

"I'm not invited."

"That isn't fair, Eve."

I stay silent. Then my boots shuffle forward and I am beside her, helping to prepare the last of the offerings.

"I heard about the boy on your team. About his death." Her eyes lick my wounds. Thankfully, they are mostly healed by now. She probably thinks they are from the Bowl, and I don't bother to correct her.

"Blue Circuit. I fight for Blue Circuit. And his name is Bruno. *Was* Bruno."

"A terrible way to go."

I don't need her telling me that. It is all I can do to keep him from invading my thoughts throughout the day, particularly that last conversation of ours. Then there's the image that Emerald painted of his death. It follows me. It colors my dreams at night. "Does Dad know?"

"He's the one who told me."

"Oh." The fact that he hasn't been by stings more now.

"Are you still planning on fighting professionally?"

My hands fold together a parcel of lentils. I am slow, rusty. "I don't know. I haven't decided. Does Dad still want me to?"

"Decide for yourself, Eve. Your life is too important to waste on other people's wants."

I stare at her with my lips undone, but she leans forward and slides open the partition that separates us from the hungry Denominators without another word. I realize as I watch her that I barely know this woman. The thought makes a sharp pain rip through my chest.

She is hardly ever like this—hardly ever normal. Usually she is engrossed in her embroidery or her thoughts, and the rest of us slide by unnoticed. I know from experience I won't have her attention for long, even though I want nothing more.

Decide for yourself, she said. *Decide for myself.*

I wait for the rush of hungry Noms to be over before I speak again. "What if my decision is selfish?"

"You do not exist in a vacuum, Eve, just as I taught you when you were young. You must always take into account the impact your actions will have on those around you. You owe it to your loved ones and to society at large."

I nod. I knew she would say something like that.

"However. Sometimes you should behave selfishly."

My head lifts to look at her, and I see unbearable sadness streaking through her eyes. I hear her screams from all those years ago, feel them hot against my cheek. "What do you mean?" I ask quietly as I drop my gaze to the floor. I can't bear to look at her. Maybe it is better when she is busy with her embroidery. Certainly it is easier to think of leaving forever when she is closed off to me and to the rest of the world.

"I mean that life is ruthless and merciless and unkind. Sometimes we owe it to ourselves to be greedy."

I wonder what she has done that is selfish, what greed she has bestowed upon herself after the unkind world of ours took her child. No. Not the unkind world—that is too vague. Too generous. Commander Katz—the leader of Eleven. Ted Bergess—the Head of Population Control. The guards. *They* took her child.

There is no chance to ask, because Monica and her son, Avery, are at the window. Besides, I don't think she would give me an answer.

"Hi, Eve. I've missed you," Monica says shyly. "So has this little guy."

I give myself a shake. "I've missed you guys, too," I reply to my friend, and I mean it. "Especially you," I add to Avery with a wink. He covers his eyes, and I laugh. "Looks like someone's feeling better."

Monica nods. "He had a rough go there for a bit. Fevered all day and all night. But now he's better, so life is good. Right, you?" She smiles deeply at him, and I notice her dimples for the first time, and they remind me of Emerald. Her hand strokes his hair as my mother gathers two parcels and two buns.

"Until next time, Avery," I say with a salute.

"Until next time, Miss Eve," he says back in his tiny voice. I laugh again.

My mother's back is straight as we watch them go, the two of them walking hand in hand. I wonder if it hurts, seeing a mother with her little boy. I wonder if it makes her think of Jack. If it makes her yearn...

I don't think she intended to break the rules all those years ago. I don't think she intended to become pregnant a second time, not with so much on the line. But once it became evident that her swollen belly could mean only one thing, her rule breaking began.

Instead of reporting the pregnancy, instead of aborting the fetus, she hid herself from view. And when the time came, she summoned a black-market specialist, one who delivered Jack in exchange for plastic goods smuggled by my father from the factory where he worked.

The relief she must have felt once he was born. Safe and whole. Firmly within her arms. Probably, she thought the odds were in her favor, when in fact the chips were stacked against her all along.

I think of the song—the one that used to lull me to sleep each night and now does again. I have an opportunity to ask her about it, but just as I open my mouth, my eyes snag on her pushed-up sleeves, on the ink that is so rarely visible. My father's name is stamped there, and my own listed next, alongside my birthdate. And then there it is. That most unwanted addition to her life story: *second child Jack Hamilton born in contravention of Rules 43.5(a)-45.8 hidden from authorities in contravention of Rules 48.1(a)-49.7(d) removed from compound pursuant to Rule III—*

It is barely legible. Scar tissue distorts each letter, and I think of her in the days after those words were inscribed, clawing at the skin until it bled, desperate to rid herself of those memories—scratching, scratching, scratching—so relentless that my father had to restrain her, had to tie her hands behind her back, bits of skin and strands of tissue everywhere—

"Howdy, Eve. Hi, Mrs. Eve." I blink and see Jules waving hello to my mother.

"Elaine. It's…Elaine."

"You used to do this job forever ago, didn't you?"

She nods. "In another lifetime."

Jules's eyes meet mine, and I notice that she wears a white sweatshirt with black cuffs around the elbows that used to be my own. Noms hardly receive any allotments. "Things going okay, lady?"

I shrug. "Can't complain."

"Looks like a few complaints are warranted." Her gaze dips down my face.

"Just the Bowl; you know how it is."

Still, her eyes are narrowed. Maybe she doesn't believe me. "We should hang soon," she says.

"You know the party's this weekend, right?"

"I did not, but my weekend is wide open, and be there I shall. You bringing that cute sidekick?"

"Huh? Oh. He's just a friend. And he might be there, yeah…" I give her a sideways look. I don't want to talk about Wren in front of my mother. Partly because he is a boy; mostly because he is a Preme.

Jules nods, and I think she understands. "Alrighty then. Well, thanks for the food, Elaine." She looks at me and winks. "See you Saturday, Eve."

After I say goodbye, I clear my throat. "Can I ask you one more thing?"

"You can ask me as many things as you like. You know that."

I sigh. Sometimes I don't think she realizes she is usually unreachable. My voice is quiet. "How exactly does forgiveness work?"

Immediately, I frown. I had planned on asking her something different. Not about the song—to bring up the past wouldn't be fair, I know that now. Instead I was going to ask her whether it was wrong to take another life if that life was evil. Maybe I didn't because I already know the answer. Or maybe I just don't care about right or wrong.

She slides the partition closed before responding. It's silent in the small room, more so than last time, when I was here with Wren. My heart was hammering loudly then; now it is still. Dead. She faces me and places her hands on my shoulders.

My shoulders, like the rest of me, are thick with muscle. My mother's hands and arms are frail, skin and bone. But they rest so heavily on me, I feel like I could fall to my knees. I have to resist the urge to squirm, to shrug myself free.

"That is a strange question to ask, Eve. Whatever greedy choice you are considering that requires forgiveness…" She looks at her feet and shakes her head. "I'm afraid I am not the right person to ask when it comes to forgiveness."

I stare into her eyes and see something deep, deep within that burns with putrid, yellow hatred. She hasn't forgiven those who took Jack, not by a fraction, not by a millimeter. And I'm willing to bet the fog she so often hides behind is her one greedy act.

CHAPTER TWENTY-NINE

The next day, I sit cross-legged in the Oracle and wait for Wren.

There was a note shoved under my door this morning, asking me to meet him here. I haven't seen him since he attacked Landry.

Outside, the sun is shining behind me, its rays too bright for my eyes. The sky overhead is a brilliant blue, and the tree leaves flutter lazily in the hot breeze. I can see the heat; I can hear it buzzing.

I let my eyes close, let my mind drift away and into nothingness. I feel myself running north—

"You lied to me."

My eyes open, and my stomach muscles draw my spine straight. He moves into my field of vision, but he doesn't sit and he doesn't smile. His right fist hangs at eye level in front of me, and I see purple scabs beginning to form over nickel-sized wounds.

"Wren…"

"You told me you didn't know who it was." His voice is

tight, and his eyes are hard. "Again and again, you swore you didn't see."

"Yeah, okay, I get it," I say. "I lied. Can we drop it?" I don't want to fight with him. But I don't feel bad for lying.

He crouches in front of me, and we are separated by only inches. "That's it? That's all you have to say?"

I exhale. "I didn't tell you the truth so you wouldn't do exactly what you did. Is he even still alive?"

"Who gives a shit?" he growls. "Since when does someone like *you* give a shit about someone like Landry, after what he did? Since when does someone like you protect her attackers like a—"

"I wasn't trying to protect them," I say, and my voice is loud, but it wavers. It isn't strong right now. My eyes cast down. "I wasn't trying to protect *them*."

"So what was it?"

My gaze skirts around him, to the blowing leaves. To the mounds of ragged rock in the distance that glint majestically in the sunlight. "I didn't want you to be sent out there."

"Why?" His voice is dismissive. "That's where you want to go."

"Yeah, *I* do, Wren. *I* do. But you don't. So…I guess I was trying to make sure that didn't happen."

His eyes are still hard, but he sits now; his muscles relax. "You don't need to protect me, Eve. Not from anything, and especially not from that."

"What's that supposed to mean?"

"Come on. You know how this shithole compound works by now. Use your head."

I take a deep breath. "You wouldn't be sent out? Even if you killed him. Even if you killed the pair of them. You're a Preme; you wouldn't be punished."

"I'm not just a Preme, Eve. I'm a well-connected one, so

yes, you're right—I wouldn't be sent out there to burn."

I shake my head. How can the rules only apply to some? Injustice pinches my stomach. I glare at him and cross my arms, but even as I do, I know it isn't his fault. "I'm still glad I did what I did," I say after a minute of silence passes between us.

"You're glad you lied to me."

"Yeah, I am. I did the right thing, Wren. Had I told you, I know what you would have done. You would have killed both of them before I could stop it, right? And yes, you wouldn't be punished for it, but you'd become a killer. On my watch. You think I want that?"

He leans forward and drops his voice. His eyes reduce down to slits. "But you're willing to become one yourself? Who've you decided on? Because I just got word that Landry's going to pull through, so he's up for the taking if you decide to pass on Daniel."

I am still. I don't even breathe. "How do you know?"

"If I were you, I'd set my sights on Daniel," he continues. "Landry's already paid for his sins, so it's time to share the fun around, don't you think?"

"Tell me how you know."

"I wasn't born yesterday, Eve. I could see it in your eyes in the cafeteria. I put two and two together, just like you did. So"—he shrugs—"you have a way out. Kill someone, and you get to die yourself. Congratulations."

"Is this why you asked me to meet you? So you could make me feel like crap?"

"Tell me how I'm wrong."

I shrug. "You're not wrong. Aside from the me dying part, that's exactly what I'm going to do."

"Only you're not a murderer."

"How do you know?"

"Because you wouldn't let me kill Landry. Because you're

honorable, because you're good."

After a nervous laugh, I stretch out my hand, curl it around his. "You're overestimating my goodness. I need to go, and nothing is going to stand in my way. Especially not ending a life that doesn't deserve to live."

"I could make things better for you, you know. Here, in Compound Eleven. A job, for instance. I could get you a job on one of the higher floors. And goods, anything you need."

"Goods?"

"Premes don't receive allotments like downstairs. If we need anything, if we want anything, it's ours. I can make it yours."

I stare at him.

"And I could get rid of both of them," he continues. "Daniel and Landry. Their friend, too. And anyone else who bothers you."

I resist the urge to shiver at his words. At his influence, his *power*. Instead I turn his hand over and run my fingers along the damaged skin. "You would do all that for me?"

"To get you to stay? I would do anything."

I blink back a million tears that threaten to burst their way into the world. I blink them back and away because I need to stay strong.

"I've already decided. There's no going back on it. Not now, not ever."

He leans forward and kisses me on the lips, and part of me aches to stay with him. To never let him go. The thought of saying a final goodbye is almost too much for me to bear. Almost.

He pulls away and sighs. "I just wish I met you before you made up your mind."

Suddenly, I wish that, too.

A moment later, he gives me a funny look. "Did I hear

you say that you don't plan on dying out there?"

"Not so much."

"Care to elaborate?"

I laugh a little. My mother's song echoes through my head. But all I say is, "You know by now I'm a survivor. Ask a different question."

He grins. Then a loud hum from the middle of the Oracle draws both our attention, and when I glance at him, I see he is already jumping to his feet.

"We have to go *now*."

The elevator. And since it only runs from the fifth floor, we have seconds before we are spotted. He grabs my hand and pulls me through the sunlit space in the direction of the trapdoor.

The elevator clicks into position, and I hear the doors slide open.

"Space is the issue," comes a woman's voice, and I recognize it as Wren's mother's.

"Is it, Cynthia? It sounds to me like we have much bigger issues on our hands than space alone."

"If the solution is another fleet of panels," she snaps, and I hear the clicking of her high heels, "then space is indeed the first issue we must tackle."

"Jump," Wren growls in my ear.

I do as he says and collapse a second later on the floor below. It knocks the wind from me, and I can't breathe; I can only watch as he silently pulls the door shut, then jumps from the top of the ladder next to me. He lands more gracefully than I did and moves quickly to the edge of the room, where he snaps off the lights. "We have to go," he says through the darkness.

He grabs me under the shoulders and pulls me easily toward the door; then, I hear the trapdoor open, and light pierces the small space. I draw my boots quickly to my chest and away from the center of the room. We are frozen, neither of us so much as breathing.

"See anything?"

There is a heavy pause, and then...

"Nothing. Must've been the wind." The trapdoor slams shut, and we are in blackness once more.

"You okay?" His voice sounds stern, and as I catch my breath, a bubble of laughter escapes, and then another. Finally, I can't hold it in any longer and I must press my hand to my mouth to try to silence it. My shoulders shake, and my stomach hurts from the effort.

"Come on," he says finally, and I can hear in his voice that he has been laughing as well. He lifts me with too much ease into the hallway, where the walls glow white around us.

There is blood on my shirt, I notice, and I see that Wren's knuckles have come apart. I take his hand in mine, my brow knotting as I examine it.

"Really, Eve?"

"What? I don't want you injured on my account."

He shakes his head. "Do you remember when we first met? I merely mentioned the fact that your knuckles were bleeding, and you chastised me for it."

"What, whether you'd ever seen blood before? It was a simple question. There was no chastising involved." I nudge him in the ribs, our hands still entwined. His hand bleeds onto mine, but I don't care.

He nudges me back as we walk, and I am laughing again. Then I realize I don't know where we are or where we're going. I turn to him. "I'm not exactly allowed to roam free up here, you realize."

"Relax, Eve. You're with me."

So I *do* relax, because in this moment I am happy. I am

happy to have him by my side. I am happy that Landry didn't die—that Wren didn't become a murderer on my behalf. And I'm happy we made it safely from the Oracle.

"I can't believe we almost got caught."

"Yeah, and by my lovely mother, of all people. God, part of me wishes we didn't run, just so I could see the look on her face."

We turn onto a busier corridor, and automatically I pull my hand from Wren's and jam it into my pocket. Second nature. A moment later, my eyes latch onto two people: one thick with the build of a fighter, the other Addison.

She is staring at me, and by the look on her face, I'm willing to bet she saw his hand in mine, or how close we were walking, or maybe the way we were smiling. I know it shouldn't make me happy, but it does.

"Haven't seen you on many of the tours," says the thick boy to Wren, and he shoves his hands into his trousers and pushes his head back so that he stares down his nose. He doesn't smile. "Eyeing your mother's office, then?"

"Like I told Addison, I'm not interested in my mother's office."

As Wren talks, I look more closely at his ex-girlfriend. I stare at freshly brushed red hair that reaches to her elbows, and I wonder, aside from her looks, what it was that he saw in her. Maybe it was how composed she is. Competent. Because even though I wish it wasn't true, she appears to be both those things. The revelation makes me scowl.

"Not paving the way for your friend Long, I hope?"

"What's that supposed to mean?" Wren's eyes narrow.

"You know exactly what it means," the boy snaps. "When are you going to stop dragging him alongside you?" His cold eyes sweep over me, and it looks like he is going to say something more, but he bites his tongue. Whoever he is, he knows not to anger Wren.

Addison, however, clicks her tongue. "Wren," she interrupts. "Can I see you for a moment?" She nods in the opposite direction.

"No," Wren replies without hesitation. He turns back to the boy, and my eyes meet hers. She reduces hers down to slits, and they drop to my boots with disdain. Lower-Mean disdain. Half my mouth curls into a smirk. For I might hail from a lower floor, but I am thick with strength, and suddenly I wouldn't have it any other way.

"Try not to worry yourself over him, Strike," Wren is saying. "After all, he only stole your girlfriend that one time."

For a second, I think Strike might attack, because his face turns red. But finally his feet draw him away. "Let's go, Addie," he says over his shoulder.

But she stays behind. "What exactly do you think you're doing?" she says to Wren, and though her gaze doesn't shift from his, I can tell she is talking about me. I can see the longing in her eyes, or maybe it's just my imagination. Then she smooths her skirt like she is agitated. "Are you trying to punish me?"

He shakes his head. "I'm just living my life. Something you should do, too."

She holds his gaze for a second more, then follows after Strike, her eyes cutting through me as she goes.

His face is emotionless. "Shall we?"

He is already walking, and I have to hurry to catch up. "What was that all about?"

"The fifth floor has more hierarchy than the rest of the compound combined. My friend Long happens to fall low on the ladder. That means his every move is scrutinized by assholes like Strike, who are scared shitless of getting grabbed around the ankle."

It isn't what I meant, but I nod anyway. "Where do you fall?" I think I know the answer.

"My mother's office is a powerful one," he says.

The admission, though expected, makes my skin prickle. Sure, my blanket hatred for all Premes has proven to be misguided. Amiss. But my hatred for *powerful* Premes, the ones who run this compound, is perfectly warranted.

He is not his mother's son, I remind myself. They are different people. They *despise* each other.

"How come you're not interested in it?" I ask casually.

He shrugs. "Politics isn't for me."

"Because...?"

"Because bullshitting and small talk are two things I'd rather not do."

"Fair enough." I couldn't picture Wren doing either of those things, even if I tried. It is one of the reasons I like him. "So what's Long's story? How do you fall low in the Preme hierarchy?"

"He's what they call illegitimate." He turns his head to look at me. "His mother is a Preme. His father is an Upper Mean. Long is the product of their brief tryst."

We walk in silence as his words settle on my brain. They don't surprise me, but still they sting. It is another reminder that Premes and Means are not meant to mix.

"You weren't asking about Long, though, were you?" he says eventually.

"No. I was asking about Addison."

He turns onto a quiet corridor. One side is walled in glass, and through the glass I spot a series of large tables with red felt lining the top. Pool tables, I think they are called, though I have never seen one. But I remember hearing that the Premes play pool. It is more civilized, I suppose, than fighting for sport.

"Well then," he says, "your guess is as good as mine."

"Mmm."

"What?"

"Nothing."

He glances at me over his shoulder. "What are you thinking?"

"I'm thinking who cares about Daniel. Maybe I'll take her out instead."

Wren's eyes narrow, but he can't stop the smile from spreading across his face. "Jealous, Eve?"

"Not at all. Just think maybe the compound would benefit as a whole without her."

"Uh-huh. There's the Eve I know. If you're not threatening my mother—to her face, I might add—you're thinking about offing my ex. Very interesting."

I punch him. "Funny. You said the same thing, more or less, about offing Daniel and Landry."

"Mine's serious," he says and punches me back.

"Mine is, too," I start, but his hands are wrapping around me, shaking me, and I am laughing, and he is, too. His lips are on mine, and I don't care that we're in the middle of a Preme hallway under lights so bright they burn my eyes. My hands curl around his waist, and I kiss him, I kiss him, I kiss him.

"We're not far, you know," he says between breaths, and his voice is low and rumbly. It lights a fire in my belly.

"From?"

"My place."

I smile a little. "Let's go."

"The lighting is much better in here," I say as soon as we slip inside his apartment.

"I thought you liked it bright."

"I'm starting to come around on this dim stuff."

"Why's that?"

"Because it's a little less embarrassing to do this." My hands grip the bottom of my shirt and pull it over my head.

Wren freezes as he stares at me.

"I was thinking, last time we made out, it really wasn't fair at all that I got to keep my clothes on."

He presses his mouth together, and his eyes flash. "Precisely my thinking." And then his hand grabs mine, and he is pulling me in the direction of the bedroom, and I am laughing uncontrollably the whole way.

"And for the record," he says into my ear as we collapse into bed, "don't use the word 'embarrassing' in relation to your body ever again. Are we clear?"

My lips find his; my hands run along his back and under his shirt. "Mm-hmm," I manage to say before his clean, masculine smell overwhelms me. He pulls himself away, but it is only so he can rip his shirt off, and then his skin is against mine, and nothing has ever felt so warm and perfect, and I feel alive in a way I have never really experienced. My heart pushes against my breastbone. Every cell in my body feels electrified.

"God you're perfect," he grumbles as he kisses me. I rope my fingers around his neck as his run through my hair, and I feel like I am consuming him and he is consuming me and it is manic and wild and free.

When his lips reach my collarbone, I shiver.

"Everything okay, Eve?"

"No complaints."

His hands trace their way down my back, and then his fingertips curl around my waist and graze my stomach. Instantly, my muscles tense up; I stiffen. I hope that he doesn't notice, but he eyes me. Then sighs. "They touched you."

"It's okay. Come on, it's okay." I push my mouth toward

his, but he shakes his head.

"It's too soon."

"It was days ago."

"Exactly. *Days*. I don't want you to be reminded of that. *I* don't want to be reminded of that." He frowns. "I should've finished Landry when I had the chance."

I smile into his chest and pull him close. "Um, Wren? Even when I *am* over it, there's a very good chance I'm going to get, you know. Nervous."

"When we…?"

"Yep." I am thankful that the lights are dim; he can't see how deeply I blush.

"Mmm," he growls in my ear. "Good point." He holds me tight in his arms and kisses my forehead, and there is that feeling again. That I never want him to let me go. But it doesn't make sense, because all I've ever wanted is just the opposite. Freedom.

And that is what I will get when I make it aboveground. That is what I will get when I kill a person. A hard pit forms in my stomach at the thought, and for a second I forget Wren lies against me, our hearts beating in rhythm. All I can think about is how soul-destroying it must be to take the light from someone's eyes, no matter how dark those snake eyes may be. All I can think about is that I might not have the stomach for it. And so I might not ever escape Compound Eleven after all. I might have to stay here, in Wren's arms, forever.

CHAPTER THIRTY

The next day, murder doesn't seem so difficult to comprehend. My eyes watch Daniel, and as they do, his flit to mine. When they lock into position, I see them sparkle with dark laughter, laughter that is sinister, that is full of ill intent. We are on opposite sides of the cafeteria, but still I can see them shine. Still I can spot their wickedness.

"Is everything okay, Eve?"

I look at Hunter and nod. "Daniel's over there. That's all."

"Too bad Wren isn't here," says Maggie as she cranes her neck to see.

"I don't need Wren to defend me," I insist, and my voice is sharp. Maybe I'm afraid that I do.

"Okay," she says slowly. "Well, that wasn't what I meant." She sighs. "So, is everyone getting excited for tomorrow night?" Her voice is strained with effort. Normally, it is light and airy, but lately it has been heavy, bogged down with reality. "We could all use a fun night," she adds.

Hunter gives her one of his shy smiles. "How come ever since school finished, life's been…"

"Shit?"

He adjusts his glasses and frowns. "Not shit. Just…tough."

"Hopefully it isn't a sign of what's to come," mutters Emerald. "You know, in the real world. On our own."

"We've had a run of bad luck, that's all," I say, and I sit straighter. "And if we let it get us down, they win. The Daniels and Kyles and Anitas of the world win."

"Wow, Eve," says Hunter. "I think that's the most positive thing I've heard you say in ages. No wait, eons. Literal eons." His eyes comb the ceiling like he is counting, and he nods. "Eons."

I kick him under the table. "Very funny."

"What's going on with you lately?" Hunter continues. "You're hardly ever around."

Maggie's eyes snap to mine, and I look sideways. I feel Emerald glance at me, too. Both of them know; they know where I've been. With Wren. And if I am being more positive lately, it probably has something to do with him, too. I think of kissing him, of the feeling of his arms wrapped around me, skin to skin, and I smile.

"Hello?" Hunter calls. He waves a hand in front of my face. "You're grinning like a fool. I think you need to take a hiatus from the Bowl before you do any permanent damage."

I kick him again, harder this time. Both of us are laughing. "Maybe I'm looking forward to letting loose tomorrow night after all."

"Know what I'm thinking, Eve?" asks Maggie. Her lime green eyes twinkle.

"Don't say it."

"Makeover!"

I roll my eyes. "I told you not to say it. What happened last time?"

Half of Emerald's mouth twitches into a smile. "Oh yeah,

I remember. You looked like a poodle."

"She looked fantastic," Maggie protests. "But okay, fine. I won't touch your hair. I'm just thinking a little makeup. That's it."

"It's not a bad idea, Eve," says Emerald. She winks. "I've seen you attempt it, and you really could use a few pointers."

I shove her.

"She doesn't need makeup," says Hunter between bites. "She looks amazing just like that."

I stare at him, but before I can respond, I am shoved from behind, and the cafeteria table digs into my sternum. I swing my legs around, but Daniel's hand lands on my chest, collecting the fabric of my shirt and forcing me to stay seated.

It reminds me of that night—his face alone reminds me of that night, but for him to grab me...

"Looks like your face has healed up okay, Eve. Too bad."

"Get out of here," Hunter says sharply from the other side of the table. Emerald jumps to her feet, but I hold up a hand to stop her. This is something I need to deal with on my own.

"What do you want, Daniel?" I whisper.

"Here's the thing. What your bodyguard did to my best friend is something I take personally—*very* personally. Do you understand?"

"Take it up with him, then. I'm sure he'd love to chat."

He shrugs. "I'd rather hit him where it really hurts, and I think I'm looking at just that." He sneers. "Why he cares about the likes of you, I can only guess, but no doubt your Lower Mean charm will wear on him soon enough. In the meantime, consider yourself warned." He bends down so we are eye to eye. "*I'm coming for you.*"

Then he is gone, and I am left with my heart thudding through to my feet. Whatever clout I had with Daniel has evaporated. I don't know if it was Wren fighting my fights for me that did it, or the attack itself. But if Daniel was ever intimidated by me, he is no longer. I'm a walking target.

I can't be a walking target.

"I'll see you guys later," I say.

"Eve—" starts Maggie, but I shake my head.

"I'll see you guys later," I repeat, and my voice is firm. Hunter and Emerald eye each other, but already I am gone. I follow Daniel out of the cafeteria in time to see him board the elevator, and then I head for the stairs. Moving over steps that witnessed my own slice of hell makes my palms slick, but I push on. Determination and anger are my guide, and I step onto the fourth floor at the same time he does. The hallways are crowded, and he doesn't see me.

I wait until he is half a hallway ahead, and then I follow. This time I am the cat and he is the mouse. Wren may have gotten revenge on Landry, but Daniel's blood is all for me. It is time he paid for his sins. It is time I see whether I have the stomach to kill.

I think I do.

He turns down a hallway that is quieter than the first. Still, there are too many people about, and the next hallway is the same. The one after that, though, is perfect. It is dead empty, and one of the lights is missing its fancy Upper Mean case. That means the bulb is glaring and uncomfortable. Bright. So I will be able to see his anguish in detail.

My heart doesn't thud anymore; it hammers with excitement. I jump on the balls of my feet, and I feel like I do in the Bowl. I haven't worked out much since the attack, so my muscles are fresh; they are looking for an excuse to engage. And I am not injured anymore, or tired, either. I've always thought I could beat Daniel, and now I will see. He is larger than me and in decent shape, but he doesn't have experience fighting.

I stare at the back of his head, at the brown curly hair cut short. It would be almost cute, that hair, if it didn't encase pure evil. It's strange; neither he nor Landry looks particularly troubling. But scratch beneath the surface, and their veins run black. I am about to find out just how much.

Right now I could do one of two things. I could run up behind him and attack, or I could call his name, make it a fair fight.

I am the kind of person who is fair, but he isn't. He wouldn't extend me that courtesy, and so I won't for him. I smile, and then my leg muscles twitch and I am sprinting as fast as I can, and by the time he hears me and turns his head, I'm on top of him. I knock him to the ground and punch him three times in a row, three quick bursts of rage that loosen his eye sockets. He is awake now, and he pushes me back with considerable force. His eyes streak red; the fight is on.

His first punch, I block, but the second I am not so lucky. I land in a heap on the floor. Normally I would jump to my feet again, but not this time. No, this time my fingers stretch into the lip of my boot, where they brush cool metal. Daniel is moving toward me, and my fingers plunge deeper, snatch the knife, tuck it into my fist.

"I hate dirty little bitches like you who don't know their place," he says under his breath, and I let him drag me to my feet. I let him shove me into the wall. I wasn't planning on killing him today. I just wanted to see if I could. But the more vitriol he spews, the more I begin to think that now is the time.

"So what, Daniel?" I say, and my voice is remarkably calm. "What, you think you're going to be the one who finally puts me in my place? Is that it?"

"Yeah, something like that"—and he releases me, then shoves me against the wall with all his force. The impact stuns me, and it burns the back of my skull, but only for a moment.

I kick him between the legs, and he doubles over in pain, into a position of weakness.

I knock him quickly to the ground, and my fist unclenches. The knife is warmed through from my palm, and the blade springs open. His eyes find it; they widen. The hate that lurked there a second earlier is replaced by fear.

"What are you doing?"

"What do you think I'm doing? I'm getting even. For when you tried to kill me!" Tears burn behind my eyes, and my breathing is ragged. Below me, he struggles to free himself, to push me off him, and if I'm not quick, he will. My fingers are deft, and they shove the blade to the side of my fist, and I punch him across the face. The blade slices into his skin as I do.

He screams.

His warm blood is everywhere, and panic overtakes his senses. But that was just a taste of what is to come…

I must act quickly. I must kill him now, or he will get me off him and he will be gone. I *must* act now.

My pulse races, and all I see is red.

I am a monster, and I am cruel, and I can't wait to see the light leave his snake eyes forever, a small payment for all his sins. I am a killer.

But more than anything else, I am a liar.

CHAPTER THIRTY-ONE

Every step I take hurts more than the last. Not my legs, not my arms—nothing physical. It is inside where it aches, and I can't think of a worse feeling. It is less painful to be black and blue and filled with broken bones. Now I am filled with despair, and everywhere I look is darkness.

It was bad enough when my first plan to escape came to a crashing end. And then along came another, fortuitously dropped into my lap as if sent from the heavens. But I had my opportunity yesterday to kill Daniel, and I couldn't do it. And if I can't kill him, of all people, I can't kill anybody. Not Landry, not Kyle, not the guard. I am not a murderer, not a monster, and that means my fate is sealed.

I will never feel fresh air; I will never have freedom. I will never have a shot at finding Jack. Instead, I will spend my life serving those responsible for exiling him to a likely death.

I should probably go back to my cell now. Maggie and the others are excited for the party; maybe it would cheer me up to spend the day with them. The past two hours have been spent walking the Lower Mean corridors mindlessly, and my feet are beginning to ache from the concrete floors. I wonder what it would feel like to walk on top of the earth. The grass, the soil. What does that feel like underfoot?

Jack experienced it; I hope he still does. I will never know.

Just thinking it makes a sob choke my throat.

I walk faster.

The doors around me are more frequent now, and I can hear children playing; I must be near the family cells. My feet move of their own accord, and soon I find myself knocking on a door I know well. The dent along the bottom, the scuff marks near the keyhole, the fingerprints around the handle are intimate details, ones that are forever imprinted on my soul. Any day now, my parents will be moved to a smaller cell, and these little details will become imprinted on someone else.

My father opens the door, and his eyebrows inch up when he sees me. No smile, not even any pleasantries.

"What are you doing here?" he demands. I shrug, and my eyes comb the space for my mother. In the corner, and my heart sinks as I look at her. Embroidery sits on her lap, and her gaze doesn't lift to see me. Her expression is placid, her eyes empty. She mutters *tick-tock* under her breath.

Gone once more.

I want to scream at her. I want to tell her to stop being selfish, tell her that *I* still exist and I need her right now. But I can't do that. I am soft and weak and good, and I hate myself for it.

My father clears his throat. "I've been checking the schedule. Care to explain what's going on?"

At first I have no idea what he is talking about, but then I realize he is referring to the Bowl. I haven't had a fight lately; I haven't signed up for any, either. "Nothing's going on."

"This doesn't have anything to do with Bruno, does it?"

"What, the fact that he *died* in the ring? You do realize

most parents wouldn't want their kid fighting after something like that, right?"

He gazes at me calmly, and it makes anger burn my insides. "It was a fluke, Eve, nothing more. Don't throw away everything you have worked toward because of a fluke."

"Actually, it's everything *you* have worked toward. I just went along with it, remember? Because prize fighters get tons of allotments, right? Enough for me *and* you."

He crosses his arms and stands taller. "What exactly are you saying? That I've been using you? That you don't enjoy fighting?"

"I hate it!" I scream at him. The words erupt from my belly. On the other side of the cell, my mother doesn't flinch; I'm not sure she even hears. "I've always hated it, and you know what? I hate *you* for making me do it!" I stalk out of the room and slam the door as hard as I can. Now my legs move quickly; my brain races. Maybe he didn't deserve that. Maybe he did.

Maybe it doesn't matter, because soon I will be gone.

After all, I didn't always plan on going aboveground, oh no. Before I broke into the Oracle, I knew only that I was finished with Compound Eleven, and that is something I can still make happen.

I can go to another compound, just like I planned.

Except I have never discovered where the tunnels are that lead to Compound Ten or to Compound Twelve, not on the many miles I've covered over the past sixteen years on the Mean floors. That means they probably run from the ground floor or the Preme floor, then.

Think, Eve.

My feet carry me to the nearest stairwell, and I turn down it. It makes more sense for them to run tunnels deep below the earth. Building a tunnel right below ground level would be unwise. It could cave in too easily; the poisonous sunlight could infiltrate it.

The first floor is more dangerous than the rest of the compound combined, but I don't care. My feet are moving too quickly for that to be a concern, and besides, right now the toxic ache in my stomach is lifting. Right now, I have a purpose.

I have never been down this far before—only to work the Denominators' food line from the feeding dock off the second floor. Nobody comes here if they don't strictly have to. It is dark, darker than the Lower Mean floor, and eventually I stop running, pull out my flashlight, even though it is doubtful the Noms carry one. I am marking myself a trespasser from a higher floor, even from a distance. Not wise.

Then I notice something: my feet hurt less down here. When I bend over and slide my hand over the ground, I know why. Dirt. Hard-packed dirt. I crouch to examine it, press my palm against it. Cold and unyielding. I breathe deeply, and it smells of must, a smell that I instantly like. I may never know what the top of the earth feels like, but at least now I know what *part* of it feels like.

After a while, I continue walking, senselessly stumbling on, always remembering my way back. I may be foolhardy and reckless, but I am not careless. Around me, the corridors are empty, silent, the Noms seemingly elsewhere. Perhaps it is getting close to their feeding, and I wonder who will be feeding them today. Certainly not my mother.

Eventually, though, I decide to change tactics. I turn my flashlight off and take a steadying breath. It isn't completely black—in every corner, there is a lone bulb encased in wire—but still it takes a few moments before I can see my way. I begin knocking on doors, trying to find someone who can point me in the right direction. When finally someone answers I blurt out, "I need a guard!" because a door out of this compound and to another is an important one. One so important it must be guarded. The woman stares at me coldly—she can probably tell I'm from upstairs—then points along the corridor.

"Two sharp rights," she mutters before she disappears.

Two turns later, I am still. In front of me stands a guard, his back against the wall, his gloved hands crossed over his chest. I can see a gun in his holster. He looks bored, but then he notices me standing there and straightens. He isn't a guard I recognize, and that is a good thing, considering my history.

This one is tall and lanky, not young. He isn't as malicious-looking as most of the other guards, and that is maybe a blessing, maybe a shame. Because I may need to force my way by this man, and that would mean violence. It is the only currency I know.

For now, though…for now, I just need to discover if the locked door next to him is the one I am after.

His eyes narrow as we stare at each other. "Something you want?" he finally asks.

"Is this your usual post?" I am feeling bold.

He leans against the wall again and swings one boot over another. "It's my usual post. Who's asking?"

"I've heard it's quite a hike to the other compounds," I say as I nod at the door. Then I hold my breath.

He hesitates, but barely. "Doesn't mean it's not doable."

Something moves through my veins. Maybe it is relief or excitement. Maybe, even, it is dread. Whatever it is, this is the spot. *This* is the door that links to a new life. "I'm curious—do Ten and Twelve both run from here?"

"Just Ten."

I nod. "You trying to keep our compound in or Ten out?"

"Both. I didn't catch your name." His cheeks are gaunt,

hollow like the Noms', though of course Noms don't become guards. Jobs aren't available to them at all.

I lift my chin. "Eve."

"You don't look like you belong down here."

"I'm from a floor up." I hold out my hands as proof.

"And why are you so interested in this, Eve?"

I shrug. "I'm supposed to pick a job soon."

"And you're interested in becoming a guard?"

I shrug again. "Not so much," I admit. He wouldn't think I could get such a job anyhow. "The tunnels interest me, though."

"The tunnels." He stares at me, waiting.

"Maintenance, construction, that sort of thing," I add. My eyes linger on the door, on the keypad. "I missed the job tour. Any chance you could open it up for me? Just so I could have a look?"

He smirks. "Afraid not."

"Where does the tunnel to Twelve run?"

"Not from down here."

"So, where?"

"You ask a lot of questions."

"Fifth floor?"

"I think you should go now."

"But—"

"I said," he interrupts, "I think you should go now." He leans his weight forward so he is standing upright.

Automatically, I am wary; I am ready to run. My boots shuffle backward.

"Denominators will be done feeding soon," he continues, "and these halls will choke up. You should go before they do."

For a moment, I just stare at him. I can't tell if he is being kind—kindness is a foreign concept here in Compound Eleven, and so recognizing it is difficult. Recognizing it from a guard even more so. After another moment's hesitation, I nod briefly, then walk away, back in the direction from which I came.

If I want to, I could get by him, that guard. I could guess the passcode. I could go through the tunnel, see what Compound Ten has in store. That was my plan, initially. To try another compound. The only difference between now and then is that I have seen aboveground and know that another compound isn't the answer.

No, that isn't quite true. There is another difference, too. Wren.

He shouldn't change anything, but he does. He changes everything. Then the toe of my boot stubs on the compact dirt underfoot, and I fall to my knees. Grit wedges into the lines of my palms, and I swear into silence.

Slowly, I stand and give myself a shake. Things with Wren have no future, not here. Illegitimate Long is one of a million examples. Wren is a Preme, and I am a Lower Mean, and we don't belong together. It's that simple.

If he changes things, it is only because I am forgetting that one simple fact.

CHAPTER THIRTY-TWO

Later, I open my cell door to a well-dressed yet somber-looking Maggie. "It's time," she says flatly. She wears a thin black headband and a short green dress with tights. A bag is slung over her shoulder.

"Time," I repeat.

Her fist opens to reveal a tube of mascara, and I roll my eyes. She laughs as she pushes her way past me. Emerald is close behind, but her face is stern. I don't think I have seen her look any other way since Bruno's passing. She wears a blue sweater—dressy by her standards—and slacks.

"Hunter's going to meet us there," Maggie says as she places the bag on my desk.

"Why? We always go together."

"He's meeting up with some of the kitchen crew. They're, like, his new best friends." She sighs. "Just another reminder of how I'm supposed to make this huge, life-altering decision soon. In case you're wondering, I still have no clue what to do, even though everyone else seems to have made up their mind."

"Everyone?" says Emerald. She kicks off her shoes and

sits heavily on my bed. "I haven't. I have no clue what to do."

I clear my throat. Making *huge, life-altering decisions* is the last thing I want to talk about right now. "Is Kyle still staying away?" I ask Maggie instead.

"So far, so good," she replies. But she looks suddenly glum, and I regret bringing it up. "It's hard, though. Every day is hard, kind of."

"What do you mean?"

Her lime green eyes sweep to the side. "Breakups suck, right? Even if he is scum. And things ended so quickly, it almost feels like... I don't know."

"Like?"

"Like it didn't really happen. Maybe I just want closure or something. Is that wrong?"

"Is it wrong?" I force myself to grin. "Well, it definitely *sounds* wrong."

"Speaking of breakups," says Emerald, "is anything new going on with Hunter and Anita?"

"That ship has sailed—she has a new boyfriend and everything. He's totally over it, though. I have a feeling he was never that invested anyways." She pulls a full bottle of liquor out of her bag and screws off the lid. "Bottoms up, ladies—Dad hasn't been using his allotment lately, so drinks are on me." She winks, takes a gulp, then looks me up and down. "You're not ready, I see."

I look in the mirror and see a tired face, hair drawn into a low ponytail. I shrug. "It's just a party."

"Eve." She crosses her arms. "Your shirt has a hole in it."

After a quick inspection, I see that she is right. I see, too, that the hem is beginning to fray.

"And you haven't brushed your hair today. That's what it looked like last night."

I finger it silently. Emerald stares at me.

"Are you sure everything's okay?"

I don't want to lie, but of course I do. "Everything's fine. I'll change; I promise. And want to know something seriously wild? I'll even *brush my hair*."

Her brow relaxes, and she laughs. One leg crosses over the other as she leans against the wall. "That's my girl. So, are Wren and Connor meeting us there?"

"As far as I know." Then I fix Maggie with a stare of my own. It has been a long day, and all of a sudden I feel like having some fun. "Connor's cute, don't you think?"

"Wren's cute, too," she says quickly. She presses the bottle into my hand, and I have a sip. It burns my throat, but I don't mind.

"Yeah, I know he is. He's my *boyfriend*." I push her. She looks at Emerald, and Emerald looks at her. And then I understand. "Oh. Right. Wren and I are together. Both of you know, you just don't know each other knows."

"How does *she* know?" shouts Maggie. "And how could you not tell me that you know?" she adds to Emerald, swatting her arm.

"Because I didn't think *you* knew, obviously." A small smile plays on Emerald's lips, finally. "I pieced it together when I caught her going out one night with blush smudged all over her face."

Maggie turns to me with her mouth hanging open. I try to push her again, but she jumps on the bed. "God, I wish I could've seen *that*. I pieced it together after Wren kicked Landry's ass in the cafeteria."

"Damn, I knew *way* before that, girl."

Maggie shakes her head, mouth open, and Emerald laughs. I raise my hands: "Okay, you guys. Very funny. Listen, Hunter doesn't know, so whatever you do, don't mention it in front of him."

"Probably a good idea," mumbles Maggie. Beside her, Emerald's smile has disappeared. She runs her hands over her face and groans.

I pause—I had been about to ask Maggie what she meant, but now I turn to Emerald. "What's up?"

"Nothing. Everything. It's just that every time I start to have fun or think of anything else—bam. There it is. His face." She shakes her head and frowns.

Maggie and I exchange a look. Suddenly, I have a thought. "Emerald, you and Bruno weren't…were you?"

She stares at me. "Oh God," she says. "No. No—definitely, *definitely* not." Her eyes slide sideways, and it strikes me that I am not the only one with secrets.

I lower my voice. "It's just that… I mean, I've been struggling too, obviously, but…he's not the first friend we've lost."

"I know that, okay? It isn't that. I mean, part of it is."

"And the rest?"

"I love fighting, Eve. I know you like it well enough and everything, but it's my *life*. It's everything. And now I don't want to step in that ring again. I just don't."

I sit on my heels in front of her. "I get it. So it's a bigger loss than even Bruno."

"I know I'm being a big downer and everything, but—"

"You are not. Here"—I pass her the bottle—"have some. We don't even have to go to the party, if you don't want. But you can't keep dwelling on what happened or you'll never get past it." After doing nothing today but dwelling on my own problems, I am not qualified to give such advice. But Maggie nods encouragingly at my words and so my gaze is steady.

"What do you think I should do about Blue Circuit?" Emerald whispers. Her large brown eyes look torn in half.

"Keep fighting," I say without hesitating. "I wasn't kidding when I said it was just as dangerous out there. You love fighting, so that's what you're going to do, whether as a hobby or professionally. Just give it a bit of time. And stop putting so much pressure on yourself right now to make a job decision. We still have two weeks."

She laughs, and I stare at her dimples. "I wish I could be as laid-back about choosing a job as you."

"Yeah," says Maggie. "Me, too. What's your secret?"

I take another drink from the bottle—a long one—enough to push the onslaught of guilt from my mind. "Let's just try to focus on thoughtless, fun stuff tonight, okay? Nothing heavy, nothing job-related, nothing sad. Deal?"

Emerald sits a little straighter. "Thoughtless stuff only. I think I can do that."

Maggie kneels next to me. "Hold still. Mascara's going on."

"Is this really necessary?"

"Oh, trust me, Eve. When I'm finished with you, Wren won't know what hit him. You are going to drive him mad tonight."

Suddenly, I am laughing, and so is she. So is Emerald. Something resembling contentedness fills my chest, and the thought of Compound Ten recedes backward, just a touch, in my mind.

When we arrive at the Upper Mean playground, it's already thick with bodies. Most people stand between the equipment with bottles in hand, but some actually use it; the teeter-totters are full, and there is a rowdy-looking line-up behind the slide. Shouts of laughter rise from all corners of the room; music, too. Lanterns provide the only light, soft and yielding. I spot Wren quickly, because he is dressed all in black and because he is the first thing my eyes tend to notice. Maybe it is his shape, tall and lean yet thick with muscle. Broad shoulders, rounded forearms. Maybe it is his kind mouth, the one that turns up slightly at the corners, or his wide-set, flashing eyes.

Whatever it is, he notices me staring, and his gaze tightens. Yes, he changes things for me. Definitely.

I push my way through the crowd in his direction, and in this moment, I don't care that he is a Preme or that I am a Lower Mean. After the day I've had, it is all I can do not to wrap my arms around him, to lean on him, to kiss him. Instead, I string my hands together behind my back and nudge him. My gaze lingers on his T-shirt, which carves gently over muscle. I am a little tipsy and hope he won't notice.

"You look different," he says bluntly. His eyes drift over my face, one augmented by Maggie's mascara and lip gloss, and my hair—loose except for a braided headband crafted by Emerald. On Maggie's insistence, I wear a tight pair of jeans. On my own insistence, I wear a plain white top.

"Who, me? That's weird—"

He presses a hand into my back and his mouth to my ear. "You look killer, Eve."

My heart beats quicker. We look at each other, and for a moment I forget the music in my ears, the people surrounding us and pressing into my sides. I forget screaming at my father, and my discovery of Compound Ten's tunnel, and my inability to kill Daniel. I forget all of it because there is something about Wren's eyes that make me feel a paradox I can't explain or even begin to understand. I feel cocooned, safe, but also as though I have all the latitude in the world.

"Killer?" I laugh. "I think you've had too much to drink."

He squints and tilts his head. "Nope," he says finally. "That's not it." Still, his hand rests on my back, and I don't want him to move it. Even though others are sure to see.

"What's she doing here?" I ask as I catch sight of long red hair.

He looks over his shoulder. "Let's see. Maggie told Connor. Connor told Long. Long told everybody. That's pretty much how it goes."

"Did I hear my name?" A hand clamps down on my shoulder, and on Wren's, too. "How are my two favorite lovebirds this fine evening?"

I glance at Wren, who looks at me and shrugs. "He knows, in case you couldn't tell. Connor, too."

"About your forbidden romance?" Long winks. "Yeah, I know."

I try not to smile, but I fail. I know it makes no sense, but I like that Wren told his friends about us. It feels more official, somehow.

"Any of your friends know?" Wren asks as Long sips from a bottle. Laughter swells from the other side of the room.

"As a matter of fact, they do. Emerald and Maggie."

"What about Hunter?"

I make a face. "He just needs a chance to get to know you better."

"Ah. And then he will give me his seal of approval."

"Exactly," I say as I tug at the bottom of his T-shirt. We stare at each other, and I think he wants to kiss me right now as much as I want to kiss him.

"Ugh. You two are disgusting." Long disappears into the crowd, and I laugh. Around us are mostly faces I recognize— Mean faces, from Floors Two, Three and Four. But there are Premes here, too, Long evidently the reason. They pay the Mean crowd around them little attention, and the Mean crowd does the same. Animosity runs deep, and it runs in both directions. But still they are here. Still we share the same space.

A few months ago—before I met Wren—the Premes were

foreign. Evil. Now the younger ones, the ones who dared to descend to the fourth floor tonight, the ones without a track record of iron-fisted, ruthless leadership, seem like more of the same. Now the compound feels smaller.

"I really should report this event to Father's office, you know," comes a voice that I'd rather not hear. "He wouldn't approve of such a security breach." Addison stands so close to Wren that her arm brushes against his.

"It's just a party," Wren says.

"Just a party?" she repeats. "Is that what your mother would say?"

"What my mother has to say is the least of my concerns."

"Wren, you're much too hard on her." She pauses as a Floor Three Mean brushes against her. I can see in her expression that she is put out, but, to her credit, she says nothing about it. "That darling mother of yours," she continues, "always went out of her way to make me feel special during our courtship. That kindness can't be overstated."

"The two of you had more in common than you and I ever did."

"Yes, ambition. A quality you used to prize in me, I might add."

"Before I saw it for what it truly was, perhaps." His voice is calm and indifferent.

"Being?"

He shrugs. "Greed."

"Admit it, Wren," she laughs. "All this Mean nonsense—it's just a way to attack her. At first I thought I was the target, but then I came to my senses. I know you would never hurt me intentionally, not after what we had. But your mother? You've hated her since the day your father died, placing all your bad luck on her shoulders. And now you've found a way to ridicule her in the most public of ways." She wiggles her eyebrows. "Don't forget I know you better than you know yourself."

Wren looks far from amused by the accusation. In fact, he scowls. "The more we speak, Addison, the more I think you've never really known me at all."

"I know you plenty well," she replies with confidence, completely indifferent to his demeanor. "I know you like spicy food and bland food but nothing in between. I know you don't enjoy playing pool because you are fiercely competitive and hate to lose. I know you have a soft spot for knee-high black leather boots—"

"That's *enough*, Addison," Wren snaps.

Maybe he is worried about how I will react. Maybe he thinks I will punch her. It is a wonder that I don't, for that list was intended for my ears. Spicy food, playing pool, knee-high boots... All frivolities unknown to Lower Means like me. These are details I cannot know about Wren. These are details that she can throw in my face.

"Fine," she sighs. "But let me say this. You aren't realizing the toll all this is taking. You also aren't realizing that your rebellion could have lasting repercussions. Serious ones. Look at this room: Premes and Means, socializing? Think of future generations, Wren. And as for me, I won't wait around forever."

"I'm not asking you to," he reminds her. "And if you want to report the party, be my guest. In the meantime, enjoy your evening." Then his hand wraps around my elbow and he is pushing me through the crowd in the direction of the swing set.

Briefly, I wonder, though, if she is right. If I am nothing more to him than a tool for revenge, a way to strike back at his mother. Addison can't be trusted; I know that. But she has known Wren for much longer than I have, and in ways that I can't, in ways that I don't. Intimate ways. Knee-high-black-leather-boot ways.

The thought makes my lips pucker with dissatisfaction.

Maggie and Connor sit side by side on the swings, and behind them, Emerald talks with Erick. She is laughing at something he says, and she looks lighter than she did earlier.

A bottle is wedged into my hand, and the glass feels cold against my skin. "Drink up," instructs Maggie. "Before Connor here drinks all of it." She nudges him in the arm, and they grin.

I have a sip and notice as I do that Wren's eyes slowly sweep the room. I elbow him. "Looking for someone?"

"Just wondering if your good friend Daniel decided to show," he says, his voice vaguely threatening.

Before I can respond, Maggie's head snaps in our direction. "He's not here, but that's only because Eve did something to him yesterday and now she's being super cagey about it."

"Thanks, Maggie," I say with a grimace. "Thanks for sharing."

"No problem!" She winks, then turns back to Connor. I watch as she grabs his swing and pulls it so they bump into each other. Wren, meanwhile, is watching me.

"What'd you do?" he says evenly.

"Nothing."

"Come on, Eve."

"I roughed him up a bit, okay?"

He squints as he eyes me. "No, I don't think that's all you did. Because fighting is a way of life for you down here, remember? You wouldn't be cagey about something like that. What really happened?"

I hesitate, but not for long. There's no sense in hiding it from Wren—not when I have shared so much with him already. I lower my voice so the others can't hear. "He got in my face in the cafeteria. Told me he was coming for me. So I followed him. I waited until he was alone…"

"Yeah?"

I shrug. "I attacked him." My gaze casts down. "With my knife."

He leans forward. His eyes are deadly serious. "Did you...?"

I shake my head. "I slashed him. His face. I didn't kill him."

I think Wren is going to ask why I didn't, but instead he straightens his back and wraps his hands around my head, pulls me to his chest. He already knows why.

His lips brush against my forehead, and we are still.

"Think he'll leave you alone?"

"Now that he knows I carry a knife? Yeah, I'd say so. For now, at least." I close my eyes and see the blade slice apart his skin. I see red, and part of me winces. The rest of me cringes at my weakness. At my inability to kill him. "Can we talk about something else, please?"

"This reminds me of when you were hiding from that guard," he murmurs eventually.

"Yeah. Before we fed the Noms."

"Back when you were still resisting my charms."

"Mmm. Is that what you call it? Could've fooled me..."

He smiles. "In my defense, you weren't all that pleasant yourself. And you did give me some killer bruises, I might add."

"So then why were you trying to charm me?"

His face is suddenly serious, and I feel his rib cage expand and contract under my grasp. "When I saw you upstairs, after you broke into the Oracle, your eyes were so...alive... They were like nothing I'd ever seen before." He pauses, and his gaze finds mine. "Besides, it's kind of hard to get a girl out of your head once she sucker punches you in the face. Never a dull moment with you, Eve."

He kisses my forehead, and I lift my lips to his, and he kisses me there instead. My eyes open once I remember where we are—surrounded by people.

He laughs softly. "Relax, Eve. I don't think you're in any danger with this crowd. Besides, everyone's too drunk to notice, and if I'm wrong, who cares." But even as he speaks the words, I feel someone staring at me. Hunter. It makes my stomach squeeze painfully into itself. When I glance at him, he turns at once back to his kitchen friends.

"Looks like everyone's up to speed," says Wren quietly.

I swallow. "Looks that way."

Before I can digest the look on Hunter's face or the feeling in the pit of my stomach, a bright voice shouts over my shoulder. "I *knew* it!"

I grin at the sound of Jules's voice. "You did not." I pull away from Wren and shove her.

"I totally called it as soon as I saw you guys, didn't I? You remember, right, hottie? By the way, Eve, this"—she points her finger at my face—"is totally doing it for me. You look like a sexed-up warrior princess or something."

"Told you, Eve!" Maggie shouts from the swing. "You need to trust me with this makeover business, okay?"

"Very funny."

"It's no joke," she insists, though she is smiling. "What do you think, Wren? Can you even contain yourself?"

"Hmm. I have notoriously found it difficult to do that around Eve," he says as he pretends to examine me. "Tonight is no exception."

"What about when you beat the shit out of her?"

I turn quickly and see that Hunter stands there, arms folded. He is staring at Wren with a menacing look on his face. "Could you contain yourself then?" he continues.

"Hunter," I begin, but Wren lifts a hand.

"Let him finish."

"What—you're telling her what to do now? Because you wouldn't be the first upper-floor asshole with control issues sniffing around my friends."

"*Hunter*," I say.

Wren, meanwhile, smiles. It doesn't reach his eyes. "An asshole with control issues. Is that what you just called me?" He takes a step closer. Hunter is tall and no weakling, but still, their difference in strength is devastating, and I remember Wren's vengeful words: *I could kill Hunter with my eyes closed.* Wren isn't cruel, but I know he could kill a person, and I know he doesn't like my friend any more than my friend likes him.

"Not just a controlling one," Hunter replies levelly. "An abusive one. One who likes to slap girls around. One who enjoys it."

Wren's body is still—too still—but then he laughs. "You think I'm like that?"

"Tell me how I'm wrong."

"I'd sooner die than lay a finger on Eve outside the Bowl, that's how. And if you want to think I'm an asshole, fine. Go ahead. Better that than a manipulative coward like yourself."

Hunter shakes his head. "She might trust you," he spits, "but I don't."

Wren takes another step closer and dips his head. "That's funny, because I was about to say the same thing to you."

Hunter's face flushes with anger, and then he grabs Wren around the collar. I'm between them in a heartbeat, even before Wren can react. "Cut it out!" I yell as I pull at Hunter's hand. "Both of you, cut it out."

Hunter stares at me, and all at once, the anger in his eyes dies. Something new shoots through them—something bare and unprotected; something that makes me feel bare and unprotected, too. Then he shoves off through the crowd. Wren touches my arm, but I shake my head, and that is when I notice someone I don't want to see.

Kyle.

I spot him before Maggie does. She is distracted, deep in conversation with Connor. The two of them sit so close that their knees touch, and I don't want Kyle to ruin the moment for her. I don't want her to have to think about him ever again.

I start forward through the crowd to head him off, but it's too late. Already he moves quickly in her direction.

I manage to get myself in front of him before he can reach her. "Get out of here," I say loudly in his ear. "You guys are over. She doesn't want anything to do with you."

Kyle's eyes, usually so smug, are filled with heat. He glares at me. "Let's hear it from her own mouth."

I am about to refuse—I made her a promise, after all— but then I hear her voice from over my shoulder, and even through an abundance of alcohol it is perfectly clear. "She's right, Kyle. I told you we were through. I told you to leave me alone."

"Come on, Maggie. It was just a fight—and don't think an Upper Mean's going to get down on their knees and grovel. I've given you some space. Now it's time to move on."

"I have moved on." Her voice is calm. "Just not with you."

Kyle's eyes dart around her and land on Connor. They shine with anger.

Maggie shakes her head. "Not with him, either. Not with anyone. I've moved on by myself, for myself. You and I are through."

"Don't do this to me, Maggie."

She inhales at his words, and her voice shakes. "You crossed a line many, many months ago. Maybe it was my fault for staying, but I don't think so. All I know is that *I* am not doing anything to *you*."

He starts toward her, but I place a hand on his chest. "Don't even think about it," I say. "She's made herself perfectly clear."

"Get your disgusting, Lower Mean hand—"

I punch him in the mouth, a single shot, one that draws blood from a slit in his lip. It isn't quite the ass-kicking that Bruno had hoped for, but still it is enough to distract him from Maggie.

He dabs at the blood, and then his eyes harden into beads. He readies himself to punch me back...but his gaze lands on something over my shoulder, and he goes still.

"I dare you," Wren quietly taunts from behind me.

Kyle looks one last time at Maggie, then turns, his shoulders squared against the crowd that he pushes through. When he's gone, I grab Maggie by the hand. "Are you okay?"

"Me?" she laughs. "You've got a mean right hook, you know that? Maybe you could teach me a thing or two."

"Next time we're at the Bowl," I agree. But a knot forms in my stomach. If I go, I can't do that. If I go, I can't do a lot of things. I feel Wren, still close, and push my fingers through his. I turn, pull him tight to my body. "Thanks for having my back," I whisper.

"Mm. Like I said—never a dull moment with you, Eve."

CHAPTER THIRTY-THREE

I butter my piece of toast and spread jam on top of that, the way my mother used to prepare it for me when I was young. Across the table, Maggie chats loudly with the others. She has been chipper since the party, much like her old self. Maybe it was standing up to Kyle, maybe it was spending time with Connor, maybe it was both.

I have been in a good mood, too. I shouldn't be. There are now less than two weeks until I am expected to pick a job, to leap into adulthood while trapped in Eleven, to dedicate my life to serving the compound and its commander. And with every strike of the clock, it becomes less and less likely that I will taste true freedom, that I will reach that famed oasis — or Jack. That leaves the tunnels, the ones to other compounds. A dangerous journey, and one with a question mark waiting at its end. So I'm not sure why I'm in such a good mood, frankly.

Maybe it's the fact that my friends know about Wren — even Hunter, which means one less secret standing between us. Or maybe it's that Addison also happened to spot Wren and me holding hands at the end of the party… I smile over my toast as I think about it.

"Let's go to the Bowl," I say suddenly. I push the rest of the toast into my mouth and look at them. "It'll be fun. I can show you how to throw a punch," I add to Maggie.

"Right now? I just woke up!"

"So? We're finished eating, and besides, we've got nothing else going on this morning. There are no job tours today, right?"

Maggie shrugs. "I guess we could…"

"It'll be fun," I say again.

Emerald clears her throat. "I've been kind of avoiding that place since, you know…"

"All the more reason we should go. Come on, we never do anything besides sit around here and mope about stuff."

They stare at me.

"Okay, that's not *all* we do. But seriously, it'll be fun. Now, how many times are you going to make me say that?" I stand, and—slowly, reluctantly—they stand, too.

I lead them out of the cafeteria, excited about the prospect of spending the morning with my friends like old times, teaching Maggie how to fight. The thick Mean crowds that clot the hallway can't even dampen my spirits.

Then I hear my name shouted from over my shoulder—or at least I think it's mine. The noise of the people swallows it immediately up, so after a cursory glance around, I walk on. But my arm is grabbed, and my right fist clenches just as it always does when I am surprised. Just as it should in Compound Eleven.

Wren, and my hand relaxes. Except that I know immediately something is wrong. His eyes are harder than usual, and there is a crease between his eyebrows. His jaw is clenched.

"What?" I ask and take a step closer. Bodies push around

us. "What is it?"

He stares at me for a second like he's lost in thought, then shakes his head. His gaze drops to my collarbone. "It's nothing. Just…listen, this is going to sound weird, and I don't have time to explain, but—" He leans his head down to my ear and lowers his voice so nobody else can hear. "You should invite Jules up. And that other friend of yours. Monica. Her kid, too."

I pull back and stare at him. "I should *what*?"

But already he is drawing away. "I'm late, Eve. Connor's waiting. Just trust me, okay? Have them up. Now."

"Right now?"

"Now."

And then he disappears through the bodies, and I am standing there, staring at the empty space he left. The others crowd around me.

"What was that all about?"

I shake my head. "I'm honestly not sure."

"I thought he was supposed to be with Connor this morning."

I turn to Maggie and wait for her to catch her balance after being sideswiped by an Upper Mean. "How do you know that?"

She shrugs. "Connor told me. The Preme jobs work a bit differently. You have to pass certain tests before you can even apply to some positions. Today is one of the main tests for the computer jobs. Didn't Wren tell you?"

Hunter and Emerald are staring at me, and I feel almost foolish shaking my head. No, he didn't tell me. I shift my weight from foot to foot and try to ignore the sound of a child wailing a few steps away.

"Listen," I say slowly. "I think we have to take a detour on the way to the Bowl."

"Where are we going?"

"To the feeding dock."

"Care to elaborate, Eve?"

"Not really."

Then I lead them silently down the stairs and push through the dimly lit Lower Mean corridors until the crowds thin and we are close. Broken glass underfoot crunches loudly with every step and wedges into the sole of my boot. I barely notice. When I pass over the place where Wren hid me from the guard, my stomach clenches uncomfortably.

"You guys wait here," I mumble over my shoulder. "I shouldn't be long."

The door is open, and the lights are on. At the bottom of the stairs, a short man with thick-rimmed glasses and black tattoo sleeves passes out portions of bread through the partition. His eyes narrow when they see me.

"I'm looking for someone," I say. My voice is even. "Do you know the Denominators well?"

"Visitors aren't authorized," he says instead. "Get out or I'll find a guard."

"Look, I do this gig, too. Lunches. I'm looking for a girl named Jules. And a woman named Monica. Do you know them?"

He gives me a cold look. "I don't do names."

"One's my age. Bleach-blond hair. Spunky. The other's a bit older with a young boy glued to her side."

He shrugs.

"Mind if I…?" I gesture to his spot directly in front of the open partition. "I'll pass out the food."

He stares at me for several seconds, then shakes his head. "You think I do this out of the goodness of my heart? I don't. Consider it my sentence for a meaningless crime. If I let you barge in and stop me from doing it, who's to say they don't make me do dinner duty, too? Sorry. Can't risk it." He shoves bread to several faces that come and go, none of them my friends.

My fingers, meanwhile, ball into fists. I don't have time for this, and I don't like to be told no. But my options are limited. He looks vaguely dangerous, for starters, and I have been working toward less violence in my life, not more.

"Fine," I sniff. "I won't interfere with you doing your job. Happy?"

"You're going to stand over my shoulder the whole time instead?"

"What's the difference," I snap. He turns and looks at me, and I raise my hands. *Keep calm, Eve.* I force my voice to relax. "You won't even know I'm here."

He passes more bread through the partition, and my eyes scan the dark room for signs of blond hair and eyes that shine with laughter. A mother and son, hand in hand.

Why did Wren say to have them upstairs? Why now? Why was it so important he risked missing a test that could determine his entire future? I try to ignore the question of why he didn't tell me about the test in the first place.

I stand there for several minutes before I finally see one of them—Jules—and she looks confused as she approaches the partition. "What are you doing here? You never do breakfast duty."

"Um," I begin. Too many secrets, too many lies. I just eliminated a major one that was standing between me and my friends—do I really want to start another? Maybe the whole thing is ridiculous. Maybe Wren wasn't being literal, or he was messing around, or he was mistaken. I stare at her and frown. "Grab your breakfast and meet me at the closest stairwell. We're headed to the Bowl, and you're coming, too."

Even though he is a Preme, even though his own mother is one of the compound leaders, I trust Wren. That is one thing

I am suddenly certain of.

Her eyebrows draw together. "Right now?"

I nod.

"It seems a little early."

She looks unsure, and so I step in front of the heavily tattooed man. "It'll be fun, I promise," I begin, but I'm distracted by a slight figure with a child positioned on her hip.

"Hi, Eve," Monica says, smiling. "Did they change your shift around?"

"No. I thought I'd pop by to invite you guys upstairs for a bit. Me and some friends are headed to the Bowl, and Avery might have fun playing with the equipment."

Silently, she collects her breakfast items and passes half to her beaming boy. "Can we go, Mama?" he asks.

She shakes her head. "I'm sorry, sweetie. And I'm sorry to you, too, Eve, but we can't go."

"But—"

"It's against compound rules. Denominators aren't allowed on the Mean floors, you know that. What would happen if we were caught?" she asks quietly, nodding in Avery's direction.

I say nothing. Because of course it's risky sneaking around in Eleven, and nobody is treated more harshly for breaking the rules than Noms. With a child…there's just too much on the line.

"Thank you for the invite," she adds. "To think an upper-floor might be thinking of us…well. It means a lot. I'll see you later, at lunch duty—yes?"

"Looking forward to it," I confirm. I wink at Avery and then wave goodbye, feeling uneasy.

"Will *you* come up, at least?" I ask Jules.

"Okay," she says, after she's taken a bite of the bread I hand her. "I'll see you in a sec."

"Thought you were just going to stand there," says the

man behind me. He crosses his arms.

"So sorry about that," I say in a rush of sarcasm. "And thanks so much for all your help." Then I am gone, up the stairs and back to my friends, none of whom look terribly happy about our unexplained detour. "We need to go meet Jules," I explain to them.

"What's going on, Eve?" asks Hunter.

I don't slow down, but I look over my shoulder and sigh. "All I know is that Wren told me to invite her upstairs, and that's what I did. Trust me, I'm as confused as you are."

"That's weird," Maggie says slowly as I head for the stairwell. "It's not like him to dictate your social life, is it? Or do you think something else is going on?"

I shrug.

A few minutes later, Jules walks up the stairs toward me. "Can't a girl enjoy her breakfast in peace anymore?"

I force myself to laugh. "Don't give me that. I know how much you like punching things. Could I really leave you out?"

"Of course not." She nudges Hunter and nods at Emerald and Maggie. "You guys enjoy the party?"

"A lot more than the next morning," Maggie replies.

"You're telling me."

The four of them laugh. When we reach the Bowl, I feel Emerald tense up beside me, so I knock her on the arm. "You doing okay?"

She tries to smile, but it looks more like a grimace. "Dandy. Thanks."

"Bruno loved this place. He wouldn't want it to be poisoned for you." Then I grab her hand and pull her through the door into the cylindrical tunnel that leads to the Bowl. "Come on. Remember all the times you warmed up here before a big fight? Remember the sound of the crowd?" I smack the punching bag closest to us with my fist. "Remember that sound?"

"It's a beautiful sound," she agrees, and half her mouth twists upward. I stand aside, and she punches it once, twice.

Hunter turns to the Bowl. "I suppose there aren't any fights scheduled for today, given how empty it is right now." Behind us, Maggie and Jules try on gloves, laughing intermittently.

"Nope."

"Let's head to the ring, then. If you're going to make us fight, it may as well be somewhere good."

I look at Emerald and see beads of sweat shining on her forehead. She looks focused, peaceful.

"You want to take center stage, Hunter?" I smile. "It's probably not allowed, but...yeah, okay. I'm game." I grab a handful of punch pads and tape, then lead them through the end of the tunnel and into the Bowl itself. My gaze casts upward and around. It is eerie, being here when the stands are dead empty, when the only sound is our boots underfoot.

"This is actually pretty neat," Hunter comments. He twists around as his gaze combs thousands of empty seats.

"Yeah," says Jules. "This is badass. I don't know how you do it with a kajillion people in the stands."

"You don't even notice them," says Emerald quickly, and when I look at her, I see her brown skin is flushed pink. Her eyes are alive. "I mean, you do and you don't. It's just such a rush, you know?"

We climb into the ring in the center of the Bowl, and inwardly I am smiling. So far, aside from Monica and Avery, my plan has worked quite well. Emerald is falling in love with fighting again, Jules is upstairs as Wren recommended, and Maggie is about to learn how to defend herself. Things could definitely be worse.

That's when I hear the first round of gunshots go off.

CHAPTER THIRTY-FOUR

The Bowl whirls around me, and the countless rows of seats that ascend to the top of the Mean floor blur into streaks. But it isn't the room itself that moves; it is me.

Bang, bang, bang, bang.

I forget to blink as I search for the source, eyeballs burning. It sounds close; it sounds far. Rapid fire, a short break, another round. Repeat.

All of it with a backdrop of screams.

Around and around I go.

Finally, the gunshots cease, and the silence they leave in their wake is heavy against my ears. The Bowl stops whirling, and I glance at the others.

All of us are stationary, mouths open. Slowly, our senses come back to us; we blink and swallow, lick our lips. Without speaking, we climb out of the ring, and our steps are deliberate and tentative, as if we are learning to walk for the very first time. Every nerve in my body prickles, and sweat pools along the crease where my palm meets my fingers. As we walk through the cylindrical tunnel, I can hear them.

I can hear their voices mashed into one, can feel their energy from here. When we open the door and join the throngs outside, it is chaos. Complete chaos. Some scream in fear; others yell with anger; everywhere, people push. I don't know where they are going, and they don't seem to, either.

A memory of being in the shooting range with Wren flashes in front of me, and I can feel cool metal in my hand, heavy and unyielding. I feel the bullet shock the gun as it speeds from the chamber; I smell the smoke that drifts backward. Deadly and destructive and terrible.

I push and am pushed, and then through the crowd I spot the first of them. One leads to several to many, all with eyes glassy and round. Denominators. The one near the front clutches at her side, and I see a purple stain on her shirt. Adrenaline must drive her, but not for long. The stain swells as I watch. My eyes slowly scan over the rest of them. Two rows back, a man's dense beard is covered in pearls of red, and the palm of the man next in line looks like it has been dipped in paint.

So the gunfire came from below.

Jules bursts past me in their direction, and before I can follow, a hand pushes at my back, too strong for me to resist.

"We need to go, now!" Emerald shouts in my ear.

"But—but Jules."

"She needs to find her family."

"And we need to help her!"

"Are you familiar with the first floor, Eve? Didn't think so. Come on, hurry up!"

And then a terrible thought occurs to me. "Monica! And Avery! I can't stay—I need to make sure—"

"No! No. Keep walking." Her hand presses harder against my back, shoving me through the crowd. "How do you know, Eve, that the danger is over? For all we know, there's a madman walking around the place, shooting everyone up! So. *Keep walking.*"

I shake my head and mutter, "It's over, Emerald. You know it is."

"Maybe from the madman, but you know how quickly a crowd can go sideways down here. We don't need to get caught up in a riot, thanks."

I look over my shoulder and see that Maggie is pale-faced, her nose is bleeding—probably from an elbow thrown inadvertently in her direction. She looks so terrified that I have no choice but to turn away from the madness.

Once we're far enough, Emerald comes to a stop and wipes sweat from her face. Her knuckles are still pink from the Bowl. "What. The. *Hell*. Just. Happened."

"Don't know," I mutter. The only thing I *do* know is that I need to speak with Wren. Unease claws the lining of my stomach and makes me nauseous. It is too unlikely that he would tell me to invite Jules and Monica up right before gunfire broke out on the first floor. It can't be a coincidence; I know that.

But how could he have known?

Probably, he isn't finished with the test yet, but I can't stand to be here for another second, images of the wounded Denominators flashing through my brain… "Go lock yourselves in your cells," I instruct, "and wait for everything to settle down. It'll be safer there than out here."

"And what are you going to do?"

"I'll be back later!" I yell over my shoulder before they can stop me. I dart toward the main corridor.

My feet move quickly—I am pent up with energy, but the main corridor is thick with bodies, and I am forced to slow. The ceiling overhead seems to linger just a smidgen lower than usual, and between it and the elbows pressing around me, it is difficult to force a full breath into my lungs.

And then I am shoved hard to the side. I see why a moment later; down the middle of the hall walk guards shoulder to shoulder. Each one is masked, and each one carries a tall stack of folded gray plastic with *Compound Eleven* stamped in white. It makes a stone fall in my stomach.

Body bags. Hundreds of them.

Something bad happened downstairs. Something very bad. I think of Monica and Avery and try not to be sick.

All around me, people shout. Ask what is going on. Demand an explanation. I wait for an answer, but of course there is none. The guards walk on as if they don't hear us, as if they don't notice our existence at all.

People mutter and swear and wring their hands with frustration, but that is the extent of their feelings.

Rage will come. Whatever happened downstairs, rage will come. People are always mad in Compound Eleven.

When I get to the elevator bank, I turn to the main stairwell, just as I often do. Less crowded, no line. But I pause. I turn back to the elevators; I wait for a spot. I feel weak right now, and I don't want to be in the stairwell ever again when I feel weak. And these are dangerous times right now — I can taste it.

My thumb punches the button for the fifth floor. My brain echoes with the sound of gunshots. Deep breath in, deep breath out. Others empty out of the elevator at the third floor, at the fourth. I am the only one going to the top.

When I step onto the fifth floor, it is into a different world. Not just because the lights shine brightly overhead; they always do. I am used to it by now. It is that the white, pristine hallways are silent. Empty. Calm.

Not at all like the chaos unfurling down below.

Since I have no idea where the test rooms are, I decide to

wait for Wren here, in the atrium. The glass front of the library lines the far side, but I don't go there now. Instead I walk to the large bronze globe that sits in the middle of the space.

Four weeks ago, I stood right here—I studied this very sculpture. And I realized that the world is a large place, that Compound Eleven occupies a very tiny sliver. I realized that the number of other compounds out there must be staggering, that I can keep searching and searching, on and on, for my rightful home…

Or can I?

What if I wake up one day and find that I spent my whole life searching for something that doesn't even exist? What if all life is…is this? Ups and downs, highs and lows. Unspeakable cruelty, sharing laughs with friends. Unwanted violence, kisses with boys. Loving, working, killing time, growing, changing, discovering.

I can have those things here.

Is there more to life, or is that it?

I don't know how long I stand here thinking about it, but slowly I realize that people pass by, that the air is alive with movement. I look up, and my eyes find his. For a second, I can't remember why I am here, but then it all comes crashing back, and I push my way to him, gunshots once again ringing in my head.

He is still, and his jaw is set, his eyes unreachable.

"What the hell happened on the ground floor?" I hiss at him. "And don't you dare say you don't know, because why else would you tell me to have Jules and Monica up right before it happened?"

He grabs my elbow and leads me to the quietest corner of the atrium, where a little girl dressed in yellow tugs at his sleeve. Nell. She must recognize that something is amiss; her eyes look startled. Instinctively, his hand slips over her hair, just enough to provide reassurance before she is pulled along with the current.

"Did you have them up?" he asks, terse once more.

"Jules, I did. We were hanging out in the Bowl when about a thousand gunshots started going off under our feet." I cross my arms and stare at him. "And Monica refused to come upstairs, by the way. Because it's against the laws of the compound and she has a little kid to think about. Who knows if they're okay. Who knows if Jules's family is okay."

He pulls a face, like he is frustrated. It passes quickly, and just like earlier, he stares at my collarbone. "Look. I don't know much about it. And I'm not supposed to say anything to anyone, but…" He looks me in the eye and sighs. "They call it a cleanse. Every generation or two they do it, or so I've heard."

I feel like something crushes against my chest, and it restricts my ability to get oxygen to my brain. I remember those whispers of how disposable the Noms are in the eyes of the Premes, and the crushing sensation worsens. "Who's *they*?"

He hesitates. "I'm not sure which office is in charge of making those decisions—"

"But the orders come from this floor."

"Yes, Eve. They come from this floor. This floor controls the entire compound."

That old hatred of the Premes wells up in me once more. "You're telling me that the leaders of our compound just slaughtered God knows how many of their own people…"

He nods. "I don't like it any better than you—"

"Bullshit!" I snap before I can stop myself.

He grabs me by the shoulders. "Eve. Stop. I understand you're furious, but I'm not the bad guy here. Try to remember that. *Please* try to remember that."

I look around at faces that come and go. Everyone up here looks as pristine as the floors. Pristine and content—the exact opposite of down there. It makes me sick. "Why would they do this, Wren?" My voice is weak.

"It's to control populations down there. The one-baby policy doesn't work perfectly—"

He goes still, and my cheeks fill with heat. "So you're saying I should feel ashamed, Wren? That my mom had a second child? You know, in contravention of the one-baby policy and everything? I guess it's her fault—people like her—and she's to blame for shooting up a bunch of innocent people, right?"

"Stop." His eyes are flashing, and he lowers his head so we are eye to eye. He squeezes my shoulders so tightly I almost wince. "Stop. Stop putting words in my mouth. Stop getting mad at me for something I had nothing to do with. Just *stop*."

But I am mad. Every fiber of my being twitches with anger. It burns in a million different directions, and I don't know which yarn to tug at. I take a step back and breathe deeply. I can set it aside; I can. "Okay," I say finally, willing my voice to relax. "Okay, fine. Let's talk about something else. Your test, then."

"My test?" He shrugs. "It went as expected."

"Surprised I know about it? Maggie told me. I guess Connor tells her more about himself than you bother to tell me."

He rolls his eyes. "Eve, that's ridiculous. You've had a lot of shit going on the past couple of weeks, so I didn't want to burden you with—"

"With what, Wren—your life? You're making excuses. An important test that determines your entire future is the kind of thing you share with your *girlfriend*."

He stares at me. "Noted. Can we drop it now?"

I shake my head and glare at the wall next to us. The test doesn't seem relevant right now, but I don't want to admit that to him. I don't know what I want to admit, what I want to talk about.

"So probably our floor is next, is that right?" I blurt out. "They shoot up the Denominators first, then move on to the second floor, take out Maggie and Hunter, maybe my parents, too?"

"I've never heard of it happening on the Mean floors. Means are valuable to the functioning of the compound—factories, food, you name it. But the Denominators…to those in charge, that's a different story." He frowns. "And in case you couldn't figure this out for yourself, there was nothing I could have done to stop it. I did my best to help your friends."

The elevator doors slide open just then, and four guards exit the elevator, then calmly walk past. Each carries a body bag, and each body bag is full. My insides seize up at the sight. I feel lightheaded, like I could vomit.

Probably, they are headed for the Oracle, then outside. Probably there is a mass grave somewhere close by, a place to dump the deceased. I picture myself playing dead to get outside, and the thought is so ridiculous, so macabre, I almost laugh out loud. Almost.

Wren is watching me closely, and I give myself a shake.

"When did you first find out about this?" I ask in a low voice. More and more guards exit the elevators, all of them with arms full. Some loads look large and heavy, some heartbreakingly small.

"I heard it was going to happen this morning. Hence why I rushed down to warn you."

I go still. "First of all, *Preme*, you didn't warn me. Secondly, you found out about *it* this morning, or you found out about the *timing* this morning?"

"Well…the timing."

I cross my arms. "So you knew this was going to happen."

"I didn't know *anything*, okay? But there's been talk of it for some time. I was doing everything I could to *stop* it from happening at all."

"Bullshit!" I shout again. I can feel my heartbeat in my throat. When I speak, my voice has gone hoarse; it is little more than a whisper. "What about when I took you down there for the feeding?"

He raises both hands. "Eve —"

That old tendency toward violence resurfaces quickly, and I lift my hand to strike him, but he grabs it, and then there is a wailing that comes from the elevator, one that grows louder as the doors slide open. One that is so coated in anguish it makes my muscles unclench, and my hand is free; it drops to my side. I stare at the elevator, at the guards who empty out of it. The last guard is slower, for there is a child clutching the full body bag in his arms.

My heart stops beating for a moment in time.

I wish that it wouldn't start up again, but it does. I keep on living, and so I have to see Avery, red in the face and smothered in tears, his little hands clenched around plastic so tightly his knuckles turn white with effort.

His mother is in that body bag. There is no question. Monica, my friend.

No. My feet are moving me forward, my own tears are falling, my voice is screaming. *No.* But before I can reach the boy, a guard wrenches him away from his dead mother's side and he is shoved onto the elevator from which he emerged. I scream his name and bang on the door, but it's no use. He is gone. And when I turn around again, the guard carrying Monica has disappeared, and it is over; it is all over.

My eyes find Wren, and I know he feels something now — something beyond a generic, requisite disgust. His back holds him upright, and his jaw is squared, but his eyes betray him.

There is a glimmer of emotion—guilt, too—and it only makes me madder.

I breathe heavily, but otherwise I am composed. My voice sounds normal, except that it is laced with fire. "Don't come near me. Don't talk to me, don't look at me, don't set foot on my floor. I never want to see you again."

And then, as fast as my boots allow, I push through the stairwell door. Gone.

CHAPTER THIRTY-FIVE

I lie facedown on my bed in the darkness and squeeze my eyes closed. Sleep won't come; I know that. I am going through the motions because that is what society dictates. At a certain time, each and every day, we change out of our clothes and brush our hair and shut out the lamp. Time for sleep.

But the sound of gunshots plays over and over again in my mind. Avery's screams do, too, sounding just like Jack's when he was taken, and I tell myself to stop, stop. But in the darkness there is no fighting it. I think of Avery's tiny face, eyebrows drawn to the top of his forehead in disbelief, in horror, his hands clutching at his mother, desperate to feel her skin against his, desperate for her to wake, to calm him down, to tell him everything will be okay. Nothing will be okay for him—not now and not ever. He is just a child, and he watched his mother die.

I pray she went quickly, before she could realize what was happening. Before she realized that her beloved boy was watching, that his life was changing by the second in the most horrible way imaginable. *Looking forward to it.* Those were my last words to Monica. Looking forward to seeing her at lunch duty, a time that never came. That will now never come. *Why* didn't I try harder to get her upstairs? I want to scream just thinking about it.

All that terror and pain and misery, just to control population growth. Surely there is a better way. A more just and humane way. But what else should I expect from the man in charge of Population Control, Ted Bergess? The same man who ordered Jack's removal—it has to be. For him, today was just more of the same.

I wonder if Commander Katz felt any remorse when he signed off on the "cleanse." Whether he so much as blinked when he considered the tremendous loss of life committed at the flick of his pen. Then I remember the ease with which he had Sully tortured, and I know that he didn't.

My pillow is already wet with tears, but still I cry harder, harder still. I cry so hard and for so long that when I do pull myself to my elbows, I am dizzy; the blackness of my cell oozes around me like tar. I need to calm down; I need to breathe.

At least one thing is crystal clear to me now. I am leaving Compound Eleven

I am not staying here, where such hideous acts of inhumanity are not simply tolerated by Katz and Bergess and the rest of our leaders, but ordered by them. I'm not even going to wait until job selections, like I originally planned. In a day or two, once I get my affairs in order, I will no longer be a citizen of Eleven.

And that is the only thought that brings me a sliver of peace.

I sit up in my bed and chew my thumb until I taste blood. The darkness doesn't bother me in the slightest. I chew my thumb because I am thinking of *him*, even though I do everything in my power not to.

Don't do it, Eve, don't.

But I can't stop. Every single time I blink, I see the look on his face when I told him I never wanted to see him again. His lips ever so slightly parted, his eyes—usually so alive with intent—dull. But goddamn it, they should be dull.

They should be full of guilt and sorrow, because he knew, he knew, he knew. Even if he didn't know for certain this was in the pipeline, he suspected it, and he didn't do anything about it, no matter what he says, and never before have I felt so betrayed. What a fool I was for trusting him—he is a Preme; he is his mother's son, through and through. I want to punch him; I want to make him bleed. But more than anything, I ache because I am sad, and I miss him, and I want the comfort of his embrace.

I straighten my back and wipe away tears. It is better this way. It will be easier to go now, without having to say goodbye. I may feel like a million pieces of shattered glass smashed to sand by the heel of a boot, but it means less pain later.

This is good. It's *good.*

Things with Wren have reached their conclusion—one I always knew would come—and though I didn't expect such a violent end to our relationship, I never really expected it to begin in the first place. And if there is one thing about life that I know, it's that it is perfectly unpredictable.

I will move on, my heart will heal, and I will pick myself back up.

I just have to get out of this godforsaken compound.

I am lying on my stomach again, but this time my friends surround me. Hunter sits at the foot of the bed, and my feet are on his lap. Emerald sits on the floor, her back against the wall, a ball passing slowly between her hands. Maggie sits next to her with her head between her knees. None of us talks. There is so little to say. So much to say, and so little.

News of the cleanse has made its way around the compound. A government-sanctioned mass murder. Unthinkable.

Finally, Maggie lifts her head. "My granddad said they did the same thing when he was a boy. He was too young to understand it but old enough to remember the sound of gunshots and people, you know…freaking. He said it sounded just like yesterday. No different at all."

I turn my head and look at her. "If they do it every so often, how come nobody does anything to stop it?"

She shrugs. "Like what? This is Compound Eleven. If you don't like it, too bad. There's nowhere else to go."

"Actually, there is somewhere else to go," I say and take a deep breath. The others stare at me. "To another compound."

"Come off it," mutters Hunter quietly.

I roll over on my back so I can look at him. "Why not? Do you have any idea how big the world is? There have to be hundreds—maybe even thousands—of compounds out there. Are you really telling me that none of them is better than this shithole? Look around, Hunter. This place is a dump. I'm sick of seeing dirt and garbage everywhere, and—and filth. Blood. Bodies. I'm sick of the burned-out lights and walking on broken glass. I'm sick of being treated like shit because I was born on the second floor and not having any decent job options. I'm sick of all of it."

"Maybe you're right. Maybe there are other compounds out there that are better than here. Maybe. But how exactly are you going to get to any of them? And what are you going to do once you get there? Ask to stay awhile?"

"I don't know what I'm going to do," I admit as I draw my

feet off his lap. I sit upright. "But I do know how I'm going to get there."

He stares at me. "How's that?"

"The tunnel to Compound Ten runs from downstairs. I've seen it. There's only one guard in the way—it'll be no problem to force my way past."

"You're serious right now?"

I take a deep breath and nod. "I'm going tonight."

There is a commotion in the hall, yelling, but it has been happening all day, and I tune it out. "The guards will be distracted dealing with that," I add, nodding in the direction of the door to indicate the aftermath of the cleanse.

"*Tonight.*"

"Tonight."

Maggie's back straightens. "Are you seriously telling me I'm losing my best friend tonight?" Her mouth hangs open, and her bloodshot eyes grow round with bewilderment.

"Not necessarily…" I hesitate. "You could come, too. All of you."

They say nothing, which of course says everything. I never expected them to come—not under normal circumstances. Under normal circumstances, I wouldn't have even mentioned it. But given the cleanse—

I shake my head. "Look, it isn't something I'm rushing into. I've been thinking about it for a long time now. Why do you think I haven't been doing the job tours? It's not because I was planning on going pro; it's because I need out. I hate it here. I hate everything about this place. I hate how unfair and unjust it is. I hate how low the ceilings are; I hate what they did to Jack. I *hate* it."

There is no point in telling them about the Oracle. About how much I crave proper freedom, how much I want to see if my mother's song holds any truth, how much I want to search for my brother even if it is a mission in futility... Even if the expense of all that is probable death. They won't understand it; few can. But they can understand this, especially now, especially after the cleanse. They can understand why I would want out — who could possibly want to stay?

Hunter makes a sound at the back of his throat. "I think you've covered that, Eve. But I'm sure Ten is just as much a shithole as Eleven. These compounds were founded by the same group of people, don't forget."

"Yeah," says Emerald. "Even without the wondrous Katz dynasty at the helm, it might be just as unfair." She throws the ball at me, and I catch it. "The ceilings might be lower."

"I know that. But it's a chance I'm willing to take."

"What about us?" Maggie says, and when I look at her I see a tear glide down her cheek. "What about us? And Wren? And your parents? How could you walk away from all of that?"

"Please don't start crying, Maggie, or I will, too. Please don't." I sit straighter in an effort to keep my emotions in check.

She wipes the tear away and frowns. "Well?"

"You know how my parents are. They won't care. And you know things are finished with Wren." My voice breaks at the mention of his name. I can't bear to think about him right now. Not now, and not ever again. Because whenever I do, my stomach feels like it is filled with lead, and it hurts so deeply it is beginning to scare me. "And as for you guys..." My hands cover my face; they try to push back the tears before they escape.

"What, Eve? We're not enough, are we? We're not enough to make you stay."

"You guys are the reason I've stayed as long as I have! I've been miserable for so long. And now...and now nothing is enough. Nothing could *ever* be enough. Think what they did to so many innocent people yesterday. Think what they did to Jack!" My face is wet, and my bottom lip quivers. "I'm going to miss you guys like hell, but I've made my decision."

Maggie shoots toward me and rests her head on my shoulder. She is crying, and I cry, too.

When the tears finally clear, I see Emerald sits on my other side, her brown eyes wet. She grabs my hand. "I don't want you to go," she says, and her voice is hoarse, "but I'm not going to stand in your way. Promise me you'll find a way back if Ten's not everything you want and more."

My eyes meet hers. "I promise," I say.

Hunter sits at the end of my now-full bed, and his eyes are dry. The hardness of his features makes all my muscles clench—he doesn't like change; he won't understand. But I need him to.

"Hunter," I begin, but he shakes his head.

"If you've been so unhappy, how come I haven't heard about it? We're *best friends*." He glances coolly at me. "Or at least we used to be. It's nothing but secrets with you anymore."

I know he is referring to Wren, and I am shaking my head, back and forth, even though I know he is right.

"Stop it. Stop with the lies. I'm so *sick* of it," he says in a tight voice.

I don't know what to say. There is nothing *to* say, not really. Nothing that could make him understand. So we just stare at each other, a lifetime of friendship and familiarity and closeness between us, until three sharp knocks pierce the uncomfortable silence. With one last desperate look at Hunter that gets me nowhere, I shove off my bed and go to the door.

Jules.

Immediately, I rub at my face to get the last of the tears away. Not that she looks much better. Her cheeks are streaked, and her blond hair is tangled with knots.

"I need to talk to you," she says before I can collect myself. She pushes her way past me, then freezes when she sees the rest of them. "Oh. Perfect. You're all here." Sarcasm. She turns to me and jams her finger into my chest. "You knew," she spits. "You knew. You *knew*, didn't you?"

"Of course I didn't know," I insist, even as I feel my face reddening. It looks like I'm lying even though I am not. I *didn't* know; I didn't.

"You expect me to believe that you just so happened to invite me upstairs right before my entire floor gets shot at? Before a bunch of my family and friends get killed?" She is yelling now. "Monica, too, by the way. Her kid is fucking heartbroken. Goddamn it—as soon as I saw your face at breakfast, I knew something was up. The whole thing about going to the Bowl and wanting me to come along—it was all bullshit, wasn't it? Don't lie to me, Eve."

"It wasn't bullshit; it wasn't." Hunter's words ring in my head, and I take a deep breath. "But...I *had* been warned to invite you upstairs. That's the entire truth, Jules. I promise. We really were going to the Bowl and—"

"What do you mean, you'd been *warned*. By whom?"

I run my fingers through my hair. It is still wet from my shower, and my fingers snag in tangles. "Wren. He caught up with me on the way to the Bowl. He told me to invite you and Monica up, but that's all he said. I had no idea what was going to happen, Jules—you have to believe me."

"But *he* knew. Is that right?"

I feel that familiar weight in my stomach. When I speak, my voice is barely audible. "I've already ended things with him, if that makes it any better."

She stares at me, and it is several long moments before she speaks again. "It doesn't," she finally breathes. "And for the record, you and I are done, too." She walks out the door, slamming it so hard the thud echoes through my ribs.

The concrete wall of my cell is cold against my back, and I slide down it until my chin rests on my knees. Five minutes ago, I didn't think I could possibly feel worse, but I was wrong.

"I guess it doesn't exactly matter, seeing as how you're leaving, but if it brings you any peace, she won't stay mad at you."

I give Maggie a look. "Did you hear her? She hates me. Rightfully so."

"No, Eve. You did *nothing* wrong. If anything, you saved her life."

I stare at my thumbs. "I trusted Wren," I say quietly. "I trusted a *Preme*."

"Yeah…that." She slides off the bed and onto the floor in front of me. "What exactly did he do again?"

My eyes snap to hers. "Are you serious?"

She shrugs. "Yeah, I am. Sorry—I don't see it. He found out what was happening, so he risked missing the biggest test of his life to make sure you kept your friends safe." She opens and closes her hands. "And you're angry at him why?"

"It isn't that simple."

"Maybe not. But I think he deserves a proper goodbye. How do you think he's going to feel when you just disappear?"

"I *ended* things with him. I told him I never wanted to see him again. I'm not saying goodbye to him now."

She looks at me, then shakes her head. "Your call."

I stare at her. I'm right; I *know* I am. So why does my stomach feel like it is twisting into knots? When did life get so confusing? I thought it was supposed to be black and white, and instead it is a million pixels in between.

Hunter stands. "I've got other things to do, Eve," he mutters. "Have a ball in Compound Ten."

I push what happened with Jules to the back of my mind—

Wren, too. Then I jump to my feet. I'm not joking about going tonight, and I'm not bluffing. This is the last time I will see my best friend, and I'm not leaving him on these terms.

Quickly, I block his path.

"Do you mind?" he asks.

"I do."

"Eve, move."

"No. You can't leave like this. You owe me a proper goodbye."

He crosses his arms. "I don't owe you anything."

"Come on, Hunter. That's not what I mean. It's just—I can't have you mad at me, I just can't. You're my oldest friend, and I love you to pieces, and I *can't* leave on these terms."

"So don't leave, then."

I tuck my hair behind my ears and look him in the eye. "I'm going, Hunter. I've already made my decision. All I need is for you—my best friend—to give me your blessing. Please. I *need* it." There is something wet on my cheek, and when I wipe at it, I realize I'm crying.

He just laughs. "If anything, the past two months have shown me that I'm not that important to you after all."

"What does that even mean? Of *course* you're important to me. You're everything to me." I grab him by the shoulders, and tears fall quickly now. I feel desperate, suddenly. As if his blessing will make everything in my life okay again, if I can just manage to secure it. "*Please*, Hunter. Please try to understand. Please know you're everything to me."

His arms wrap around mine. He says in a low voice, "Everything? So what about *him*?"

"Him?" I stare into eyes so familiar that I recognize every speck. I stare into them and try to understand.

"You know who I'm talking about."

Wren.

My head is shaking. My pulse is unsteady. Words form on my tongue, but they are jumbled and uncertain. Hunter is everything to me. Hunter is *everything* to me.

It is *his* blessing I need.

But no…Hunter is a friend. He is more than that—he is family. There is too much on the line. And there is too little time; I am leaving soon—that much I know. That much I must remember.

So I take a step back, and our arms uncurl. I take another step, and they fall to our sides. "What does he have to do with anything?" I hear a voice say. I know it is mine, but still it sounds foreign.

His expression sours. But just as quickly as his anger came, it disappears again. His voice is restrained. "It doesn't matter. Not now. You want to leave so badly, good riddance." He pushes past me, and my insides turn to acid.

I will not get his blessing.

But he stops at the door. "Only one thing," he says. "Compound members aren't allowed to come and go as they choose, Eve, and you may know where the tunnel out of here is, but that doesn't mean you're getting through it. So maybe I'll see you around tomorrow, maybe I won't."

"Nothing's stopping me, Hunter," I say in a voice muffled by tears. But it's no matter; already he has slammed the door, and another relationship lies bloodied at my feet.

I spend the rest of the afternoon retrieving the gun from the storeroom and passing time with Maggie and Emerald. Though the mood is heavy, we do our best to keep the conversation light. *Don't worry about Hunter*, they assure me. *Or Jules*. Instead they indulge me, like good friends would. Together we brainstorm all the great things awaiting in Compound Ten—unlimited croissants, cells built aboveground, music—and despite the silliness of it, it makes me more excited to go. It is an adventure, just as Maggie said, and what is life if not a great adventure?

My time in Compound Eleven has been the opposite of a great adventure, and now is the time to right that wrong. My pulse is quick as I collect myself, as I prepare to slip downstairs and never see these hallways again.

That is the good news.

The bad news is that my hand shakes as I run a brush through my hair. The bad news is that my pulse isn't simply quick; it ticks so furiously that a light sheen covers my skin and I am faintly nauseous. I am wracked with nerves and guilt and sorrow. Part of me doesn't want to go; it wants those old feelings again. The ones I get with my friends, or when my mother is lucid, or before Wren and I broke up.

I stare at myself in the mirror and breathe. I am strong. And I deserve more than Eleven.

That is when I hear something at the door, something I haven't heard before. Scraping, the sound of metal, a thud. But then it is gone and there is nothing but silence. I turn back to the mirror.

No bruises today. Just a plain face, one free of violence. That is what the surface says, anyway. It almost looks foreign, that smooth skin the same color. I want to examine it further, but instead I look again at the door.

Someone was out there. But who? And why?

I shake my head. I know where my brain is going, and I am desperate to stop it. Maybe it was Hunter, ready to make amends. Or maybe it was *him*.

I can't help it—my eyes comb the bottom of the doorframe.

Nothing, and my stomach drops.

How careless and shallow and weak. What a hopeless romantic I have become. So I slap myself; I force myself to refocus.

Time to go. I have said my goodbyes to my friends as best I can, and I do not plan on extending the same courtesy to my parents. Anger bubbles in my stomach whenever I think of them. No, no—my friends are my family, and I have said a proper goodbye.

I turn to my boots, but before I pull them on, I walk instinctively to the door. No harm in taking a look—it had been an unusual noise, after all.

And then something strange happens.

When I pull at the door, it doesn't give. My fingers move to the lock; I have locked myself in.

But no, that isn't it.

I haven't locked myself in, but…*I am locked in*.

I yank at the door again. I turn and twist the door handle and pull with all my strength, but the door doesn't budge. I take a step back and stare at it. My brain seems to move like molasses. I am locked in.

Why am I locked in?

Maybe the lock itself is jammed or malfunctioning. The others will notice; they will come by my cell, knock on the door…unless they think I have already left. What a cruel twist of fate that would be.

Or maybe…maybe I have been locked in by those in charge of Compound Eleven. But surely not. Surely that wouldn't happen to me. Besides, why would the compound care to lock me in my cell? I haven't done anything wrong.

But something claws at the back of my brain. My plans to go to Compound Ten are against the rules. Hunter was right—I'm not permitted to come and go as I choose. If the authorities know, I will be locked in here until my punishment is determined.

But they couldn't possibly know.

I try the door again and rattle the handle until I am out of breath, until sweat beads against my forehead and at the back of my neck. The effort makes me thirsty, so I go to the bathroom and fill a tin cup with water. I swallow it down in one gulp.

They couldn't know. Of course they couldn't. It's a coincidence, the fact that my door is locked just before I am about to escape. Nothing more.

Only I don't believe in coincidences. I sit on my bed with my back straight and stare at the wall in front of me. I swallow the saliva that pools in my mouth and think. Either my lock is broken or they know.

And if they know, only one of three people could have told them. Maggie, Emerald, or Hunter. Nobody else knew of my plans for tonight.

Deep down, I know which one of the three to blame. But I can't accept it, and I won't believe it. I shake my head back and forth and back and forth until the thought is gone.

Time has passed, but still I haven't moved from my seat on the bed. And so when there comes a knocking and shouting from the other side of the door, I am startled. It takes a moment for my feet to find feeling again, but eventually they rush me to the door, which I pound with the heel of my palm.

"Eve?" Maggie shouts, and I know she must have her lips pressed close, because these doors are thick and sound doesn't pass easily through.

"*Maggie. Help—I can't get out!*" I don't know if she'll be able to understand me, but I keep thumping my hand so she knows I'm here.

I can feel her jiggling the doorknob, pulling against it— metal thuds quietly, but still the door doesn't open.

Useless. I'm locked in. Compound Eleven knows my secret. Security knows, the guards know—whoever needs to know about a possible security breach knows—and now I am locked in. And next I will be punished. A chill runs down my spine at the thought.

I heard once they snipped off a man's index finger—Sully, in fact—and now both are missing. I heard about a young child forced to clean toilets every day for five long years. I have heard of people sent to live on the floor below, of family and friends being severed, of job opportunities squandered. I have heard so many things over the years, and now they twist around my brain and I can't hear Maggie anymore—I can't hear anything anymore. I sit on the floor, and when I come to again, my cell is silent.

CHAPTER THIRTY-SIX

I should try to get some sleep.

Certainly there is nothing else to do. My stomach aches with hunger, but I ignore it because that isn't a problem I can solve right now.

Since I can't think of a problem I *can* solve, I take off my white sweatshirt and fold it into a neat square. I place it on my desk. Next, I take off my pants, and I fold these, too. Normally I don't bother with such rituals, but right now I do these things without thinking. My mother taught me to fold my clothes when I was small; my father enforced it after she left. I haven't bothered since I moved into my own cell.

The cell I am now a prisoner of.

I slip between the sheets, and they feel cold and unwelcome against my bare skin. I turn out the lamp beside my bed and stare into blackness. It is strange, this feeling, like I'm alive and dead all at once. Hunter's betrayal stings my eyes every time I blink, but it keeps my heart ticking, too. I don't know why. I don't feel particularly vengeful; all

I feel is sorrow kicking me straight in the gut. But I will. I think that is it. I will be vengeful, and so I must persevere until I can exact my revenge on someone whom, until today, I treasured and loved and who I thought loved me, too.

Funny—ever since I was little, I was taught to be forgiving, and this thought makes a laugh slip between my teeth. The same woman who admits to me now that she knows nothing about forgiveness, that she isn't capable of such things, taught me to always forgive those who falter.

Perhaps we don't teach our children what we know—only what we ought to know.

If I had children of my own, I would teach them what a sham forgiveness really is. And I would make them cold and hard so they couldn't be gutted. I would make them cruel, because that is what this world is. Cruel. Those with soft hearts can't survive, not in peace.

I kick the cold sheet off and turn on my side. I wrap my arms around my stomach and think to myself: *That is what my father did.*

He tried to make me a monster. A tough, hardened, violent monster, one cruel enough to survive Compound Eleven. I stare into the darkness and turn it over in my mind. Perhaps he wasn't angling for allotments; perhaps he wasn't pining for a son. Perhaps he was acting in my own interest all along. Perhaps I have been wrong about him.

I roll onto my other side and shake my head. *Lies.*

This must be what it feels like to lose your mind. Thoughts become warped; they twist inside your head until you're too confused to move a muscle. What I need more than anything is to quiet my mind. That must be the key to sanity.

Like my mother. She has quieted her mind to keep her sanity.

Another laugh.

So maybe quiet minds drive us insane. Maybe they *are* insane.

I roll onto my back and thump my palms against my cheeks. I am losing it. I know I am, because I can hear scraping and thudding and it is thunderous inside my brain. Now I see neon, my vision is no longer true—

"Eve."

My arms flatten against my bedsheet. Terror. But once I look up, I see a familiar figure standing over me. I see, too, that his face is carved out of the blackness by the neon light shining from the hall, and that means my cell door must be open.

And it isn't just a familiar face.

It is *him*.

I don't think about my actions—I simply act, I simply *react*. The balloon in my stomach lifts me from the bed and into his stiff frame. It is hard and unyielding, but I wrap my arms around him anyway.

It is Wren, and he got my door open. I am free.

His hand grips the back of my head, and his mouth is in my ear. "Are you okay?"

I am shaking my head back and forth as a million thoughts tumble inside. I am not okay. I am not, but I am, because he came. "You saved me," I whisper.

"Only so you could go save yourself." He pulls away and adds curtly, "I need to close the door."

I watch his long body as it shuts out the neon light from the hall. We are swallowed by blackness until my fingers switch on the lamp. In his hand, he holds a padlock with a keypad on it, and he places it on my desk next to my folded-up jeans. I remember that I am almost naked, other than an undershirt and underwear, but I don't care. Of all the things to care about lately, that is not one of them.

Before he can turn to me, I am twisting my arms around his chest, sealing out any air trapped between us. Maybe if I hold him close enough I won't remember the fact that my best friend betrayed me. Or that I am leaving now, going to Compound Ten. Or that I broke up with him and he came to my rescue anyway.

Maybe I won't remember the massacre that happened beneath my feet or the sound of Jack screaming for my mother and me.

I breathe deeply, letting the smell of his skin and his shirt soothe me, and it must work, because my pulse slows and I feel almost peaceful.

Then I realize that other than a hand on the back of my head, he doesn't hold me. I am clutching him like I never want to let go, but one of his arms hangs limply at his side. It is a simple thing, but it sends pain radiating through my chest.

I know I ended things. I don't know if I was right or wrong when I did it, but I know it doesn't change the fact that it happened.

"Eve."

Too many thoughts, too many emotions. I push them aside and wrap my hands around his neck. I stand on my toes and kiss him, and for a second I think he is going to resist, but then the hand that hangs by his side wraps around me, and he tugs me close, and, for a fleeting moment, life is good.

It doesn't last long. He pulls himself back several inches and says my name again. His voice is heavy, somber.

I shake my head. No. Don't want to hear it. I can't accept whatever he is about to say. I don't want to be reminded of the fact that we broke up and shouldn't be kissing right now. And I don't care if it's messy and confusing; right now, he is my rock. I step forward and kiss him again.

This time, I kiss him hard; I squeeze his shoulders, I push

him in the direction of the bed. I can feel him starting to resist, so I push harder, like I am fighting in the Bowl, and once he sits, I straddle him. My fingers run under the hem of his shirt, and his fingers find my bare legs, dig into flesh. He kisses me now just as hard as I kiss him.

Just as my lips curl into a small smile, I am pushed from his lap, shoved toward my desk.

"Put your clothes on." His voice is cold and level. He drags his palms over his face, then stares at me.

"Why?"

"What do you mean *why*? Because this is a mistake. I know why you're doing...that. And I'm not being a part of it."

"A part of what?"

He gives me a look. "I'm not a child, Eve. You're doing this because you're a wreck and you want a distraction."

"No, I'm doing this because I like you. A lot."

"That's a quick change of heart."

"That was yesterday. I was angry. This is now."

"I'm not talking about the fact that you broke up with me, although we should probably discuss that. I'm talking about the fact that until you were locked in here a few hours ago, you were planning on leaving for Compound Ten. Tonight."

I am still. When I try to swallow, I realize my throat has gone dry.

"You weren't even going to say goodbye," he whispers. "After everything." His gaze drops to the floor, and it makes me hurt.

"Wren—"

"If you want to think I'm a monster, that's fine. I get it, trust me. But there was nothing I could do to stop the cleanse. I did the best I could for you, Eve, and I'm sorry it wasn't enough."

"A monster?" I let out a nervous laugh. "Not for one

second—not from the moment we met and you kicked the shit out of me in the Bowl—have I believed you were a monster." I look him straight in the eye. "You're not, and don't let anyone ever tell you otherwise."

He stares at me. I feel like he is looking not at me, but through me, deep inside to the darkest recesses of my mind.

"What?" I finally ask.

"You're serious?"

I turn my palms to the ceiling. "Of course I am."

"Even after yesterday."

I let out a deep breath. "Even after yesterday."

He shakes his head again, but this time he is smiling. "I take it from the welcome I just received you've had a change of heart about us breaking up."

I shrug. "That was a mistake."

"But still. I didn't handle the whole thing very well. I would promise to do better in the future, but I guess there's no point." Suddenly, his smile is gone.

"There's not, no." I need to change the subject. Fast. "So. How'd you know I was stuck in here? I assume, since you know of my plans to go to Compound Ten, that it was Maggie who tracked you down." I cross one foot over the other and lean backward onto my desk.

His eyes graze my hips. "You assume correct. Can you put some clothes on?" He shifts, and his gaze pushes sideways. "Please."

I tug my sweater over my head, smiling. "So she tracked you down, and you happened to know the passcode?"

"Not quite."

I close my eyes as I understand. "Addison." She had mentioned it enough times—her father's office oversees security. Jeffrey Sitwell, lord of the guards that I loathe so deeply.

He nods, and jealousy ripples through me.

"She agreed to let me into her father's office."

"In the middle of the night."

"Something like that."

"I'm surprised she would do that for you after seeing us together at the party."

He frowns but says nothing more. Immediately, I know why she did it. She knows we broke up. *Deep breath, in and out*, I remind myself. I am leaving. I am leaving Compound Eleven. How Wren chooses to spend his time from here on out is none of my concern. It is none of my business.

"Did Maggie mention how my plans to go to another compound were leaked in the first place?"

"She didn't, but it doesn't take a genius to figure it out."

I twist away to hide my shame. Pull on my jeans instead. "Yeah, well, I must be quite the fool, because I didn't think in a million years he would do that."

"Sometimes it's hard to see the flaws in people we love."

"Maybe that's the problem," I mumble after a while. I sit beside him on the bed and draw on my boots, shove my gun into my waistband.

When I am finished, he strings his hands through mine, and they are impossibly warm. For a moment, I feel almost mended. The hole that Hunter's betrayal left in my heart doesn't ache right now. Nothing aches. I stare at Wren, and as I watch him take a deep breath, I see something strange sweep over his eyes. A flash of emotion, and then it's gone, and I wonder what is passing inside that great mind of his.

"I have something for you," he says finally. Every word seems strained, unnatural. Not like Wren at all.

"Okay..."

"I don't want to give it to you, because..." His voice trails off, and he shakes his head. "I'm going to give it to you because it's the right thing to do, and because I know it's what you want above all else."

My hands, which are twisted in his, clench. My spine draws me upright. "Okay," I say again, this time in a whisper. I can barely breathe.

"Freedom. It's…freedom."

"What—"

"I used my connections for something good for once. I found a way for you to get aboveground."

I am perfectly still, but the edges of my cell seem to quiver in my peripheral vision. I can see Wren, but I can't; the world is both crisply defined and a blur.

Slowly, I pull my hands free from his and coil them around his neck. Our foreheads touch, and tears fall from my eyes to the bedsheets below. *Freedom.* I am going to have freedom. I am going to reach the oasis; I am going to reunite with Jack.

I hug him so tightly that I think I might press his chest into mine and our hearts will beat truly as one. "Thank you, Wren."

He nods. "We should go. Now."

CHAPTER THIRTY-SEVEN

Once we are in the Lower Mean hallway with my knife and flashlight tucked inside my boot, Wren's hand grabs mine. "We need to go to the storeroom."

I look at him in surprise, and his face is full of sunken shadows under the glare of the neon light that hangs across from my cell. "I can get to it through the kitchen."

He nods. "You lead the way."

I guide him down the hall with my hand snug in his. The dark may not scare me anymore, but since these hallways are ripe with danger—especially now—his presence next to me is welcome. "I thought we would be heading to the Oracle," I say.

"You thought wrong," he replies under his breath.

"Care to elaborate?"

"There's another exit."

"What?" I stop in my tracks and stare at him through the darkness. "You're kidding."

He looks at me. "Not one that's easy to access, mind you. But it definitely won't be guarded, and it won't require a passcode or a handprint to get outside."

Another exit. My heart thumps with excitement. "Where is it?"

"Remember where the controls are for the solar panels?"

I do. In the outbuilding at the foot of the hill.

He looks past me as he speaks. "Inside, there's a trapdoor that opens onto the top net of the storeroom. It's for the engineers—so they can access tools."

"But the storeroom is four stories high."

"Like I said, getting out won't be easy." He glances at me, and a shiver runs along my spine. "But somehow I think you'll find a way."

Another exit. Not one intended for humans to pass through, but that is what makes it so genius. So perfect. "How did you find out?"

He exhales noisily. "I spent the afternoon yesterday touring my mother's office."

"Wow, first the security office, now energy. Decided that politics is your thing after all?"

"Very funny. It was a ruse, as if you couldn't figure that out. When she finds out my intentions were far from serious, she won't be happy. I'm fine with that, and you should be, too."

"You mean you toured her office for the sole purpose of—"

"Of finding a way for you to fulfill your dream of breathing fresh air?" He pulls his hand from mine and shoves it into his pocket. "Something like that."

He is conflicted; I know that. He is giving me the gift of freedom, but we both know it is probably a death sentence. I want to tell him that it's okay, but I can't bear to. Because if we discuss it, I might be forced to say that I would rather die than be with him, and that isn't something I can handle right now—or ever. Because it isn't true. It is true, but it isn't.

Maybe I am just as conflicted as he is.

"Why would you do that for me?" I finally ask. My voice sounds weak. "After everything…" *After I broke up with you*, is what I mean to say.

"Maybe I'm the fool."

I grab his arm; I stop him. "Not to me. You're brilliant. And selfless. You're the most amazing person I've ever met."

He laughs an impossibly shy laugh. "I've never known you to be so full of compliments, Eve."

I want to tell him how much he means to me, but instead there comes the sound of heavy footsteps fast approaching, and I am distracted by them, by my muscles clenching.

A bright light erupts from the end of the corridor—a blinding one that could only come from the flashlight of a guard. My hand finds Wren's, and I drag him backward, away from the light.

"Stop right there!" the guard yells, and his voice sounds tinny in the tight corridor. Just as I have always done, I listen to what the man in power orders and do the opposite. My legs burst into a sprint, and my hand pulls at Wren's. Around the corner we go, and only just in time, because I hear a gunshot blast behind us, and it sounds too close, too close.

We run in silence, but my mind screams. It was strange for the guard to fire his weapon so soon. Usually they wait until you punch them before they try to shoot you dead. But these are desperate times.

I can tell by the echo of footsteps that the guard is in the same corridor as us now. Ten more paces and we can turn the corner, taste a sliver of safety until he nears again. *Nine.* Vulnerability makes my ears ring. *Eight. Seven.* I wait for a bullet to rip through me, or worse—through Wren. *Six. Five. Four.* Please don't let it hit him. *Three.* He has done so much for me. *Two.* He has risked so much. *One.*

The blast is thunderous as I dive. My fingers slip from Wren's, and as I fall to the ground, they snap backward, snatch at nothing but air. Where is he, where is he, *where is he*?

As soon as I land, my feet are under me again, and I rush back, toward the line of fire. I will find Wren, no matter the cost.

But my hand is grabbed, and he is there, here, and whole. He gives me a strange look through the darkness, and then we run on, but now I am smiling. I force him to take a quick right, then another. The beads along the crevice where floor meets wall stream into long lines of light, and for a moment I feel like I am flying.

"Are you laughing, Eve?" he asks through heavy breaths.

I am too winded to reply. Relief has flooded my veins, because I can lose the guard now. These are short corridors and ones I know well. And because for a fraction of a second I thought he had been hit by the bullet. Now I feel like I do after a nightmare: joyous to be awake.

I didn't know I would die for him, but I know that now. I know, too, I have never been willing to die for someone before—not seriously—aside from Jack.

With my brother, it's easy—I love him. Always have, always will, whether he beat the odds and survived up there or not. So with Wren...does it mean that I love him, too?

Am I *in love* with Wren?

I try not to think about it as our pace slows. We walk, no longer seized by panic, no longer pursued by the guard. He is probably out there somewhere, ready to shoot again, but for now, we are safe.

Wren wraps his arm around my back, and his thumb touches bare skin. "You realize that unless that was Ben, there was no reason for you to run?"

"Ben?" The laughter is gone.

"He's the one who put the lock on your door. None of the other guards on duty right now would realize you should be in your cell."

"I guess old habits die hard," I reply bitterly.

He walks close enough to watch me, then stops and pulls me to his chest. I know we should be moving, putting more space between us and the trigger-happy guard, winding our way back to the kitchen. But instead I loop my arms around him and let my palms rest on his shoulder blades. "I'm sorry you've had to deal with this bullshit your whole life." His voice is low and rumbly, just like I remember it.

"It was worth it, getting to spend these last two months with you."

His eyebrows lift at my words, and quickly I turn away, lead him into the night. I have said too much.

"What exactly does that mean, Eve?" he asks from behind me.

I walk in silence for several seconds as I try to think of something to say that doesn't give me away. "It means I like hanging out with you."

He laughs to himself. "Sure. Well, if it helps—I like hanging out with you, too." We hold hands again, and I turn in the direction of the kitchen, more careful this time, listening for the sound of footsteps.

"What are you going to do once you're out?"

"I'm going to run north." I say it bluntly. Matter-of-fact. "I'm going to run as fast as I can. I'll sleep somewhere safe and shaded during the day, then I'll keep going. On and on, until I find Jack. Until I find paradise."

He looks at me, confused. "I can't tell if you're joking or serious."

"Does it matter?"

Instead of replying, he squeezes my hand. The magnitude

of what I am about to do begins to sink in, so I squeeze his hand in return and feel calmer. I focus on him walking next to me, the rhythmic sound of his breathing, and feel calmer still.

I pull him around the last corner before we reach the kitchen and freeze.

A figure up ahead, and I can see by his uniform that it's a guard. Not the one we just ran away from—another one, one that is faintly familiar to me. Old habits die hard indeed, and right now I fight every instinct in my bones to turn and run. But Wren is right; there is no need to run from the guards right now unless that guard happens to be Ben. And the man ahead of us certainly is not.

I take a deep breath. We are out for a walk, nothing more. Frowned upon, yes. But not strictly prohibited. He will ask us what we are doing, and we will tell him, and he will let us walk on. I will be inside the kitchen, then the storeroom, in a minute or two.

And so we continue forward, hand in hand, and even though Wren's presence steadies me, it isn't enough. The guard looks familiar; I know that.

I don't know why until we're within feet of him. A shudder grips my shoulders, and my boots stall. I have to run—I know it is risky, but I have to. Yet Wren's hand holds mine too tightly—I couldn't go even if I tried, and he pulls me closer and closer to the man who tried to kill me. The man whose nose I broke.

I see the outline of a gun in his holster, and I shudder again; my feet drag. He turns to look at us, shines his flashlight over us, and I shield my face from the light, from his prying eyes. If he recognizes me, I am dead.

"Odd time to be out of bed, isn't it?" he says, and the sound of his voice makes me tremble. Black bead eyes glare at us.

"Not if you feel like going for a walk," Wren replies levelly. My hand is still held over my face, even though the flashlight is pointed at the ceiling. We are almost past him, but then he moves quickly; he stands in front of us, and we are forced to be still.

"You look familiar," he says to me. I try not to look at him, but I can't help it, and I see the recognition dawn quickly across his features.

"I know you," he spits at me. "You coldcocked me, you bitch."

"I think you have me confused," I say, and I am surprised by how bold my voice sounds. It doesn't betray how fast my heart hammers.

"I don't have you confused," he hisses, and quickly his free hand grabs his gun and digs it into my stomach. Panic flares inside my brain. "I'm good with faces. Now, turn around and walk to the elevators or I'll shoot you. *Happily.*"

Wren's hand releases mine, and I close my eyes. Less violence. All I want is less violence. And so it brings me no pleasure to slip my hand to the back of my waistband, to dig my hard-earned weapon into the guard's side before he knows what I am doing.

"You don't have the guts to shoot me," he snarls.

"Sure I do," I reply, even though I don't know whether I mean it or not. But then I remember the journey to this moment. I remember the despair I have endured down here in Eleven and the desperation to find a way out. I remember the soaring highs I experienced as I crafted plans to escape and the crushing lows as those plans were dashed. Now... against all odds, I hold the threat of death over a guard. And that guard is the only thing standing between me and a future of my choosing.

I have come so far; I am so close to finally tasting freedom, to having a shot at finding Jack…and suddenly I know I mean what I say.

Sure I do. Sure I have the guts to shoot him.

"She does," Wren confirms, as if he can read my mind. "But she doesn't need to."

"What are you talking about?"

I expect Wren to pounce, to disarm him. Instead he says, "Jeffrey Sitwell. Does the name ring a bell?"

The guard's muscles contract. "My boss," he says between clenched teeth.

"Your boss's boss. The Head of Security. He's a family friend. That's how I know your name is Dennis Grove. Your wife is Penny, middle name Lynn. Your mother is Gertrude Grove, though she goes by her maiden name, Frank. Your father is Evan. You and your wife reside on the fourth floor in hallway 16K. Shall I continue?"

The face of Dennis Grove is paper white, and I'm not sure if it's from Wren's words or the weapon I press into his side.

"Drop your gun and walk away," Wren commands. "Don't look back. Don't come back. Don't do anything that would make me give the word to Sitwell."

"Give the word," he repeats slowly. Then he smirks. "What, you're going to get me fired?"

Wren smiles in return. "Not quite."

The guard stares at him. He peers at me. One eyelid twitches ever so slightly. But then slowly, against all odds, the gun pointed at my hip drops to the floor; the metal clatters loudly against concrete. With a stony face, he walks by and into darkness. I listen carefully as his footsteps fade into another section of the compound, and I breathe once, twice, three times.

Wren picks up the discarded weapon. "You okay?"

My chest heaves, but otherwise I am still. I don't know if I am okay or not. I just had a gun pointed at me; I just pointed one at somebody. I don't know why it bothers me, other than the fact that the same type of weapon slaughtered hundreds if not thousands of innocents just yesterday, including Avery's mother. I hate it. I hate them.

"Why didn't you attack him?" I ask. "Force the gun away when he was distracted by mine?"

Wren looks at me out of the corner of his eye. "I guess I didn't feel like more violence would solve anything," he says carefully.

I grab hold of Wren's hand at this, press his palm tight to mine. Then I lead him to the kitchen door. We are close. We are so close.

My fingers enter the code under Wren's watchful gaze, and the door swings open.

Inside, a man I recognize from the job tour chops onions at one of the cutting boards. I saw him at the party, too, with Hunter. My stomach squeezes at the thought of my old friend. Now my enemy.

The man stares at us. "This room isn't public access. How'd you get in, anyway?"

I step forward and let the door swing closed. "Hunter," I reply, and I try but fail to suppress a smile from stretching across my mouth. "Hunter sent us. He told us to get him some lemon squares."

The man looks affronted. "That isn't allowed. Hunter should know that. What—he gave you the passcode for the kitchen?" He stands up straighter. "I told him that in confidence, and only because he'll be starting soon, so long as his application is accepted."

"He did tell us. Probably a lot of other people, too. Take it up with him tomorrow, and make sure you mention the lemon squares. Now, get out."

"Are you kidding? I'm not going anywhere. I've got prep to do for the morning. You two get out, or I'll get a guard in here faster—"

"Come back in an hour," interrupts Wren. His voice is heavy, and he steps around me so the man can see him clearly. More accurately, so the man can see the gun he still holds by his side.

The man's eyes round slightly, and then he wipes his hands on his apron, pulls it over his head, and drops it on the cutting board. "Hunter's going to hear about this," he mutters as he pushes out the door.

"Perfect," I say once he is gone.

"Lemon squares. Aren't they your favorite?"

"Yep. Consider it a calling card. So, before I forget to ask— are you going to tell me how you knew that guard's name?"

"Grove? He tried to kill you." Wren shrugs. "I looked him up after the feeding dock."

I lead him through the kitchen to the storeroom, and I am glad that he can't see my face, because I can't stop myself from smiling. We weren't a couple that day, but still he cared enough to do his homework. The rush of emotion makes my stomach tighten when I think about what is going to happen next. I am going to leave him. Forever.

I give myself a shake and enter the passcode for the storeroom. 11000200.

"It's different," Wren says from over my shoulder. "It doesn't follow the same pattern."

"It's an important room."

"So how do you know it?"

I push the door open before I answer. "I came here, once, with…him. Hunter. A job tour—the only one I went on. Funnily enough, the only reason I went was to try to make amends with him."

"And?"

"And the leader of the tour took us in here. I made a point of standing close."

I throw on the lights as Wren closes the door behind us.

"Shit," he says when he turns.

"I assume you've never been."

"You assume correctly."

"And you're telling me that way up there, above the very highest net, there's a trapdoor into the building that houses the controls for the solar panels."

"That's precisely what I'm telling you."

"And there's no code or anything stopping me from going outside once I'm up there."

He shakes his head. "No. There's a keypad on the outside of the building. 1100061 is the passcode, in case…" He breathes deeply for a second, and I know what he is thinking. In case I change my mind. Then, calmly, he carries on. "There's nothing on the inside. The trapdoor is an access hatch for tools, not humans."

I nod and crane my head back. It's impossible to see much from here. Nothing but net after net slung at intervals all the way to the top of the towering room.

"You aren't afraid of heights, I hope?"

"Not that I know of."

He sighs. "Then I guess…I guess this is where I leave you."

A lump forms in my throat. I don't want to say goodbye to Wren; I don't.

I loop my arms around his waist and breathe deeply to keep away the tears. He smells like he always does, and I wish I could take that smell with me aboveground. If I don't make it to paradise, I would be happy to die with his smell embracing me.

Once I feel like I'm not going to cry, I force myself to

smile. Just another conversation with my boyfriend. "What will you do now?" I ask.

He shrugs as he holds me. "Go back upstairs. Sleep like a baby. Shoot some pool in the morning." He kisses my forehead.

"Very funny. Besides, I didn't mean right now. I meant… in general."

It's a few moments before he responds. "I passed the computer test, so I'll get whatever position I'd like. And I'll spend time with my friends. I don't know. I don't really want to think about it—life without you."

I don't want to think about it, either. It makes me feel physically ill. Like when I realized that Hunter had betrayed me. Except that only hurt in my gut, and this hurts everywhere. "Will you…and Addison…?"

He pulls back and looks at me. His eyes are suddenly hard. "You can't have it both ways, Eve. *You* are deciding to leave, and that includes leaving me. I get that you have to do this. I understand it, I do, but you can't have it both ways." He sighs and pulls me close again, roughly, so that my cheekbone thumps against his chest. "But to answer your question, no."

It's silly, and he's right, but still I smile. "You smell so good," I say, and my voice is muffled by his shirt; it is weak with the tightening of the belt looping around my heart.

He laughs softly. "Is that a fact?"

"It is a fact. It's one of the things I love about you."

I feel his stillness, and it makes me realize that I said the word. *Love.* I squeeze my eyes shut so hard that white stars pop through the blackness, but it is the only thing stopping the tears. I breathe in. I breathe out. Enough with the lies, with the secrets. They have clouded the past few months, and now I need to clear my chest, lift this weight. I can do this. I can do this because I am brave and strong and fierce.

When I open my eyes, I see he is watching me.

"Wren."

"Eve."

I rest my forehead against his chin. I can't look him in the eye right now; I can't. "I'm in…" I breathe. In, out. "I'm in…with you."

I shake my head. I'm being ridiculous. Of all the things we have been through together, why is it so hard to say one little word?

He pulls his head back, and his hand lands under my chin; he raises it several inches so I am forced to look into those flashing eyes that look like the sun. "I'm in…with you too."

A quick laugh pushes between my lips, and he catches it with his own. He kisses me, and then we relax into each other's arms, and I feel like my heart is several times too big for my chest. It feels warm and swollen with happiness. I am not a novelty, not something to laugh about with his Preme friends, not a tool for revenge against his mother. His feelings, like mine, are true. But after seconds pass, then minutes, the significance of what is about to happen sinks further and further through the layers of my skin until it strikes at my heart. Tears leak from the corners of my eyes. "Don't let go of me just yet," I say as soon as his grip loosens, and he obliges.

But finally the clock runs out.

"It's time, Eve," he whispers. I nod. He lets go of me, and I feel cold and exposed without his embrace. When I look into his eyes, I am surprised to see they are slippery with emotion.

He takes a step toward the door, and I swallow. I don't want him to go. Another step. I feel like something is sitting on my chest, and it is a weight I can't sustain. Another. I am going to be crushed by this weight, smashed into particles at any second. But when he reaches the door, he forces a smile, and seeing his final act of strength makes me strong, too.

This is my destiny. It is time to get a grip.

"Enjoy your freedom, Eve."

All I can do is nod.

He turns and is halfway through the door when I lunge forward and grab him by the arm. My voice rings through the silence. "If you ever doubt yourself again, remember you made a very miserable girl very happy. Please. Please carry that with you."

He looks at me, and then the sun in his eyes disappears, and I shut mine quickly. He grabs my hand and squeezes it.

He squeezes it so hard it hurts, and then he is gone.

He is gone, and I am alone.

CHAPTER THIRTY-EIGHT

I stare at the door with only my beating heart as company. The sadness I feel right now is unbearable. It hurts a thousand times worse than I imagined it would, like I am being crushed from above and below and either side. It is terrifying.

So I look at the ceiling, and then my eyes comb the walls for the nearest ladder. I need something to distract myself from the feeling that sits inside my chest like a poisonous lump, and climbing to the top of the storeroom is just that.

Deep breath, in and out.

The closest ladder is attached to the wall near the corner, and I walk there on unsteady feet. My fingers curl slowly around cool metal. Silver has given way to tarnished gold on either side of each rung, and it comforts me, this. I am not the first person to climb this ladder, and I won't be the last.

But I will be the first person to climb it for the purpose of going aboveground. My nerves tingle with a blush of excitement, and the lump in my chest shrinks ever so slightly. Soon I will occupy the same space that Jack occupied—maybe still does. Soon I will taste freedom. *That* is what I need to focus on right now. Not him.

Not him.

I pass by net after net after net, all slung at three-foot intervals. Goods litter each one, but I don't turn to examine them; my only goal right now is to reach the top.

The nets themselves are constructed of rope, coarse and sturdy, and they fasten to the corners of the room through thick hoops of metal. If I stick my leg out behind me right now, or maybe even my arm, I could touch one.

I don't want to do that, though. Right now I am a single story up, no more, and already my heart is thumping harder than it normally would. My muscles are beginning to ache from the effort, and if I waste too much time, they will tire.

When I am halfway to the top, I look down. Panic floods me like liquid lead; if I fall now, I will die. The thought makes my palms wet, and so I close my eyes and wait for my pulse to slow. Sweaty hands will slip. I need to relax, or this will end badly. Very badly.

I need to think of something else. Anything else.

Hunter. He will be in trouble with his soon-to-be colleagues, and this thought alone makes me distracted enough that I smile. And he will see that the lock on my door is gone in the morning and that I am, too, and my smile grows. He didn't win. I did.

I wipe my hands one by one and continue to climb.

Next I think about my parents. The fact that I didn't say goodbye weighs on me. Not much, no, but it is there. A remnant of guilt — one I didn't want to carry with me aboveground. But who am I kidding. I am choosing to be selfish by the very act of going, and saying goodbye to my parents wouldn't alleviate that, because they wouldn't accept it.

Or maybe they would. Maybe when I spoke with my mother that day she fed the Noms, she was giving me her blessing to do whatever selfish act I wanted. Maybe she can find it in her heart to make peace with my decision. After all, if there's any chance of her children reuniting, side by side, just like she used to sing, this is something I must do.

Now I am three-quarters of the way there. Breathing is becoming difficult because my heart beats so quickly, and everywhere my skin is tacky. I am fearful, yes, but there is also something exhilarating about being so high, doing something completely new.

What would Maggie say if she could see me right now? She would be shrieking at me to get down but cheering me to go higher. I smile, and my boot lifts to the next rung of the ladder.

I wonder what Wren will tell her. Whether he will let her think I have gone to Compound Ten or if he will tell her the truth. That I craved freedom, and, thanks to him, I got it.

I wonder if he will tell her that I am likely dead.

Because by the time the morning comes, I could be.

I shudder, and my boot doesn't land firmly on the next rung; it grazes the edge, and I slip. The ticking of my heart is replaced by thick, meaty thumps in my throat as my fingers snatch around metal, as my feet scramble for position.

It was a careless mistake—one I can't afford to make again. I swear under my breath.

Now my heart is beating much too quickly, and when I lift a hand to wipe it on my jeans, I see it is shaking. It shakes so deeply, it must be controlled by a mind that isn't my own. Okay. Okay, I could climb onto the nearest net and wait for my heart to slow, wait for my palms to dry, or I could force myself to keep climbing, to not worry about the danger that presents itself with each and every step.

I bag up my fear, and I set it aside. Up and up and up, until just ten rungs separate me from the top of the storeroom.

Seven rungs, and I will stand inches below the earth's crust.
Five.
I climb quicker now.
Two.
I am almost there.
One.

The top of the ladder—the top of the storeroom. If I reach up, my fingertips will graze the ceiling. If I look down, I will vomit on the floor below.

Every muscle in my body is clenched, rigid and taut. The joints in my fingers scream with pain; they have been forced into position for too long—I am asking too much of them.

I will my left hand to open.

It does, but slowly, and it moves sideways on an uneven trajectory until it wraps around the thick girth of rope that leads to the highest net. A shiver of excitement courses through my veins as my boot lifts from the ladder. Another breath, in and out. I tremble and shake and push off with my leg and let go of the ladder completely.

Okay.

All I must do is shuffle along the ropes until I am in front of the nets. Except it occurs to me as I do that I am suspended in midair, that a great bubble of space separates me from the floor—the same one that usually runs directly under my boot.

The idea makes a bite of laughter rattle my tongue.

I inch left, again and again, until the nets are in front of me. Three of them: the one my boots stand on, the one my hip bone digs into, and the one that my hands grip. It is the latter one I care about. My eyes comb it greedily, and I notice that it holds very little compared to the rest of the nets—a small pile of metal in the very center and nothing more. Slowly, my gaze lifts.

Carved in the shape of a perfect square is a small trapdoor.

I stare at it, and a smile spreads across my mouth, exposes my teeth. I'm not even sure I believed it was there, until now. The only problem is that the net is slung directly below it; there is barely any room for me to crawl over and up.

I will figure out a way onto it, I will, but first I must rest. Carefully, I draw one leg up, then the other, so that I sit on the edge of the second-highest net in the storeroom, and before thinking about it I twist so that I lie down, so that I give my arms a much-needed reprieve. I catch my breath; I rub my muscles. Then I am still, and all I can think about is the feeling of Wren squeezing my hand, of the look on his face when we forever parted ways.

The trembling in my muscles is replaced by overwhelming sadness.

So I stir; I draw myself back to the edge of the net, back to where my pulse races. It is better this way. Because here, I need to focus. I need to focus on getting to the net above me.

A simple task, except completing it will be anything but easy.

I am much too close to the ceiling to stand. The only way for me to hook my boot onto the top net is to let my arms carry my weight. But my arms are tired from being held over my head for the past ten minutes—blood isn't flowing to my muscles as it should, and they protest loudly at the idea. I don't like it, either, but there's no alternative.

I string one arm through the top net and clench my other hand around it to lock it in place. I let my weight fall, then lift both my legs and hook them around. I am nauseous and cold, yet a new padding of sweat spreads across my skin.

So close. I am so close. I just need to swing my body up, and I will have done it. *Soon, Eve.* Because right now I can see the floor so many feet below me, and it makes my stomach lunge. Because right now my arm is beginning to ache, and if

I don't act now, I will fall.

My abs contract, and I shift my weight up, my legs straightening to lock in my progress. Every muscle in my body is engaged, and my breathing is shallow. I am perfectly horizontal, hugging the edge of the top net in the storeroom. So close. I am so close.

I lunge upward once again, and this time my arm that serves as a lock lets go. It reaches around, desperate to grab the top of the net.

It is an error.

I lose my balance. I fall. I scream. Then my left hand snatches closed, and it is around rope.

The only thing standing between me and death. I taste something acidic at the back of my throat. Vomit.

My feet are kicking, desperate to latch onto something, desperate to give my fingers a break, to save myself. I didn't realize how desperate I was to live until now. At first I screamed, but now I sob. I think of my family and friends, and I think about Wren. I want them all, and I love them all. I picture their faces, I imagine their embraces, and my limbs grow still.

Focus.

I need to curl my left arm, to use every last ounce of strength to bend it, to draw my body up to a spot where my right hand can reach the net. That is step one. I can accomplish step one. Already, my arm throbs, but it is my only chance, and so I force my sob to turn into a grunt, and I pull, I pull, I pull.

An inch, and another, and finally the fingers of my right hand curl over rope, and now two limbs hold me from falling to my death.

Now for the final test of strength. One leg springs up and hooks around the top net, and I use the strength in this leg to wrestle the rest of my body weight up and up and up, and now my hands reach deeper onto the net, and I am on, I am on, I am on.

I roll until my back digs into metal, and I breathe deeply and laugh; I let out a shriek.

I did it.

I just about died, but I will live another minute. I will taste freedom after all.

It was strange, though. When I almost fell, I didn't want to go. I was scared of death, scared of the unknown.

Is it death I am not ready for, or merely death without freedom first?

It isn't a question I can answer—not here.

And then, all of a sudden, that song starts up in my mind, the one my mother used to sing, playing at full volume. The last stanza thunders in my ears:

Children dearest hear me roaring, release the ticking clock
Relieve your pain, don't be scared, smash apart the lock
Drift to gentle paradise, it's there that we shall talk
Children dearest side by side, tick tock

When everything is silent again, I know it in my bones. Maybe I knew it all along.

That famed oasis, paradise, the one I am chasing—it doesn't exist. There is no north night hawk, no green canopy, no burbling stream—not in actuality. It is the afterlife my mother was singing about.

It is *there* where I will reunite with Jack, side by side in a field of hollyhock…

Those murmurs under my mother's breath—always about a clock…it was the song. An act of self-care, maybe—a reminder of the gentle paradise awaiting her, where she, too, can finally reunite with her beloved boy…

A breath rattles my lungs. The afterlife. The *afterlife*. Jack is dead. He likely died within hours of being released aboveground. And I may be a survivor, but against that burning ball of fire known as the sun, I don't stand a chance.

Fists cover my eyes, but they don't stop the tears. Nothing could. I have been chasing an idea and nothing more, blinded by hope, clinging to a whim that offered much-needed solace at the expense of reason. I will never feel Jack's delicate hands strung through mine, not until I bid goodbye to everything, to *life*—

And that's just what I will do if I step foot outside, into the scorching outdoors.

I squeeze the sides of my face; I squeeze until it hurts. Not *if*. When—*when* I step foot outside. Because I may not have a shot at finding Jack in the flesh and blood—or paradise, for that matter—but I do have the opportunity to escape Eleven and experience true freedom, even if it is short-lived.

And that is still something I think I want. So I lift myself gingerly over tools until the trapdoor is directly above me. Carefully and with trembling fingers, I push.

Maybe it will be locked, maybe it won't open, maybe I have come this far for naught.

But no.

It opens silently, and I am greeted by darkness and a musty smell that reminds me faintly of the first floor. I pull myself upright, into the building itself. The building that will see my last moments of Compound Eleven confinement.

My fingers are shaking, but this time it isn't from fear or terror or whatever it was that saw me here. I don't know what it is. Perhaps it's excitement, but I don't think it is so simple.

I reach into my boot, pull out my flashlight.

The first thing I see is that there are no windows. Next, I see that there is no locking mechanism on the door, just as Wren said. My fingertips brush the door handle. Nothing stands between where I am now and the sweltering world outside. A world I now know without a shadow of a doubt will kill me.

One wall is full of buttons and levers; the rest is empty. There is a lightbulb overhead, but I don't bother looking for the light switch. Instead, I set the flashlight down on the plank floor so that the small space is illuminated, then lean my forehead against the door.

This is it. This is what it has all been about, what I have been working toward, what I have been dreaming of. Escaping Eleven. I can't balk now; I just can't. Even if I wanted to, what cruel punishment would await me below? I am a criminal now, known to authorities. And all thanks to my best friend.

No, I don't have a choice. I have to go outside. I was going to kill a person to get here. This is what I wanted above all else, and even when I believed I actually had a chance of survival, I knew, too, there was a likelihood of death. So why does it feel so bittersweet?

I don't think it's the prospect of certain death doing it—not fully. I think I know the answer but I don't want to admit it to myself. Because I used to be hardened and tough and self-sufficient, desperate to leave the cruel corridors of the compound at all costs. Then I fell in love.

Just do it, Eve. It's like lemon juice: The first jolt is the worst. The heat will sting, it will take my breath away, but then it won't hurt so much.

I look at my knuckles and think of my parents and realize that I was wrong not to say goodbye. I was wrong not to have one last moment with them that wasn't a fight. Maybe they are worthy of my anger, maybe they aren't, but regardless of it all—they are family. I breathe deeply and try to set the pang of regret aside. It isn't a problem I can solve right now;

it is too late. If I come back in another lifetime, I will be wiser.

Right now, all I can do is breathe.

Breathe, Eve.

I thump my head against the door, again and again, and after a while, my trepidations slowly give way, smacking into one another and down like a house of cards.

This is what I came for. This is what I want. When I open this door, I will be free.

So what if I am swallowed by unbearable heat—so what that I will never see my loved ones again? I will be free. I will die a happy girl because I will be free.

My shaking fingers graze the door handle, and then my palm grips it tightly. The muscles in my arm stand at attention, and I can feel them rippling under my skin, fatigued from the effort it took to reach this spot but still resilient. I stand up straighter and breathe. In. Out.

In.

Out.

This is it. I am going now. I am brave and strong and free. Finally, I am free.

Time for the lemon juice to spill. I am turning the door handle when something stirs behind me.

"Eve."

CHAPTER THIRTY-NINE

I am frozen like ice that even the heat on the other side of the door can't melt. I can't move; I can barely breathe. But finally I let go of the handle.

I let go and turn and gaze into flashing eyes. Breathing hard, he steps forward; I am in his arms. Something warm spreads through my veins as he wraps me tightly in that clean, safe smell.

I didn't think I would ever see him again.

His hands cradle my face, and he kisses me, and for a second I forget where we are, what I am about to do. For a second, everything feels right.

"I'm coming, too," he breathes into my lungs.

My eyes open, and I push against his chest. The second is over.

"Don't," I hear my lips say. I don't remember formulating the word; I don't remember saying it. But I mutter it again and again.

"Eve," he says loudly. "If you're going outside, I'm coming with you."

Already I am shaking my head. I step back and feel the door handle dig into my spine, then lift my eyes to his under the glow of the discarded flashlight. "No," I say weakly. "I'm not letting you."

"I'm not asking for permission."

I take a deep breath and straighten my back. "But you have a life down there. A good one—one you don't want to leave."

He steps closer, but this time he doesn't wrap his arms around me. He just stands there, and I feel small in his shadow. "I don't want to be in Compound Eleven if you aren't. Don't you get it, Eve? Don't you see? *You're* the reason my life is good down there. It's *you*. If you're gone…" His gaze touches my collarbone, and he shakes his head.

Tears threaten to burst from my eyes. His words make me weak, but I force myself to be strong. "I can't let you die for me. I'm sorry." I squeeze out from his shadow and turn away from him, dragging in oxygen through hoarse, uneven breaths. "I just can't."

"I know you were willing to die for me down there, when we were running from the guard. I saw you turn around."

"That was different," I start, but then I look into his eyes, and the sun blazes inside them so fiercely I can feel it against my skin.

"You made your decision to leave Compound Eleven, and now I have, too."

The only thing that will stop him now is violence, and I have been trying for less violence in my life, not more. I smile at this thought—at its absurdity right now. Then my fingers lace through his, and he squeezes them.

"I read once that there's no such thing as death," I say.

"I remember. Only a change of worlds."

I nod.

He gazes at me steadily. "Let's go find a new world, then. Together."

"On the count of three," I say slowly.

"One." He pulls our entwined hands to his mouth and kisses my fingers.

"Two"—I stand on my toes and kiss him lightly on the lips. I am not shaking anymore.

"Three."

I turn the door handle and shove it open, and my boots go with it.

I gasp.

CHAPTER FORTY

Beside me, Wren is still. But I can see how hard his features are out of my peripheral vision, under the light of the moon.

It isn't the taste of freedom that has taken my breath away. It isn't the feeling of fresh air rippling through my lungs. We glance at each other, and a slow smile spreads across my lips, then across his. We are side by side and hand in hand. And despite all we have heard, all we have been *taught*…a crisp, cool breeze sweeps my hair and tickles my skin.

END OF BOOK ONE

Want to find out what happens next? Turn the page to read the first three chapters of the next book, Unraveling Eleven, *for FREE!*

UNRAVELING
ELEVEN

JERRI CHISHOLM

CHAPTER ONE

"Eve. Don't move."

The voice is low and hoarse in my ear.

A moment ago, my fingertips grazed the back of his neck as we kissed. My other hand curved over his large shoulder and pressed firmly into muscle. It was the first time we had stopped walking since escaping Compound Eleven, the first time we had even acknowledged each other, because for the past hour we have been too preoccupied and too overwhelmed.

Too mesmerized.

I think it's the feeling of earth beneath our boots that's to blame. That and the twinkling night sky overhead. We are used to concrete below and concrete above. But more than anything, it is the staggering realization that the heat won't kill us after all.

It won't even hurt us, despite all we've learned, all we've been taught. Everyone back in Eleven thinks it's a sauna up here, a killing field—practically upon impact. Yet an hour ago, we discovered that nothing could be further from the truth.

In time, as our shock wore off, our pace slowed, and we held each other—we kissed, celebration thundering like laughter in our ears. Then Wren went still.

Now his tendons stiffen. They lock him in place. He murmurs to me again, "Don't move."

The stars overhead offer enough light to see that he stares at something over my shoulder. His gaze is steady and his mouth is tight. I think it's the closest thing to alarm that his face can register.

Around his neck, my hands curl into fists, ready for violence—always ready for violence. My stomach binds. For a fleeting moment, I feel like I'm belowground again. I start to laugh the thought away, but then I hear it: the rustling of leaves, a gentle yet poignant indicator that we are not alone. An image flashes in my mind of guards decked in protective suits, dragging us back by our ankles, guns trained on our temples—

No. It's impossible they know of our escape.

Except nothing is impossible.

We thought it was impossible to survive aboveground, then we stepped outside. And so against Wren's words, I turn.

I turn and see something I have never seen before.

Something completely unexpected, completely foreign to those who dwell in tunnels below the earth's crust. "An animal?" I mutter, and as I do, the large beast's ears twitch. Like it knows it's being talked about. My arms drop to my sides; otherwise I am still. Back straight.

It stands in a clearing twenty feet away, and if it weren't for its beady eyes that catch in the moonlight, it wouldn't be noticeable at all. It would fade into darkness. I stare at it, partly with fear that is inborn, but also with awe.

If only the beast weren't so vaguely yet distinctly threatening…

Maybe I'm imagining it. Maybe my muscles *could* defeat it—I grew up in the Combat League, after all. I've been fighting those larger and seemingly stronger than me since I was nine years old. Or maybe it *is* a gentle beast.

But I know that can't be true, and Wren knows it, too. Silently his hand wraps around mine. He pulls me backward: one step, two. The beast watches us retreat, then its heavy skull lifts ever so slightly. It takes two steps forward.

Now I can see its paws, and they are the size of Compound Eleven's dinner plates. Curved knives line each one.

"Should we run?" comes a strained voice that I barely recognize as my own.

Wren shakes his head. "I don't think so." Once more, he tugs at my hand. So once more, we retreat like we're walking barefoot on glass, and this time the beast is still. This time it doesn't follow.

Suddenly I am hopeful.

Off in the distance comes a sharp cry—one of the birds that calls this strange world home. The beast's ears flick.

Another two steps back we go.

This is good; this is very good. Soon we will slip out of sight, nothing but a distant memory. And more importantly, we will be nothing but a distant memory to the guards of Compound Eleven, too. They will not drag us underground after all. Nothing will.

And then the heel of my boot hits something hard along the ground. A root, maybe, or the lip of a rock. I catch myself before I tumble.

Still, it was jarring. Still, my pulse quickens.

It must have been jarring for the beast, too, because now something has changed.

Now its head is lower than a second ago and its ears are flat. Now a sound reverberates from its stomach, bubbly and guttural at the same time. Now my heart pounds twice as loudly as before.

"We need to—" Wren begins urgently, but there's no chance to finish.

The beast charges.

Immediately our muscles spring into action, propelling us away, hurtling us into a sprint for our lives. Twigs snap underfoot as we shoot further into darkness, up a small hill, then down a steep slope littered with narrow trees. We are fast, our bodies built for speed.

But Wren's legs are longer than mine; he is faster. Under the glow of the moon, I see his head shift in my direction, and I see his gait slow.

As his hand reaches for mine, I scream at him to keep going—

Maybe he listens. I doubt it, but maybe. I wouldn't know, because something strikes my back with enough force to break my neck. A fraction of a millisecond passes since impact, then I'm facedown. My fingernails wedge with dirt. My forehead opens on a jagged rock.

On your feet, Eve.

Before I was fearful, an advantage to the beast. No longer, because now the lemon juice has spilled. Now I'm primed, and I'm ready. A fighter.

But then it pulls itself onto its hind legs, and it's taller than even I am. Half a second later, a mitt sized with blades slashes at me, and I swing backward in time to hear it slice the air, my innards barely spared. A heartbeat later, I punch it square in the nose.

I'm used to the feeling of a human nose squashing under my fist. I'm used to the sound it makes and the stinging of my knuckles. I'm used to the look of shock and panic shooting through my opponent's eyes. But this is different. There is no dull crack of bone, and there is no shock, panic, or pain. All that happens is that the blackened lips of the beast pull away in obvious anger, and as they do, they reveal a terrible sight. Yellow daggers, some of them as long as my ring finger.

This is not an opponent I can defeat.

There is no sense in punching or kicking. There is no sense in rooting around my boot for my blade. This creature is already equipped with blades. And speed. And strength.

Just as when I stare down the barrel of a gun, I'm completely powerless.

The gun.

Instead of groping around my waistband for my own weapon, I launch myself at the beast and throw my arms around its neck, tuck my head against coarse fur. This is the safest spot until Wren can shoot it. Otherwise it will gore me with its claws, gut me with its teeth—all before I can pull the trigger.

I hold on with every ounce of strength and scream at Wren to shoot. I hold on, but barely.

It resists my grip as fiercely as I fight for it. It jerks and shakes, and through it all, I wait for Wren. He must be near. He must.

He must have the gun cocked.

He must.

I can't hold on for much longer. And as the thought passes through my head, its paw is beneath me, my grasp is wrenched free, I am thrown onto my back so that the inky night sky is spread out before me.

The sound of fast, heavy footsteps, then my vision is clouded by blackness.

CHAPTER TWO

Blackness. I was born into it, and I will die in it, too.

At least I was able to taste freedom first. That was my goal; it was always my goal. And it is better to be dead and free than caged and alive.

I must not forget that as I take my last breaths.

That's when I finally hear the blast of a gun.

The beast collapses on me, its weight as devastating as the daggers lining its mouth, and I scream. Or I would if I could force air to my lungs. Claws tear through my clothes. Pain clouds my vision.

Then it lifts.

Oxygen. And the ability to move, even if gingerly. Blood rushes to my extremities and dribbles from rips in my skin. When my eyes clear of tears, I notice that the beast has lost interest in me. Its sights are set on Wren and Wren alone, and the realization makes me smile.

The blast of another bullet, then another. Another. They echo through the trees like poetry. Belowground they explode, like a punch to the face. Normally I hate the sound, but right now the shots wash over me in waves. Then the earth tremors.

I don't know how many bullets it took to defeat the deadly creature, but I hear the clatter of discarded metal on rock and know we are down a gun.

Then Wren is above me, concern rippling over his handsome features. Quickly it passes. Now a scowl contorts them—those wideset eyes, his kind mouth, that straight nose.

"Are you *laughing*?" he shouts. "I thought you were dead!"

Now I laugh harder.

He sighs. His hand turns my head, and his fingers trace the wound over my eye.

"A rock," I explain as I catch my breath.

"Mm. I think you'll live. What about the rest of you?"

Hands slip down my body, and I wince as his fingers find the tears in my clothing that have given way to tears in my skin. "They're not deep," he says eventually. "You're lucky."

I wrap my arms around his neck. "Next time, shoot quicker."

"I defend my timing completely," he says as he presses his forehead to mine, angling it away from my cut. "I wanted to see what that thing was made of." He glances at the fallen beast through the darkness. Then he glances at me, and I see humor dancing in his eyes. "I wanted to see what *you* were made of, too."

I laugh softly. "And?"

He frowns, then presses his mouth together as if he's deep in thought. "Tough as nails, Eve," he finally concludes.

I grin; I can't help it. Because we are free. We can kiss, and shout, and run. We can search for my little brother, Jack, who was cruelly expelled from Compound Eleven at the tender age of three. We can do whatever we like—forever.

There's no more need to fear Daniel or Landry. There is no need to cower at the sight of the guards, not that I ever gave them the satisfaction—that particular form of torture is finished. Same with the low-hanging ceilings and the recycled air. The injustice at being born on the second floor where I'm treated like garbage, where my job options are so severely circumscribed. No longer am I a citizen of a ruthless regime, one that massacres its own people at will.

Now I am free. Forever free. Forever *free*. Because the

scorched earth is scorched no longer. We can survive up here.

Wren and me—and the thought sends a shiver down my spine. How did an unlucky person like me get so lucky?

No matter that my body is bruised from the beast—I pull him as close as possible so no air can separate us. I feel so light; even with his weight on top of me, it's like I could float to the night sky. I feel so secure; I could let my muscles go soft. I feel so happy; I can't believe that even for a second I was ready to die.

For a long time, we just lay there, breathing in unison, digesting it all. Then Wren says in a husky voice that tickles my cheek, "We should get some sleep."

I lift my head to better look at him. "Here?"

"Or maybe we could find a bed nearby," he says, pinching me. "Of course *here*."

I laugh, and as we make ourselves comfortable, I realize what a new experience this will be. Not just sleeping on the ground instead of a hard, dusty mattress. Not just sleeping aboveground instead of below. But sleeping with a boy next to me, as well.

I decide to be brave and tuck myself into the curve of his body where it's warmest, and I find that it's not scary at all. It feels safe here next to Wren—it feels like home.

In time, our breaths grow longer. As my eyes become heavy, I know not only will I go to sleep with a smile on my face, but for the first time ever, I'll wake with one, too.

Sometime later, the call of the birds lifts me from my slumber, and I find myself grinning ear to ear—just as I predicted. It's because lightness fills my retinas, and I didn't even have to switch on a lamp. It's because I'm not just waking up to sunshine; I'm waking up to *freedom*.

It's everything I ever wanted. No, that's not true. It's *more* than I ever wanted, because I have Wren here by my side. And now we have nothing but time on our hands—nothing but time to explore this strange new world and search for Jack. Because even though the beast we encountered in the night, the one that lies in a crumpled heap nearby, was dangerous and clearly deadly, there's too much beauty up here. It's paradise. And it's impossible to believe that Jack perished in paradise.

Dying underground, on the other hand, is easy. Compound Eleven is hell—death is just a small sidestep away, a trip to the left, a tumble to the right. Yet Jack was released into this oasis, and I know he thrived.

Just like Wren and I are going to.

Gingerly, I move Wren's arm from around me, then sit upright. I wipe sleep from my eyes and gaze around—left and right, up and down, in every direction. The problem with my certainty that my brother is still alive, I think, is the vastness of the space up here. It's completely foreign to someone like me. It's unfathomable, hard to get my brain around. And it means he could have gone in any direction, could have traveled endlessly—still, to this day.

But maybe not. Maybe he stayed nearby, living among the surrounding trees, because it's the closest thing to home that he knew. My chest expands with excitement at the thought.

Then I draw away from Wren, careful not to wake him. The morning air feels dewy and fresh, and aside from the endless call of birds, it's silent. So silent, I can hear my boots as they echo dully along the forest floor, toward the fallen beast. I drop to my knees next to it, then run my fingers over its coarse fur.

Now that I'm not fighting for my life, I can appreciate the texture of the coat and the thickness, too. I study its claws, note how beautiful the arc of its skull is. I even begin to mourn the fact that this sprawling creature died under our hand. Because the last thing I want to do up here is destroy.

But as I finally settle myself onto a large rock nearby, I realize that I don't want to be destroyed, either. So maybe life up here is a balancing act. Maybe in the old world, things skidded off center. Maybe humans, left unchecked, destroy, destroy, destroy.

I can't let that happen.

Wren's voice pierces the silence. "Enjoying yourself?" He is awake now, watching me.

I let my legs dangle over the edge of the rock. "Just a little," I say, and my tone is playful.

For a while, he says nothing—he simply contemplates me with his brow furrowed, like he's deep in thought. "It's good to see you so happy," he finally says. Then, before I can respond, he adds in a lighter tone, "I take it you don't object to the constant chatter those things make?" He gestures to the treetops. As if on cue, a black bird caws into the morning.

"Things? I believe they're called *birds*, Wren."

"Ah," he says theatrically. "Aren't you knowledgeable."

I bow my head.

"They're loud." And he stifles a yawn. "A few more hours of sleep would've been nice. And maybe a proper mattress."

"Of course you'd want a fancy mattress," I scoff. *"Preme."*

He chucks a stick at me, grinning.

I kick aside the stick and throw a stone in his direction.

"Not great aim, Eve." His expression is full of feigned seriousness. "You should keep practicing—it might be the best protection we've got the next time we run into one of those things." He turns his attention to the fallen beast, no longer joking.

"I was wondering about that, too," I admit.

He walks over to me and lets his arms drape over my shoulders and down my back. "And? Did you figure out what we're going to do once we're out of bullets?"

"Run faster?" I suggest. I loop my arms around his waist and pull him close.

He bends down and kisses me on the forehead, then the nose, and finally on the lips. "We'd need a motor to outrun that thing. Do you think they can climb trees?"

I lean back and give him an incredulous look. "Why? Can *you*?"

He smiles. "Good point. Not that there was a need, but it's too bad they didn't teach us how to outwit shockingly large, strangely ferocious animals back in Eleven."

I smile, too, but then the phrase *back in Eleven* echoes through my head, and my smile falters. The problem is that I'm up here—free and happy—and my friends and family are stuck in a situation that is just the opposite. Caged and miserable.

Back in Eleven. If only there was a way to get word to them that the world has cooled. Because the twinge of guilt I feel that I get to live up here and they don't isn't one I want to endlessly carry with me. And more than that, I don't want them to be stuck underground forever.

Maybe they'll figure it out for themselves when they realize that Wren and I have vanished without a trace. Maybe the Premes in charge—like Wren's mother—will figure it out, too. Maybe all of Eleven will join us up here in the coming days.

Then Wren asks, "What's for breakfast?" and all my thoughts dissipate at once.

I blink up at him. Breakfast? It isn't something I've

thought about, not even once, not since we bid goodbye to the compound. But now that he mentions it, I *am* hungry. Thirsty, too, and a small flare of panic ignites in my stomach at the realization. "Maybe we should walk around and see what we can find?" I suggest, careful to hide the unease in my voice.

"Sure."

I slide off the rock and consider the ring of trees surrounding us. "Which way?"

He shrugs, then points behind me. "That's the direction we came from last night, which means the compound is that way. Do you remember seeing any food last night?"

"I didn't notice any cafeterias," I joke. But beneath my easy tone, that flare of panic grows larger. Because Wren and I have always been served food. Food that's been grown underground, in commercial greenhouses and factories, and prepared in a kitchen by trained staff—and there's none of that up here.

So. What the hell are we going to eat?

"Let's keep heading in the same direction," I say after a while. "I'm sure we'll find something."

A minute later, we start picking our way through the close-knit trees, my gaze no longer dancing along the treetops or admiring the sun that rises slow and steady from the horizon. No, instead my eyes are trained on the ground, searching for something—*anything*—that resembles food.

CHAPTER THREE

Time passes. My brain flips from jubilation at being up here, to guilt over those back in Eleven, and finally to hunger, then back again. A nonstop cycle that becomes lopsided toward food with every hour that passes. Movement is slow through the thicket of trees, my boots are coated in dirt, and my clothes are sticky with sweat. The giant rock face that sits to the north of the Oracle is now behind us, far off in the distance, but every so often, I stop to glimpse it through the trees. Right now, it's the most familiar sight I know.

Wren is as quiet as I am, both of us focused on the task at hand—finding sustenance—but finally he breaks the silence by asking, "What's that?"

I look around, spotting nothing out of the ordinary—nothing out of our *new* ordinary, that is. "What?"

"You can't smell it?"

I walk a bit farther, and then I nod. It's a scent I can't pinpoint, and yet it's sweet and very strong. I gesture to a swell of plants that tower over Wren and me, all their branches covered in tufts of purple flowers. We edge closer, and as I run my fingers over one of the tufts, the scent becomes even stronger. Then I jerk my hand aside as a black-and-yellow insect appears, landing delicately on the petals.

"Wren," I whisper, eyeing it. Together we watch as it moves from flower to flower, pausing now and then, like it's eating or maybe collecting something. "What do you think it's doing?"

"I have no idea."

"Do you know what it's called?"

He shakes his head. Then he adds, "Do you think we can eat it?"

I gaze at him. He must be hungrier than I am. "Maybe," I say, even though it doesn't exactly look palatable. I reach my fingers forward until they wrap carefully around it and I can feel its wings beating against my palm. I start to laugh at the sensation until it's replaced by white-hot pain.

I jump, and I scream, and then Wren pulls back my fingers. Part of the insect flies away, but the rest remains embedded in my palm, surrounded by a fast-growing welt. It looks vaguely like the splinter I got when I was five, from an old can that Hunter and I were playing with. My father had to hold me down as my mother dug it out with a fork she'd swiped from the cafeteria, except she couldn't get it all, and it became infected. After weeks of sickness, I finally healed, and I was told I was lucky I didn't lose my hand. I was lucky, even, to be alive.

Right now, I carefully grip what remains of the insect, my heart thumping in my throat with a volatile mixture of fear and intrigue, then yank it free. I dig my thumb into the welt to try to numb the pain, then shout, "What *was* that thing?"

"I'm not sure," admits Wren. Then he grins. "It probably wouldn't have tasted very good, though."

I try to kick him—but I'm still doubled over, and even though I feel like crying, I find myself laughing instead. Wren watches me with an amused look on his face.

"Here," I say a few minutes later, once the throbbing begins to ease. I tear a handful of flowers from the plant and push them into his hand. "If that insect *was* actually eating them, maybe we can, too."

"That does sound logical," he says, holding them to his nose. "Except they don't smell like food. They smell like… perfume. Don't you think?"

I roll my eyes. "You think I know what *perfume* smells like, Preme? That wasn't exactly an allotment offered on the second floor."

"Your loss," he says, nudging me, then he pushes the entire handful of flowers into his mouth. Immediately he makes a face and spits them back out.

"No good?" I ask, trying to hold back my laughter.

"No good," he confirms. "I'd rather eat month-old mashed potatoes from the Mean cafeteria."

Mashed potatoes. Normally I hate those glutinous mounds of starch, which have no taste, no flavor. Right now, I realize, I'd give my ring finger for some.

A few hours later, the sun has arced high in the sky, and it's far warmer than the middle of the night, or even the morning. My clothes are soaked from sweat, and I'm more thirsty than before. Funny: I had envisioned the world up here to have large stores of water—I've seen plenty of pictures in the Preme library of land ending and water claiming its place. Yet we've been walking for hours and haven't spotted a single drop.

Wren and I no longer joke or chat—we just focus on stomping through the overgrowth in search of sustenance. Too bad we don't know what to look for. Nothing up here resembles those mashed potatoes or shriveled peas that I was served underground. There are no tin cups waiting next to a chipped sink, either.

The flare of panic I felt this morning intensifies, filling my empty belly, and all thoughts of searching for Jack vanish as I zero in on the most pressing need standing before us.

Since I can't think of anything else, I try to remember the last time I ate. It's been a while. I was locked in my cell without food before leaving the compound, because my supposed best friend Hunter betrayed me. Before that, I was too busy mourning the Noms who lost their lives in the government-sanctioned mass murder on the ground floor—called the cleanse—to eat a thing. It's been days, I think, since I've had a proper meal.

The longer we walk, the less energy I have. Wren, too—I can tell by the slouching of his shoulders and the shortening of his stride. As the sun drops lower in the sky, our pace is no longer slow simply because of the densely packed trees. I feel like my muscles have gone soft, like pools of molasses, and navigating up and down steep slopes leaves me dizzy. My head throbs, and without the warmth of the midday sun, I find myself shivering.

Finally, after several more hours of fruitless searching, we decide to sleep next to an overturned tree, and we're both so exhausted from spending the entire day walking, so weakened from having no food or water, that we fall immediately asleep before we can say good night to each other at all.

The next morning when I wake, I listen to the happy chatter of the birds, feel the gentle morning sun against my cheek, even remember that I am waking in total freedom.

But I do not smile.

Wren's not in a good mood, either, and we quickly begin our search for food and water all over again.

Monotonous hours pass. Futile hours. My stomach gurgles, and hurts, and my headache returns with a vengeance. With every step, I imagine us stumbling upon water—see it sparkling under the sunlight, wide and vast like the pictures I've seen in those Preme books. With every step, I'm disappointed. At the same time, a steady stream of visuals competes for space in my brain—visuals of everything I've ever eaten back in Eleven— even simple things, like toast. I salivate at the thought.

More and more hours slide by, and that now-familiar feeling of panic grows even worse. What are we going to do? What's going to happen? Just as I start to lose all hope, I hear Wren say in a thick voice, "Eve. Over there."

I follow his gaze and spot something slinking between the trees. At first I think it's just a mirage—another trick of the eye or deceit of the brain. But when I move closer, I see that something is definitely moving, and it resembles water, except that it's brown and murky. We stumble closer, barely daring to believe it, and finally I step off the land, feel the liquid seep through my boots. I kneel down and dip my hands in, examining how it falls through my fingers, behaving exactly the way water does. "Do you think…?"

"It doesn't look like water belowground," Wren says, and I note how weak his voice sounds.

"No," I whisper. "It doesn't."

He sighs, then crouches next to me and scoops the rust-hued liquid to his lips.

"How does it taste?"

"It tastes like water," he confirms. "Just…dirty water."

It must not be that bad, because he drinks down handful after handful, and a moment later, I do the same. Because even though dirty water doesn't sound very appetizing, I've never been this thirsty in all my life, not even after a full day training with Blue Circuit—my Combat League team.

Wren is right: it doesn't taste like the water we're used to—but it's satisfying, and slowly the all-consuming panic that gripped me a few minutes ago ebbs. And maybe it's because of that—because of my sudden clearheadedness—that I spot the red berries growing along the water's edge.

I've seen food like this on occasion underground. It isn't often that Means are served fresh fruit, but once in a while we're served the leftovers that the Premes aren't interested in, and I think that's why it looks familiar. I wade through the murky water as quickly as I can, stopping when I'm right in front of it, then examine the bright red spheres.

"Have you had these before?" I ask Wren.

He stands over my shoulder and shakes his head. "They look like blueberries, aside from the color. Have you had blueberries before?"

"Not that I know of," I mutter. Then I pull a berry free and roll it between two fingers. "Is there such a thing as *red*berries?"

He tries to grin—I can see the corners of his mouth pull up, but it looks more like a grimace. "Evidently," he says.

Since we don't have anything else to eat, I shove the morsel into my mouth. Bitter, and I almost spit it out again. But it's been so long since I've had food that I swallow it down, then I pick more, fill my stomach with them, and Wren does the same, both of us ignoring how we gag with each bite.

When finally the berries are gone, we wade out of the water and sit on the forest floor, more content than before. My head no longer pounds from thirst, my stomach no longer consumes itself from hunger, and I lay back, stretching out so that I'm spread-eagle, staring at the blue sky and the billowing clouds overhead. I feel exhausted, and I realize I've never walked so far or for so long in my life. I've never come so close to starvation, which is saying something, considering how strictly Compound Eleven rations food.

Right now, though, all is good. All is calm. I watch the leaves shimmering in the breeze and the clouds rolling by.

I realize that my hand is no longer swollen and sore from whatever caused such pain yesterday, and for that I feel grateful. I feel *hopeful*.

Everything will be okay up here in paradise.

Then, just as I think about searching for Jack, Wren draws himself unsteadily to his feet. He disappears into the bushes.

At first I think he's spotted something—I almost follow him. But when I hear him vomit, I go still. All that hope and gratitude are replaced by concern, by fear, and a few minutes later, I feel it, too. Nausea. It creeps up my stomach and swirls around my brain. My skin is no longer tacky from the sun—it breaks into a cold sweat that drenches my clothes. Those shimmering leaves overhead distort sideways, then I roll onto all fours as my stomach heaves.

The vomiting is unending—again and again and again, along with the tremor in my bones and the blistering fever that leaves me curled into a ball at the foot of a tree. Somewhere off in the distance, I hear Wren groan, and I spot through my warped vision him clutching his stomach. I wonder if it hurts as much as mine does right now.

And as time marches on, as the symptoms refuse to vanish, as the world spins around me, I begin to wonder if we'll die here.

Look for
Unraveling Eleven
wherever books are sold.

ACKNOWLEDGMENTS

I would like to thank my ever-reliable, always-helpful agent, Rachel Beck, and my incredibly talented editor, Stacy Abrams, for believing in this project and offering invaluable insight along the way. Without the pair of you, this book would literally not exist, so, thank you…THANK YOU!

I would also like to express my unending gratitude to everyone at Entangled Teen for their hard work, creativity, and patience. I am so honored, so blessed, to work with such an outstanding team.

And lastly, I would like to thank my friends and family for their love, support, and much-needed words of encouragement over the course of this journey. Thank you!

Escaping Eleven is a pulse-pounding, action-packed dystopian novel full of romance and intrigue. However, the story includes elements that might not be suitable for some readers. Violence, bodily harm, sexual assault, death of a child, mental illness, and police brutality are included in the novel. Readers who may be sensitive to these elements, please take note.

Let's be friends!

@EntangledTeen

@EntangledTeen

@EntangledTeen

bit.ly/TeenNewsletter

entangled teen

an imprint of Entangled Publishing LLC